Praise for Peter Spiegelman's

Red Cat

"Lustrous. . . . Elegant. . . . The fashionable aesthetics of 'noir porn' are presented here in high style."
—*The New York Times Book Review*

"A taut little number . . . [with] enough shady characters to keep readers guessing whodunit." —*Entertainment Weekly*

"A dark journey into the parts of New York that few tourists visit. . . . An intriguing, intelligent book." —*The Economist*

"Fast-paced, witty and utterly believable, *Red Cat* is as exhilarating a read as you are likely to find on the shelves today. . . . A must-read." —*Shots Magazine*

"Spiegelman's sharp prose pulls the reader straight through to the bittersweet end." —*The Wall Street Journal*

"Clever. . . . Entertaining and fast-paced. . . . Artfully converts March's investigation into an insider's guide to various Manhattan milieus." —*Pittsburgh Post-Gazette*

"Filmic, fun . . . [with] a winning narrator and lots of arty but dirty sex." —*The New York Observer*

"Peter Spiegelman has made the transition from banks and brokerages to bandits and bullets look easy."
—*Pittsburgh Tribune-Review*

PETER SPIEGELMAN

Red Cat

Peter Spiegelman is the author of *Black Maps*, which won the 2004 Shamus Award for Best First P.I. Novel, and *Death's Little Helpers*; both novels feature private detective and Wall Street refugee John March. Prior to becoming a full-time writer, Mr. Spiegelman spent nearly twenty years in the financial services and software industries and worked with leading banks and brokerages around the world. He lives in Connecticut.

Red Cat

Red Cat

PETER SPIEGELMAN

VINTAGE CRIME/BLACK LIZARD
Vintage Books
A Division of Random House, Inc.
New York

FIRST VINTAGE CRIME/BLACK LIZARD EDITION, FEBRUARY 2008

Copyright © 2007 by Peter Spiegelman

Grateful acknowledgment is made to Alfred A. Knopf, a division of Random House,
Inc., for permission to reprint an excerpt from "Siblings" from *The Night Parade*
by Edward Hirsch. Copyright © 1989 by Edward Hirsch. Reprinted by permission
of Alfred A. Knopf, a division of Random House, Inc.

The Library of Congress has cataloged the Knopf edition as follows:
Spiegelman, Peter.
Red cat / Peter Spiegelman. —1st ed.
p. cm.
1. March, John (Fictitious character)—Fiction.   2. Private investigators—New York
(State)—New York—Fiction. 3. Brothers—Fiction. 4. Adultery—Fiction.
5. Extortion—Fiction. 6. New York (N.Y.)—Fiction. I. Title.
PS3619.P543R43 2007
813'.6—dc22
2006049529

Vintage ISBN: 978-1-4000-9704-3

Book design by Virginia Tan

www.vintagebooks.com

Printed in the United States of America
10   9   8   7   6   5   4   3   2   1

For Nina

The story of siblings is the story of childhood,
Experienced separately and together, one tree
Twisting in different directions, roots and branches,

One piece of land divided into parcels,
Acres and half-acres, parts of a subdivision,
Memories carved into official and unofficial versions.

—Edward Hirsch, "Siblings"

Acknowledgments

Thanks are due to many people for their help with this book. To my early readers—Nina Spiegelman, Barbara Wang, and Jan Taradash—who once again were so generous with their time. To Denise Marcil and her team at the Denise Marcil Literary Agency, for their ongoing efforts on my behalf. To Sonny Mehta, Pat Johnson, and Gabrielle Brooks at Knopf, for their insight, encouragement, and support. And to Alice Wang, who makes it all possible.

Red Cat

1

I'd seen him angry plenty of times. I'd seen him dismissive, contemptuous, reproachful, and mocking too—and, more often than not, I'd seen that bad karma pointed in my direction. But in the thirty-four years I'd known him, I'd never seen my brother quite like this before. I'd never seen him scared.

David ran a hand through his ginger hair and knocked it from its slick alignment. He rose from my sofa and whisked imaginary dust from his spotless gray trousers and paced again before the long wall of windows. I shook my head, as much from the surprise of him turning up at my door on a Monday morning—or, indeed, any time—as from what I'd heard.

"Jesus Christ, David—on the Internet? What the hell were you thinking?"

He stopped to look out at the rooftops and at the sun, struggling up an iron January sky. Reflected in the window glass, his face was lean and sharp-featured—fairer-haired, lighter-eyed, more sour and lined than my own, but still too similar. At six feet tall he was barely an inch shorter than I, but he seemed smaller than that now. His smile was tight and bitter.

"Is this your usual approach with prospective clients—to interrupt their stories so you can exercise your own disapproval?" He flicked at a speck of nothing on the sleeve of his suit jacket.

The irony of him complaining about my disapproval was lost on David just then, but I fought the urge to point it out. Nor did I comment that he wasn't so much telling his story as wandering around the edges of it. I knew it would be futile. Unsure of what to do with his fear, and unused to discussing it with anyone, least of all with me, David was falling back on more familiar and reliable behaviors, like annoyed and patronizing. I'd seen clients go through it before; fighting didn't help.

David turned and made an elaborate survey of my loft—the kitchen at one end, the bedroom and bath at the other, the high ceilings, cast-iron columns, bookshelves, and sparse furnishings in between. He pursed his lips in disapproval. "I haven't been here since it was Lauren's," he said. Lauren was our younger sister, and still the owner of the apartment. I'd been subletting the place for the past five years. "She did more with it," he added. I kept quiet. David wandered to a bookshelf and eyed the titles and smirked.

"Do people still read poetry?" he said. "People besides you, I mean."

I sighed, and tried to bring him back to at least the neighborhood of his problem. "You exchanged names with this woman?"

His smirk vanished. "First names only, and not our real ones. At least, the one I gave her wasn't real. I called myself Anthony."

"And she . . . ?"

"Wren. She called herself Wren."

"But now she knows your name—your real name."

David smoothed his hair and smoothed his steel-blue tie. "Yes. When I think about it, it wouldn't have been difficult. My wallet was in my suit jacket, and my suit jacket was in the closet or on the back of a chair. She could have gone through it while I was in the bathroom. I should have been more careful about that sort of thing, I suppose, but I assumed we both wanted anonymity. That is the point, after all."

"The point of . . . ?"

David lifted his eyebrow to a familiar, impatient angle. "The point of the websites. The point of using words like 'casual' and 'discreet' in your posts."

I nodded slowly. "You're pretty familiar with the conventions." David looked at me and said nothing. "By which I mean: I assume it wasn't the first time you'd used one of these sites."

"It wasn't."

"How many—"

He cut me off. "How is this relevant?"

I drained my coffee mug, rubbed the last smudges of sleep from my eyes, and counted to ten. "I don't know what's relevant and what's not. I'm still trying to get the lay of the land."

David sniffed. "Suffice it to say, there were other sites and other women."

"Were they all one time things?"

He walked back to the windows. A few sooty snowflakes were drifting down onto Sixteenth Street. David watched them drift. "Some, and some were three- or four-time things. Wren was four times."

"None of the other women—"

"None of the others ever called me on the phone, John. None of them has shown up at my house. So can we drop them and stick to Wren?" His voice was shaky.

"You saw her four times, over what period?"

"Two months maybe."

"From when to when?"

"From October to December. The last time was about six weeks ago."

"When did the calls start?"

"New Year's Day. She left a message on my office voicemail."

"And since then?"

David turned toward me. Beneath the flawless Italian tailoring, his arms and legs were stiff as wire. His normally ruddy face was paper white. "In the past two weeks I've gotten four more calls at the office, three on my cell, and three at home. Four days ago she dropped by."

"Does she say what she wants?"

"The two times she's managed to get through to me she's said she wants to meet again. She doesn't seem to get the point of *no*."

"She doesn't say anything more?"

David examined his cuticles intently. "She says plenty more. I've saved a couple of the messages; you can hear for yourself."

"Maybe you could give me a preview."

He sighed impatiently. "She *demands* to see me; she won't be *dismissed* or *ignored*. It's a whole *Fatal Attraction* shtick. And she makes it clear that she knows where I work—not just my office number, but what I do and where. She mentions Ned, and threatens to call him if I don't get in touch with her." Ned is our brother, the eldest of the five of us. With our uncle Ben's retirement the previous June, he'd also become the managing partner at Klein & Sons—the head guy at the merchant bank our great-grandfather started a few generations ago. Which also made him David's boss.

"How are you supposed to get in touch with her?"

"The same way we arranged things before, by e-mail."

"What else does she say?"

David stared at me. His blue eyes were weary but they didn't waver. "She knows I'm married," he said finally. "She mentioned Stephanie's name, and a couple of events Steph has been at recently—fund-raising things. She threatened to call her."

I nodded. That was more than a glance through his wallet, though the research wouldn't have been hard. David was a reasonably high-profile guy in some circles, and Google would do the trick. I recalled the mentions in the trade rags, last August, of David's promotion to head of mergers and acquisitions at Klein. Those articles would probably appear at the top of the search results, but Stephanie's name would come up too, along with a skein of social contacts.

"She's done some homework," I said.

Irritation rippled across David's face. "You think?" He stalked to the kitchen counter and picked up his coffee mug. He drank from it and grimaced and emptied it in the sink. "Cold," he said. He made it an accusation.

"Has she made good on her threats?"

"Do you think I'd be here if she had? There wouldn't be much point, would there?"

I counted to ten again, and then to twenty. I was getting good at it. I'd had a lot of practice with David. "Has she tried to make good on them?"

"Does her little visit to my place count? Thank God Steph wasn't home for that. Thank God I took care of the fucking doormen this Christmas."

"So Stephanie doesn't know about her?"

"No," David said. His voice was empty of emotion again. "And neither does Ned, and I intend to keep it that way."

A fine ambition, I thought, though perhaps not realistic. "Does Stephanie know about the other wo—"

"No, goddammit, and can we stick to the point here?" David's fingers were white on the edge of my kitchen counter. I was running out of numbers.

I took a deep breath. "What happened when you and Wren were together?"

David's look was a mix of irritation and *are you some kind of idiot?* "What do you think happened? And if you're looking for details, forget—"

"I'm not. But did she say or do anything out of the ordinary—anything to make you think she had another agenda?"

"There was nothing," he said, shaking his head. "Conversation tends to be . . . limited, and that's how it was with her. She was maybe a little quieter than some of the others, a little more . . . inwardly turned . . . but that's all."

"And you didn't say anything to her? Anything that might lead her to believe—"

"To believe what, that we were going to run off together or something? Get a cottage by the sea and raise a new generation of Marches? Do you think I'm stupid?" It was one of many thoughts that were colliding in my head, and that I'd so far managed to keep to myself. But David wasn't making it easy. He jabbed his fingers at me. "And what happened to sticking to the fucking point?"

"That would be a lot easier if you would tell me just what the fucking point *is*. What is it you want from me?"

"I want you to find this Wren, for chrissakes—to find out who she is and where she lives. To find out as much about her as she has about me. And then I want you to talk to her. Make it clear that I have no interest in seeing her—or hearing from her—ever again. Make it clear I won't sit still for extortion or manipulation or . . . whatever the hell she has in mind. Make her understand there are consequences." His voice was shaky at first but steadied with talk of action. The fantasy of control over this sorry situation was short-lived, though, and worry filled the silence when his speech was done. His gaze, fixed on me, was more desperate than resolute.

"You have the wrong idea about what I do."

David snorted. "I know just what you do, John. You rummage around in people's lives—you go through their garbage and their dirty laundry. You find them, and you find out about them, all the things they want kept private, all the secret things. I know exactly what you do, and this is right up your alley."

"I don't do kneecaps, David."

He raised his eyebrows and shook his head. There was genuine surprise in his voice. "You think that's what I'm asking for? Jesus— what kind of person do you think I am?" It was a good question, and I realized then that I didn't have a clue.

"What kind of *consequences* did you have in mind, then?"

"I don't intend to have my life overturned, or to have my pocket picked. If she won't take the hint from you, the next message will come from a lawyer—a high-priced, tireless, nasty one, with a taste for human flesh. That's the message I want you to send."

I thought about that for a while. "Assuming I can find her—"

"*Assuming?* I thought you were good at this."

"I am good at it, but there's nothing certain in this work. Assuming I can find her, and deliver your message, there's still the possibility that lawyers might not frighten her." David's face said the notion was unfathomable. I went on. "She might not have any assets worth going after, or—if she's nuts enough—she might not care. She might even like the attention."

A shudder went through him and he pulled his hand again and again through his glossy hair. "We'll burn that bridge when we get to it," he said finally. "First find her." He shut his eyes and pressed his fingers to his temples and looked smaller still.

"You could just let her find you, you know—just wait until she calls and agree to a meeting and send your message in person."

"I'm done waiting!" David said, and smacked his fist on the countertop. "I won't have this hanging over my head any longer, and I won't dance to her tune. If she calls, fine—I'll agree to a meet, and you can go, but I'm not sitting on my hands until that happens."

I carried my coffee mug to the kitchen and filled it and wandered to a window. David eyed me warily and I looked back. He was just two years my senior, but in the gray morning light, with the color wrung from his eyes and his expensive woolen skin hanging sadly from his narrow shoulders, he might have been a hundred.

"What is it?" he asked finally. "If it's money you're worried about—don't. I don't expect a family discount or anything; I'll pay full freight."

Full freight. Jesus. I shook my head. "There are other PIs in the world, David. Why do you want to hire me?"

"You think I *like* the idea? Trust me, I don't. But I like even less the thought of going to a total stranger. That's all I need right now is some sleazebag careening around in my life, upending things or . . . God knows what." David paused and the small sour smile came and went again. "You're at least a sleazebag I know. You're the lesser evil."

I looked at David and nodded. It was the first really straight answer he'd given me all morning.

Hendry's was a sleek boutique hotel in NoLita—a luxurious, low-key sanctuary built inside the sandblasted shell of what used to be five adjoining brick tenement buildings. The patrons these days ran not so much to huddled masses as to movie people, rock stars, fashionistas, and, on three afternoons this past fall, David and Wren. According to David, Wren had suggested the place and had taken care of booking the rooms, and I went there on Tuesday morning in the hope of charming, confusing, or otherwise persuading someone to let me have a look at the registration records. Other than establishing that Wren had expensive taste, it was mostly a waste of time.

Given the nature of their clientele, the Armani-clad people who manned the polished perpetual twilight of Hendry's lobby were exquisitely sensitive to matters of privacy, and quite immune to my manipulations. The records were a nonstarter and so was peeking at security camera footage, and I found only one person with more to offer than a tastefully muted threat of removal from the premises.

Her name was Vera, and when she wasn't checking people in and out of Hendry's, she was a film student at NYU. She was black Irish, wry and elfin, and red-cheeked from the cold when we met at a Starbucks on Houston Street during her break. I bought her a latte and gave her the description of Wren that David had given me: about five foot nine and about thirty years old, with thick auburn hair to the shoulders, fair skin, brown eyes, narrow face, longish nose, wide mouth, slim, athletic build, soft voice, no jewelry, plain but expensive clothes, in mostly black and gray. I didn't mention the smiling red cat tattooed very high up on the inner part of her left thigh, or the skimpy French underwear, or the birthmark shaped something like Florida on her ass. Vera shook her head.

"Could be half our feckin' guests," she said. "And if you tell me she's twenty pounds underweight and halfway a junkie, it could be two thirds."

"You get many who want rooms for only an hour or two?"

Vera grinned crookedly. "You'd be surprised," she said.

"If I gave you three dates, you couldn't take just a quick glance at your computer?"

She laughed. "Sure, if you could just pick up the fees for my last two semesters in school."

"How about just one date then?" I asked. "November eighteenth." It was the one time David and Wren had met someplace other than Hendry's. "You recall anything happening at the hotel that day?"

Vera squinted into her cup for a moment and nodded. "Sure—that whole week—and it was a feckin' zoo, I'll tell ya. They were givin' out music video awards or some such shite uptown, and we were booked solid."

I thanked Vera, who gave me one more crooked grin, shook my hand, and left. I stayed put, nursing my drink and thinking.

I hadn't fared much better yesterday, when I'd spent most of the morning trying to put some meat on the bones of David's story. He hadn't made it easy.

"It isn't enough to know I met her on-line?" he'd said. "What do you need the particulars for?"

"Gee, I don't know, David—maybe on the off chance they could help me locate her."

"I don't see how."

"You don't need to see how. That's what you hired me for."

" 'Hired' is the key word there—it means *you* work for *me*."

We went around like that for a while and finally David relented. He was sullen at first but eventually a note of pride crept into his voice, and I realized he was quietly pleased with his shrewdness.

He could quote Wren's posting on MetroMatchPoint.com, the dating website he'd used to find her, almost word for word. "Slim, leggy redhead, twenties, healthy, tasteful, and discreet, seeks professional man 35–55 for casual meeting. Manhattan only, downtown preferred." He'd sent a note to the e-mail address in the ad, and had established what he called his "ground rules."

"Half the people on these sites who claim to be women, aren't—so before I waste any time, I get a photo." I didn't quite gulp.

"Tell me you haven't been mailing your picture around the web, David."

He gave me a *get real* look. "For chrissakes, no. I get photos from them; I don't send anything out."

"A little lopsided, isn't it? What if the other party doesn't agree?"

"So be it." David shrugged. "If she won't play by my rules, I move on."

"And how do you know the photos you get are for real? What's to stop someone sending you a picture of someone else entirely?"

"It happens, but that's why I insist on a first meeting at Third Uncle." I knew the place; it was a café on Charlton Street, off Varick. "It has that huge front window and you can see everyone in the place from the sidewalk. If I like the view, I go inside and take a closer look. If I don't, I just keep walking." The voice of authority.

"So you've never been fooled?"

He squinted at me. "Fooled how?"

"You didn't see *The Crying Game*?"

"Jesus," David said. His face wrinkled in disgust. "You think this is some kind of joke?"

"No joke, David. It's a big city, and full of all sorts of people."

"Fuck you. I know the difference between a man and a woman."

"Whatever. Exactly how many of these look-sees have you gone on anyway?"

His face went blank and his voice dead flat. "You have more questions about Wren, or not?" he asked.

"Let's hear those messages," I said.

David blanched. "I deleted the ones she left on my office voicemail and at home," he said, and he pressed some keys on his tiny phone. "But I saved the ones on my cell." He held the phone to his ear and then passed it to me. His hand was shaking a little as he did it. In a moment I understood why.

There were three messages and they were brief but operatic. Wren's voice was quiet, educated, and medium-deep, and when it wasn't steeped in anger or bile or plain craziness, it was pleasant, if a little tired sounding. The first one was the least strident.

"David—it is David, isn't it?—it's Wren calling. It's been so long, David, and I missed you over the holidays. I thought of calling you at home, but then I thought that might be awkward with Stephanie, so I left you a message at the office. When I didn't hear back I thought you might be taking a break from work, and not checking your voicemail. I imagine you could use a vacation, considering how busy you must be at Klein & Sons—your new job and all. Are you traveling? Are you someplace warm? I wish I could join you in the sun, David. I want to see you. Write me soon."

If you didn't know the context, there was something only slightly creepy in the way she kept repeating David's name, and in her neediness. The volume went up in the second message, and so did the harpy quotient.

"It's been two days and I haven't heard from you. I know you're in town, David—you were at that benefit last night, you and Stephanie. You suddenly seem to have so much time for her, David, and none at all for me. I never thought you would be cruel in this way, or so rude. But I won't be ignored, David—and I won't be disrespected. I want to see you, and if I don't, I'll keep calling. And who knows what number I'll dial . . . or who will answer? Maybe your big brother or one of your other partners. Maybe your bitch wife." Her voice was charged with venom at the end, and traveled through anguished, indignant, and imperious to get there. The third message had apparently been left after one of Wren's phone conversations with David.

"You're not picking up anymore, David? Well, fine—don't. You were such a rude bastard when we spoke this morning—so nasty and cold—I'm not sure I want to talk to you just now anyway. I know you like talking dirty, but this was different, David. This was . . . brutal and coarse and not sexy at all. Tell me, do you talk that way to Stephanie? Does she like it? I'll have to remember to ask." There was a frightening slyness in Wren's voice, and something almost triumphal too. She was in control and relishing her power.

The message ended and I looked at the cell phone display. "The call comes through as *private*," I said, and handed the phone to David. "Otherwise I would've looked her up myself," he'd muttered. It wasn't long after that he'd left, still white-faced.

I tossed Vera's cup and my own into the trash, stepped out into the frost and glare, and headed west on Houston. An icy wind was blowing off the East River and it bullied me along in its rush to Jersey. Cold as it was, it felt good to be out in the air, good to walk. I hadn't run since Thursday, and at some point over the weekend, a thick, logy feeling had settled behind my eyes and a plank of dull pain had fastened itself to my forehead. I felt slow and half hungover, and my failure yesterday to find hide or hair or the smallest feather of Wren on the MetroMatchPoint website had only reinforced my sense of being slightly stupid.

The e-mail address Wren used for her correspondence had led me nowhere. Like the one David used, it was provided free of charge by one of the big web search sites and was untraceable without a subpoena or a court order. We weren't to that point yet, and in any event there was no reason to believe that Wren had been any more truthful in the information she'd provided to establish her account than my brother had been in establishing his own.

David had given me the keywords he'd used to find Wren's posting on MetroMatchPoint: *age 25-35*; *Manhattan*; *white*; and the all-important *casual* and *discreet*. The search criteria had helped me cull a thousand women-seeking-men entries down to fewer than a hundred, but even so the list seemed endless. And, after the first couple of dozen, endlessly grim.

Some tried for sexy or funny, but their authors lacked the skill to carry it off in twenty-five words or less, and they came across as crude or incoherent or both. Most of the postings, though, aspired to nothing more than businesslike: a listing of the advertiser's alleged physical attributes, and those she sought in a partner; a few words on specific restrictions or inclinations; and an e-mail address. These were no doubt useful as transactional devices, but the aggregate effect was one of grinding loneliness, and a bleak and relentless hunger. I'd tweaked and twisted David's search criteria but found nothing remotely like Wren's posting, and after three hours I'd called it a day.

A plastic shopping bag blew past me, and so did three pages of a Chinese newspaper and a Mexican takeout menu and a hundred or so cigarette butts—and so, eventually, did my headache. By the time I crossed Sullivan Street, my ears were numb but my brain was full of chilly oxygen.

It was late for breakfast and too early for lunch and I could see through the big window that David had found so useful that Third Uncle was nearly empty. There were a couple of skinny girls behind the steel counter, ministering to the espresso machines, and a pair of drowsy dilettantes paging listlessly through the *Times* at a steel-topped table up front, and no one else in the black-and-white-tiled room. I went inside and my face burned in the sudden warmth.

I sat at the counter and hung my coat on the back of the stool and ordered a hot chocolate. By the time I was halfway through it I'd discovered that the girls were only dimly aware of their customers, even the ones right in front of them, and in any event they had worked there only since November. It had been a long shot, and I was only slightly disappointed.

I checked my watch. I had nearly an hour until my meeting, and the dilettantes had abandoned their newspaper and their table. I carried my coat and my hot chocolate over and sat in a ragged patch of sunlight. One of the skinny girls put on a CD—Nellie McKay. I listened to the flex and twist of her clever voice, and scanned the front page, while the wind roiled the dust outside. The news was more of the same and all bad—a relentless slide backward and down, an inexorable slouching toward a new Dark Age. I was grateful to be following it with only half a mind. The other half was still reeling from what David had told me.

I suppose it shouldn't have surprised me: as my brother himself had observed, secrets were my stock-in-trade. As a PI, and as a cop before that, nearly all the people I met had something to hide, and often very big things—a drug habit, an offshore bank account, a lover or two, a husband or a wife, a whole secret family sometimes, with kids and fish and a secret mortgage on the secret house. Why should David be any different? Just because he was my brother? Just because I knew him, or thought I did? Though, of course, I didn't.

Before he leaned on my intercom button a day ago, I would have said differently. I would've looked into his pale blue eyes, so like our mother's, and said that I knew all I cared to about David March, and certainly all the important stuff—the prickly outer shell of disdain and disapproval; the prickly inner shell of smug superiority; the deeper layers of barely clothed ambition, impatient intelligence, and rigid self-discipline; and the clenched and thwarted core, so quick to take offense, so certain that the rewards that came his way were over-due and never quite enough, never quite his fair share. And I would have said that Stephanie was his perfect match, her ambition and self-satisfaction and ready reproach so well suited to his own. They met the world with the same sharp elbows and bitter mouths and appraiser's eyes: a united if unappealing front, or so I'd thought. But what the hell did I know?

David's questions played over again in my head. *Do you think I'm stupid?* No, not stupid, David, not even close, but maybe a little crazy—maybe more than a little. *What kind of person do you think I am?* Twenty-four hours later I still had no answer. That too familiar face had become a mask, and those blue eyes had gone suddenly opaque.

By the time I finished my hot chocolate and my browse through the newspaper, it was time to meet Victor Sossa.

The wind had quickened a knot or two, and my coat might have been sewn from cheesecloth for all the good it did on my walk to Lispenard Street. My face was brittle when I stepped into the mini-malist lobby of the building just off Church Street, and my eyes were full of grit. Victor Sossa was there, inspecting a tiny crack in the pol-ished stone floor and waiting for me.

Victor was somewhere in his fifties, a compact, muscular man with skin the color of light coffee. His face was wrinkled as a tobacco leaf, and his bald head was covered by a green knit Jets cap. His eyes were black and bright and skeptical. He looked at his watch and at me.

"You March?" he said. I nodded. "You're right on time." Wherever his accent had originated, it was now mostly from the Bronx.

Victor Sossa was the building's nonresident manager—the super—and I'd gotten his name and number from the building's managing agents. Victor and his crew tended to several properties in the neighborhood, all high-priced apartment houses converted a few decades ago from what had been warehouses and factories. Once upon a time, thirty or so years back, the building we were standing in had housed a textile company. More recently, on November 18—when Hendry's was overflowing with rock stars—it was the spot where David and Wren had whiled away an afternoon. David could recall the address, and that the apartment was a large one-bedroom on the fourth floor, but he didn't know the apartment number or its owner's name. I was hoping Victor could help me out.

I had a little story for Victor about investigating an auto accident that had occurred on the eighteenth, and about trying to trace someone who might have witnessed the whole thing from the window of a fourth-floor apartment. He listened politely and nodded, but I'm not sure if it was my story he believed, or my fifty dollars. Either way, he smiled and told me what I wanted to know.

3

It wasn't quite three when I returned home, but already light was draining from the sky. Gray bars of cloud were stacking in the west and the sun looked like a patch of old snow. I paused in my apartment doorway. There was a long black coat slung across the back of my sofa and an open bottle of tonic water on the kitchen counter, next to a bottle of vodka, a paring knife, and three-quarters of a neatly quartered lime. There was a midnight-blue Kelly bag on my long oak table. I smelled Chanel and heard the shower running. Clare.

I'd started seeing her again about six months back, after a long hiatus. Two years ago she'd decided that what passed for our relationship wasn't particularly healthy, and that I wasn't particularly fun, and I couldn't argue with her. I hadn't changed much since then, and certainly not for the better, so when Clare called me last July I could only assume that she'd revised her thinking on health and entertainment.

I'd given her a key in October. It made things more convenient, but I still wasn't used to it. Not that she ever dropped by unannounced; Clare was nothing if not a considerate guest, always calling first and always bringing a little something—orange juice and croissants in the morning, cheese and grapes in the afternoon, and on those evenings when her husband was out of town, cut flowers, takeout Indian food, and an overnight bag. So it wasn't surprise that unnerved me so much as a long habit of solitude. I was still unaccustomed to opening the door on anything other than silence and dust.

I hung my coat on the hook, and Clare's as well, and checked my messages. There weren't any, and hadn't been for a while. David's case was the first new work I'd taken on in a month, and besides him I hadn't heard from any of my siblings in a year and a half. And the handful of acquaintances who used to call occasionally did so less frequently nowadays, maybe because I so rarely called back. I pressed my fingers to my temples. My headache had returned and I poured a glass of water and swallowed a couple of aspirin. I looked down the long line of windows and thought about running but had gotten no further than that when Clare came out of the bathroom.

She was wearing my terry robe, and her pale blond hair hung damp and heavy halfway down her back. She had a towel in one hand and an empty highball glass in the other. From across the room she was model pretty, with pointed chin, straight nose, sculpted cheeks, and a wicked widow's peak, but on closer approach the impression changed. There was something skeptical in the arch of her brow, and something mocking in the curve of her lips, and altogether there was just too much irony and intelligence in her face to make her an effective shill.

"Your water pressure is great," she said, "but you need some new shampoo. I used that green crap in seventh grade, and even then it smelled like funeral flowers." Her voice was scratchy and intimate and always vaguely amused. Her laugh was single-malt. Clare kissed me on the mouth and barely stretched to do it. She left an odd mix of tastes behind—vodka, tonic, lime, and Crest.

There was an intent look on her face as she built herself another drink, and a scientific glint in her narrow gray eyes, as if she were repairing a watch or performing minor surgery. Her sharp features blurred and softened in the evaporating light, and her cheeks faded from pink to porcelain as the shower's heat dissolved. She finished her work with a wedge of lime and some ice cubes from the freezer, and she looked me up and down.

"You look like shit—pale and tired, and look at the bags under your eyes. You're going to screw up those nice pores if you don't watch out." She took a tiny sip of her vodka tonic. "If I didn't know better, I'd say someone got hammered last night." She reached out a long-fingered hand and patted my chest. "How about you come lie down for a while."

Clare was gone when I awoke, and so was the day. Snow was falling in tiny flakes, lit pink by the streetlights. I fumbled on the nightstand for my watch. I'd slept for an hour but I wasn't rested. My headache was still there, joined now by a soreness in my thighs and a tightness in my lower back: the aftermath of Clare's athleticism. I rolled onto a cold, damp spot, and kept on rolling—out of bed and into the bathroom.

A long shower and a peanut-butter-and-jelly sandwich revived me enough to get some work done. I dug through my coat pockets for the notes from my meeting with Victor Sossa and I picked up the telephone.

Victor knew his properties and their owners, and he'd told me enough about the apartments on the fourth floor of the building on Lispenard Street for me to identify which one David had visited: 4-C, the only one-bedroom on the floor.

The apartment was owned by Mr. and Mrs. Martin Litella, who had bought the place for their daughter, Jill. According to Victor, the daughter was an actress, a petite blond who went by the name Jill Nolan, and who was fortunate enough to have steady employment in the road company of a popular musical comedy about the Spanish Inquisition. Nolan had started touring four months ago, Victor said, and she had another three months left on the road. She returned to New York only infrequently—once every six weeks or so—and stayed for just a night or two. He didn't recall her being back at all in November, and thought she was currently in Seattle. Best of all, he had her cell phone number. She answered on the third ring; I said my name was Fitch.

Jill Nolan told me I'd caught her during her no-fat, no-whip, extra-hot decaf mocha break, right between spinning class and her Bikram yoga session. Usually she was able to fit a box-ercise class in too on Tuesday afternoons, but not that Tuesday, because Mandy, the girl she was rooming with—the little redhead who plays the part of the rabbi's daughter from Salamanca who dies at the start of act two—had her boyfriend in from Cincinnati, and to give the two of them space Jill stayed the night with Brittany from the chorus, who forgot to set the alarm and so they were late getting up and it threw off the whole effing day, from breakfast right through to picking up the dry cleaning and returning the boots she'd bought last week. It all came out of her in an endless rushing breath, in an almost hypnotic, singsong voice that rose and fell and tumbled and frothed, and seemed to fill my head with suds.

Finally, she inhaled. "You got my phone number from Victor?" she asked.

"I did," I said, and I repeated my tale about the accident and the search for a witness who'd seen it all from a fourth-floor window. She seemed to take the story more seriously than Victor had.

"Was it a bad accident? Was it with one of those effing bicycle messenger guys? The way they ride, I swear it's a wonder more people aren't killed. Can you believe I actually dated one for a while? That was a trip, let me tell you."

"I'm sure."

"He called himself Storm, like he was a superhero or something. Can you believe it?"

"I'm struggling. Were you by any chance at home on the eighteenth?"

"November eighteenth, you said?"

"November eighteenth."

"No, I wasn't home at all that month."

"Could anyone else have been in your apartment then?"

"Anyone like who?"

I tried not to sigh. "That's what I was hoping you'd tell me."

"Well, I don't know. My parents have keys and they use the place sometimes, but usually they mention it, and anyway they've been in Palm Beach since Halloween. They won't be back till March."

"There's no one else?"

"No one else . . . ?"

"No one else with a key."

Jill Nolan thought about that, which must have been even more trying for her than it was for me. It went on for a while, but eventually she finished. "Well . . . there's Victor, I guess—but you already talked to him. And there's Holly. She has a key, but it's only for emergencies—like if something happens when I'm out of town and my parents are away too."

"Away, like in Florida?"

"Yes, like that. But nothing happened at my place. I mean, I've never called Holly to ask her to go over for anything. I haven't even spoken to her for like five months."

Listening to Jill Nolan hadn't robbed me of quite all my ability to think. I looked at the jelly jar still sitting on my kitchen counter. "I understand," I said. "And this would be Holly Welch you're referring to, yes?"

"Who's Holly Welch? I'm talking about Holly Cade."

"Of course," I said, and chuckled—*silly me*—while I copied down the name. "And you're sure Holly would've told you if she'd gone there?"

"I'm positive," she said.

"Is it possible she stopped by your place, but hasn't had a chance to mention it yet?"

"That's nuts. Holly knows my number—she would've called if she'd gone over."

"How can you be so certain?"

"Because I've known her since, like, second grade—that's how."

"I see. Could you describe Holly for me, Ms. Nolan?"

"Could I what? What does that have to do with your accident thing?"

"Maybe nothing, but my client is sure he saw a woman looking out on the accident scene from what turned out to be a window in your apartment. Tell me, does Holly have blond hair?"

She laughed. "You're way off base. Holly's got red hair, and she's had it all her life. So your client must be wrong, Mr. Fitch. Maybe he got the windows mixed up."

"I didn't say that my client saw a blond, Ms. Nolan. In fact, what he saw was a tall, thirtyish woman with thick auburn hair, fair skin, a narrow face, and a slender build. Does that sound familiar?"

Her response was slow in coming, and when it did, confusion and surprise vied with anger in her voice. "That sounds like . . . But she would've . . . You . . . you tricked me."

"And I'm sorry about that, but does the description fit Holly Cade?"

A few moments more of silence, and anger won out in Jill Nolan. It made her smarter. "How could your client see someone so clearly from all the way down in the street, anyway? You lied to me, Mr. Fitch—if that's your real name—and I don't think I'll talk to you anymore."

"I'm sorry you feel that way. If you give me Holly's number, I could finish up with her directly."

I wasn't surprised when the line went dead, and I wasn't dissatisfied, either. I had a name to work with now, and maybe the name of my little bird. Holly Cade.

Holly Cade who had no listed phone number and no address, no car registration or voter registration, no real property in her name—almost no presence at all in the on-line world. Almost.

I found a reference to her on the website of some sort of performance space in Williamsburg, Brooklyn, on its calendar of events. The event in question was the staging of a play entitled *Liars Club*, by a theater troupe called the Gimlet Players. *Liars Club* was a one-act work, penned by one of the Gimlet's founders, a certain Holly Cade. Unfortunately for me, the performance had taken place three Aprils ago, and in the meanwhile the Gimlet Players seemed to have disbanded.

The only other trace I found was a brief mention of her in a back issue of something called *Digital Gumbo: The On-line Journal of Emerging Video Arts*. Clicking through the website didn't tell me much about "emerging video arts" or anything else, and most of the articles read like muddled pastiches of Jacques Derrida and Roland Barthes. The reference to Holly was in a review of a group show at the Krug Gallery, in Woodstock, New York. Holly was one of four artists who had exhibited their video works there nearly two years ago. The review was lukewarm, and Holly's piece rated barely two sentences. Like the Gimlet Players, the Krug Gallery hadn't stood the test of time; it had closed last May. Which left me, as the evening wore out, knowing not much more about Holly Cade than her name. Except that I remembered what Jill Nolan had said.

"Because I've known her since, like, second grade . . ."

Holly Cade was mostly invisible on the Web, but Jill Nolan was not. I found a one-paragraph biography of her on the touring company's website, and a headshot of her bland, pretty, bright-toothed face. The bio was mostly a list of stage and TV credits, but near the end was the nugget I'd been looking for. "Born and raised in Wilton, Connecticut . . ."

Forty-eight hours was more time than David wanted to wait for a progress report. I was happy to report what little progress I'd made over the telephone, but David wouldn't have it. He was typically specific in his other demands too: no stopping by his office, no meetings south of Park Row or anywhere on the Upper East Side, and definitely no house calls—not to his house, anyway. In the end, we met at the Florida Room, an airy, high-concept diner around the corner from my place. It has a lot of jalousies and slow-turning ceiling fans, and enough background noise for private conversation. There's a row of booths along the back wall and I was in one, working on a bowl of oatmeal, when David arrived. He kept his coat on and sat and stared out the windows at the pedestrians and cars.

"Holly Cade," he said again, and shook his head. "Never heard of her." He dug his hands into his coat pockets and seemed to shiver. The waitress came and David ordered orange juice and nothing else.

"How about Jill Nolan?" I asked.

"Not her either," he said softly.

He was turned out in pinstriped navy, crisp and spotless despite the messy sidewalks. But David also looked smaller today, and older and more distracted too.

"Is this Nolan going to tell her pal about your call?" he asked.

"Maybe," I said. "Probably. And I don't expect it will take Holly long to figure out what it was about."

"That's fucking great," David said. "What happened to discretion?"

"You think she'll be surprised that you're looking for her? It's not like she ordered you not to try to find her, after all. Hell, she might even be flattered. Maybe it'll make her get in touch."

"Fucking great," he said again. David's juice came, but he just looked at it for a while and went back to peering out the window. He looked east and west and east again, searching for something along the length of Seventeenth Street.

"Has she called again?" I asked.

David snorted. "Don't you think I would've mentioned it?"

I was by no means certain, but I nodded anyway. "Did something else happen, then?"

He stiffened and shook his head slowly. "What the hell are you going on about?"

"You seem a little jumpy."

David stared at me for a long moment, his eyes feverish in his waxen face. "Don't think you know something about me now, because you don't," he said. He tugged at a tiny scrap of skin over his Adam's apple, a nervous habit he'd had since he was a kid but that I hadn't seen in years. And I thought of something I hadn't thought of for at least as long.

I couldn't have been much older than ten, which made David maybe twelve. It was springtime, I remembered, because the French doors were opened onto the terrace, and a table was set outside with our parents' breakfast on it, though no one was eating. And I remembered it was a weekday, because Irma, the woman who took care of us back then, was orbiting raggedly around Lauren and me, trying to get us ready for school. But her efforts were in vain that morning; we were even less cooperative than usual, distracted as we were by the tension congealing around us, and the dangerous hum in the air.

It was what happened when the usually simmering border war between our parents heated up to something more overt. We never knew the substance of their conflict, or the particulars that brought things to a boil, but we knew more or less what to expect: lowered voices, raspy whispers, quick footsteps and slamming doors, and a thick, oppressive silence in between. Familiar, but frightening nonetheless.

We hadn't seen our mother, but only heard her voice in jagged fragments. Our father had made a brief appearance, unshaven and still in his striped pajamas and robe—he'd given up going to the Klein & Sons offices years before. He breezed through the kitchen with a bottle of seltzer under his arm and ruffled his hand through my hair. His smile was lopsided and his eyes were unfocused. He breezed off again, in the direction of the bedrooms, and I followed at a distance. I found David outside the double doors to their room, his ear cocked. He turned away as I approached.

"What are they saying?" I whispered. He didn't answer. "Can you hear?" Again, nothing. I stepped up to the door, to listen myself, and I saw David's face—the tears in his eyes and on his cheeks. It was the first time I remember seeing him cry.

"What the fuck are you looking at?" he snapped.

"Nothing."

"Then get out of here."

"Can you hear?" I asked again. "What are they talking about?"

David wheeled and wiped his arm across his face and shoved me in the chest. "You, you little faggot—they're talking about what a fucking loser you are, and how they're sending you to military school. So you better run now, before the Marines show up to take you."

I stumbled backward until I hit the hallway wall. My eyes were burning. "Fuck you, crybaby," I whispered.

David stared at me and tugged at a tiny scrap of skin over his Adam's apple. He looked for a long time and then his fist came up from what seemed like nowhere and split my lower lip.

It was the first time for that too.

I shook my head and shook the thought away and the restaurant din returned. David was still looking at me across the table.

"So where the hell does this Cade live—in Wilton?"

"Somebody named Nicole Cade lives there—the only Cade in town; I don't know if she knows Holly. But Jill Nolan grew up there, and she and Holly were childhood friends, and—"

"Yeah, yeah, yeah—I get it," David said, and looked up and down Seventeenth Street some more. "Just call me when you get back."

The waitress came to refill my coffee cup, and when she left David did too.

Wilton was just over an hour's drive from the city, north and east on 95 and then north on Route 7—chaotic interstate followed by strip malls followed by pricey clapboard suburbs. Concrete and slush gave way to pines and stone fences and still white snow, and the cars were fewer but more expensive. I turned off 7 onto Route 33, toward Ridgefield, and turned again when I came to Cranberry Lane. It was a quiet road and the houses were large and far-between along it. My rent-a-car fishtailed through two miles of scenic turns before I reached the Cade place.

It was a red-doored, black-shuttered white colonial set well back from the road, and set handsomely in its landscape. The big lindens in front would make for nice shade in summer and nice color in fall, and the conservatory at the south end, while certainly not original, was well proportioned and well matched to the lines of the roof and the flow of the façade. The plantings around the stone foundations were wrapped in neat burlap. Snow lay like cake frosting on the brown bundles and covered the broad front lawn in a pristine blanket that was painfully bright under the noontime sky. The curving drive was plowed to a layer of ice and packed gravel and I took my time driving up, parking in the turnaround by the garage, and walking back down the shoveled flagstone path. The man on the front steps, fussing clumsily with a screwdriver and the hinges of a storm door, watched me the whole way.

He was middle-aged and bulky, and soft-looking all over, and his dark eyes were vaguely nervous behind rimless glasses. He took off his Red Sox cap and his brown hair was messy and thinning underneath. He wiped his brow on the sleeve of his corduroy shirt, and cursed when he dropped his screwdriver into the snow. He stooped to retrieve it and the storm door swung against his hip. I caught him by the elbow before he tipped.

"Thanks," he said softly. He steadied himself on my arm as he rose. His face was small and bland and fleshy around the jaw. A web of shattered veins darkened the pinched end of his nose, and embarrassment colored his unshaven cheeks.

"Mr. Cade?" I asked.

His mouth puckered in annoyance. "My name is Deering, Herbert Deering. Who are you looking for?"

"Nicole Cade," I said. Nicole Cade was the name the public records search had returned—the owner of this house, its purchaser six years back from a Fredrick Cade.

The man's annoyance heightened for a moment, and then was gone. "Nicole's my wife, but she didn't say anyone was stopping by. You are—who?"

"John March. Is your wife at home?"

Deering slid the screwdriver into the back pocket of his jeans and wiped his hands on his thighs. "What is it you want to see her about?"

I looked past him through the open door, into the entrance foyer and down the wide center hall. I saw a brass chandelier, cream-colored walls, glossy wood floors, and dark Persian rugs, and I heard sharp footsteps, like blows from a tack hammer. A shadow crossed the hallway near the back, beyond the staircase.

"Holly," I said. "I'm here about Holly."

Deering nearly dropped his hat. His voice grew softer and more anxious. "What about Holly?"

A woman's voice interrupted. It was deep and impatient and something like a wood rasp. It seemed to scare Herbert Deering. "Who is it, Herbert, and what do they want? I'm *trying* to get some work done, for chrissakes."

The hard footsteps grew closer and a woman came down the hall. I looked at her and looked for some resemblance to the Wren David had described. The height maybe, and maybe the hair. I didn't speculate on the tattoo or the birthmark.

She was north of forty, tall and gaunt, with angular shoulders beneath her green turtleneck and thin, hard-looking legs in snug jeans. Her face was bony and weathered, any prettiness there worn down by wind and sun, and carved into a wedge of suspicion. Her arctic eyes peered out from a thicket of lines, and her mouth was a bloodless seam beneath the blade of her nose. She pushed faded red hair behind her ears and folded sinewy arms across her chest. Nicole Cade looked several years older than her husband, and many times more formidable. She tapped a loafered foot on the floorboards and turned her gaze on Deering, who wilted beneath it.

"This is Mr. March, Nikki," he said, and he took his screwdriver from his pocket and retreated to the front steps. "He's here to talk to you. About Holly." With that, Deering scuttled off the steps and down the flagstone path toward the garage.

Nicole looked me up and down and took in the paddock boots, the black cords, the gray sweater, and the leather jacket. She nodded minutely and glanced at the big runner's watch on her bony wrist. Her mouth grew smaller. "What's this about my sister?" she said.

"Would you mind if we spoke inside?"

"In fact, I would. Now what's this about my sister?"

I took a deep breath and told my little story again, about the accident and the witness. Nicole didn't consider it long enough for belief or disbelief. "And what is it you want from me?" she asked.

"I was hoping you could help me get in touch with Holly."

She looked at me for what seemed a long time, tapping her foot all the while. Her face was motionless and set in well-worn lines of distrust. "That assumes I know something about my sister's life, Mr. March, and that I have some interest in helping you. But neither assumption is true, I'm afraid." Nicole Cade looked at her big watch again and back at me.

I almost smiled at her rudeness, and at how much it reminded me of David's. "I suppose I should have called first."

"Of course you should have—that's just polite—but it wouldn't have changed my answer. I haven't spoken to Holly in some time."

"Do you have an address for her, or a telephone number?"

"I thought I'd made myself clear: I don't know about my sister's life, and I don't care to. Now if you'll excuse me . . ."

"Sure," I said. "Do you think your husband might know something more?"

"Certainly not," she said, and looked as if I'd asked about flying pigs.

"How about any friends in town?"

Nicole Cade pursed her thin lips and a hard light came up in her eyes. "Holly's not in touch with anyone from Wilton," she said evenly.

"You're probably right," I said, "but it never hurts to ask. Maybe I could start with the neighbors."

The hard light turned speculative, and she tapped her foot for several beats. "Is that a threat, Mr. March," she said quietly, "that you'll make a nuisance of yourself, or embarrass me, if I don't talk to you? Is that the kind of sleazy thing they teach at private detective school?" The anger in her voice was tamped down, and covered with a layer of satisfaction: I'd lived down to her expectations.

I gave her my most innocent smile. "I'm just trying to do my job, Ms. Cade."

She checked her watch again, more elaborately this time. "You're lucky I've got work to do, and no time for this nonsense," she said. She walked down the hallway and took a left at the end, and she was back in under a minute, with a black notebook.

"This is the last address I have for her. I have no idea whether it's still good." It was an address in Brooklyn and I copied it down.

"Is she still acting?" I asked.

She sighed impatiently. "Acting, writing, video—Holly's dabbled in a thousand things, and as far as I know not one has taken. I have no idea what she's doing now."

"She can support herself doing that—dabbling?"

Impatience morphed into suspicion, and Nicole Cade squinted at me. "Ask Holly, if you can find her—though how it's relevant to your accident case escapes me. And now goodbye, Mr. March." The storm door swung shut and the front door closed behind it, and I was left standing in the cold.

I made my way down the path toward my car. I rounded the corner and found all three garage doors open. There was an immaculate Volvo sedan in one bay, a filthy VW wagon in another, and Herbert Deering in the third, standing by a green metal tool cart and fumbling with a socket wrench. He looked up and dropped the wrench on the concrete floor. The clang made him wince.

"Catching up on some chores?" I asked.

He ducked his head nervously and made a small, rueful smile. "Plenty of time for that now—the wonders of outsourcing." I nodded sympathetically. Deering opened a drawer in the tool cart and picked through whatever was inside. "You through with Nikki?" he asked.

"More like she's through with me."

Deering smiled again. "I didn't think it would take long, not when you said you'd come to talk about Holly."

"I guess they don't get on too well."

Deering shook his head. "They have nothing to do with each other," he said, and looked up at me. "Is Holly all right?"

"As far as I know," I said, and I trotted out my accident story yet again. I was getting to like it, and Deering seemed to have no complaints either. "Your wife gave me an address," I concluded, "but she didn't know if it was still good."

Deering nodded vaguely and opened another drawer. "Holly moves a lot, and like I said she and Nikki don't keep up. It's one of those things where one says white and the other has got to say black. It's a thing with sisters sometimes."

And not just sisters, I thought. I nodded at him. "Is Holly still making a living as an actress?"

Deering thought about it a while and shrugged. "I don't know. I don't know that she ever made much of a living at it."

"How does she pay the rent, then—waiting tables?"

"That's never been her problem," Deering said, shaking his head. "Her mom left some money." He looked around and then looked at me. "You going over there? To Brooklyn?" I nodded. "Well . . . tell her hi if you see her."

"Will do," I said, and I dug in my jacket for the car keys. I found them and thought of one more question for Herb Deering. "Who is Fredrick Cade?"

Herb nearly dropped his wrench again. "Fred is Nikki's dad—my father-in-law. Where'd that come from?"

"This used to be his house?"

Deering grimaced a little. "The girls grew up here. We—Nikki—bought it from him a few years back."

"And where did he go?"

"North of here, up to Brookfield. He's in an assisted living setup. Why?"

"Do you think Holly might be in touch with him? Just in case this address is out of date."

He blanched. "God, no. The one person Holly gets on worse with than Nikki is Fred. No way she's in touch with him. And even if she was, he wouldn't know it, not the way he is now." Herb Deering tapped a forefinger to the side of his head. "Alzheimer's," he said.

I nodded and started to thank him, when a knob turned at the back of the garage. Nicole Cade was a rigid silhouette in the doorway, and her voice was colder than the air. "I thought we were finished, Mr. March—in fact, I know we were. What are you still doing here?"

"Getting directions back to town," I said, "and a recommendation of someplace for lunch."

"Well, we're not the auto club, and Herbert has better things to do with his time, I'm sure."

I smiled to myself and shook my head. The garage doors dropped before I made it to my car.

It was nearly three when I got home. Much of Sixteenth Street lay in shadow, and the slush had begun to refreeze underfoot. The lobby of my building was empty and the hallways were quiet. My apartment was filled with winter light, like a vast gray sheet over the furniture. Nobody home. I put my jacket on the kitchen counter and poured myself a glass of water, and started when I heard music from upstairs.

A lawyer moved in up there a year ago, on a two-year sublease. He's generally pretty quiet, and even when he's not his music is inoffensive, but I jumped every time I heard it. Every time, I thought of Jane Lu.

It was two years last November that she'd bought the place upstairs, and shortly after that we'd become lovers. It wasn't even six months later that Jane had gone away, first on an extended vacation to Italy and then to another of her CEO-for-hire gigs, this time in Seattle. She'd wanted me to go with her, on the vacation part at least, and if I had, she might still be living upstairs. But I hadn't gone and she hadn't stayed and maybe it wouldn't have made a difference, anyway. Maybe it was doomed from the start.

Certainly there wasn't much left of me by the time I met her. By then it had been three years since my wife, Anne, had been killed—shot neatly and precisely and left to die within yards of our front porch, the last of many victims of a man who wouldn't live to see the end of that day. It was my biggest case by far as a sheriff's investigator up in Burr County, and my last one, and I'd fucked it up from start to finish. My stupidity and ego had let Morgan Furness run loose for too long, and let him turn the investigation around on me and into an elaborately constructed suicide by cop.

For months afterward I was consumed by chaos—by anger and guilt and annihilating grief, and a hurricane of alcohol and drugs. When the storm passed, I was no longer a policeman and I'd succeeded in burning down most of my life. From the charred bits that remained I'd fashioned something else, something small and simple, made of work and running and solitude. It was modest craftsmanship, but it was all that I could manage.

It was nineteen months since I'd seen Jane last, and listened to her last scratchy message on my telephone.

"I can't do this, John. I thought I could, but I was wrong. I tried to keep things at arm's length—tell myself you were like Nick Charles or something, and your work was clever and glamorous, and somehow separate from you. But that's bullshit, and I can't pretend otherwise.

"There's nothing amusing about being followed. There's nothing witty about beatings and guns and emergency rooms. There's nothing funny about getting shot. I don't know why you want that in your life, John, but I know I don't.

"Maybe it would be easier if I knew what you were looking for from all this—from us. Or maybe there's no mystery to it. Maybe you're not looking for anything at all. Maybe your life is already just the way you want it."

Doomed from the start.

I ate some aspirin and drained my water glass. I took out my notes from Wilton and carried them to the table and started reading. I was dozing over them when the intercom buzzed and I jumped again. I went to the wall unit and watched the grainy image emerge on the tiny video screen. It wasn't memory that disturbed me this time, but a more surprising visitor: my sister-in-law Stephanie. David's wife.

I hit a patch of black ice coming off the curb at East Third Street, crossing Avenue B, and my ankle turned and I almost went down. But not quite.

"Shit," I hissed as I caught myself, and the middle-school kids crossing the other way laughed. Not even four miles gone and I was panting like a hound. It served me right for laying off so long. A wet snowflake landed on my eye. I brushed it off and huffed forward, headed west and sometimes south.

The snow had made it that much harder to drag myself up the deep well of sleep that morning, and to drag my ass onto the road, but snow was only part of it. The night had been filled with dreams I couldn't remember, but that left behind a nagging sense of something unfinished or mislaid or abandoned. And then there was the nightmare I couldn't forget: Stephanie's visit.

She'd stood in my doorway for a full minute, legs together, arms at her sides, hands jammed in the pockets of her navy blue coat. Her wiry hair was shorter than I recalled and bound precariously by a tortoiseshell clip. Her pale face was pinched and stiff, and her overlarge eyes skittered around me and all around the apartment. Her little mouth was twitching.

"Why don't you come in," I'd said finally. My voice made her flinch, but she came. Her steps were tentative and rigid, as if onto thin ice. I offered to take her coat but she seemed not to hear. She'd picked her way around the room, teetering first by the kitchen counter, then by the bookshelves, then the windows, and finally by the sofa. Then she sat. I sat too, at the table, and closed my laptop and my notepad.

I knew she was working again, as an equity analyst at a firm downtown, and she looked as if she'd come from the office—black pumps, dark hose, dark striped skirt, ivory blouse. She kept her bony knees together and kept her coat wrapped around her narrow body like a cocoon. Her eyes hopped around for another minute and she clutched her hands together and finally spoke.

"What are you doing to him?" she asked. Her voice was brittle.

"Stephanie, I don't know—"

"Oh, don't even bother to lie! Just don't, John. What are you doing to him?"

"I'm not doing any—"

"Of course you are! Why else would he come here? Why would he visit you?"

I pulled a hand down my face and sighed. "I think David's the person to ask about that." But she wanted no advice.

"You've never liked me."

Jesus. "That's been mostly a two-way street," I said.

She waved that away. "And you never made a secret of it, and now that I need something from you, you're just going to lord it over me."

I shook my head. "I don't know what you're talking about, Stephanie. I'm not *lording* anything over any—"

"Then answer my goddamn questions," she said. "What are you doing to him? What kind of thing have you gotten him involved in?" Her voice was like breaking glass.

I bit back my first three answers. "You need to talk to David," I said again. She ignored me.

"It wouldn't be the first time you dragged your family into the gutter, though, would it? But I won't let you do it to David."

My breath caught in my throat and I think even Stephanie knew she'd gone too far. "You should go now," I said quietly. But she didn't. Instead she walked to the window and stood stiffly where David had stood.

"Or are you saying he came to you for help of some sort? Is that it? But what kind of help would that be?"

"The only thing I'm saying is that you should go," I repeated.

Stephanie bent her head and a shudder went through her back. I heard sniffling. Shit. After a minute, she hitched her coat higher on her shoulders, did up the buttons, and headed for the door. She paused when she got there and turned to me.

"It's about that woman, isn't it, and those phone calls?" she'd said. She hadn't waited for an answer.

I had another mile and a half in by the time I came lumbering up Sixteenth Street to the wrought-iron steps of my building. I was still winded and soaked in sweat, but my headache was gone. I crawled up the stairs and into the shower, where I stood for a long time with the spray in my face.

After Stephanie had left I'd phoned David, to tell him about her visit and about my trip to Wilton. We never got to the Wilton part; his questions were all about Stephanie. "How much does she know?" "How did she find out?" "Did that crazy bitch call her?" "Tell me again what she said." After the third go-round I stopped answering.

"I don't want to be in the middle of this," I told him. "I didn't hire on to lie to your wife."

"Who's asking you to lie, for chrissakes? I just expect some confidentiality."

"Slice it as fine as you want, I don't want to be in that position with Stephanie again."

"Who knew you were so sensitive?" he said, and hung up.

I fumbled for the faucets and turned up the heat.

An hour after my shower I was riding the L train to Brooklyn. Though the real-estate people keep moving the borders, the address Nikki Cade had given me was more Bushwick than Williamsburg, and not convenient to any subway station. I picked the Montrose Avenue stop and worked my way south along Bushwick Avenue, leaning into the wind all the way. It was a short walk from trendy to just getting by;

vegan bistros and handbag ateliers gave way to bodegas and auto parts shops and boarded-up shells in the space of a few blocks. By the time I got to Holly Cade's street, there was nary an artisanal cheese market in sight.

Her building was five stories of dirty red brick, with a gray stone stoop, friable-looking fire escapes up the sides, and liberal coats of graffiti all around. There was a smell out front like burnt garbage, which beat the hell out of the festering-wound odor in the vestibule. There was an intercom box on the wall, with a mangled speaker grate and worn plastic buttons with apartment numbers next to them. The name next to 3-G was written in green ink on a strip of masking tape. Cade.

I leaned on the button for a while and got no response, and I was thinking about what I might do to the massive lock on the inner door when a pack of teenaged girls came boiling off the elevator and down the short hallway toward me. I didn't ask why they weren't in school, and they paid me no mind as they passed in a swirl of perfume, hairspray, bubblegum, and cigarette smoke. The inner door was gaping in their wake, and I walked up to three.

The stairwell was narrow and dark and smelled like a urinal, and the third-floor corridor wasn't much different. The door to 3-G was at the end of the hall to the left, adjacent to 3-F and the trash chute. The door was metal-clad and once upon a time it had been painted black. When I put my ear to it I heard someone moving around on the other side. I knocked hard and the moving stopped but no one answered. On my third try I heard a bolt slip and hinges squeak behind me. I turned in time to see a narrow gap in the door to apartment 3-F close quickly. When I turned back to 3-G, the door was opening.

The man in the doorway was an inch or so taller than I and maybe forty pounds heavier, none of it fat. His shoulders barely cleared the doorframe as he stepped into the hall. He closed the door behind him, locked it with a key, and put the key in the pocket of his gray parka.

"What do you want?" he said. His voice was surprisingly soft. He crossed massive arms on a massive chest and strained his sleeves to tearing. His blond, crewcut head was large and square, and affixed to the rest of him without benefit of neck. His face was broad, pale, and smooth, and his close-set features looked stunted and abandoned in the center. His mouth was a pink ripple below a pinch of nose, his brows no more than sketch marks above blue eyes that were empty of curiosity and everything else. His hands were like steaks and there were blurry green tats on them that looked like prison work. I put his age at thirty, tops.

"This your place?" I asked.

"I got the key," Babyface said. "Now what the fuck do you want?"

"I'm here to see Holly."

"She's not here," he rumbled. "What do you want her for?"

"Who are you, the husband? The boyfriend? The secretary, maybe?"

Color rose on his flat cheeks. "I'm the guy who'll plant his boot up your ass, you don't say why you're banging at the door."

I shook my head and smiled. "Let's not get stupid too fast," I said, with more nonchalance than I felt.

Babyface squinted at me and a wrinkle formed on his smooth forehead. "You a cop?"

"Why would a cop be looking for Holly?"

"You're a cop, lemme see some ID."

I smiled some more. "You didn't answer my question: why would a cop be looking for Holly? Or maybe it's you they're looking for. Maybe you're the one who should be showing ID."

The wrinkle deepened and his big face got dark. "You're no fucking cop," he said. "And you're pissing me off."

"Get Holly out here and you won't have to talk to me anymore."

Babyface shook his head. "You don't listen," he growled. "Now, you say who you are and what the fuck you want or we're gonna have trouble."

He flexed his large hands. I looked at the ink on them and took a deep breath and took a chance. "Do you talk to your PO like this? I don't expect it goes over too well."

Surprise, anger, and fear flickered through his eyes at the mention of his parole officer; I figured I'd struck a nerve. I was sure when he hit me.

His forearm was a tree trunk in gray nylon, and it whipped around like it was driven by a storm and banged me on the side of the head. I bounced off the door to 3-F on my way to the floor, and I caught a glimpse of Babyface's biker boots and the frayed hem of his jeans flashing by.

"Asshole," he muttered. I heard his footsteps down the stairs, and then all I heard was a ringing in my ears and all I saw was dirty linoleum.

I took a few deep breaths and prodded at my temple and slowly hoisted myself up. My head stayed where it belonged and so did the rest of the world, and I was reasonably sure that nothing was broken. I looked up and saw the door close again on apartment 3-F. I stepped over and knocked.

The voice that answered came from somewhere near the peephole. It was a man's voice, reedy and old and with a faint Spanish accent. "Get the hell away," he said. "Get away or I'm calling the cops."

"I'm trying to get in touch with Holly Cade," I said. "You know how I might do that?"

"I don't know nothing, except I'm tired of all the noise and shouts and comings and goings, and the next time this shit happens I'm calling the cops."

"I can understand that," I said. "Do you know who that guy was?"

"I know nine-one-one, and unless you leave now, I'm calling it."

I took a card from my wallet. "I'm going," I said, "but do me a favor, will you: give me a call the next time you see Holly around." I slipped the card under the door and almost instantly it came sliding back.

"Get away from me with this—I don't want anything to do with it or you."

"You don't have to be involved in anything," I said. "Just give me a call. I can make it worth your while."

"Nine-one-one, mister. I'm not telling you again."

I held up my hands. "All right, all right, I'm going."

"Then go."

I took my time down the stairs and saw no sign of Babyface. I stopped in the vestibule and buzzed 3-G again, and again got no answer. The name next to the button for 3-F was Arrua; I copied it down and left. It was still cold outside but not as windy, and the burnt-garbage smell had subsided under a blanket of new snow.

The cold air tasted good after the reek of Holly Cade's building, and the snow helped numb my aching face, and so I walked over to Broadway and kept on walking, north and west, deep into the hipster heart of Williamsburg. Block by block the neighborhood changed, from mostly Latino to Hasidic to well-heeled bohemian. By the time I got to Bedford Avenue my hair was white with snow and I might as well have been in TriBeCa.

I found a coffee bar with Citizen Cope playing at low volume and some fat chairs by a window and a pretty Asian girl with a gold ring through her nose behind the counter. I brushed myself off and ordered a double espresso and sipped at it slowly while I scratched down some notes about my visit to Holly's place.

I got a good description of Babyface on paper and some questions about him too: Who was he? What was he doing in Holly's apartment? What was his relationship to her? But I had no answers for any of them. All I knew for certain was that he was strong and fast, and that if I ran into him again I would watch out for his right and for his very short fuse. I finished writing and drank some more coffee and flipped back through the pages of my notepad.

Holly Cade was so far my only line on the mysterious Wren, but I still knew precious little about the woman, and I had yet to actually lay eyes on her. Knowing where she lived was progress, but until I had a photograph and a positive ID from David, she would remain just my best guess. I could, if I had to, hire some freelancers to set up outside her building and wait until she came home, but I hadn't quite gotten to that point yet. That approach was neither cheap nor subtle, and I still had a bread crumb or two left to work with. I read through another few pages of notes and wondered if I might eke something more out of my trip to Brooklyn than a shot in the head and a pricey cup of coffee.

Null Space was south and west of the coffee bar, off Bedford Avenue, in a gray brick building that long ago had been a tea warehouse. It shared the ground floor with an art gallery and a Chinese fusion restaurant, and it was the venue, three years back, where the Gimlet Players had staged a production of Holly Cade's play, *Liars Club*. It was a large, chilly space with black walls and a dense array of lights and speakers hanging from the high ceiling. Any lingering fragrance of tea was obscured by the odors of paint and cement, and by the smell of lemongrass from next door.

The manager was a sturdy, fortyish woman with dark, messy hair, a pleasant gap between her teeth, and a plaid flannel shirt. Her voice was flat and Midwestern and her name was Lisa. Besides a squad of underfed guys stacking chairs, she was the only one at home when I knocked on the big metal doors. She'd worked at Null Space for six years, remembered the Gimlets well enough, and didn't ask what business it was of mine. It made for a near-perfect interview.

"They did three or four one-acts here, over the course of eighteen months or so," she said. "*Liars Club* was the last of them." We walked into what passed for the office, a gray, square room that almost had a view of an alley through a window black with dirt. The furniture was mismatched metal, too ugly for government work. Lisa took a seat behind the desk and placed her can of Diet Coke before her. I sat in a banged-up beige guest chair that was even less comfortable than it looked.

"Were they any good?" I asked.

She shrugged. "I remember the plays being very *heavy*, in a theater-class kind of way. A lot of disjointed dialogue and fucked-up families. And I remember the Gimlets being kind of a pain in the ass."

"How so?" I asked.

Lisa drank some soda and ran a hand through her hair. "They were always complaining about something—the seating, the lights, publicity, the audience or lack thereof. And they were always in the midst of some crisis or another."

"Such as?"

"Amateurish crap, like actors not showing up on time, or at all, or losing props, or just bickering."

"Any idea about what?"

"Who knows; stars on the dressing room door, maybe. I tried not to pay attention. Whatever it was, it seemed like they could never get their shit together."

"I'd guess you get a fair amount of that in this line of work."

"Like you wouldn't believe," Lisa said, smiling. "And the bands are usually the worst. But it gives you an idea of how whiny the Gimlets were that they stand out three years later."

I smiled back. "How many of them were there?"

She thought for a moment. "Four or five, maybe."

"And all of them complainers?"

"Not all of them; it was mainly the two who kind of ran things."

"Was Holly Cade one of them?"

She nodded again. "Holly, yeah, the redhead, a very pretty girl. Her boyfriend was the director and she was the writer."

"What was the boyfriend's name?"

Lisa drained her soda can and dropped it in the trash basket with a bang. "Now you're asking the hard questions," she said. "For that I need to dig."

The digging was done in a closet stacked almost to the ceiling with cardboard file boxes. There was evidently some method to their stacking and Lisa knew what it was. With only a modicum of shifting and shoving she brought out a box and heaved it onto the desk. A cloud of dust swirled up and Lisa coughed. She took off the lid, flicked through some files at the back of the box, and came out with a green folder.

She shuffled through the contents and pulled out some paper. "Ta-dah! It's the program we did for *The Nest*—another of their one-acts." She read the sheet and looked up at me. "Gene Werner, that was his name. Truth be told, he was the bigger pain in the ass."

"Can I see that?" I asked. She passed it over.

I scanned down the short list of cast and crew. Besides being director and playwright respectively, Gene Werner and Holly Cade were also in the cast. Gene played someone named Fredrick; Holly played a character named Wren. I read it twice more to be sure, and heard blood pounding in my ears. Wren.

"You mind if I keep this?" I asked.

Lisa shrugged. "Okay."

I looked at the program and thought some more. "You remember what Gene Werner looked like?"

She chewed her lower lip and thought it over. "Not that well. Dark hair and tall, good-looking—a male model type."

"A bodybuilder?"

"You mean all bulked up?" she asked. I nodded. "No, he was more like you—kind of lean."

Not Babyface. I pointed at the file box. "Any photos of the Gimlets in there?"

"I can check," she said, but my luck went only so far. Lisa rifled through the files from back to front and found no pictures—but she didn't come up empty-handed. She pulled out programs for the other two plays the Gimlets had performed at Null Space, and scripts for *The Nest* and *Liars Club*. She let me take them along when I stepped out into the snow and headed back to Manhattan.

It was two-thirty when I got home. I ran a towel through my hair, pulled on a pair of dry socks, and made a tuna sandwich, then spent the rest of the afternoon on my laptop and on the telephone, tracking down former members of the Gimlet Players. Which turned out to be easier said than done. Lisa was right about there having been four or five people in the troupe. Unfortunately, it wasn't always the same four or five people. Counting Gene Werner, there were seven names on my list. By dusk I'd left messages for three of them, including Werner, failed to find any trace of three others, and actually managed to speak with the remaining one.

Moira Neal told me that the Gimlets had never been a close-knit group, and that she hadn't kept in touch with any of them after the breakup. She had acted with the troupe for just a year, and the experience had helped to drive her out of theater altogether and into website design.

"And let me tell you, the personalities are a whole lot easier to deal with." She laughed. Her voice was smart and pleasant, and as empty of accent as a newscaster's.

"The Gimlets were a difficult bunch?"

"Holly and Gene were, and it was all their show."

"Difficult how?"

"Gene was a prima donna and a bully—which, let me tell you, is not a winning combo. He thought he was another Mike Nichols or something, but he didn't have the chops to back it up. And he took great pleasure in being a Grade A prick, a real nasty son of a bitch. Holly was a little easier to take; she was just on another planet most of the time."

"Meaning . . . ?"

"Meaning she was very serious about her work, very . . . *intense*. I don't know how much the real world ever penetrated when she was working on a play."

"Was she any good?"

"As a playwright, not very—at least, I didn't think so. Her stuff was really autobiographical, and there was a big part you just couldn't get if you weren't Holly. The part you could get was kind of juvenile: lots of evil-parent stuff and lots of proclamations."

"How was she as an actress?"

"That was a different story altogether: Holly was great. It helped that she was gorgeous and you couldn't take your eyes off her, of course, but it was more than that. She was totally committed to every part she played, and she could transform herself completely. It was a little scary, to be honest. I always wondered if she could do it in a part she hadn't written."

"And she and Werner were romantically involved?"

"They slept together, on and off, if that's what you mean. As for 'involved'—that I don't know. I'm not sure how involved Holly could be with anyone but Holly."

"I heard that besides the writing and acting, Holly made videos too."

"Not while I knew her, but it wouldn't surprise me. She tried her hand at lots of things—painting, photography, even woodworking, I think." Moira Neal paused and a little smile entered her voice. "You really need to know all this for an accident case?"

I smiled back. "You never know what you'll need to know," I said. "Speaking of which, did you happen to know someone named Wren when you were with the Gimlets?"

She thought about it. "That was one of Holly's characters, wasn't it—one of the nut-job roles she played."

"But no real person by that name?"

"No," she said, "no real person."

Clare's hair was spread like a fan on her naked back, and her breathing was slow and silent. I pulled the blanket to her shoulders and pulled on my robe and went into the living room. Sleep, I knew, was impossible, and I drank a glass of water and looked out the window. The midnight streets were empty, and a sliver of moon wandered over the skyline, drained of color by the city lights and lonely as a wedding ring in a pawnshop. I refilled my water glass and picked up the scripts to *Liars Club* and *The Nest*.

Two readings later, neither play made much sense. Both Lisa, at Null Space, and Moira Neal, the former Gimlet Player, had been spot-on in their critiques. The plays were dense with family psychodrama, incoherent speechifying, and abrupt and confusing changes of time and place, and they depended heavily on a set of symbols and references so personal and hermetic as to be impenetrable.

As far as I could tell, *The Nest* took place on a spaceship in the distant future, and *Liars Club* was set in contemporary suburban Connecticut. And while it was difficult to tease a sensible narrative out of either piece, they both seemed mostly about a vain and tyrannical father, his flagrant and chronic infidelities, and the devastating effect that these had on his wife and daughters.

As self-conscious and opaque as the plays often were, they were not entirely laughable. There was real emotion in the dialogues between the cruel fathers and the daughters, and their exchanges were wrenching and sad—sometimes frightening. And, I realized on my second readings, they were frighteningly reminiscent of the telephone messages that Wren had left for David.

I was tired and my eyes slid off the pages and drifted to the window, and to the sky that was brightening over the city. My mind stumbled over scraps of Holly Cade's life—her luckless Gimlet Players, her sister's harsh voice and suspicious eyes, Babyface looming in her apartment doorway, the nosy, frightened man in 3-F. I put the scripts down and thought about going for a run. I put on some coffee instead.

It was ten o'clock when Clare arose, and the loft was filled with hard winter glare. She padded across the living room wearing a scowl and little else. I was at the table, drinking coffee and reading the *Times*, and she squinted at me with shadowed eyes.

"There more of that?" she whispered, and cocked her head at my mug.

"You want some?" She nodded and I went to the kitchen and poured her a black one.

"God bless," she said, and she took the mug and her overnight bag into the bathroom. Thirty minutes later she returned, smelling of soap and wearing jeans and a short Norton Motorcycles T-shirt. Her hair was in a loose, shiny braid and her feet were bare. Her coffee mug was empty.

"Refill?" I asked. Clare nodded. I poured her another and she took a couple of sections of the paper and headed for the sofa. I picked up the scripts again.

I understood them less the third time through, and began to find them irritating. Having extracted what I could from the dialogue, I paid more attention to the character names. In *The Nest*, besides Wren and Fredrick, there was the mother, Lark, and the older sister, Robin. In *Liars Club*, the father was again named Fredrick—Fredrick Zero—

and the daughters were Cassandra and Medea. The mother was Helen. Birds and Greeks. Was there anything to that? Buried on my shelves were some yellowed paperbacks of Aristophanes and Euripides. I hadn't looked at them since college and wondered if they might be the keys to Holly's work, or if, like so much else in her plays, the classical allusions had been encrypted for Holly's eyes only. I sighed and tossed the scripts on the table.

Clare was still sprawled on the sofa, her bare feet propped on cushions. She'd read the *Times* and the *Journal* both, and now she was working her way through a thick biography of Andy Warhol that she'd produced from somewhere. She heard my sigh and looked at the scripts and at me.

"You going into show business now?" she asked. She stretched her legs and ran a small, pale foot across the top of the sofa.

"Isn't everybody—for fifteen minutes, at least?"

"I figured you for the one holdout."

She shut her big book and sat up and went to the window. A pair of gulls wheeled and swooped above a rooftop across the street, fighting over a scrap of something. Clare wrapped her arms across her chest and watched them.

"You buy a car yet?" she asked after a while.

"I'm still renting."

"You want to rent one tomorrow—maybe drive someplace for the day?"

This was new. I took hold of my coffee mug. "Someplace like where?" I said slowly.

"Anywhere—I don't care—someplace out of town. Someplace we won't run into anybody, and we can walk around."

I thought about it while Clare watched the gulls. "I've got some things to take care of, but if I can get through them today, then sure."

Clare nodded, her back still to me. After a while, she pulled on her boots, picked up her coat, dropped a pair of dark glasses on her nose, kissed the corner of my mouth, and left.

Her perfume still hung in the air when I picked up the telephone. It was nearly one o'clock and I hadn't heard back from Gene Werner yet, or from the other ex-Gimlets I'd left messages for. I tried Werner first, but didn't even get the answering machine. I gave up after a dozen or so rings. I tried Kendall Fein, out in LA, with much the same result. I had better luck with Terry Greer. He still lived in the city and still acted in way-off-Broadway theater and, best of all, he was actually at home.

I put another couple of miles on my accident story and Greer was eager to talk. His voice was youthful and friendly, and though his story was nothing I hadn't heard before—that he hadn't kept in touch with any of the Gimlets; that, when he knew them, Holly and Gene were prickly and self-absorbed; that Holly's plays were problematic, at best, but that she was a hell of an actress—he nonetheless turned out to be a little pot of gold. Greer had pictures.

"My girlfriend was just cleaning out that drawer last night. I was going to dump those old photos, but she put them in a box. They're not great art or anything, just snapshots from when we all went for drinks after the last performance of *Liars Club*. That was the last thing we did together."

"Snapshots are better than what I've got now," I said.

"I guess so." Greer chuckled. "Well, you can pick them up whenever—there's usually somebody around."

Pictures.

I called David's cell and got his voicemail and, eventually, a call back. He was in a car, on the way to the airport and not alone. I heard a man's voice nearby, my brother Ned's. David listened silently while I told him about my trip to Brooklyn, my conversations with the former Gimlet Players, and Greer's pictures. His voice was full of business and studied neutrality when he spoke.

"That all sounds reasonable," he said. "I'm back Tuesday night; we can follow up on Wednesday."

He hung up and I headed for the door.

Greer lived not far from me, in a beaten-up brownstone on West Twenty-second Street, off Tenth Avenue. His apartment was on the second floor and, to judge by the number of names on his mailbox, he shared it with at least three other people. Greer wasn't in when I buzzed but, as promised, someone was. The roommate was a lanky, twentysomething guy with blond hair and a bad beard; he came to the apartment door in a Columbia sweatshirt and a cloud of reefer smoke. He gave me an envelope and a nod and he shut the door.

"Thanks," I said to the empty hall.

I opened the envelope in the little lobby of Greer's building. There were two photos in it. They were in color and they showed two men and three women around a scarred wooden table in a corner booth in a bar somewhere. There were beer bottles on the table, and a few empty highball glasses and a candle burning in a red hurricane lamp.

A pale woman sat at the edge of the group, on the right, looking beyond the camera and maybe beyond the walls of wherever they sat. Her hair was a heavy russet mane, swept back from an angular, icon's face. Her nose was long and delicate above a broad, mournful mouth, and her eyes were shadowy smudges. She wore a black T-shirt that fit like paint and her breasts were round and full beneath it. One white forearm rested on the table.

Even poorly lit, she looked like Wren as David had described her to me. More arresting than I'd pictured, more frankly beautiful, but I was almost certain it was her. According to the note Terry Greer had scribbled on the back of the envelope, it was also Holly Cade.

"She's just not that into him," Clare said. She was sitting at my kitchen counter, sipping at a vodka tonic and looking at Terry Greer's photographs. Late-afternoon light came through the windows and warmed the color of her hair. "He's into her, but she could give a shit."

I was mixing a cranberry juice and club soda and eating the cold sesame noodles Clare had brought back. "Who's not into whom?" I asked.

"The redhead, and the guy sitting next to her."

The guy, I knew from Greer's note, was Gene Werner. He was dark-haired and ponytailed, clean-shaven except for a short, neat beard that covered his square chin. There was a rope braid around his wrist, a small gold ring in his left ear, and a handsome smile on his lips as he looked at Holly. I stirred my drink and swallowed some and picked up the photo.

"You think?"

"It's in the body language," Clare said, and she was right. Werner was turned toward Holly, one arm along the back of the booth, trying to encircle her, the other on the table, a barrier against the rest of the group. His eyes were fixed on Holly's face and there was worry and uncertainty in his smile. Holly was leaning away from his hopeful arm, and her eyes were in another zip code.

Clare played with the lime wedge in her drink. "She must be used to the attention," she said, "wanted or otherwise."

"How so?"

"That whole Renaissance sex-kitten thing she's got going—it's hot." I looked more closely at the photos, at Holly's pale skin and slender fingers and wide, sad mouth. Clare had a point.

"You're looking for her?" she said. I nodded. "What for?" I smiled and shook my head. Clare held up a hand. "Forget I asked." She took another sip of her vodka tonic and opened her Warhol biography.

I carried my drink, the noodles, and the pictures to the table, where my laptop and notepad waited. My notes were nearly up to date: I'd covered my conversation with Greer, and the photographs, and I'd summarized all I'd learned about Holly Cade. It took a page and a half but as I reread it, I wondered if it was what David had in mind.

I want you to find this Wren, for chrissakes—to find out who she is and where she lives—to find out as much about her as she has about me.

I'd done well enough on the first two items, though I needed David's ID to be certain; it was the third I had doubts about. Assuming Wren and Holly were one and the same, how much did I really know about her beyond her name and address? The strained family ties, the forays into writing and acting and video, and the decidedly mixed results, the striking looks and the self-absorption—what did they add up to? What had she been doing since the Gimlets had folded and her video show had gone nowhere? Who was Babyface, and who was he to her? Why was she trolling the web for a guy like David? And, having found him, what the hell did she want from him?

8

Clare and I drove to Orient Point on Saturday morning, at the far end of the North Fork of Long Island. It didn't go well. We were back in the city before dinner and she didn't take her coat off in my apartment. She disappeared into the bedroom and reappeared a moment later with her overnight bag on her shoulder. She paused on her way to the door, and her voice was more tired than angry.

"You know, you have a real knack for fucking up a good thing," she said.

Her footsteps receded down the hallway and echoed in the stairwell. I shut the door and turned on the lights.

The Long Island Expressway had been ugly but empty that morning, and my head had been full of Holly Cade and David as I drove. Of Holly I knew only bits and pieces, not enough yet to understand—or even expect to understand—her actions. But David was a different story; he was my brother and I was supposed to know him. Or something like that.

I'd wondered about his serial infidelity, and wondered why. I thought about other cheating-husband cases I'd worked, and about the rationalizations I'd heard before: "I have needs"; "She doesn't understand me"; "It's just sex"; "It has nothing to do with her"; "Out of town doesn't count"—all the usual suspects, and all so ordinary. It was hard to imagine David subscribing to any of them. Of course, it was hard to imagine him doing anything so dangerous—so potentially self-destructive—as these anonymous trysts either.

Clare had been mostly silent beside me, sometimes reading from her big book, sometimes fiddling with the radio, sometimes just watching through her dark glasses as the asphalt unfolded before us. But the farther behind the city fell, the more she seemed to lighten and uncoil, the more some tension I hadn't known was there seemed to dissipate. By Glen Cove, she'd put her feet up on the dash; by Melville, she was singing softly with the radio.

We'd taken the LIE until it gave out in Riverhead, and then made our way onto Route 25. The landscape flattened around us and the pale, immaculate sky grew larger and brighter with light off the water. We'd passed wineries, and acre after acre of bare vines. They were gnarled and tough looking, and mustered in strict rows behind wire fencing. Clare took off her glasses and ran the window down, and a cold, marine wind rushed in.

We'd stopped for breakfast in Southold, at a tiny diner with a view of a harbor. It was filled with locals and the men had eyed Clare surreptitiously over their eggs and waffles. She'd eaten an omelet and stared at the buttoned-up boats rocking at anchor. I'd had pancakes and thought more about David.

A few of the errant husbands I'd tracked had offered a kind of diminished-capacity defense when they were caught in the act—a story about judgment impaired by the sudden rush of blood to points south of the belt buckle. As an excuse it had done them no good with wives or divorce court judges, but as an explanation it had a certain honesty. I wondered if that was David's story. But he'd always been such a directed and self-disciplined bastard, and always so smug about it too. It was hard to picture him surrendering to impulse, or besotted with anyone.

I'd wondered if these encounters were an outlet for all that restraint, but ultimately didn't believe it. There was something else going on. I remembered David telling me about his screening procedures, and how satisfied he'd been with his cleverness. "If she won't play by my rules, I move on." He liked pulling the strings.

We'd strolled around the harbor after breakfast, Clare wrapped in her black coat and dark glasses, and with a black Mets cap on her pale blond head. We'd walked to the end of a street, at the end of a hook of land, to a bench with a view of Shelter Island. We sat and watched a small ferry crawl across the water, and Clare leaned into me and put her hand into my pocket. After a while the wind picked up and chased us to the car and we drove farther east, to Greenport.

Route 25 became Front Street in Greenport, and met Main Street at the harbor. Both streets were lined with low clapboard buildings and they were more crowded than I'd expected on a midwinter day. People shopping, running errands, just walking, and they all seemed to know each other. We parked the car and got out. Clare took her hat off and ran a hand through her hair.

"It's like frigging Bedford Falls or something," she'd said, but she'd been laughing.

An antique store was just opening up, and she'd led me inside, and up and down the single crowded aisle. She smiled at the guy behind the counter and left without buying. Out on the sidewalk, she'd taken my arm again and we'd wandered up the street. My thoughts wandered back to my brother.

Power and control, ego and anger: beyond the rationalizations and lame excuses, most of the cheating husbands I'd tracked were driven, down deep, by one or more of these. But David had become a mystery to me since Monday, and harder to read than any of those guys had been. Constructing a secret world, laying down its rules and regulations, and watching people jump through his hoops—that was all about power and control; but what about the rest? Was David's ego so fragile that he needed the attentions of strangers to shore it up? Or was it anger driving him, and if so, anger at what, or whom? Stephanie was one answer, but maybe not the only one. His marriage, his career, his reputation, even the reputation of Klein & Sons—David had put them all at risk.

We'd walked the shop streets until the shops had run out and Clare had gotten hungry. There was a hamburger stand at the bottom of

Main Street that was open for lunch and she'd led me there and ordered something messy, with onions. I'd ordered the same and we found another bench by the water. Our burgers steamed in the cold air and a couple of gulls had stared at us hopefully.

We'd driven the last ten miles to Orient Point after lunch. We crossed the causeway and Route 25 became Main Road and ended at the ferry terminal and the state park. The park was open and we walked in. There was scrub oak and red cedar along the sandy path, patches of snow in their shadows and a white rime at the edge of the pond. Beyond the trees and the pond and the long brown grass were rough beach, gray water, and sky, and they were bare, bleak, and gorgeous. Clare took off her glasses and opened her coat and walked at the water's edge. I thought about Holly and David and Stephanie as I watched her.

After a while Clare came back. Her face was pink and her hair was a tangle of gold. She leaned against me and put her mouth on mine. Her body was warm and firm and I could smell the ocean in her hair. "My hands are cold," she said, and she put them inside my coat and under my shirt. We stayed that way until I spoke.

"Why do you do it?" I'd asked.

"Do what?" Clare whispered into my neck.

"Why do you see me, when you're married?"

Clare stiffened in my arms and let out a long sigh and otherwise didn't move for over a minute. Then she took her hands off me and stepped away.

"Why do I cheat on him, you mean?" Her voice was flat and empty. I nodded and a grim little smile crossed her face. "All of a sudden you're curious?"

"I'm just looking for some insight."

Clare snorted. "Into what, for chrissakes?" She put on her sunglasses and buttoned her coat and said something else that the wind snatched away. Her face was rigid and the sun flared on her black lenses.

"You want to hear all the desperate details? Fine. He's twelve years older than I am; his first priority is his business; I'm wife number three; and my best guess is he's been fucking other women since before we were engaged. No one in particular, but a rotating cast of characters.

"There's a certain type he goes for, a kind of well-bred shopgirl type, young, nicely schooled, a little arty maybe, but impressionable and deferential, used to keeping the customers happy. The girl who manages the art gallery he buys from sometimes, the fund-raising girl on the hospital committee, the one handling PR for the museum benefit—that kind. I was surprised when I found out—hurt, even—but it's not like I didn't know what I was getting into. I was working at Christie's when I met him, appraising some prints he wanted to sell. He was married at the time and never made a secret of it.

"We don't discuss it, but he's discreet and I try to be too, and it is what it is—an arrangement that works well enough for both of us, at least for now. Not what I had in mind in high school maybe, but better benefits than at Christie's."

She'd stood with her hands in her pockets and said it matter-of-factly, like a slightly boring school recitation, and when she was through she'd turned up her collar and walked past me.

"I'll be in the car," she'd said.

"Shit," I said to myself. My notes were stacked on the table from the night before and my laptop was still on, and for no other reason than that I didn't know what else to do with myself, I took off my coat and started looking again for Holly Cade.

Despite my best efforts, and all the permutations of "Holly" and "Cade" and "Wren" and "Gimlet" I could think of, Google did no more for me this time than it had before. I made a peanut butter sandwich and went back to the MetroMatchPoint site and searched again for any postings from Wren. And came up just as empty. And then I thought about the names of the other characters in her plays, and about how many other aliases Holly might have used. I searched MetroMatchPoint for Robin, Lark, Helen, Cassandra, and Medea. There were no Medeas but plenty of the rest, though not one that sounded remotely like Wren. So back I went to Google.

It wasn't quite dumb luck, but neither could I claim it was rigorous procedure or faultless logic either. It was a more oblique strategy that involved typing the names of Holly's characters into Google and seeing what popped out. It took much sifting of chaff, but eventually I brought forth a kernel of wheat: Cassandra Z.

The connection was through Cassandra Zero, the doomed young daughter in *Liars Club*, and Orlando Krug, the man who'd owned the now defunct gallery in Woodstock where Holly had held her forgettable video show two years ago—the same Orlando Krug who now owned Krug Visual in the West Village, and who represented the work of a video artist by the name of Cassandra Z. Persistence and synchronicity—the detective's best friends.

Cassandra Z had a low profile on Krug's website: an entry on the list of artists that he repped, a one-line biography—"Cassandra Z lives in New York"—and a note, the only one of its kind on Krug's site, that Cassandra's videos were not publicly exhibited. "Viewing by appointment only, to qualified collectors." Which perhaps explained why I'd been unable to find any reviews of her work. I wondered what qualifications Krug had in mind.

The handful of other references to Cassandra were in an art blog called Candy Foam, and in—of all places—*Digital Gumbo: The Online Journal of Emerging Video Arts.* They were fairly recent, within the past eighteen months, and they started a ticking worry in me.

The first mention on Candy Foam was in the midst of a muddled, sophomoric thread on art and pornography, and whether these were mutually exclusive classifications. Someone calling himself BeatTilStiff offered up Cassandra's work as an example of both, and triggered a long digression in which Candy and Beat—apparently the only parties to the debate familiar with her stuff—one-upped each other with bits of in-crowd arcana about the videos, all without actually describing what was in them. Candy and Beat were at it again a few months later in an exchange about the import of Cassandra's work.

Candy wrote: "It's her insight into sexual power politics, and her obsession with liminal moments and tectonic shifts—with those instances when control is abruptly transferred, when the dominant becomes the submissive, when denial becomes surrender, and language breaks down—when the whip changes hands, so to speak. And don't get me started on the deconstructionist aspects . . ."

To which Beat replied: "Two words, Candy—'*forest*' and '*trees.*' And as always, you miss the one while plowing into the other. You got the sex right, and the power, but the actual point escapes you entirely: Cassie's doing *noir porn,* fucktard! It's about hunger and voyeurism and inevitable doom and, above all else, PAYBACK. Check out her lighting! Look at her #5 and then at anything by Musuraca or Seitz. Go watch *Out of the Past* for shit sake! And BTW—you're reading too much William Gibson again."

To which Candy replied: "ESAD."

The reference in *Digital Gumbo* was more straightforward. It was in a month-old issue, in a gossipy column called "Secondary Market," and the columnist noted that two of Cassandra Z's works—#3 and #8—were rumored to have changed hands recently, at six figures each. Whatever she was doing, people were paying good money for it.

I ran on Sunday morning, in a gritty wind I thought would sand the skin from my face. After a long shower and a bowl of oatmeal, I went out in it again and walked into the West Village. Orlando Krug's gallery was on Perry Street, between an antique shop and a store that sold extremely expensive men's pajamas, and behind a frosted-glass door with small black lettering on it. The inside was done in grays and whites and creams, and the interior designer had somehow made peace between the wainscoting and beadboard and William Morris rugs, and all the big flat-panel monitors mounted on the walls. There was footage of gray tenement rooftops playing on the screens, with pigeons that morphed occasionally into vivid tropical flowers. The air smelled of sandalwood.

A small, thin man sat behind a partners desk in the back corner. He was maybe twenty and his vaguely ferretlike face was covered in a neat three-day scruff. His hair was five shades of blond and arranged in careful chaos. He wore his French cuffs dangling but his blue shirt was well tailored and so was his look of boredom. He glanced up at me when I came in and went back to fiddling with his iPod. He looked around when I spoke, as if I weren't the only one in the place.

"Orlando Krug?"

"No."

"Is he in?"

"And you would be who?" His voice was nasal and arch, and as bored as his look.

"The guy looking for Orlando Krug. Is he in?"

The man shrugged. "No need to be grumpy," he said, and he pushed away from the desk and went through a doorway in the back. He knocked at a door at the end of a short hall and opened it and went in. He came out a moment later and so did another man.

He was about sixty and tall, and his skin had the color and hard gloss of polished teak decking. He wore pressed jeans and a black sweater, and his white hair was cut very short. His brows were precise arches over wary blue eyes, and there was something in his gaunt face that reminded me of a monk. The abbot, perhaps, of a prosperous and deeply tanned order.

He had a deep voice and an accent that almost wasn't there and that I couldn't quite place. "I am Krug. How can I help you, Mr. . . . ?"

"March. I understand you represent Cassandra Z."

Behind the desk, the blond man perked up. Krug glanced at him. "Ricky, make me an espresso, would you?" Ricky rolled his eyes but stood. Krug looked at me. "And one for you, perhaps, Mr. March? Ricky does quite a good job." I nodded and Ricky disappeared. Krug sat behind the desk and waved me to the chair opposite.

"You're familiar with Cassandra's work?" he asked. His blue eyes were shining.

"Not familiar, but intrigued. I was hoping to learn more."

Krug smiled. "Her work is indeed intriguing, Mr. March, though not widely known." I nodded but said nothing. Krug kept smiling. "How did you become aware of it?"

I shrugged. "Idle chatter from informed people. A comment here, a comment there . . . eventually it adds up."

Krug steepled his long tan fingers beneath his chin. "Indeed. What other artists do you follow, Mr. March?"

Ricky came in with two coffees on a small silver tray. I smiled more widely. "Eisner, Ditko, Infantino, Adams, Miller."

Ricky set a demitasse cup in front of each of us, squinted at me, and left. Krug pursed his lips. "Comic-book artists."

"I'm ready to broaden my horizons."

"And you wish to start with video, and with Cassandra's work?"

"I hear such interesting things about it."

"From whom, Mr. March?"

"People who know."

"I know all the people who know, Mr. March. If they know, it's because I arranged for them to know. So if one of these people has referred you to me, please don't be shy in saying."

"And if they haven't?"

Krug sighed. The lines on his face seemed to fold in on themselves and he looked like a dour walnut. "Then we can drink our coffee and discuss the work of any number of other artists."

"But not Cassandra's?" Krug gathered his brows in a look of minuscule sympathy and shook his head. "Interest alone doesn't qualify me?" I asked.

"Cassandra's work is very challenging, Mr. March—not easily accessible. A collector new to the medium, lacking the context . . . I would be doing you a disservice."

I chuckled. "I'm grateful for your concern. Would money have an effect on my qualifications?"

Krug played with the thin gold watch on his thin brown wrist. "None, I'm afraid. Cassandra's work deserves to be appreciated, not merely bought and sold."

"I thought buying and selling was your job, Mr. Krug. Does Cassandra know that you're so . . . discouraging?"

"These are her directives, I assure you." His blue eyes were cold in his shiny face.

"Maybe I could talk to her about that."

Krug sighed deeply and sat back in his chair. "The only thing Cassandra is more concerned with than how her work is disposed of, Mr. March, is her privacy." He looked at his watch. "Now, if there's nothing more . . ." He raised his cup.

"Just one thing: Do you still represent Holly Cade?"

Krug sipped at his coffee and never spilled a drop. One white brow rose minutely. "Holly who?"

"Holly Cade. She was part of a group show at your Woodstock gallery."

Krug's apologetic look was barely perfunctory. "I'm afraid I don't recall the name."

"No, of course not," I said, rising. "It's been a long time, after all."

There was a health food store on the corner and across the street. It carried an amazing array of soy products, and its large window had an unobstructed view of Krug Visual. I browsed the spelt cereals and green teas for half an hour before Ricky came out. He was wearing a topcoat bigger than he was, and he headed east on Perry Street, struggling against the wind. I followed.

Ricky was a man with a mission, and the mission, apparently, was lunch. He turned on West Fourth Street and again on West Eleventh and went into a gourmet deli and spoke to the man behind the counter. He came out ten minutes later with a white plastic grocery bag and began retracing his steps. I came up beside him on West Fourth.

"That was good coffee, Ricky."

He jumped. "Jeez!" he said. "I almost dropped the effing soda."

"Sorry. I just wanted a quick word."

Ricky drifted to the corner and stopped. His ferrety eyes narrowed. "A quick word about what? I've got to get this back to himself or never hear the end of it."

"Cassandra Z," I said.

Ricky put up his free hand and backed away half a step. "Forget it, Grumpy. I need this job. And even if I knew anything about her—which I don't—why should I tell it to you?"

I shrugged and took my hand from my coat pocket. "For fifty bucks, maybe?" The bill was crisp and new. Ricky looked furtive and reached for it. I put it away. "On the other hand, you say you don't know much."

"If you're looking for a name or phone number or whatever, I guess you get to keep your money. She's too good to mingle with the help when she comes around. She only deals with O, and he plays her very close to the vest—especially since that other guy came in."

"What other guy?"

Ricky looked at me and grinned nastily. "Looks like I know something after all." His hand was out again.

I took out the fifty but held on to it. "What other guy?"

"O banished me to the back room, but I could hear. He was a lawyer type, and he worked for one of Cassie's interview subjects. He wanted to get in touch with her, or for her to get in touch with him."

"Interview subjects?"

Ricky looked impatient. "As in the titles of her videos—*Interview One, Interview Two,* and so forth—you know."

I didn't but I nodded vaguely. "What did he want to get in touch about?"

"He didn't say."

"And this was when?"

"A month or so ago."

"You hear any names?"

"I don't remember," he said. He saw the look on my face. "No shit—I really don't." Ricky eyed my fifty. "So, how about it?"

"Nearly there," I said, and took my other hand from my other pocket. "Anybody here you recognize?"

Ricky looked down at the photo and tapped a finger on the woman sitting at the edge of the group. "That's her," he said. "That's Cassie." I sighed. Holly. Wren. Cassandra Z. "Do I get the cash now?"

"Sure," I said, and the bill vanished from my hand.

Ricky turned and headed toward Perry Street and I called to him. He turned around, impatient.

"Now what?"

"What are her videos like?"

Ricky smirked and shook his head. "Cassie's stuff? Like nothing else I've seen, Grumpy, and I've seen a lot."

10

"I told him you were shopping," Chaz Monroe said, "and that you had money to spend." He smiled and groomed the small triangle of beard on his chin with the back of his hand. He looked like a pudgy cat doing it. "All of a sudden he was glad to help."

He slipped his cell phone into his jacket pocket and sat down across from me. He examined his wineglass and decided it was too close to empty. He lifted the bottle of Syrah and tilted it in my direction. I shook my head and he shrugged and filled his glass.

"Todd's always happy to serve the cause of art," Monroe continued, "and especially if it improves the value of his own collection." He drank some wine and heaved a satisfied sigh.

"Did he say when?" I asked.

"Tonight. He'll call me back with the time." Monroe bent again to what remained of the lunch I was buying. He speared the last of his cassoulet even as he scanned the dessert menu.

Finding Chaz Monroe hadn't been hard. I'd returned home on Sunday afternoon with Ricky's words still playing in my head, and with my worry ticking louder. I thought about Holly's videos and knew that if I wanted to understand what she was about—and maybe figure out what she wanted with my brother—I'd have to see them for myself.

I returned to the Candy Foam blog and followed BeatTilStiff's postings from there to another contemporary-art blog called ArtHaus Polizei. It turned out to be Beat's home turf. Polizei was an edgier version of Candy Foam, and besides Beat's musings on recent gallery shows, museum exhibitions, and auctions there were long riffs on anime, music videos, sneaker fashion, and tattooing. "Fucking" was apparently his adjective of choice.

I'd clicked on a "Profile" link and learned that, besides being the proprietor of Polizei, Beat was "a New York–based freelance writer, art critic, and art acquisitions consultant." I'd lingered over that description for a while and then clicked on the "Contact Me" link. I'd been vague in my e-mail about what kind of consultation I needed, but I was pretty clear about my ability to pay. I'd included my telephone number, too. The market for freelance writer–art critic–art acquisition consultants must've been a little thin, because I didn't wait an hour for his call.

I told him I was interested in Cassandra Z's work, and that I was looking for help in seeing some of it. My problem didn't surprise him.

"I take it you spoke to Don Orlando?" Monroe asked. His voice was hoarse and ironic.

"We didn't exactly hit it off."

He snorted. "Which puts you in good company, my friend. O's very control-freaky, and particularly when it comes to Cassie. I used to think it was a German thing, but now I think it was always fucking strategy. All that mystery and exclusivity has built a real buzz in certain circles, and done wonders for her prices."

"Wonders," I said. "Can you arrange a viewing for me?"

"A viewing with an eye toward acquisition?"

"That's the general idea."

We'd talked about his fee, but I hadn't bargained hard. I wanted him motivated, and in any event it was David's money I'd be spending. I'd heard a cigarette light when we settled things, and Monroe had seemed relieved and eager to get started.

"I'll make my calls and we can touch base tomorrow, let's say for late lunch."

He'd picked Cousin Dupree's, a new and much hyped bistro on the Upper East Side, and he'd kept me waiting for twenty minutes. He was talking on his cell and smoking a cigarette when he almost stepped through the door—a rounded, fortyish man in a gravely abused camel hair coat and wilted Gucci loafers. The hostess had stopped him at the threshold and pointed him and his cigarette at the sidewalk, but he'd taken it affably enough. I'd watched through the window as he puffed away and made more phone calls. His tangled hair was black and shiny, and so were his eyes. They sparkled above his ruddy cheeks and, along with his sly, puffy mouth, gave him the look of a seedy cherub.

Monroe drained his glass. "No dessert for you?" he asked. I shook my head and he looked suspicious and ordered a flan. He was looking over the list of Sauternes when I cleared my throat.

"How many of her videos have you seen?" I asked.

Monroe answered quickly. "Five: *Interviews Two* through *Five* and *Interview Eight.*"

"How many are there?"

"Twelve so far."

"What are they like?"

He thought about this longer. "I won't ruin things for you by trying to describe them," he said finally, "and in any case I wouldn't do them justice—but I will give you my opinion, which is that they're fucking brilliant. Weird shit, definitely, strange enough to give a sick kind of thrill, but fucking brilliant. You'll see."

Monroe's flan came and he was halfway through it when his cell phone burred. He raised his eyebrows and excused himself to the bar again. He wore a satisfied smile when he returned.

"Nine o'clock," he said, "at Todd's place."

Which left me five hours to kill when I said goodbye to Monroe. I disposed of one of them with a cold, stiff-legged run along the Hudson, up into the twenties and down to TriBeCa. The phone was ringing as I came through the door. It was Clare.

"I was wondering if you wanted your key back," she said. I heard street noise in the background.

"I was a little surprised you didn't leave it behind on Saturday."

"I thought about it. I thought about throwing it at you too. Do you want it back or not?"

"Not," I said. "Where are you?"

She was quiet for a moment. "In the neighborhood," she said eventually.

"You want to stop by?"

"I don't know," she said, and hung up. But she was there when I got out of the shower. She was perched in the sofa with her coat still on and blue dusk falling around her. She turned the key over in her hand.

"Still thinking about throwing it?" I asked. I belted my robe and sat at the table.

Clare's gray eyes were clouded and her voice was low. "It's too light," she said. "It wouldn't do any damage."

I smiled. "I'm sorry about Saturday."

"Sorry about what part?"

"About prying."

"Was that prying? I'm sort of amazed you never asked before. Anyway, it wasn't that."

"Then what was it?"

She sighed massively and stood and paced slowly along my bookshelves. Her hair was white in the twilight and she swept it off her shoulders. "Timing. Your timing sucks."

I nodded. "Then I'm sorry about the timing, and about being insensitive."

Clare's laugh was short and bitter. "*Insensitive?* A few years of therapy, some medication maybe—and *maybe* you can work your way up to insensitive." She leaned against a cast-iron column and folded her arms across her chest. "Besides, 'insensitive' is boyfriend talk. Is that what you think you are?"

"A friend, anyway."

Another small laugh. "A friend with privileges? A fuck buddy?"

"What do you call it, if not a friend?"

She said something I couldn't make out and I crossed the room and stood in front of her. Her head was bent and her shoulders quivered in the shadows.

"What do you call it?" I asked again. My throat was tight and my voice sounded far away.

Clare leaned forward and rested her forehead on my shoulder. She tapped me lightly in the chest with my house key. "Hell if I know," she murmured. "You're the fucking detective, you figure it out." Then she put the key in her pocket and turned her face up and kissed me.

Clare was sleeping when I got into the shower and gone when I got out. I dressed quickly in gray flannels and a black turtleneck and headed for the subway and Brooklyn.

Chaz Monroe was waiting on the corner of President and Hicks streets, smoking a cigarette, talking on his cell, and stamping his feet in the cold. The collar was up on his camel hair coat and his dark eyes glittered in the streetlight. He said his goodbyes and snapped his phone shut.

"Bring the popcorn and soda?" he said, smiling. He took my elbow and led me toward Henry Street and he talked the whole way to Todd Herring's house.

"Todd's a major music-biz lawyer," Monroe said. "He bought this place two years ago—the same time he traded in his wife for a newer version—and he's been renovating ever since. About the only thing he's managed to finish is the home theater, which is lucky for us. He'll be showing us *Interview Two* and *Interview Four* tonight."

Herring's place was a wide four-story brownstone, with a construction Dumpster parked outside and scaffolds climbing up the front. There were broad steps from the sidewalk to a pair of tall, deep-set black doors. Monroe leaned on the doorbell and smiled into the video intercom.

A lanky, red-haired man in jeans and a FUBU T-shirt ushered us into a high-ceilinged entrance hall that was decorated in dropcloths and plaster dust.

"Chaz, my brother," the man said. He had a deep, radio voice, and he wrapped Monroe in a stiff-armed, stylized hug, and pounded him lightly on the back with a fist. Monroe endured it with amusement.

"Todd, my man," he said, and kept nearly all the laughter from his voice. "This is John March."

"Good to meet you, bro," Todd said, and held a fist out to me. I tapped it lightly with my own.

Todd Herring was tall, skinny, and abundantly freckled. His carroty hair was expensively cut but salted with white, and despite the business with the fists and the "bro" talk I figured him for fifty.

"We'll go downstairs," he said, and he led us past a curving stair-way and many paint cans to other, narrower stairs going down.

The brownstone's garden floor was thickly carpeted, heavily pan-eled, and flush with recessed halogen lighting. We followed Todd down another hall, past a well-equipped kitchenette.

"Drinks for anybody?" he asked. I declined, but Monroe hit him up for a beer. Todd fetched a Carta Blanca and a frosted mug and led us to the theater. He flicked a switch and muted lights came up on the walls and from the ceiling. There were twenty thick, theater-style seats, arranged in four curving rows before a large screen. Todd went to a black cabinet at the back of the room and fiddled with some technol-ogy inside.

"Sit anywhere," he said. He flicked a switch, and a large flat moni-tor swiveled quietly out of the ceiling at the front of the room.

Chaz took a seat in the second row center and put his beer bottle and glass into the slots built into the armrest. I wandered to the front of the room, and looked at a pair of glass-fronted wooden boxes lean-ing against the wall. They were the same size, about twelve inches by fifteen inches by four inches deep. One was made from cherry wood and one was bird's-eye maple, and there were shelves and cubbyholes built inside of them, and little objects mounted there. They reminded me of Joseph Cornell boxes and I walked closer and knelt for a better view. A chill went through me.

"She calls them reliquaries, bro," Todd said. "She makes them by hand, and there's one for each of her videos, but I'd wait until after-ward to look at them. They make more sense, and the impact is . . . bigger."

I looked at Chaz and he nodded. "It's a context issue," he said, and he swallowed some beer.

I nodded back and took a seat behind Chaz. Todd hit the lights and the room went black and I wondered what context would make sense of what I'd seen behind the glass.

11

"You don't want a real drink?" Chaz Monroe asked me. "Because you look like you could use one."

"Ginger ale is fine," I said. Monroe shrugged and wedged into the pack at the bar to order. In fact, he had a point. I felt wobbly and somehow disoriented, and the walk from Todd Herring's house to Smith Street had made no dent in that. "Like nothing else I've seen," Ricky had said. Ricky hadn't lied.

I found an empty table in a corner of the crowded room and slid along the green banquette. Monroe wasn't long in coming and he handed me my drink and took the seat opposite. He tilted his glass to mine.

"To art, bro," he said ironically. He swallowed some scotch and gave me a speculative look. "So, what did you think?"

I shook my head. "Are they all like that?"

"The particulars are different, but the narrative arc is the same— all the ones I've seen, anyway: the e-mail, the first meeting, the dominance and submission, the investigation, and the final interrogation."

"Do you ever see the men's faces?"

Monroe shook his head. "They're always digitally masked, the faces and anything else that might identify them—scars, tattoos, that kind of thing. And their voices are distorted. It depersonalizes them— destroys their individuality and turns them into objects, into nothing more than their desires and demands. At least, until you start feeling sorry for the poor fucks."

"But you always see Cassandra?"

"All there is to see—and you always hear her voice too. Nothing masked there."

Not much, I thought, and shook my head. "Jesus," I said.

"Indeed," Monroe said, and he drank off the rest of his scotch. "Too quick," he sighed. "Another soda for you, or maybe something stronger?" I declined and he headed for the bar. I looked into my glass and thought again about the videos. It wasn't easy to do, but it was impossible to stop.

They were each about fifty minutes long, and they both began with hand-held, documentary-style camera work—close-up, fidgety images of printed e-mail. The *To* and *From* fields, and any other information that could have identified sender or receiver, were redacted with thick black lines, and the messages themselves were brief—guarded, two- or three-line responses to an on-line personal ad. A woman's voice read the text as the camera panned across the pages. Flat and emotionless as it was, I recognized it from David's cell phone. Wren.

The first video, *Interview Two,* cut from the e-mail to hidden cam- era footage taken at tabletop level in a blurry bar or café. There was a man at the table with Cassandra, and I came to think of him as Skinny. His face was a mass of flesh-toned pixels, and his speech was synthesized and mechanical. But for the expensive tailoring, he could've been a government informant or the emcee on some hostage video.

"Late afternoon works for me—five-thirty or six. . . . I'm not into drugs, and if you are, we can stop right here. . . . I like to talk while we . . . you know."

The robot voice seemed at first too deep for Skinny's narrow frame, and too detached for the awkward situation. But after a while, it was the human bits that remained in his speech—the coughs and sighs and breathing, the pauses and small stutters—that seemed out of place.

For her part, Cassandra was demure throughout. She nodded agreement to nearly everything Skinny said, and when she spoke, her words were few and just above a whisper.

"I have a room a few blocks from here. Would you like to go now?"

And then came the sex.

It began without segue, in a dim hotel room with yellow light spilling from an open bathroom door and bleeding through a tiny gap in the drapes. The images were fuzzy and the visual style was amateur Internet porn: greenish, ghostly figures, the weightless movements of moonwalkers, and nothing left to the imagination. Eventually, I realized that the scene was actually several scenes, a montage of many late afternoons, and I realized there was a progression to the sex: from the more to the less conventional. From the variety of the angles, I guessed Cassandra must have had three cameras hidden around the room, and with them she captured a full catalogue of trajectories and thrusts. Through it all Skinny called the shots, tentatively at first, and then without reservation.

"You like that, don't you . . ." "You want it there . . ." "Tell me you want it there . . ." "Say it like you mean it . . ." "Say it again, bitch."

The soundtrack was dominated by his synthesized commands and exhortations, and by his unadulterated panting, grunts, and huffing. The unprocessed sounds were startling in their intimacy, and more unsettling than his words.

Beneath Skinny's dictates and the other noises he made, Cassandra's voice was a leitmotif of gasping obedience. She did what Skinny told her to do and said what he told her to say, and when he told her to say it again, she did. She moaned and cried out and pleaded, sometimes in pleasure and sometimes not, and her white, limber body bent and twisted beneath Skinny's cubist face. Her own icon's face, when it was visible, was pale and empty-eyed.

What Monroe had called the investigation segment began with what seemed a pause in the sex montage, and with a gradual change in the sound and look of the video. The commands and moaning faded away, and the noise of a running shower grew louder. Colors bled from the screen and were replaced by a smoky black and white. The tang of seedy sex dissipated and a sweaty paranoia took its place.

The bathroom door was opened wide and Cassandra was alone on the wrecked bed. Her naked body was luminous but her movements were stiff and achy as she rose and moved to a chair, to a jacket hanging there, to a pocket and a wallet inside. She looked over her shoulder as she rifled through the wallet and withdrew some cards. She held them to the camera lens, and though their surfaces were masked it was plain that they were credit cards and business cards. I'd thought of David when I saw it. *My wallet was in my suit jacket . . .*

I'd thought of him again as the scene shifted to another blurry interior and a shot of Cassandra, dressed now and hunched above a telephone. Skinny's wind-up voice was distant on the other end, but the fear and anger in his words were close at hand and unmistakable.

"Don't call here, for chrissakes . . ." "How did you get this number, you crazy bitch . . ." "Why are you calling me . . ." "What do you want from me . . ." "Fucking bitch—I'll kill you, you call again . . ." "Just leave me alone . . ." "Please . . . just leave me alone."

But she wouldn't. I'd heard Cassandra's side of the conversation before, on David's voicemail. Her words were different in the video but she covered the same scary ground, and she was relentless.

"Why don't you write me anymore? Why don't you call? You think you can just ignore me? If you won't take my calls, maybe your wife will."

Their back-and-forth was a tortured accompaniment to more images of Cassandra on the telephone, and to shots of a blur-faced Skinny walking the streets, hailing taxis, entering and leaving unidentifiable buildings, and completely unaware of the camera trailing him. In the course of maybe ten minutes of video, his initial surprise gave way to anger, his anger mutated to fear, and his fear dissolved in desperation. By the end of it, Skinny's synthesized words were lost in human sounds—quavers, sniffles, maybe tears—and I was surprised by the bud of sympathy that had grown for the bastard.

"Just leave my wife out of it, for chrissakes. Please, she's got nothing to do with this—nothing at all. Just tell me what the hell you want from me. Please . . ."

Finally Cassandra did:

"I want to see you again, one last time."

Like the investigation sequence, the final scene—the interrogation, Monroe called it—was shot in black and white, though the blacks were somehow deeper and the grays more silvery. It brought Cassandra and Skinny back to what looked like the same hotel room, where the drapes were still drawn but the bed was made up. Skinny was awkward, and stiff with anger, but he sat as directed in a straight-backed chair. Cassandra was perched on the edge of the bed, with her white hands on her knees. She wore a white blouse, a dark suit jacket, and tailored pants, and her auburn hair looked black and lacquered. Her bearing was military and her tone was clinical. Her questions were simple and direct.

"Why did you do it . . ." "Did you think about your wife or your children—what would happen if they found out . . ." "Did you think of the risk . . ." "Was it just the sex . . ." "Is that all it takes?"

Skinny reached for defiance at first, but he was beaten before he ever walked through the door. His resistance degraded quickly, from combative, to petulant, to whiny, and the last fight went out of him in a shuddering breath that left him folded and shrunken before the camera. But when his first answers came, they didn't please Cassandra.

" 'I don't know' is no answer . . ." "How can you say it has nothing to do with her . . ." "I didn't *just happen*—you came looking for me, and you came back for more." She shredded Skinny's evasions like a terrier and flung the scraps aside until he was spent and she had the bone in her teeth.

"I did it because I wanted to, because I wanted you. Once we got started, the things we did—I couldn't think of anything else. It made me feel handsome—powerful. I didn't think about her or the kids . . . I didn't give a damn about them."

Skinny's voice wound down like a tired spring and his narrow frame slumped in the shadows. Cassandra was perfectly still and her face was a white mask.

"And you'd do it again, wouldn't you?" she asked. "You'd do it now if you could?"

Skinny looked at her, dazed and uncertain. When he spoke, there was pleading in his voice. "If I could," he said softly. The screen went dark.

A shadow fell across the table and Chaz Monroe returned with his drink and a bowl of salted nuts. The noise of the bar crowd came back with him. He raised his glass to me again and drank.

"Hard to get out of your head, aren't they?" he said. I nodded. "They have that squirmy-sexy thing going on: the utter submission of a beautiful woman to a nameless, faceless man, and all before the cameras—except that she's the only one who knows the cameras are there, and she's the one who set the whole thing up. Abuse, self-abasement, voyeurism: it's quite the trifecta. And then she turns the tables." He tossed some cashews into his mouth and washed them down with scotch.

"Todd didn't steer you wrong on the reliquaries," he said. "They only make sense after you've seen the videos, and then they pack a punch."

They did indeed. An empty condom wrapper, Cassandra's torn hosiery, her underpants, a soiled washcloth—all last seen on screen, in Cassandra's hands or in Skinny's. Their presence behind the glass of the curio cabinet gave the events in the video a reality, an immediacy, that was undeniable and invasive. But those mementos, from *Interview Two,* were positively quaint next to the souvenirs in the other cabinet: the spent matches, the dollops of melted candle wax, the green silk tie from the hotel drapes, the white plastic grocery bag, the neatly cut square of bed linen, stained with what looked like blood. A chill went down my spine.

Monroe saw me shiver and caught the drift of my thoughts. "Have you ever heard the word 'bitch' so overused?" he said. "I don't sleep with women myself, but I certainly like them more than Cassandra's fellows seem to. And it's fascinating how similar their notions of the erotic all seem to be. The pervasiveness of popular culture, I suppose." Monroe played with his little beard. "There're two or three doctoral dissertations in there, at least."

"At least," I said. "Are the other videos as rough as *Interview Four*?"

Monroe gave it some thought. "It's one of the grittier ones, I'd say, and mostly on account of Bluto. He required no prompting."

"Bluto?"

He smiled. "It's what I call Cassandra's costar in *Four*."

I'd thought of him as Sunburn, for his vivid tan line and the skin peeling off his beefy shoulders, but Monroe's name was a better fit. I thought about the squat, hirsute body, and about the things he said to Cassandra, and did to her, and I shivered again.

"What do you mean by 'prompting'?"

"I mean that in some of her later works, Cassandra encourages the men to their extreme behavior. Or maybe 'goads' is a better term." Monroe shook his head. "As if she weren't taking enough risk."

More images of Cassandra and Bluto ran through my head: his thick hands on her supine body, the melting wax, the plastic bag stretched over her face, the green cord around her neck. I felt another chill.

Interview Four began no differently from *Two*, with e-mail messages and hidden camera footage of a first meeting in an unidentified bar. Where Skinny had worn a sedate blue suit, Bluto was dressed in a checked sport coat and chocolate-colored trousers, and where Skinny had been full of stipulations, Bluto was all accommodation, rendered in a high-pitched, synthesized voice.

"Sure, whenever you want—my schedule is flexible and I'm easy . . ." "Uptown, downtown, it's all the same to me . . ." "Around the corner, right now? Hey, I'm good to go."

Things changed in the hotel room. The colors were more vivid than in *Interview Two*, and so was the sex, which started out edgy and quickly went over the edge. Each of their encounters began with Bluto explaining—in graphic detail—what he intended to do, and with Cassandra acquiescing.

"Will it hurt?" she asked.

"It won't hurt me a bit, baby," Bluto said, and laughed.

"Will it hurt me?"

"Probably. Do you care?"

"Not much," she said. Her voice was soft and without affect.

Cassandra's pursuit of Bluto played out differently, too. Her first phone calls elicited only derisive laughter from him, and following him yielded only distant shots of a bulky man getting in and out of a black Town Car. It took a threat to visit his in-laws, somewhere in the wilds of New Jersey, to get his attention.

Unlike Skinny's, Bluto's anger didn't falter into fear. His was instead slow burning and rumbling, and when Cassandra wouldn't fuck off as ordered, he seemed almost to welcome the prospect of meeting her one last time. He swaggered into the hotel room, shoulders rolling, and stood by the bed with his hands on his belt. He barely waited until she'd shut the door to speak.

"Okay, bitch, you wanted me and here I am. So drop your drawers and bend over and we'll get to it quick."

Cassandra's laugh was small and tight. "That's not what I had in mind this afternoon."

"It's not your mind I'm talking about, bitch," Bluto said, and he grabbed Cassandra's arm and threw her on the bed. He stood over her and unfastened his belt buckle. "Now bend over."

Cassandra shook her head and pointed to the clock on the nightstand. "What time does that say?" she asked calmly.

"What?"

An edge came up in Cassandra's voice. "Are you going deaf? I asked you what time was on that clock."

"What the fuck—"

"Because at three o'clock exactly, and every twenty minutes after that, I have a call to make. And the party on the other end gets very nervous if I'm not prompt. Very antsy."

"What are you talking—"

"Knowing where I am and who I'm with isn't enough, I guess. This party still wants to hear from me. Every twenty minutes. Promptly. My voice."

Bluto was quiet, and it was almost possible to see the calculations playing across his pixilated face. When he spoke again his voice was softer. "What? That's supposed to scare me?"

Cassandra laughed again and got off the bed. She smoothed her jacket and tucked in her blouse. "Not you, tough guy. Now sit down." She pointed to a chair and after a brittle moment Bluto sat in it.

He was hardly pleasant after that, but he didn't raise a hand to Cassandra again. She worked him for what seemed a long time, pausing periodically to step into the bathroom and make her calls. Bluto was more familiar with his own appetites than Skinny was with his—more fond of them, and certain that they required no explanations or excuses. So there was no hemming or hawing when he finally ran out of obstinacy and decided to answer Cassandra's questions, no heavy sighs or tears, and but a single regret.

"No, I didn't think about my wife and kids—and why the hell should I? What business is it of theirs? I thought about fucking you six ways from Sunday, and nothing else. You had a lot of promise and I'm only sorry you turned out to be such a freakin' headcase." It was impossible to say whether that satisfied Cassandra, but she seemed to know that she'd gotten all she was going to get.

Images of Bluto's blurred face, looming above her, were insistent, and they made my jaw ache. I heard Monroe's voice from far away. "You're sure about that drink?" he asked.

I shook my head. "Are the others as bad as Bluto?" I asked.

Monroe thought about it. "He's the most brutal, I think, but there are tense moments in all the interrogation scenes." He drank some scotch and ran a hand over his chin. "Of all the dangerous things she does in her videos, I think those segments are the scariest."

He was right. Alone in a hotel room with an angry, scared, and cornered man—she was juggling chainsaws. There'd been just a hint of danger with Skinny, a moment when her back was turned and his hand went up, but it went no further than that. There'd been more than a hint with Bluto.

"Does she always get them talking at the end?"

Monroe bumped ice around in his glass and looked up at me. His eyes were blurry and his little beard was dusted with salt. His words were nearly lost in the din of the place. "Always," he said. "They posture and threaten and evade and lie, but in the end they answer."

It didn't surprise me. From what I'd seen, Cassandra was good at getting people to talk, very good. She was patient and firm and seemed to have an innate understanding of the theater of interrogation—of the fragile chemistry of power, fear, and empathy that drove it along, and the cocktail of guilt and vanity and fatigue that could bring it to confession. She would've made a good cop that way.

I paid off Chaz Monroe and poured him into a taxi, and I walked up Smith Street in the general direction of the Brooklyn Bridge. Besides some bar stragglers and a few late diners, I had this stretch of Brooklyn to myself. But if the cold and wind had cleared the sidewalks, they did nothing for my head, which was still full of Holly Cade. Holly, Wren, Cassandra—the equation played and replayed, cut with lurid images from her videos and snippets of dialogue from her bad plays, a bleak and desperate loop. I'd completed one part of the job David had hired me for: I'd found out who Wren was, and what it was that she wanted from him. Now if only I knew what the hell to do about it.

12

The sky was freighted with heavy clouds on Tuesday morning, and the local news was freighted with snowstorms, churning up the East Coast, driving down from Canada, and colliding all over New York. The timing was uncertain—maybe tomorrow, maybe the next day—but the predictions were dire.

"Bullshit," Clare muttered, and tore a piece of toast in half. "They get all hysterical but they never get this stuff right." She smeared some strawberry jam on the bread and went back to the *Times*.

She'd arrived early this morning, as I was getting back from my run, and we'd been sitting in amiable silence since, she leafing through the paper and I writing a report for David. I drank some orange juice and read it over.

The facts were straightforward, albeit strange: Holly was making another video and, unbeknownst to him, my brother was her costar. She'd shot most of it already, and now she was gearing up for the grand finale. For that she needed David to make a return appearance.

What to do with these facts was the problem. Ignoring Holly's demands was one option, though a risky one. She had proven relentless in pursuit of her quarries, and the hours of video documentation she presumably had of her sessions with David would give her a lot of leverage. But leverage ran two ways. Orlando Krug had said that Cassandra was jealous of her privacy, and the kind of art she was making required anonymity—so the threat of revealing her secret identity might actually pull some weight. But Holly was also demonstrably nuts, which made her motives hard to read and her reactions impossible to predict. I sighed and ran my hands through my hair. The speculation was pointless, I knew—a little game I was playing to keep from dwelling on the videos themselves.

Twelve hours or so had given me perspective enough to see them as unique and beautifully made works. And I knew also that Holly's former colleagues Moira Neal and Terry Greer had understated her talents as an actress. She was remarkable, and her ability and willingness to abandon herself to a role was frightening. But the queasy, sticky feeling the videos evoked still lingered. The desperation they depicted left me bleak, and their contempt and studied cruelty made me angry.

And it was impossible, of course, not to cast David as one of those faceless, mechanical men—impossible not to think about what had brought him to Holly, and what she'd captured of him with her hidden cameras. Impossible not to wonder what reserves of rage and brutality she'd tapped, and how much encouragement he'd needed. The more I thought about him the less I knew; the more he was a silhouette, receding down a darkened hallway.

Maybe it was the smell of toast that brought the memory back. Maybe it was the threatening light in the sky.

It was a bleak February Wednesday and I was home from boarding school, not for vacation but because I'd been caught, for the third time, smoking a joint in the woods behind my dorm. The dean of students said a month's suspension might teach me a thing or two, and he'd been right. I'd learned that I could buy decent weed at decent prices from our building's late-shift doorman, and that the weeknight bartenders at Barrytown, over on First Avenue, wouldn't card you if you tipped well enough. I'd slept until three that day, and would've slept later if not for the noise. It was my parents.

My mother had delayed her midwinter pilgrimage to Boca that

year, and my father was making a rare foray from his study, and they'd decided to have it out right outside my bedroom door. As was often the case in those days, I was the convenient excuse. It was nothing new and I tried to tune it out, but they were uncharacteristically loud.

"What's he doing with himself?" my mother said.

My father chuckled. "He's finding his way. He's only fifteen, after all."

"He's sixteen, and as far as I can tell he's not finding a goddamn thing."

"Must everyone in this family grow up to be a banker?"

Then there were footsteps in the hallway, and David's voice. He was at Columbia by then, but kept turning up at home, looking for a meal or clean laundry or something. He was going on about the dean's list and about sitting in on someone's graduate seminar, and the sound was bright and penetrating. There was a silence when he finished, though not a long one; then my parents took up just where they'd left off.

"Apparently, *not* everyone must be a banker," my mother said. "But must they be undisciplined and immature? Must they be so goddamn self-indulgent?"

My father's laugh was grim. "And who, exactly, are we talking about now?" His words hung there for what seemed a long time. Then I heard more footsteps and figured everyone had retreated to their corners, but I was wrong. There was a shuddering sigh in the hall, muttered words, and a single curse.

"Asshole," David said.

I'd stared at the ceiling for a while, and when it was clear there'd be no more sleep, I'd wandered into the kitchen. I was reading the paper and eating burnt toast when David came in. He wore a coat and tie and his hair was freshly cut, and he looked like a poster boy for some Bible-belt college—the debate captain, maybe. He made a show of checking his watch.

"Up early, I see," he said. "Busy day, I guess. Plenty of TV to watch, lots of dope to smoke?" I ignored him, and he smirked. "What, no smart remark today? Maybe you're a little fuzzy still—still buzzed from last night."

"If I was, you just killed it."

David's laugh was chilly. "There it is, that winning attitude that's done so much for you. Keep it up, Johnny, it'll take you right to the top." I shot him the bird and he laughed. "Keep that up, too—it'll help when you're interviewing for those burger-flipping jobs." I ignored him some more, but David kept at it.

"How long do you think before they bounce you out of this school? Another semester? Less? And that'll make how many? I keep telling Mom she's throwing good tuition money after bad, but—"

"But she doesn't listen to a fucking word you say, David—neither one of them does. Yet you keep on talking. And here I thought you were such a smart guy."

David's face darkened, and he tugged at the skin on his neck. "Smart enough not to get caught three times."

I laughed. "Caught doing what? With all that ass-kissing and back-stabbing, you've got no time for anything else."

"You'd be surprised," he whispered, and he balled his fists and stepped toward me. I stood up. He had half an inch on me then, and twenty pounds, but I didn't care. "Faggot," he hissed, and brought up his hands. He dropped them when our father came in.

His hair was rumpled and his smile vague. He was still in his pajamas. "Am I interrupting?" he asked. David's face tightened, and he turned on his heel and walked down the hall.

Where had it come from, whatever drove David to these assignations—grown from what kernel, planted where? We'd slept under the same roof—David and I, Ned, Liz, and Lauren—and eaten at the same table. Had this weed been growing in secret even then? Were we so self-absorbed, so intent on keeping low in the crossfire between our parents, that we'd somehow failed to notice it taking hold of David? Or were we necessarily blind to it, because the same dark vine had wrapped itself around us all?

"You want coffee?" Clare asked, and brought me back with a start from thoughts of body snatchers and damaged goods. "Or maybe you're jumpy enough." She smiled but there was concern in her eyes.

"I'll have some."

"You find that girl you were looking for?" she asked.

"More or less."

"She all right?"

"I wouldn't describe her quite that way," I said after a while.

"No?" Clare gave me a questioning look and for an instant I was tempted to tell her about it—about Holly, and David, and the videos: all of it—and to ask what she thought. To ask her to make sense of it for me. The impulse took me by surprise, but I kept my mouth shut, and Clare scowled when I didn't answer. She went back to her newspaper and left at noon, with barely a goodbye.

By one o'clock a lethargy had settled on me, along with a headache. I ate some aspirin and lay on the sofa and waited in vain for the edge to come off. The afternoon passed in a dozen books whose first chapters I couldn't finish, and a dozen albums I changed before the second track. It was a familiar listlessness, a sort of post-case hangover that had grown worse as my cases had grown less frequent. Investigation over, at least for now. Reports written, i's dotted, t's crossed, nothing left but to meet with the client. Nothing to do. Nowhere to go. Nowhere but my own head. No, thanks. At some point I drifted into useless sleep.

My phone stayed quiet until after ten, and I was in bed when it rang. It was David, headed home from JFK. He was hoarse and weary but he brightened when I told him I'd found what he was looking for.

"Morning's booked solid," he said, "but I'll try to make it after lunch." As it happened, it was sooner than that.

It was just past dawn when the intercom buzzed, and at first I thought I'd dreamed it. A rain of ice was falling against the window glass, and the sound of it made a fine case for pulling the covers over my head. I had just closed my eyes when the intercom erupted again. My brother was gray and hunched on the little video screen. His head was bare and the collar of his overcoat was up, and he was clutching a newspaper to his chest.

"Let me in," he said, before I could speak. I pushed the button and opened my apartment door and in a moment I heard footsteps in the stairwell. He came in with head bent, and cold air clinging to his clothes.

"What happened, David?"

"I was on my way to the office," he said. His voice was choked and his skin had a drowned look to it. So did his eyes. "I almost never buy the *News*, but today I bought one. I don't know why." He put the newspaper on my kitchen counter.

"What happened?"

He opened the paper three pages in, and I followed his shaking finger down the columns. It was alongside an article that bore the headline "Woman's Body Pulled from River," and it was murky: a photograph—an extreme close-up—of a red cartoon cat standing on its hind legs and grinning insouciantly. Enlargement made the image grainy and washed the color out, but still you could tell that the cat was a tattoo, inked upon a patch of gray, dead-looking flesh.

13

The *Post* named her the Williamsburg Mermaid, because her body had washed up under the Williamsburg Bridge, at the west end. That bit of poetry aside, the article contained nothing I hadn't read in the *Daily News*. She'd been found on Sunday evening by a man collecting bottles, and she was, so far, a Jane Doe. The police described her as white, aged twenty-five to thirty-five, slim, with reddish-brown hair and a distinctive tattoo on her leg. As to time of death they were still uncertain, but noted that she'd been in the water "for a while." As to the circumstances and cause, they said only that these were "suspicious." A search of missing persons reports for women matching her description was under way, but detectives from the Seventh Precinct asked that anyone with information call the toll-free number.

I looked at the *Post*'s photo of the red cat; it was identical to the one in the *News*. The cops hadn't yet released any pictures of her face, not even sketch work, and I wondered about that, and about how long she'd been drifting in the East River. I closed the newspaper and tossed it on the big oval table. David looked at me for a moment and resumed his pacing. I sat back in the soft leather chair and drank some of the soda water that Michael Metz had left us when he'd asked us to wait in his conference room.

Mike is a senior partner at Paley, Clay and Quick—a very good and pricey lawyer at a very staid and pricey firm. His well-deserved reputation as smart, tough, relentless, and icily calm in the face of chaos keeps his calendar perpetually full, but he'd made time for David and me that morning—not only because he was my frequent client, but also because he was my oldest friend. The only one left from college, and that despite all the calls I hadn't returned.

I'd more or less dragged David to Mike's office, though shock and fear had taken any serious fight out of him. It was only in the taxi, locked in traffic on the way to midtown, that he'd come around enough for the anger to bubble up.

"Fuck this!" he'd shouted, and hammered on the Plexiglas partition. The driver glanced back and shook his head. "I have no time for this crap," David said. His voice was shaky. "I've got to get to the office."

"The office will wait. You need to talk to someone about this."

He shook his head. "I don't need shit," he said, and he reached for the door. I put a hand on his arm.

"You need a lawyer, David."

"Bullshit," he said, and shrugged off my hand. But he sat back, and for the rest of the ride had peered silently out the window, his eyes full of nothing.

In Mike's conference room, ignoring the view of office towers shrouded in cloud, and wearing a hole in the expensive carpet, David found his anger again. "She was making fucking movies?" he said, and made it sound like my fault.

I'd gone over my report with him three times and was getting tired of repeating myself, and anyway it seemed beside the point now. "Videos," I said. "She made videos. But we've got other things to think about."

"Whatever." David shrugged and crossed the room again. I took a deep breath. There'd been questions buzzing in my head since I'd first seen the photo of the tattoo, questions I wasn't eager to ask my brother, but had to nonetheless.

"When's the last time you spoke with Wren?"

He stopped pacing and squinted at me. His mouth got tight. "We went through all that last week. Nothing's changed since then."

"Everything's changed. Did you hear from her after you hired me . . . or see her?"

He gripped the edge of the conference table, and his knuckles turned white. "What the fuck are you implying?"

"I'm not implying anything, I—"

"The hell you're not!" He slapped his palm on the tabletop. "Next you'll want to know whether I've got an alibi. Jesus, I thought you were working for me."

"I am, but I need to know where we stand. Mike will need to know too."

"Then don't dance around it—you think I had something to do with this."

"That's not what I was asking," I said, but I wasn't sure it was true. David was sure it wasn't.

"Bullshit," he said. His shoulders slumped and the air went out of him, and he turned to the window. "I haven't heard anything from her since before I hired you. I had nothing to do with this."

"Where were you this weekend?"

David made a sour laugh. "I knew we'd get to that."

"I'm just trying to build a timeline."

"Right," he snorted. "I was in London. I left Friday afternoon and came back yesterday, and I was in meetings most of the time. Is that good enough?" It wasn't, not until we knew when Holly had died, but I didn't tell David that. I took another deep breath.

"What about Stephanie?" I asked.

He stiffened. "What about her?"

"What does she know about Wren? What did you tell her?"

"Why does that matter?" I looked at David and said nothing. "What—now you think she was involved?"

"It's a question the police will ask."

At the mention of the police he took a half step back. He ran a hand over his gray face. "I didn't tell her anything," he said. "We didn't talk about it. I don't know what she knows."

"She knew something, that much was clear when she came to see me. How could you not—"

"We didn't talk about it," he said tightly, and turned on his heel to the window again. Mike saved me from asking more.

He paused in the doorway, a tall, slender figure in impeccable gray pinstripe and a wine-red tie. Partnership had etched fine lines around his narrow features, but his face, still pink from shaving, was somehow still a student's face, easier to imagine bent over some dusty tome than hypnotizing juries and scaring other lawyers. He ran fingers through his thinning black hair and glanced from me to David, and back again. A smile appeared.

"Sorry to have kept you waiting so long," he said, and put out a hand to David. "I've heard a lot about you." David gave him a disbelieving look but there was no irony in Mike's voice and nothing but sincerity in his smile. He was good at that.

"I saw you on television a few weeks ago," David said cautiously. "Court TV."

"A very slow news day," Mike said, and smiled modestly. "And now, why don't you tell me what's going on."

And we did. David was hesitant at first, staring at the carpet or at the architectural prints on the wall, but he gritted his teeth and got the facts out. I went over what I knew, reciting once more the refrain: Holly, Wren, Cassandra. Mike listened closely and made notes on a yellow pad. He interrupted only a few times with questions, and all of those were about dates and times. David concluded with an exhausted sigh and sat back in his chair, looking at Mike and for a light at the end of the tunnel.

Mike tapped his chin with long fingers. When he finally spoke, his voice was without emotion. "We don't know the circumstances of this woman's death yet. The police are calling it suspicious, which in theory could mean suicide, but . . ." He looked at me.

"They're being cute with their language," I said, "and close to the vest about the condition of the body and the cause of death. And besides the tattoo, they haven't given out any pictures. Reading between the lines, I wouldn't bet on suicide."

Mike nodded. "I agree, and in any event we have to plan for the worst, which in this case means a finding of homicide."

"Jesus," David muttered.

Mike gave him a sympathetic look and continued. "If the circumstances were different, it might be possible to sit this out. After all, if media attention to the story remains relatively low, it's entirely plausible that you could've missed the articles in the papers, or not recognized the descriptions they give, or the picture of the tattoo. In which case, you might just wait for the police to contact you. It wouldn't win you a good citizenship award, but it's not illegal and it would probably be the safest course of action. And I imagine it's what the other men in her videos are doing right now—holding their breath, keeping their heads down, and praying. Those of them who saw the story in the paper and recognized the tattoo, anyway. But, unfortunately, that's not our situation.

"Our situation is that this woman was actively harassing you—calling, coming by your home, threatening you. And we must assume the police will learn this fairly quickly, if and when they identify the body."

"Learn it how?" David interrupted. "How the hell will they connect me with her?"

I answered him. "Dumping Holly's phone records will probably be enough, but they'll also search her place, and who knows what they'll find there. Her videos, I'd guess, and whatever information she collected about you." I didn't think David could get much paler, but somehow he managed.

"To the police it will suggest motive," Mike said. "Which means they'll be keen to speak with you, and with your wife, as well. And they'll look at you even harder when they find that you were disturbed enough by the harassment to hire a PI to locate Holly. If you were upset enough for that, they'll reason, you might've been up for something more desperate. They'll find it hard to believe that you missed the Jane Doe story in the press, and they'll wonder why—if you have nothing to hide—you didn't come forward on your own.

"That's not an appealing picture, David, and that's why I don't think you can wait for the police to find you. You need to get out in front of this, and go to them."

"Go to the police?" David nearly jumped out of his seat. He went to the window and sank his hands in his pockets and rocked from one foot to the other. "Jesus Christ," he muttered.

"It demonstrates that you're cooperative," Mike said, "that you have nothing to hide. You lay out all the facts yourself and you defuse a lot of suspicion."

But David wasn't listening. " 'If and when,' you said—'if and when they identify the body.' There's a chance they won't."

"Not a good one," I said. "Holly had family and friends and people she worked with. Even if she wasn't close to any of them, they knew her. One of them will see the stories and make the connection, or get worried enough to file a missing persons with the cops, and they'll make the connection themselves. And that's without worrying about whether her fingerprints are on record someplace, or her DNA, or if there was a dry cleaning tag in her clothing. It's just a matter of time."

Still David didn't seem to hear. "If I go to the cops and the press gets hold of it . . . that's the end."

"Talking to the police is no crime," Mike said.

"Being dragged into this . . . a dead girl, sex videos . . . no, that would be it." David rubbed his forehead. "What if it turns out she's a suicide? What if it turns out the girl in the paper isn't even her?"

Mike's voice was steady and soft. "I know people in the department. I'll put out feelers. If it turns out the police think her death was suicide, then obviously there's no need to do anything. As for whether she's Wren or not, we can try and get a better description of the body—where exactly the tattoo is, birthmarks—but beyond that, I'm not sure how much we can know beforehand."

David breathed a long, shaking sigh. His legs wobbled and he collapsed into a chair and looked at me. The bottom had fallen out of his eyes. "So what you're telling me is I'm fucked. The police will identify her, find her videos, trace her calls, and—bang—I'm the prime suspect. And my only choice is whether I'm fucked now or later."

Mike pursed his lips. "The police will be interested in you, but—from what John has said—you won't be alone. For starters, they'll want to talk to every other man Wren videotaped. On their own, those guys make for plenty of reasonable doubt—and apparently one of them succeeded in finding her. And then there's the guy John ran into at her apartment, not to mention all the usual suspects: boyfriends, family, business associates."

"Who's to say the cops can find those guys?" David said. "I thought all the faces and voices on the video were masked."

"They were," I said, "but there are the phone records, and if they get hold of the unedited videos, or if she made notes, those will point them in the right direction."

"Too many fucking ifs," David said, and smacked the table again. "How long will it take for all those ifs to happen? And in the meantime, it's me the cops are talking to, and my house with the fucking camera crews out front." He shook his head. "No way. I'm not signing up for that."

"There aren't many levers for us to pull just now," Mike said. His voice was calm and reassuring. "We can't change the fact that the police are likely to notice you, but we can change how they feel about it when they do."

"By having me walk in there?"

"Trust me," Mike told him, "there's a big difference between going in on your own and being invited."

"Maybe, or maybe I'm just serving myself up on a platter. Who's to say that once they have me in their sights, the investigation won't stop right there? Can you guarantee they won't decide it's easier to make a case against me than to go chasing after a bunch of nameless men?" He looked at Mike and then at me, and neither of us had an answer.

"And no matter how it goes," David continued, "the press will be all over me."

"Going to the police on your own gives us some influence over that. We can get assurances of confidentiality from—"

"Right." David snorted. "I'm sure those count for a lot. Who do I complain to when somebody makes the first anonymous call to Fox?"

Mike looked at me and raised an eyebrow. "It's a risk," he said softly.

"It's fatal, is what it is. If this becomes public, it's fucking fatal." David put his head in his hands, and no one spoke. Only the whoosh of air in the ducts relieved the heavy silence.

"You can't wait for them," I said after a while. "If they come for you—"

David straightened. Some color returned to his face. "If I go to them, I'm not going alone."

Mike nodded. "Of course not. I'll be there, and so will John, and you'll have the full resources of this firm behind you as well."

David waved his hand impatiently. "That's not what I mean. If I go talk to them, I'm not going in empty-handed. I'm going in with other names."

Mike looked at me, confused. He wasn't the only one. "What names are you talking about?" I asked.

"If I go in there and the police have no other suspect but me, there's a chance they're not going to look any further. And even if they do, for as long as mine is the only name on the table, I'm going to be the only news story. But if I go in with other names—the guys in the other videos, the guy who hired the lawyer, the guy who punched you out, boyfriends, whoever the hell else you can find—then I'm not alone. There are other people the cops can build a case against, and other guys the press can chew on." He looked at Mike. "Like you said, plenty of reasonable doubt."

My mouth opened, but it took a moment for the words to come. When they did, they sounded far away. "*Whoever I can find?* You're asking me to investigate Holly's death?"

David waved again. "Her death, her life—whatever. I need names I can bring with me to the cops—anyone they'll be more interested in than me."

I looked at Mike, who tapped his chin. There was a glint in his eye, and it was familiar and unwelcome. I shook my head. "Have you forgotten that this is an active police investigation?" I said. "The NYPD is not overly fond of strangers pissing in their garden, and even less when the stranger's a PI and the brother of a likely suspect."

Mike nodded slowly. "Of course, but David does have a point. This woman led a high-risk life—her videos are testimony to that—and it's important that the police be made aware of this as they're setting the course of their investigation, and before they settle on a suspect. It should also give the DA's office something to consider, when they're thinking about cases that are winnable and cases that aren't." I shook my head more vigorously, but Mike ignored it. "And it's not as if you haven't done this sort of thing before: checking stories, finding new witnesses, identifying inconsistencies—developing alternative theories."

"But usually it's postindictment, when we've got charges and a defendant and a trial coming up, and when the police have finished their investigation—'finished' being the operative word there. In this case, they haven't started yet."

"But you *have* done it before. Your relationship to the client is something of an issue, but not insurmountable. You'll need to be meticulous with your reports, and chain of custody on any evidence you may find—but you're careful about those things anyway. The police won't be thrilled, but it should be manageable."

David squinted at me. "I need you to do this, dammit," he said. "And since when do you care who you piss off?"

It was almost eleven o'clock when David left for the Klein & Sons offices, still brittle looking but with necktie straightened and at least some of his abrasive composure back in place. Mike had assured him several times that he'd call if he learned anything about the dead woman from his contacts in the NYPD, but cautioned him against optimism. Even so, David was all too hopeful when he walked out the conference room door. Mike sighed and helped himself to what remained of the soda water.

"I should be annoyed that you don't return my calls," he said, "but at least when you finally show, you bring new business along. I guess we'll call it even."

"Give it time. A few more meetings with David, you may wish I was still MIA."

"He is . . . intense." Mike smiled. "And given what you've said about your family, he's not a referral I would've predicted."

"You and me both."

"So this isn't a rapprochement?"

"It's a job."

Mike peered into his glass and mostly hid a skeptical look. "You have a plan in mind?"

"I know where to start: looking at her place, talking to the neighbors, to the family, to Krug and anybody else I can find—all the usual stuff. After that, it's read and react."

"How about her friend—the actress?"

"Jill Nolan? That's a tough call. I'm not sure how far I'd get with her on the phone—her hackles were raised pretty high when we spoke—and if she hasn't seen the mermaid stories in Seattle, I don't want to get her thinking more about Holly than she is already."

Mike nodded and drank off the last of his seltzer. "I assume your brother's hobby took you by surprise," he said. I nodded. "You think he's told us all there is to tell?"

"I know he hasn't," I said. "He won't talk about Stephanie, for one thing."

"You think that's all there is?"

"If you're asking me to vouch for the guy, I can't. I know less about him every day."

"I'm just wondering if there are shoes waiting to drop."

"Clients lie."

Mike frowned. "Your brother has a lot on the table here—his marriage, his job, potentially, not to mention the black eye all this would give Klein & Sons. His situation is shaky enough without keeping secrets."

"You're preaching to the choir," I said. "If I was the cop who caught the case, and I had a choice of spending my valuable investigating time on a guy who'd already been strong-armed into being in one of Wren's videos, or the guy she was in the process of strong-arming when she died, I know who I'd pick."

Mike nodded gravely. "And the window we're working in isn't big. If Jane Doe really is Wren, the police could be coming around soon."

I nodded. "A week or two, I figure. No more."

14

The ice gave way to lashing sleet by afternoon, and the sidewalks were glazed and perilous in Brooklyn. Meltwater dripped from my parka and puddled at my feet as I stood in the vestibule of Holly Cade's apartment building, which still smelled powerfully, though of bleach now rather than decay. The intercom speaker was still banged up, and if I wasn't mistaken, a few more names were missing from the buttons.

I pressed the button for 3-G, Holly's apartment, and got no response. No surprise. I tried her irate, curious neighbor, Mr. Arrua, in 3-F. Silence there too. I pushed another six buttons at random, but the three voices that replied—one in English and two in Spanish—wanted to know who the hell I was before they'd buzz me in. The inner door was firmly locked, and though I had vinyl gloves, a screwdriver, and a small pry bar in my pocket, I wasn't sure I wanted to use them just yet. I went outside.

There was a short flight of metal stairs under the stoop, and a metal door at the bottom. It was heavy and imposing and accessorized with a fat deadbolt that would surely have secured the basement against all comers, were it not for the folded paper coffee cup that someone had used as a doorstop. I went in, and past the darkened laundry room to the elevator.

The door to 3-G was still locked, and no more scuffed than it had been last time; I was relieved to see no crime scene tape on it. I knocked, expecting nothing, and wasn't disappointed. Then I turned to 3-F. I rapped twice and heard shuffling and a scrape of metal by the peephole.

"Yeah?" said the reedy voice from behind the door.

"Mr. Arrua? I was here last week, looking for your neighbor, and I—"

"I remember you. You gave me your card and I told you to leave me alone."

"That was me," I said. "I was wondering if we could talk."

"I had nothing to say then and I got nothing to say now."

"Have you seen Holly lately?"

"You remember that number: nine-one-one?"

"I don't need a lot of your time, Mr. Arrua, and I can pay for what I use."

"I guess you're still hard of hearing," he said, but he didn't threaten to call the cops. "You're what, a private detective or something?"

"Yes."

Arrua chuckled behind his door. "So, what's my time worth?"

"You tell me."

It was quiet for a while and I thought I'd lost him, but I hadn't. "What's the weather like outside?" he asked.

"Crappy," I said. "There's sleet coming down and the sidewalk's like an ice rink."

"Wait," Arrua said. He shuffled away from the door and shuffled back in under a minute, and a slip of notebook paper appeared by my foot.

"The market's around the corner," he said.

It came to two bags of groceries: coffee, condensed milk, eggs, a sack of rice, a jar of dulce de leche, two papayas, a loaf of bread, and paper napkins. Arrua opened the door to 3-F and took the bags from me, and I followed him down a short hallway to his living room.

He was a small man, worn but well-kempt in khakis, a gray cardigan, and a white shirt. His apartment was much the same. The living room was a narrow rectangle with white walls, beige trim, and a hard-wood floor that had seen rough use, but also a recent waxing. There were two windows that looked onto a fire escape, and that were forti-fied by metal accordion gates. In front of them was a sofa covered in gray fabric, with arms that had frayed and been carefully mended. There was a bookshelf in the corner, stocked with Spanish titles, and some pictures hanging above it. A photo clipped from a newspaper and yellowing under glass: Argentine soccer players in white and sky blue, and Maradona's infamous "hand of God" goal against England. Next to it, a plaque commemorating twenty-five years of service to the Metropolitan Transit Authority—hail and farewell, Car Mainte-nance Engineer Jorge Arrua. Next to that, another photo, black and white, of a pale, pretty, sick-looking woman in a high-necked dress. Wife, mother, sister, daughter—whoever she was, I got the impres-sion that she hadn't survived her illness, and that it had all happened long ago.

Arrua pointed at the sofa and went into an alcove kitchen. I sat and watched him put his groceries in the half-sized refrigerator, and fix a pot of coffee on the half-sized stove. While the smell of brewing coffee filled the room, he toasted thick slices of bread and opened the jar of dulce de leche. A tabby cat appeared from somewhere and threaded itself between his legs and looked at me sideways.

Arrua was seventysomething and thin, with a soldier's posture but a faltering stride. His hair was metal gray, cut short and slicked against his head, and his sallow skin was like parchment. He was clean-shaven and there were deep grooves around his mouth and pale eyes that gave him a stubborn, argumentative look even as he poured coffee and set the mugs on a tray. He carried the tray to an oak coffee table and sat opposite me, in an armchair. He added condensed milk to his coffee and sipped at it and sighed.

"Breakfast's all I like now," he said, "so I eat it every meal." He spread some dulce de leche on toast. "Help yourself."

I poured condensed milk in my coffee and drank. It was thick and sweet and powerful. I sighed too.

"When's the last time you saw Holly, Mr. Arrua?" I said.

"I guess you can call me George. I saw her in the hall, a couple weeks ago maybe. I don't keep track."

"Do you usually see her more often?"

He shrugged. "I see her three, four times in a month. I go to bed early and get up early, and she's on a different schedule, I guess. It used to be I knew this whole building—all my neighbors—but not now." He shrugged again.

"So you don't really know Holly?"

"I know her to say hello."

"Is she a good neighbor?"

Arrua looked at me and drank some coffee. "Sure."

I raised an eyebrow. "Last time I was here, you were complaining about the noise."

"You made a racket outside my door."

"You made it sound like it wasn't the first time."

He tilted his head. "I got no problem with her," he said. "She keeps to herself and mostly keeps quiet. It's the people she has over who make trouble. Shouting, banging, slamming doors—it sounds like they're coming through the walls sometimes."

"Are they fighting or partying?"

"It's no party," he said. The tabby rubbed its head against his trouser cuff and purred loudly.

"Is it yelling-fighting or hitting-fighting?"

"It's yelling and throwing things. As far as anything else, I don't know."

"Have there been a lot of fights?"

Arrua thought about it. "Maybe ten altogether."

"Recently?"

He shrugged. "Last time was a couple weeks back, I think. Before that, not for a long time—not since summer or beginning of fall."

"Who is she fighting with?"

He took a bite of toast and shook his head. "I'm too old to be in the middle of anything."

"I'm not putting you in the middle, George—I wouldn't do that to somebody who makes coffee this good." A smile flickered above his skeptical look. "This goes nowhere besides me."

Arrua nodded slowly, as if against his better judgment. "Her boyfriend mainly—her old boyfriend, I guess. They went at it pretty good."

"Any idea what about?"

Arrua shook his head. "I'd hear him yelling and banging stuff around, but I don't know what he was saying."

I drank some coffee and thought about that for a while. "Did you complain?" Arrua nodded. "And?"

"I knock on the door and she says she's sorry and things quiet down for a while—but sometimes not for long."

"You never went to the super or anything?"

Arrua colored a little. "I'm seventy-nine years old, for God's sake. I don't want to get into that kind of thing."

"What kind of thing, George?"

He shifted in his seat and ran a thin finger around the rim of his mug. "The last time I went over there, the boyfriend answered. He tells me to mind my own fucking business, and if I don't he'll . . ." Arrua colored more deeply and looked down at his cat, asleep on his foot. "I don't know . . . he talked some trash about what he'd do to Diego here." He shook his head. "She tried to stop him but he pushed her away. After that, I quit complaining. Like I said, I'm too old."

I let out a long breath. "You know this guy's name?" Arrua shook his head. "What does he look like?"

"White guy with dark hair, in his thirties, I guess. Tall—taller than you, I think."

"When did he stop coming around?"

"I don't know, maybe in July or August."

I thought for a while. "You said the fighting was *mainly* with the old boyfriend," I said. "Does that mean she has other noisy visitors?"

"A month back there was a guy banging at her door pretty loud."

"What did he want?"

"I don't know. I don't know if he ever got to see her."

"You see him before, or since?"

Arrua chuckled and shook his head. "He wasn't the type that hangs around here usually."

"What type was he?"

"Looked like a banker to me, or maybe a lawyer—white hair, dark suit, white shirt, wore a tie. Not somebody I see at the community center."

I nodded. "Anybody else come around?"

"There was a woman here a couple weeks ago, did her share of crying and yelling. Dark hair, thirty-five, forty maybe—I didn't get a good look."

"Anybody else?"

"There's the new boyfriend."

"How new?"

"A few months, maybe."

"Do they fight too?"

"Not that I hear."

"You know his name?" Arrua shook his head. "You know what he looks like?"

"Sure—and so do you." I raised an eyebrow and he smiled. "He's the guy who kicked your ass in the hall."

I had no other questions for Jorge Arrua, so I finished my coffee and thanked him and listened to him lock his door behind me. Then I took the stairs up.

There was a sign on the metal door to the roof that warned of an alarm, but the wires dangling from the push bar made it less than convincing. It opened only to the brief creak of hinges. Outside, the sleet had turned to snow and the air was white with it.

"Great," I whispered. I walked to the edge of the roof and looked down the narrow passage between Holly's building and its neighbor.

The fire escape was crusted in ice and slush and decades of rust underneath. The little gate where it met the roofline shrieked like a subway when I pulled on it, but no windows opened below, and no heads peered out. I slipped and slid a half-dozen times on the way down, and I crouched by Holly's windows with bruised elbows and sodden knees.

Her windows were locked tight and, like her neighbor's, guarded by a metal gate. I peered through the lattice into the apartment beyond. It was even smaller than Arrua's, a single square room with a pocket kitchen at one end, bath at the other, futon in the corner, and what looked like all of the apartment's contents scattered across the floor. I put away my pry bar. Someone had beaten me to it.

"Burglary?" Mike Metz asked.

"I doubt it," I said. I propped the phone on my shoulder and spooned some yogurt into a bowl. "At least, not the traditional kind. The windows were intact and so was the door, so whoever it was had a key—and no interest in the television or the iPod or three fairly expensive flat-screen monitors."

"You saw all that?"

"The apartment's not big. What I didn't see, though, were her computers or any video equipment."

"You think that stuff was there to begin with?"

"There was a table with a modem and a printer and all the monitors on it, and lots of loose cabling hanging off the side. And there were factory boxes on the floor—three of them—for digital video cameras. Two of them were opened and empty. I couldn't see into the third one."

Mike made a clicking sound. "Anything else not there?"

"There was a file cabinet tipped on its side. The drawers looked empty from where I was, but I didn't see any file folders around. I didn't see any disks around, either, or video cassettes."

"So, someone looking for . . . what?"

"Her work would be my guess."

Mike swore under his breath. "Someone interested in her work and someone with a key."

"I suppose she could've let whoever it was in—but either way it implies someone she knew."

"Like the new boyfriend. Or maybe the old one."

"That's the hopeful answer," I said. "Talking to them is way up there on my list."

"The neighbor didn't know their names?"

"No, but I'm hoping the sister or the brother-in-law will. I'm going again tomorrow morning."

Mike made a noise of vague assent. "How about her other visitors—the woman, and the guy in the suit—did the neighbor know anything about them?"

"Just the vague descriptions."

"They ring any bells?"

"The suit could've been the lawyer Krug's assistant told me about. Or not. The woman could be anyone."

Mike was quiet for a while, and I could almost hear the gears turning. "You didn't go inside?" he asked finally.

"I would've had to force the window and the window gate, and that would mean nothing but heartache with the cops. B and E is bad enough, but screwing up a possible crime scene is worse, and if they find out you've done both it makes it that much harder to convince them you haven't tampered with evidence. And speaking of cops, how are you doing with your contacts?"

"I'm taking a guy to lunch tomorrow," Mike said.

"Rough work."

"You haven't seen him eat."

Mike rang off and I ate some yogurt. Outside, the slush had frozen over, and the night sky was streaked with cloud. This afternoon's snow had been a feint, not the promised onslaught but merely a scouting party. Still, the local TV news crews were giddy with anticipation. They prattled on tirelessly about plows and salt and closings and delays, and only war would've made them happier. The storm was good news for David, too, as was any story that sucked up air time and column inches, and pushed the Williamsburg Mermaid far from the public's view. If he got really lucky, the snow would be followed by an ugly celebrity divorce.

On television, a stiff-haired woman gestured toward a weather map that was white from Maryland to Massachusetts, and west to the Ohio Valley. I turned up the sound. The forecast called for the storm to hit New York sometime tomorrow afternoon. I only hoped it would hold until I made it back from Wilton.

Nicole Cade was in Toronto, Herbert Deering told me, stranded at the airport by the storm that hadn't reached us yet, and deeply unhappy. Which explained why, on my second visit, I actually made it inside the house.

"They don't know when they'll clear the runways," he said. "And who knows what the airports down here will be like by then. It could be days before she makes it back." The prospect didn't seem entirely devastating to him.

He led me to a book-lined study with a striped silk sofa and matching slipper chairs, and a fire in the small brick fireplace. It burned silently behind glass doors, throwing off light but no heat. I sat on the sofa and Deering perched his bulk on a slipper chair, as comfortable as a hippo at the opera. He looked at me and looked nervously around the room, as if he wasn't usually allowed in there and expected at any moment to be ordered out. He ran a hand over his messy, thin hair.

"I thought Nikki gave you Holly's address," he said.

I nodded. "She did, but I haven't been able to reach Holly there. I was hoping one of you might have some other ideas of where I might find her."

Deering rubbed his chin with the back of his hand. He'd shaved today, and nicked himself in several spots. A tiny scrap of toilet paper, punctuated with a dot of blood, still clung to the side of his neck. His eyes were red and his voice was furry, and I wondered if he wasn't hungover.

"I don't know," he said. "Like I told you last time, we're not in touch."

"You must know some of her friends, though. A boyfriend, maybe . . ."

Deering shook his head and rubbed his hands on the legs of his corduroy pants. "Really, we don't. Even when we heard from her more often, we didn't know those things."

"No?" I said, and smiled in what I hoped was an encouraging way. "When was it that you used to hear from her more often?"

He squinted with confusion. "When—?"

"I mean, was it months ago, years? How long?"

"She and Nikki were never close, and she pretty much stopped calling after her first year in college. We heard from her even less when she moved to the city."

"Did you know any of the Gimlet Players?"

The name took him by surprise. "That theater group she was with?" I nodded. "We never saw any of those plays—we never saw her in anything."

"Did you ever meet any of the players?"

"There was a guy who came here."

"What guy?"

"An actor, from the group. He drove her up here a couple of times, to pick up some of her things. I think they were seeing each other."

"Gene Werner?"

Deering shrugged. "It could've been. I don't remember."

"When was this?"

"The first time? A couple of years ago, maybe. And then again last summer."

"This past summer?" He nodded. "Do you remember what he looked like?"

Deering tugged at the cuffs of his flannel shirt and thought about it. "A tall guy, with brown hair, long I think, and a little goatee. Handsome guy, looked like he could've been an actor or something." Gene Werner.

"And he's her boyfriend?"

"It seemed that way."

"Have you seen him since then?"

"Just those two times."

"Did she ever bring anyone else here?"

A log popped and crumbled in the fireplace, and Deering started. He shook his head. "She barely comes here herself."

"Not for holidays or birthdays?" Deering shook his head. "When was the last time she was here?"

He squinted at me again and shrugged. "Maybe in the summer, when she came up with that guy, or maybe there was a time after. Whenever, it was a while ago. Months."

"Would your wife remember better?"

The thought that I might ask her horrified Deering. "The summer was the last time—I'm pretty sure."

"How about friends in town? Are there any she's in touch with?"

Deering took off his glasses and cleaned them on his shirttail. "Not that I know of," he said.

"How about people from college?"

Deering shrugged vaguely. "Sorry," he said.

I nodded. "And Holly doesn't go to Brookfield, to visit her father?"

Deering blanched. "No," he said.

"How do you know?" I asked. He peered at me. "I mean, how would you know if she just went up there to see him?"

Deering shook his head. "She wouldn't. She has nothing to say to him."

Another log collapsed in the fire, and Deering and I watched the ash and embers drift. "What happened with Holly that she doesn't talk to her family?" I asked after a while.

Deering gave another cautious glance around the room, as if someone, maybe Nikki, might appear in the doorway. He pinched his blurry chin between thumb and forefinger. "It's just one of those things," he said quietly. "The parents fought a lot and the girls chose sides—Nikki with her dad and Holly with her mom—and then their mom died, just when Holly was starting high school. That's a tough time for a kid, and Holly's been angry ever since—at Fredrick, at Nikki, even at their mom. As long as I've known her, she's been mad at pretty much the whole world."

Deering stared again into the dwindling fire. Outside the window, snow was starting to fall.

16

The storm started slowly, and with no wind, and though the roads were crowded with people fleeing work or school, or making last, desperate runs to the supermarket, I returned to the city without incident and returned my rented car in one piece. Back in my apartment, I listened to a message from Clare—"I'll be over later, snowshoes and all"—then I poured a glass of water and opened my notebook.

A lifetime ago, when I'd been trying merely to locate Holly Cade, Gene Werner hadn't returned any of my telephone calls. Ultimately I'd been able to get where I was going without his help, and I'd had no need to push. But that was then. Now I knew that Werner and Holly had been seeing each other as recently as last summer, and now Jorge Arrua's vague description of Holly's belligerent old boyfriend— "white guy with dark hair, in his thirties . . . tall"—sounded less vague. I leafed through my notes until I found Werner's phone number and address.

A deep, newscasterly voice came on the line, but it was just his answering machine, apparently back in working order. I left another message. I looked at his address, on West 108th Street. I looked outside, at the city going white, and decided what the hell. I put on jeans and boots, and a parka over my turtleneck. I left a note for Clare, and headed for the door.

The snow was coming harder when I stepped outside. My hair was white by the end of the block and frozen by the time I walked down the subway stairs at Fourteenth Street. When I walked up again, at 110th Street and Central Park West, a wind was blowing and streetlights were coming on. I headed south and west.

Werner's block was a mixed bag—a few lovingly restored seven-figure brownstones, a few of their beaten, boarded-up cousins, a seventies-ugly housing project, and an even worse senior center from the 1980s—all bookended by slouching brick tenements. There was a coffee shop at one end of the street and a pizza parlor at the other. Werner's building was in the middle, a four-story brownstone, not boarded but by no means restored. It was soot-streaked and the front door was wire glass and metal bars. The intercom was outside, mounted in the recessed doorway.

There were three apartments to a floor; Werner was in 2-B. I leaned on the button but got no answer. I tried his neighbors and got the same. I stepped back from the building and looked up. All the second-floor windows that I could see were dark. There was a narrow passage between Werner's building and the one next to it, and I could see a side door about twenty feet along, under a security light, but the alley was protected by a high metal gate that no one had been considerate enough to prop open with a coffee cup. I pulled out my cell phone and tried Werner's number again. Again the machine. I dropped my phone into my pocket and walked to the corner and into the pizza place.

There were a half-dozen tables, all empty, to the right as I came in, and to the left a counter. The guy behind it was rolling out dough and listening to forró on a loud radio, and he barely glanced up when I came in. I ordered a slice and a Pepsi, and he slid a large piece of pizza into the oven and filled a tall cup with ice and soda. I took the cup to a table by the window and waited for my pizza and stared through the snow at the front of Werner's building.

I made the pizza last, and the soda too, and the whole time I ate, I saw only one person pass through Werner's door. She was a small, round woman, with a long, puffy coat and frizzy hair exploding from under a white knit cap, and she was inside the building before I could make a move. A minute later I saw a light go on on the top floor. I was throwing out my greasy napkins when the second person came along. He wore a red parka and he was tall, and underneath the snow on his head, there was dark hair. He had two sacks of groceries, and he set them on the sidewalk as he dug in his pockets. I ran out the door, zipping my coat as I went.

"Gene," I called, as I crossed the street. He didn't look. "Hey, Gene," I said again, coming up beside him.

He pulled a heavy key ring from his pocket and stooped for his bags. He looked at me curiously.

"Huh?" he said.

Unless Werner had developed an overbite and bad acne scars since Terry Greer's bar snapshots had been taken, this wasn't him. "Sorry," I said. "Wrong guy. I was supposed to meet Gene, but he hasn't shown up yet. Gene Werner—you know him?"

A wrinkle of distaste crossed the man's face. "I know who he is."

"I was supposed to meet him here half an hour ago. Have you seen him around?"

"Not lately," the man said. He slid his key into the lock and pushed the front door open. I followed behind him and stepped into the doorway. He turned and elbowed the door shut. I stopped it with my foot.

"You mind if I wait inside? It's pretty cold out here."

He shook his head. "No can do—building rules. Sorry, man." He leaned against the door.

There was nothing to be gained from a shoving match; I moved my foot back. "Do you remember when you saw him last?" I asked as the door swung shut.

The man shrugged and shook his head. "Sorry," he said again. He carried his bags to the elevator and watched me through the glass until I walked away.

It was full dark now and snowing harder. The wind was heavier too, swirling between buildings and spinning the snow in dizzying vortices. Spikes of icy air ran down my collar and up my sleeves. Across the street, lights were going out in the pizza parlor, and at the coffee shop the roller gates were already down. I headed east, toward the subway.

I spotted him in less than a block, when he stepped out from the shadow of the senior center and began trudging along behind me. He couldn't have been worse at running a tail if he'd been pounding on a drum. And I recognized him right away too, from the gray parka and biker boots and big shoulders, and from the wide face with tiny features: Babyface, Holly's new boyfriend.

I knew he hadn't tailed me to 108th Street—it would've been impossible to miss him on my way there—which meant he'd picked me up at Werner's place. Which meant he'd been staking it out. I'd have to remember to ask him why. I paused at the corner of 108th and Central Park West and made a show of checking my watch. Babyface ducked behind a van. He was nothing if not earnest.

There was little traffic on CPW: a few cabs cruising slowly south, slewing when their brake lights flared, a FedEx truck double parked at 106th Street, delivering God only knew what in the middle of a blizzard, a Number 10 bus lumbering uptown, and another headed back down. Across the street, Central Park was a landscape through static: bare trees, footpaths, streetlamps, and stone walls, all gray and grainy and dissolving in a whirl of snow. The northbound bus was still three car lengths away when I sprinted across the avenue, and its horn was still braying when I went into the park at a run.

The footpath was slick and I skated downhill and slid to a stop where the path forked north and south. I paused to make sure Babyface was with me. He was—standing by the entrance, backlit and steaming. I moved under a streetlamp, to make sure he could see me, and then I headed south. The path curved uphill and was sheltered from the sideways snow by rocky outcroppings to the left and by a canopy of branches overhead. I stepped off the path and into the gap between two large rocks, and I waited.

I heard Babyface—his fraying breath and scuffing boots—before I saw him, and then a broad expanse of gray nylon passed, like the side of a freighter. I let him go fifty feet up the path and then I stepped out.

"Gets cold, just waiting," I called.

Babyface spun and his hands came up in a dishearteningly practiced way. "What the hell do you want?"

"Same thing you do, I guess: Gene Werner. You see him around?"

"All I see around is you, and I'm getting fucking sick of it."

"You get sick of Holly too? Is that what happened to her?"

At the mention of her name, Babyface stiffened and took a step toward me—and stopped in his tracks when a Samoyed came around the corner behind him. The dog was dragging a well-bundled woman on a red nylon leash, and he froze when he saw Babyface and emitted a nasty growl.

Babyface looked at the dog and the woman and then back at me, and looked like he might growl too. Instead, he said, "Fuck it," and turned and ran up the path, past the woman, and around the corner. The Samoyed barked and snapped, but Babyface never looked back. The woman reeled in her dog, and her mouth was a perfect "O" when I ran past.

I didn't get far. Babyface sprinted, arms pumping and shoulders bouncing, and took a sharp left where the path forked again. I did the same and I was gaining ground until the next turn, when I hit a wide crescent of ice. My boots flew up and my legs churned in the air like a cartoon, and I came down hard on my ass and elbows and on the back of my head.

Through the rush in my ears, I heard his footsteps fade in the distance, and I thought about hauling myself up and going after him. But my legs had emptied out and my head had filled with sand, and all I could manage was to lie there, while snow fell on my face and wind carried my breath away.

I took inventory in the morning, in the bathroom mirror. The worst was the purple egg on my left hip, followed by the cuts and bruises on my elbows and the knot on the back of my head. I was stiff and limping on my way to the kitchen, but there was coffee at the end of the road, and a note from Clare: "Back later. Coffee's fresh." I ran my fingers over the neat lines of tape and gauze on my elbow.

The people on the subway the night before had scrupulously ignored my wet and muddy clothing, and avoided even looking in my general direction. Clare was less circumspect.

"Jesus Christ, what happened to you?" She'd dropped her book and sat up on the sofa as I limped through the door.

"Slipped on some ice," I said. I dropped my coat and eased into a chair and winced. Clare bit her lip. I fumbled with the laces of my boots and she'd brushed my hands away and untied them for me.

"Shouldn't you say some shit like 'You should see the other guy'?"

I stretched out my leg and winced again. "I am the other guy."

Clare shook her head. "I don't do the Florence Nightingale thing," she'd said. But as it turned out, she did, carefully and with surprising tenderness.

I filled a mug and stared out the frost-framed window. The wind had died since last night, but snow was still falling in small, relentless flakes. The TV news said it was the calm before the second—the worse—storm that was due to arrive that night. The anchormen read long lists of things that were closed, and likely to stay that way for a while, and field reporters trained their cameras on impassable roads and on the dazed and hapless at the airports. I looked down at Sixteenth Street. The only cars I saw were at the curbsides, buried until spring, and the only people were gray smudges, trudging—one snowshoeing—down the middle of the road. I wondered what errand Clare was on.

A shower loosened my limbs, and three cups of coffee got my brain cells spinning, but still they found no purchase when it came to Babyface. He was Holly's new boyfriend. He had a key to her place. He was looking for something or someone—maybe Gene Werner. He had a bad temper. And twice now my conversations with him had ended in bruises. I thought again about the crude green tattoos on his hands, and added some speculation to my paltry pile of facts: he's maybe been inside recently. It was still adding up to nothing when the phone rang.

It was Mike Metz, who'd somehow made it to his office. I told him about my conversation with Herbert Deering, in Wilton, and about my livelier encounter with Babyface.

Mike was quiet for a while when I was done. "It'd be good to know his name," he said eventually, "and whether he actually was inside—and, if so, what for. It'd also be good to know where he was a week ago last Tuesday, or thereabouts. And the same goes for Werner."

"Why a week ago Tuesday?"

"That's when the ME thinks she went in the water, or so my lunch date told me. They think she was in about five days."

"They have a time of death?"

"Sometime that day—Tuesday—but nothing more precise yet."

"And the cause?"

"Shot in the face, four times."

I took a deep breath. "Not your typical suicide, I guess."

"Not really."

"But it explains why no pictures."

"Yep."

I thought about the timing. David's London trip did him no good, and I wondered if he had a story for Tuesday. I didn't relish asking. "In the face is . . ."

Mike found the word for me. "Intimate."

"Anger like that, you think *lover*—which doesn't necessarily narrow the field with Holly."

Mike made an affirmative noise. "According to my friend, the gunshots weren't all of it. Sometime before she was shot, she was beaten, and pretty badly."

"Jesus," I sighed. "How long before?"

"Days, they think. Apparently the bruises had started to heal."

"The cops think it was the same person that did both?"

"My guy says they're still debating. Why—you have a theory?"

"Not even close," I said. "Holly seemed to make a lot of people mad, or scared, or both."

"I just wish we knew who some of those people were."

"I'm working on it." My voice was louder than I intended.

Mike's voice was quiet. "I'll let you get back to it, then," he said, and hung up.

Four times, in the face. Jesus.

Getting back to work was dragging on a pair of jeans and a turtleneck, and making another call to Gene Werner. I got no answer and left no message, and afterward I called Orlando Krug's gallery. The deep, faintly accented voice answered after five rings, and there was a long silence on the line when I told him who it was.

"Like most of the city, we are closed today, Mr. March."

"I guess that leaves you time to talk."

"We've already discussed Cassandra's work; I don't know that I have any more to say."

"It's not Cassandra's work I want to talk about, Mr. Krug. It's Holly."

There was another long silence, and finally Krug spoke. "I will be in the gallery for another few hours."

The walk to the West Village was slow going through stabbing cold on mostly empty streets. A few hardy shopkeepers shoveled their patches of pavement against the tireless snow, and were rewarded

with the business of a few desperate souls—coffee and bagels and cigarettes, diapers and beer. I limped in the road, and moved aside now
and then for the churning orange mass of a snowplow.

Orlando Krug hadn't bothered to clear his piece of Perry Street,
but the security gate was up on the door of his gallery. I rapped on the
glass and he let me in. Krug was still neatly pressed, but he was pale
under his dark tan, and his blue eyes were clouded. I followed him
through the gallery and into his office, a snug, bright space with more
beadboard, a red and green kilim on the floor, and a big cherry desk in
front of a shuttered, deeply recessed window.

"You've come through the snow; I suppose the least I can do is
offer you coffee." Krug went to the windowsill and poured coffee from
a steel carafe into a heavy mug. He handed the mug across and settled
into a tan leather chair.

"I was surprised to find you here today," I said.

"No more so than I. I'd planned to wake up in Palm Beach this
morning."

"I was surprised you agreed to see me too."

Krug's nut-brown face creased more deeply for a moment. "You
piqued my curiosity, Mr. March, which I assume was your intention."

"When's the last time you saw Holly, Mr. Krug?"

Krug smiled thinly. "Who is this Holly you keep mentioning?"

I sighed. "You didn't make me shlep over here for this, did you?
Because it's cold out there and my socks are wet, and if all we're
going to do is dance around, the coffee doesn't cover it." The little
smile went away and Krug's face fell again into tired folds, but he said
nothing.

"I know that Cassandra Z is Holly Cade, and that Holly Cade is
Wren," I said. "I've seen two of her videos. You're not violating any
confidences."

"What do you want with her?"

"I'm a private detective." The news didn't seem to shock him. "I'm
trying to find Holly, but she hasn't been home for a while now."

"On whose behalf are you trying to find her?" I shook my head and
Krug laughed harshly. "But I am supposed to trust you?"

"I promise you, I mean her no harm."

"This from a man who has lied to me from the moment we met."

I drank some more coffee and stretched my leg out and looked at Krug. "Did you invite me here out of curiosity, Mr. Krug, or out of worry?"

Krug pursed his lips. "It's been nearly two weeks since I've heard from her."

"Is that a long time for you two?" He nodded. "You're close?"

" 'Close' is difficult with Holly. There are things she discusses with me, and things she never mentions, and always she is jealous of her privacy. But I'm fond of her, Mr. March, and I'm not fond of many people."

"Is there anything in particular that's making you anxious?"

Impatience flitted across Krug's face. "If you've seen her videos, you know the risks Holly takes for her art. They're reason enough to worry."

I nodded. "How long have you known her?"

"Since that group show at my upstate gallery, two years ago now. She came to see me several months later, to discuss Cassandra's work, and I must confess I was surprised."

"Surprised how?"

"When we first met, I'd pigeonholed her as a girl of a certain type. A beautiful girl, unquestionably, but just one of many, I'd thought, who come to the city with expensive educations, vague artistic aspirations and precious little in the way of talent. You must know the kind. They float around town for a few years, and play at painting, or acting, or what have you, and fill space in the clubs until they settle down with their pudgy little bankers. But then I saw the early edits of *Interview One*, and I knew I'd been wrong about her."

"She has talent."

"*Talents*—plural—and a remarkable vision as well, and there's nothing dilettantish or lazy about her."

I nodded some more. "Have you tried to reach her?"

"At her apartment. As you said, no one's been home for some time. I don't know where else to look."

"How about friends or family?"

"I don't know Holly's friends, Mr. March, and all I know of her family is that she's not in contact with them." Krug's eyes narrowed. "I assume you have tried them yourself."

"Only her family, who know next to nothing about her. As far as friends go, I haven't found many, at least none who've been in touch lately. I'm trying to locate her boyfriend."

His eyes narrowed some more and his brown face hardened. "You're referring to Gene?"

"Gene Werner—he's one of the men I'm looking for, though I understand they stopped seeing each other several months ago."

"That is my understanding as well," he said. He looked unsure of whether to say more.

"Do you know Werner?"

"I saw him once, waiting for Holly when she left here one day, but we were never introduced." There was distaste in Krug's voice.

"You have any idea why they broke up?" Krug gave me a speculative look but didn't speak. "I've been trying to reach Werner for days now," I said, "and he seems to be missing too. Frankly, it makes me a little nervous."

Krug sighed. "It's not as if Holly sobs on my shoulder about her love life, Mr. March, but my sense is that the relationship was always fraught. He was, by the sound of things, quite obsessed with Holly. She was less invested, but she let things go on—I'm not sure why. Perhaps she liked being the object of his mania, or perhaps staying with him was the path of least resistance; perhaps she liked the element of abuse that I think was there; but, whatever the reason, she allowed the relationship to carry on for years. Then—sometime in late summer or fall—he found out about her videos."

"He hadn't known?" I felt my brows go up. "Privacy is one thing, but to hide something like that from someone you're involved with . . ."

Krug shook his head. "She takes pains to insulate her life from Cassandra's work, but you're right, it's odd, and I don't claim to understand it. Perhaps she thought it was none of Werner's business, or perhaps she was afraid of his reaction."

"What was his reaction?"

"Anger. Jealousy. More anger. I don't know the particulars, but I know that Holly was very upset, and that it went on for weeks. He called here countless times looking for her, and there was an ugly scene out front. I think there may have been some violence too."

"He hit her?"

"It's speculation on my part, but . . . I saw bruises."

"You said there was an element of abuse in their relationship—does that mean there'd been violence before?"

He nodded. "It wasn't the first time I'd seen bruises."

"Could they have been from Cassandra's work?"

Krug shrugged. "Of course they could have. As I said, it's speculation."

"What finally happened with Werner?"

"His anger seemed to play itself out after three or four weeks. Holly stopped talking about him and she seemed less tense. And a little while after that, she told me she was involved with Jamie."

I took a slow breath. "Jamie is the guy she's seeing now?"

Krug nodded. "Holly seems happy with him, as happy as I've known her to be."

"Do you know Jamie's last name?"

Krug shook his head. "I haven't met him or even caught a glimpse; I just know him as Jamie."

"Any idea of where he lives?" Another head shake. "How about where he works?"

"He works at a place in the East Village, the 9:30 Club. Holly met him there."

"When?"

"I don't know precisely, but she hired him over the summer to do some work on the side."

"What kind of work?"

Krug pursed his lips and ran a manicured finger across his chin. "Security, for some of her filming." The puzzlement showed on my face, and Krug went on. "Filming the closing scenes of her pieces can be dangerous. Her subjects are agitated, and they sometimes become . . . hostile. Holly finally decided to be sensible and have someone close by. Jamie is apparently an imposing fellow. He was a fighter, Holly tells me, and she intimated that he'd spent time in prison."

"He sounds wonderful. How close does she keep him while she's filming?"

"Not in the room, of course, but nearby, and reachable by telephone."

I thought about *Interview Four,* and Bluto, and Holly's telephone check-ins. I looked at Krug. "Was he on the other end of the phone in *Interview Four*?"

He smiled thinly. "She made that long before she hired Jamie."

"Was it you?"

"It wasn't me, either, Mr. March. It was acting. There was no one waiting for Holly's call when she filmed that scene, but she made that man believe there was, and she made you believe it too."

I sighed and shook my head. "She has quite an appetite for risk."

"What work of art worthy of the name isn't risky?"

"I wasn't talking just about her art."

Krug gave me a speculative look. "An artist's life and work necessarily run together, Mr. March. Holly's work is dangerous and . . . extreme, and I suppose her life is too, though she takes pains to keep the two separate."

"The alter ego thing, you mean?"

He nodded. "Anonymity enables her to work. It keeps her safe."

"But her secret identity isn't so secret, is it?"

"Your presence here is proof of that."

"And I'm not the first to come calling." Krug ran a hand through his snowy hair and tapped his chin and said nothing. "I'm talking about the lawyer who came here a couple of months ago," I said. "The guy working for one of Holly's interview subjects."

"I know who you're talking about, Mr. March."

"Do you know who he was working for?"

"I don't."

"Or what he wanted?"

"He wanted Cassandra, though he wouldn't say why. In fact he said very little, though he did it in a very threatening way. Despite that, I told him nothing."

"Did you know that he'd found her anyway? Did Holly mention that?"

Krug's eyes narrowed. "She did not. I told her about his visit and gave her the information on his business card, and that was the last we discussed it."

"He gave you a card?"

Krug rummaged briefly in his desk and took out a large leather-bound diary. He opened it, flicked through a thick sheaf of business cards, and handed one to me. It was heavy stock and plain white, with simple black print. *Thomas Vickers, Attorney.*

I copied down the name and number and handed the card back to Krug. I finished my cold coffee and asked a few more questions that he couldn't answer, and he walked me to the door. When I thanked him for his time he stared at me. His face was like a weathered stone and his eyes were full of worry.

"Just tell her to call me," he said. His voice was low and tattered and it followed me through the snow, all the way home.

When I have questions about lawyers, I call Michael Metz. I heated some soup from a can and watched a taxi skate sideways down Sixteenth Street while I waited for Mike to come to the phone. When I said Thomas Vickers's name to him, he went quiet.

"You know this guy?" I asked after a long silence.

"I do."

"And?"

"And Tommy Vickers is a very good lawyer. A very expensive and discreet lawyer. A lawyer about whom there is much rumor and speculation, none of which has yet been substantiated."

"Rumor and speculation about what?"

"Tommy is in the tax consulting business these days—at least that's what he calls it. Tax shelters, offshore corporate shells, and byzantine trust arrangements are the specialties of the house. Rumor has it that his client list is heavy with Wall Street types, and speculation is that his services run right to the edge—maybe over the edge—of tax evasion and money laundering. Our crackerjack Justice Department has apparently been looking at him for years without any joy."

"How do you know so much about this guy?"

Mike chuckled. "Back when he was a litigator, a dozen or so years ago, he cleaned my clock in a civil case. I like to keep track."

"I didn't know you'd ever had your clock cleaned."

"What can I say, the ink was barely dry on my law diploma. It was all very educational."

"No doubt. What does he look like?"

"Somewhere in his fifties by now, medium-sized, silver-haired, and very old-school. Always the dark suit and white shirt and dark tie, like a G-man, and always the closed mouth."

"Fits the description I got from Holly's neighbor. What's his firm called?"

"It's called the Tommy Vickers All by Himself Firm. He's not big on trust and sharing."

"So what's a high-priced tax consultant like him doing chasing down Holly Cade?"

"Only one reason comes immediately to mind."

"And that is?"

"Because a very important client asked him to."

I laughed. "I'll call him today and find out who."

"Get him to say more than twenty-five words, I'll buy you lunch."

I was about to ring off but Mike wasn't through. "I spoke to your brother this morning, and told him what I'd learned about the cause of death, and the timing."

"How did that go?"

"Not well. The news upset him—no surprise there—and he wasn't particularly cooperative when I asked him his whereabouts that Tuesday."

"Uh-huh."

"And when I asked about Stephanie, he pretty much hung up on me."

"Uh-huh."

"You know I've worked with painful clients before—worse than David, if you can believe it—and I manage them fine, but he's not doing himself any favors here. And of course it makes me wonder, and worry."

"You want me to talk to him?"

"He needs to get past this angry denial crap soon. God forbid the cops call and we still aren't straight about where he was that Tuesday, or about what your sister-in-law knows."

"I'll talk to him," I said. For all the good it would do. Shit.

My appetite was shot, but I ate my soup anyway, and thought about my brother and his angry denial crap. I didn't see him getting past angry anytime soon: he had too much to spare, deep wells of the stuff, and it was too dependable. Anger anchored David, and organized his world, and it gave him comfort somehow—though from what I didn't know.

Denial was something new, though, and it spoke of an irrationality I wouldn't have expected from him. David had always fancied himself a realist—pragmatic, unsentimental, and supremely logical; tough-minded, he liked to think. Refusing to answer your lawyer's questions didn't fit that picture. But then, what about this case fit any picture of David that I'd ever had? A wind was kicking up outside, and little funnels of snow spun up from the rooftops. I watched them rise and vanish in the air.

I put my soup bowl in the dishwasher and called Thomas Vickers. A frail-sounding woman answered and took my name and put me on hold. Vickers came on the line five minutes later. I started to introduce myself and he stopped me.

"I know who you are," he said. "You're a PI." His voice was soft and raspy and it came from somewhere in Nassau County.

"I'm calling about Holly Cade," I said, "or maybe you know her better as Cassandra Z."

"What makes you think I know her at all?"

"Maybe the fact that you were at Krug Visual a while ago, looking for her, and that you were seen at her apartment last month."

"Looking isn't the same as finding."

"Did you find her?"

"I'm not clear on how it's any of your business."

"Would you rather it be cop business?"

Vickers made a coughing sound that might have been a laugh. "So much for romance."

"I don't want to waste anybody's time. Should we get together?"

"I need to make a call," he said. "Give me your number." I did and Vickers rang off.

I spent the next couple of hours not calling my brother, and thinking about what I'd say when I finally did. I picked up the phone a half-dozen times and put it down again, and while I wasn't calling him, I tried the 9:30 Club. I was surprised when someone answered.

The man's voice was reedy and annoyed. "Sure we're open tonight—why not? Half my staff is stuck here, what the hell else should I do?"

"Is Jamie working tonight?"

"No, she's in Wednesdays and Thursdays."

She? "I'm talking about the Jamie who's a guy—a big guy—and works the door sometimes."

The man was quiet for what seemed a long while. When he spoke again, his voice was rushed and nervous. "Must be another place you're thinking of," he said. "No Jamie here." And then he was gone.

I put the phone down and wondered. It was possible that Krug had been mistaken about where Jamie worked, but the man on the phone hadn't been confused, he'd been tense. I recalled the tattoos on Baby-face's hands, and what Krug had said about Jamie having perhaps been in prison. If that was true, it might explain the tension: places with liquor licenses—places like the 9:30 Club—weren't supposed to hire convicted felons.

The apartment door opened and Clare came in. Snow dusted her long black coat and glistened in her pale hair. Her cheeks were red and her gray eyes were shining. She handed me a brown plastic sack and pulled off her gloves and whisked snowflakes from her sleeves. There was an overnight bag slung on her shoulder, and a larger bag rolling behind her on its own set of wheels. I wondered where her husband was, and how long he'd be snowbound, but I decided not to ask.

Clare laughed. "Well, they got it right this time," she said. "It's starting to blow out there." I looked in the plastic sack. The smell of cilantro wafted up from the takeout containers.

"Thai?" I asked. Clare smiled and nodded. "Where'd you find a place that was open?"

"This is the center of the fucking universe, pal, haven't you heard?" She unbuttoned her coat. "Put that stuff in the fridge and take a bath with me. We'll see how those bruises are coming along."

It was six o'clock and dark when the phone rang. Clare stirred and muttered something, and I rolled out of bed to get it. It was David. His voice was at once sleepy and combative, and it took a while for me to realize he was drunk.

"I talked to your pal Metz today."

"You should think of him as your lawyer, David, not as my pal."

"If I think of him that way, I'm not too impressed. In fact, I'm thinking he's more sizzle than steak, and maybe I should get somebody else."

"What did he do that was so unimpressive?"

"As far as I can tell, he hasn't done anything at all. I still don't know for sure who Mermaid-girl is, and your pal couldn't seem to find out from the cops."

"Find out what? The police haven't identified her yet, for chrissakes—something for which you should be supremely grateful."

"So he doesn't know who she is, but he still wants me to go talk to the cops? How fucked up is that?"

"Be serious, David: how many women do you think are walking around with that tattoo on their legs?"

"How do I know? And why should I fucking bet my life on the chance that there was only one?"

"If it's not her, then all it costs you is a little embarrassment in front of a few cops. If it is her, then—"

"*A little embarrassment?* How do you know what's big and what's little? You don't give a shit what people think, you never have, so don't lecture me, Johnny."

"I don't lecture drunks. I learned it was a waste of time when I was a cop."

David laughed nastily. "It took till then? Shit, I figured it out listening to Mom lecture Dad."

I took a deep breath and let it out slowly. "Where were you the Tuesday before last, David?"

"Your fucking pal was after me about this too. I don't want to talk about it."

"We have to talk about it. Where were you?"

"Where was I when?"

"Don't fuck around, David."

"Where the hell do you think I was? I was at work, for chrissakes, just like every fucking day. You should try it some time."

"What time did you get in?"

"Probably the usual time—seven, seven-fifteen the latest."

"What does 'probably' mean?"

"I got in at the usual time—okay?"

"You came direct from your apartment?"

"Of course I did."

"And you were in the office all day?"

"What's all day? I had meetings, I had a lunch—I was in and out."

"What time did you leave?"

"I don't know—six, six-thirty."

"You went right home from there?"

"Sure."

"Is that the same as yes?"

"Yes, I went right home."

"And then?"

"And then nothing. I had dinner; I read some reports; I went to bed."

"You didn't go out?"

"I told you: I ate; I read; I slept."

"Was Stephanie with you?"

"What the fuck does that mean?"

"Was she there with you the whole time?"

"I'm not talking about—"

"Don't start this shit again, David. We need to know where you were. We need to know where Steph was. We need to know how much she knows about all this. And you need to get it through your head that you're in the deep water now. The cops will ask these questions, and a lot of others, and they won't be as nice about it. And you can't ignore them, or make them go away by being arrogant or angry. Cops like it when a suspect acts that way—it makes them think they're on to something—and when the suspect is somebody like you, it makes it just plain fun."

"*Suspect?*" David laughed again, crazily this time. "I ain't no steenking suspect."

I ground my teeth and thought hard about hanging up. Then I heard a noise like glassware in the background. "Where are you?"

"Why, you gonna join me? I thought you pretended not to go in for this stuff anymore."

"Where are—"

"I'm in the only open bar south of Fulton Street—the only one I could fucking find, anyway."

"Jesus—you're talking about this in public? What the hell's wrong with you? Are you trying to blow up your life?"

"You're the last person to be giving out life advice, don't you think, Johnny-boy? Like you've done such a bang-up job with your own— that swell career, and all those friends."

I counted, I breathed, and finally I gave up. I put down the phone and turned around and Clare was there, leaning in the bedroom door. The light from the street was softened by the snow, and it fell in pale pink bands across her arms and legs and small, bare breasts. Her face was in shadow, but even so I could see the worry in her eyes.

Clare wanted to come along to the 9:30 Club, but between the snow, and my dissuasions, and maybe the gun behind my back, she gave up on the idea.

"What the hell is that?" She froze with a forkful of pad thai halfway to her mouth.

"It's a Glock 30, a forty-five caliber semiautomatic handgun."

"I see it's a gun. What are you doing with it?"

"I'm putting it in its holster and fastening it to my belt."

"Don't be funny. Why do you need it?"

"I'm hoping to find the guy I romped around Central Park with last night, and I'm hoping for a more sedate conversation."

"You're going to . . . shoot him?"

"I'd rather talk, but it's nice to have options."

"Jesus," she breathed.

Clare ate her noodles and watched gravely as I dropped the clip out of the Glock, checked the load, worked the spring and the slide, ran the clip back up, and tucked the gun away. I was pulling a waterproof shell over my fleece jacket when she spoke again.

"Was that your brother on the phone before?"

I looked at her, surprised. I'd never discussed my family with her, and had no clue what, if anything, she knew of them. Her face was still and her gray eyes said nothing. "One of them," I said slowly.

A rueful smile came and went. "I know the tone. My sister gets it when we talk on the phone sometimes; I get it too, I suppose. A kind of 'I'm going to explode and I'm going to strangle you all at the same time' thing. Only family can make you crazy like that." I nodded. "He's your client?" she asked.

I shook my head. "I can't—"

Clare held up her hand. "It doesn't matter. I was just going to say that, whatever it is you're doing, the work agrees with you." She saw my surprise, and smiled. "Dents and dings aside, you look better than you have in a while. You're eating better and sleeping better, and that cloud above your head is not so dark." She went back to her dinner and looked startled when I kissed her goodbye.

There were no taxis or Town Cars in front of the 9:30 Club, and if there was a velvet rope, it was buried under a foot of snow. I leaned on the bar and drank my cranberry juice and surveyed the room. It was a big, rectangular space, dimly lit and done up like a seraglio in a pumpkin patch. Acres of green and orange silk covered the walls, and leafy green pennants twisted down from the high ceiling. A dance floor dominated the center of the room, flanked by round green tables on one side, and on the other by curtained alcoves with fat orange sofas. A wide stairway with translucent green risers climbed up a wall in back and emptied into more alcoves and the VIP rooms. The bar was opposite the stairs, an orange crescent topped in green frosted glass. There was a row of flat-panel monitors above it, just then looping footage of Copacabana Beach. The sound system was pumping out a low-key techno rhythm, and there were a dozen bodies on the dance floor, doing all they could with it.

I counted fifty people scattered around the place, dancers and staff included—nothing close to a typical Friday night, I was sure, but not bad for a blizzard. The shared disaster of the storm made everyone a friendly castaway, happy to be alive and happy to be there, and it lent a faintly manic tang to the proceedings. The kitchen was serving what food there was without charge, though the drinks were still ringing at full price.

Babyface—Jamie—wasn't in the house, but the reedy-voiced man I'd spoken to on the phone was. His name was J.T., and I'd found him at the end of the bar, looking dolefully over the room. He was a skinny thirtysomething, with a tangle of peroxide hair, three days of dark beard, and a *Buffy the Vampire Slayer* T-shirt. He was the manager, more or less, and he hadn't been happy to see me.

"Fuckin' A, you're the guy who called," he'd said. I'd nodded, and he'd frowned. "I told you, the only Jamie working here is a girl."

"So if I ask your staff, none of them will know another Jamie?"

The frown deepened. "What are you, some kind of cop?"

"Not a cop, and not from the State Liquor Authority, either."

J.T.'s eyes darted away, and he ran a nicotine-stained hand down his narrow face. "What's that mean?" he asked.

"It means I don't give a shit about your hiring practices. Martians, felons, it's all the same to me."

He shook his head and grimaced. "No good deed, man, no fuckin' good deed."

"I'm not looking to make trouble, J.T. Not for you, or Jamie."

"Then go away."

"Talk to me about Jamie, and I will."

J.T. fished a cigarette from his pocket and dangled it, unlit, from the corner of his mouth. "I don't know what I can tell you. It's not like we're running buddies."

"You know his last name?"

"Coyle," he said, and he spelled it for me.

"How long has he worked here?"

"About ten months."

"Off the books?" J.T. nodded. "Because he was inside?" Another nod.

"You know what for?"

He shook his head. "I don't press."

"What does he do here?"

"Mostly he works the door, but he helps out with other stuff too."

"Like?"

"Like behind the bar sometimes, or security in the VIP lounge."

"He work every night?"

"Two, three nights a week, usually, until he started this no-show crap."

"No-show?"

"He hasn't been around for going on three weeks. He hasn't called, either."

"That's not like him?"

"Nope. Before this he was Mr. Dependable—on time, on top of things, never any bullshit."

"And his work was good?"

"I had no complaints," J.T. said. "He knew when to be cool and when to be scary, and he knew how to keep the messes out of sight."

"You didn't worry about his . . . prior experience?"

J.T. squinted at me. "I put him behind the bar, and that's all cash back there. I wouldn't do that if he worried me."

"You know his girlfriend?"

"Nope."

"You have an address for him, or a phone number?" J.T. pulled out a multifunction digital doohickey, and had at it with his thumbs. He read me a phone number and a P.O. box, and I copied them down. "Kind of a risk for you, taking on a guy like that," I'd said.

He'd shrugged. "My wife's kid brother was up in Coxsackie," he'd said. "Jamie looked out for him." Then J.T. had wandered off, in the direction of the deejay's booth.

I looked up and saw him still there, smoking by an open window and sorting through stacks of CDs. I finished my drink and put the glass on the bar. There was a waitress doing nothing near the passage to the kitchen, so I went over.

Her name was Lia. She was young, not much over drinking age, and nearly my height, and her unruly, strawberry-blond mop went well enough with her freckles and blue eyes to be natural. Her mouth was wide and her chin was pointed, and I imagined her agent described her as a well-scrubbed waif. She scanned the crowd lazily as we spoke.

"I haven't seen Jamie in, what, a couple of weeks, which is weird for him."

"You friendly with him?"

She shrugged. "I guess."

"He a nice guy?"

"Sure. I mean, he's a little scary at first, but once you get to know him, what's not to like?"

"Scary how?"

"You know, he's all big and broody, and he doesn't say much at first. But really he's a teddy bear, and he looks out for all the girls."

"Looks out for what?"

"Like, for when a customer gets too touchy, and thinks the tips buy something more than thanks."

"That happen a lot?" Lia smiled regretfully and nodded. "What does Jamie do about it?"

Her smile broadened. "Basically he scares the piss out of them."

"Just scares them?"

"You mean does he actually like beat them up?" I nodded and Lia thought about it. "There was one guy, a few months back, a real big guy, and a real groper—legs, asses, tits, anything he could grab or rub up against. This one night he was all over Sheri, who was brand new then, and really freaking out. She'd been avoiding him the whole shift, when finally he corners her on her way to take a piss. Now Sheri'll blow away in a strong wind, and this guy's like six two and double-wide, and he's got her by the arm in the hallway when Jamie comes along.

"Sheri told me he said something in the guy's ear—she didn't know what—and the guy lets go of her and turns around and throws a punch at Jamie. And Jamie catches it—just like that, Sheri said." Lia made a fist with one hand and covered it with her other. "And then she tells me the guy just starts turning red and kind of crying, and he falls down on his knees with Jamie still holding his fist."

"And then what?"

"And then Jamie makes him apologize to Sheri, and he picks the guy up by his belt and throws him out the back door." She grinned. "That part I saw for myself. It was cool."

"No doubt. You know Jamie's girlfriend?"

Lia furrowed her freckled brow. "That redhead—the one who makes indy films or something?" I nodded and Lia nodded back. "She's been in. I heard they were a thing but I didn't know for sure. She's hot."

"She in here lately?" A shrug. "They get along pretty well?"

"I don't know; they seemed to. I don't pay attention." She looked at me, curious for the first time. "Why do you want to know all this stuff? Jamie's not in trouble, is he?"

I shook my head. "I'm just trying to get in touch."

Lia studied my face and looked worried. "Look, he's a good guy," she said, "and I don't know how to reach him." And she disappeared into the kitchen.

Lia didn't come out again, and the bartender and the other waitresses had less to say than she did. I hung around for another half hour, and watched people troop in, in twos and threes, frosted and windblown and happy to join the lifeboat party.

It was close to eleven when I left, and the route home was straight into the wind. Even with head down and jacket zipped high, the cold was crushing. In two blocks my face went from frozen to burning numb, and in two more my limbs followed suit. By Avenue B, walking had devolved into an endless struggle with the next step, and all sense of time was lost. The wind pried at my lungs and howled around my ears as I pushed forward, and Lia's words repeated in my head— "Look, he's a good guy"—and echoed alongside the last thing Orlando Krug had said—"Just tell her to call me." After a while, I wasn't sure who had said what.

I had a hard time with the key to my building, and I stood for a while in the lobby, catching my breath while pricking pain spread across my face. I rode the elevator up and opened my apartment door and Clare was standing across the room. She was holding a towel and looking at me and at the sofa, and her expression was a mix of puzzlement and disgust. I stepped inside and the smell of vomit hit me. I looked over the back of my sofa and found the source: my brother David, spattered in puke, slumped over, and passed out.

20

We got his clothes off—the sopping cashmere overcoat, the sodden English shoes, the Italian suit, soaked and stained from the knees down—and cleaned him up as well as we could with a damp washcloth. I levered him into sweatpants and a T-shirt, and Clare put sheets on the sofa and covered him with a blanket. He muttered and flailed a little, and threw up once more, but I'd wrestled less cooperative drunks before.

"He showed up maybe twenty minutes ago, and I didn't know what to do with him," Clare whispered. She was in the kitchen, drinking tonic water and watching David sleep. "He was leaning on the buzzer and saying he was your brother, and he was covered in snow from the chest up. I couldn't just leave him out there."

I nodded. "You don't have to whisper," I said, "he's gone. From the look of him, he must've walked uptown."

"Good thing he didn't stop to rest along the way—they'd be chipping ice off him for a month."

"Did he say anything?"

"Besides that he was your brother, nothing that made sense. Is he like this a lot?"

"Passed out drunk, you mean?"

Clare nodded.

"This is the first I've seen it, but . . . I don't really know what he's like."

Clare looked at him and looked at me and shook her head. "Jesus."

I came awake in the middle of the night. Clare was breathing slowly beside me, and we were both sunk deep into the mattress. Beneath the wind and shaking windows, I heard a stifled cough from the living room, and the rustle of bedsheets. I got up carefully and pulled on a T-shirt and went out.

David was cross-legged on the floor. He was wrapped in a sheet and his back was to one of my bookcases. His skin was pale and his hair was damp-looking. He had a book in his lap and he was turning the pages. He looked up at me. His eyes were still confused, and his face was somehow out of focus. I closed the bedroom door.

"You should sleep," I whispered.

"Things were spinning," he said quietly.

"You want anything?"

"Water, maybe."

I went to the kitchen and filled a glass. I carried it over and David took it and drank. I looked at the book he held. It was a big coffee-table volume with frayed covers and a cracked spine, a collection of Brassaï photos I hadn't opened in years. David set the glass on the floor and turned a page, to a picture of a fog-wrapped Paris avenue. He turned again, to a picture of a woman under a streetlamp.

He laughed softly. "The first time I went to Paris, I had in my head it was somehow going to look like this. I was just out of college and, boy, was I disappointed. I was expecting fog, and hookers on every corner, and I thought it would be all smoky and romantic. Then I saw that fucking Pompidou Center. After that, I didn't feel so bad that Mom hadn't let me spend junior year there." There was a sheen of sweat on his forehead, and he shivered as he spoke.

"I didn't know you'd wanted to."

"Oh, yeah," he said absently. "Instead, I did an internship at Beekman Quist that year." He turned another page—a sedan idling on a cobbled street. He chuckled to himself. "There was a receptionist there who gave me head in the supply room every Friday afternoon. Now, *that* was educational." He reached for his glass and emptied it.

"You want more?" I asked. He nodded. When I returned, he was examining the book's cover.

"I used to look at this thing all the time," he said. "It was on Daddy's desk." He turned it over and ran his fingers over the torn dust jacket. "It's really falling apart now."

"You should get some sleep," I said.

David ignored me, and turned the book over again, and opened the front cover. There was a bookplate pasted inside—a white rectangle, yellowed now, with a line drawing that was supposed to be the Widener Library. Printed across the bottom were the names Philip and Elaine March. Our parents.

He looked at me. "How'd you end up with this?"

"I'm not sure. I ended up with most of Dad's books."

He nodded vaguely and ran his fingers over the bookplate, over their names. "What was it with them, anyway?" he said.

"I don't—"

"I mean, why stay together, if all you do is fight? Why get married in the first place, for chrissakes? And why have children, when you don't have a single fucking clue of what to do with them—or any interest in finding out? You'd be better off on your own."

Old questions, and I certainly had no answers. I shook my head. "You should get—"

"And what the hell were they looking for in their kids, anyway, that they could never seem to find in me? Did I not have the password, or something—the secret charm?" He looked up at me again, and his eyes were shining and angry. "How did that happen, Johnny? How is it that you got all the fucking glamour, and I got none?"

He took the glass and drank the water in one swallow, and a shudder ran through his shoulders. He squeezed his eyes shut and held his head in his hands. His skin went from white to gray, and I knew his world was spinning, and that he was fighting to hold on. I went to the kitchen and came back with a garbage pail. I took the book from David's lap and held the pail while he retched.

.   .   .

By morning the storm had passed, and the city was a frosted fantasy of wind-carved snow and glistening ice, achingly bright under a lapis sky. Squinting out the windows at the Gaudí curves and spires, I forgot for a moment about David, who was in the shower, and had been for a long time.

"You think he's drowning himself in there?" Clare asked. She wore yoga pants and a sleeveless T-shirt, and her hair was pulled into a loose ponytail. She looked maybe twenty.

"Feel free to check."

She smirked. "I'll give it another hour or so."

We were eating oatmeal and watching news reports about the storm when David appeared. He was pale and drawn and wrapped in my bathrobe. His ginger hair was damp and roughly combed and his eyes were painful to look at. When he spoke his voice was hoarse but devoid of embarrassment.

"Where are my clothes?"

"In there." I pointed to a black plastic garbage bag in a corner.

David walked over on brittle legs, and opened the bag and looked inside. He drew his head back quickly and closed the bag. "Shit," he said. "You have something I can wear?"

I nodded and went into the bedroom and pulled a pair of jeans and a turtleneck from my closet. When I came out, David and Clare hadn't moved, but were eyeing each other over the kitchen counter. The look was one I'd last seen exchanged on the Nature Channel, between jackals and lions over an antelope carcass. David took the clothes and went into the bathroom. Clare frowned.

"Friendly guy," she said. "Very warm."

"Always."

"Not like you."

"Don't even joke."

Clare laughed and kissed the corner of my mouth. "Not as cute, though."

The news showed endless scenes of plowing and digging—snow from roads, cars from snow, people from cars—from D.C. north. In the city, the mayor, mindful of the storms that had permanently buried the careers of some of his predecessors, struck brave and resolute poses astride plow trucks and sanders, assured us that all was well, and pledged not to rest until asphalt was showing on every street in Queens. In fact, surface transportation was only just beginning to recover, though the people skiing down Fifth Avenue seemed in no rush to have it back.

David returned wearing my clothes, which were too long in the leg and too snug at the waist. He squatted by the black plastic bag and wrinkled his nose and began sorting through it. "Where the hell are my shoes?"

"They're in there," I said.

He pulled through the wet wreckage and came out with them and dropped them on the floor, disgusted. More clawing yielded his wallet, his watch, and his cell phone. He popped the phone open and pressed some keys and in a moment he was shouting.

"The roads are *your* problem, not mine. *My* problem is getting home—and unless you want to lose the Klein & Sons account, you'll fucking solve it for me."

Clare suppressed a laugh and looked at me, eyebrows raised. David pressed some more keys on his phone. When he spoke again his voice was a low monotone.

"I stayed with John. Yes, my brother John. He was walking distance, that's why, and I couldn't get a car. There were no taxis, Stephanie, and the trains were all screwed up. Why, you want to talk to him? I didn't think so. How are things in New Canaan?"

He said his goodbyes and closed the phone and looked at me. "There any coffee?" he asked.

I poured a mug and handed it to him. Clare excused herself, shaking her head, and went into the bathroom and shut the door. In a moment, I heard water running.

"Who's she?" David asked.

"A friend."

David snickered. "I figured that out. She have a name?"

"Clare."

He nodded. "Nice looking. I thought you were seeing that Chinese girl."

"Not for a while now. Stephanie's in New Canaan?"

"With her parents."

"Is she . . . okay?"

David scowled. "She's great. Is there more coffee?"

I refilled his mug. "And what about you?" I asked. "Are you great too?"

He squinted. "Don't start with me, all right? I had a little too much on an empty stomach, and—"

"Enough bullshit, David. What the hell is wrong with you?"

"Nothing's wrong. I didn't have lunch yesterday, and I—"

"I'm not just talking about the drinking, or the wandering around in a storm. I'm talking about all of it—the Internet sex, not cooperating with your lawyer—"

"I slept on your fucking sofa one night; that doesn't give you—you of all people—the right to lecture me."

"Fine, don't listen to me. But don't waste my time, either."

"What's that supposed to mean?"

"It means don't ask people to help you when you won't help yourself—when you're actually making things worse."

David's pale face went red; he opened his mouth to shout, then shut it again. "Worse how?" he asked.

"Mike needs to know what's what, and so do I. Surprises make our jobs harder, and, trust me, they're already hard enough. You want your lawyer's mind on solving your problems, David, not on wondering about what you haven't told him and why."

He tugged at his turtleneck collar. "Is that what this is about—you and Metz have doubts about me?" I looked at him and said nothing. "You son of a bitch, you think I did it."

"I think you're not being upfront with me, and I don't know why."

"I haven't seen that girl in months," he said. His voice was low and hoarse. "I had nothing to do with her death."

I nodded. "How much does Stephanie know about . . . all this?"

David reddened again. "She knows . . . I guess she knows that I've seen other women. I . . ." His voice broke and he ran shaking hands through his hair. He took a deep breath. "That's enough," he said finally. "I'm not talking about this anymore."

I started to speak, but the bathroom door opened and Clare came out. She looked at me and at David.

"Am I interrupting something?"

"Not a thing," David said quickly. "I need to eat."

I made him toast and he sat on the sofa, eating in silence and looking like a sick old man. Two hours later his car came. He slipped on his still-damp shoes, hoisted the black plastic bag, and left without a word.

"What the hell is his problem?" Clare asked, but I had no answer. She opened a window and let some icy air climb in.

Clare had finished the Warhol biography and had started another, this one of Diane Arbus. She sprawled on the sofa and read. I tried not to think too hard about my brother, and opened my laptop instead.

The phone number J.T. had given me for Jamie Coyle was answered only by a synthetic voice and an out-of-service message, and I found no corresponding billing address for it in any of the reverse directories on-line. The post office box had a zip code in Peekskill, New York, and it too did me little immediate good. J.T. had told me that Coyle had done time in Coxsackie, so I plugged his name into the always helpful New York State Department of Correctional Services inmate search, and got lucky.

According to the DOCS database, Jamie Coyle, d-o-b August 11, 1979—the only Jamie Coyle in the system—had been convicted of Assault II, a class D felony, and had been sentenced to no less than two and no more than five years in prison. He'd spent three years in Coxsackie and was paroled a year ago, and he'd behaved well enough for the next ten months to have been discharged from parole, free and clear, last November.

Googling him yielded little—an article in a Westchester newspaper about his arrest, and another, a few weeks later, when he pleaded out. The arrest piece played up a local-hero-gone-bad angle, and squeezed some pathos out of Coyle having been a high school football star and Golden Gloves champ who'd fallen in with a bad crowd after blowing out his knee in the last game of his senior year season. The bad crowd belonged to a local loanshark for whom Coyle had become a collector, and Coyle's arrest was apparently the result of some vigorous debt rescheduling with the owner of a Peekskill video store. Skull fracture, facial lacerations, fractured jaw, detached retina, and fractured ribs—with that list of injuries, I was surprised that Coyle had only gone for Assault II. Good lawyering. I took down the details and the name of the reporter who'd written the pieces.

Clare sighed massively and put down her book. She stretched and walked to the window and looked down at Sixteenth Street.

"I want to go for a walk before they plow it all away. You want to come?"

I was surprised: Clare was usually very careful about us and public places. Maybe the storm had swept away her caution. I nodded. "Let me just call this guy again," I said. "I've been trying to reach him for days." Clare pulled on a sweater and I pushed the buttons for Gene Werner's number yet again. And was stunned when he actually answered.

21

I wrong-numbered Gene Werner, pulled on boots, coat, and sun-glasses, and made my apologies to Clare, who took them stoically. In fifteen minutes I was at the subway station, where the subway gods were kind, and in thirty minutes more I was climbing the snow-covered stairs at the 110th Street station.

Werner's block was a mess, barely plowed and badly shoveled, with only the narrow path of other people's footprints to walk in. I saw no sign of Jamie Coyle, which didn't mean he wasn't hiding in a drift. I stamped my boots at the door to Werner's building, brushed snow from my legs, and pushed his intercom button. His newscaster voice was tinny through the speaker.

"Who is it?"

"It's John March, Gene—the guy who's been leaving you messages for what seems like forever." Silence. "Gene, I'm getting cold out here."

"You're who?"

"John March. I left you phone messages. Several of them."

"And you want . . . ?"

"To talk about Holly." More silence. "Holly Cade."

"What about her?"

"How about I tell you indoors, Gene?"

The buzzer sounded, and I walked up to the second floor. Werner was in the hall outside his apartment. He wore jeans and a black checked shirt, and he pulled the apartment door shut behind him.

He looked much as he did in the snapshots, though the straight, dark hair was shorter now—just long enough for a stubby queue—and the goatee was trimmed to little more than a stripe down the center of his square chin. The handsome face was leaner too, and there was a vulpine cast to his dark eyes that the camera hadn't caught, and a cruel stamp to his mouth. Neither had the camera caught the aura of snaky strength that surrounded Werner. He was a sinewy six-three, lithe despite his size, and there was something coiled and nasty about him that made the hallway seem dangerous and too small. Werner pushed his sleeves up over muscular, hairless forearms.

"I didn't think anyone would be out today," he said, and made it a question about my judgment. I ignored it and we shook. His grip was strong and rubbery. He looked me over and shook his head. "Been too busy to call you back. Now, what did you want about Holly?"

"I have some questions, and it's probably better if we talk inside."

"What questions? I haven't seen her in a long time."

"That was one of the things I wanted to talk about. I'm trying to locate Holly."

"Locate?"

"I don't think you want to discuss this in the hall, Gene—unless there's some problem with going inside."

Werner squinted at me. "Whatever." He dug a key from his pocket and I followed him in.

We walked into a tiny foyer, and from there into the living room. It was a high-ceilinged space, with white plaster walls, dark wood molding, and a scuffed wooden floor, and there was a bay window at one end, flooded with white light.

The furnishings were spare and thrift-shop chic—soft and faded, but still solid-looking. Green sofa, brown easy chairs, tables in dark, battered cherry, oak bookshelves stacked with plays. The artwork was mostly framed posters, big reproductions of French and Italian advertisements from the 1920s, with stylish devils and sultry fairies perched over giant coffee cups or lounging on bars of soap. The only other pieces on the walls were a half-dozen framed photographs—white-clad, mesh-masked, sword-wielding figures, leaping and lunging: fencers in mid-duel. A look at the newspaper clippings mounted with each photo revealed that the big guy in the pictures was Werner himself, ten years before—the star, apparently, of his college fencing team.

Werner stalked around the room, watching warily as I eyed the photos, took off my coat, and opened my notebook. When I sat on the sofa, he struck a graceful pose near the fireplace. He leaned an elbow on the dark wood mantel and looked into the mirror above and absently groomed his beard. When he was satisfied, he tossed a thumb at the photos.

"Hell of a sport," he said. "Incredible physical conditioning, and great training for the theater. And there's nothing like competition to let you know where your balls are."

I didn't recall ever misplacing mine, but I resisted the urge to comment. "About Holly," I said.

"She's missing?"

"My client has been trying to reach her for some time."

"Are you working with the cops?"

I paused half a beat. "Not yet."

"Why not? If she's missing . . ."

"From what I gather, Holly is sensitive about her privacy. My client wants to respect that."

"And this client is . . . ?"

"Someone who's concerned about her."

"But not someone you'll name?"

"Confidentiality is part of what clients pay for."

Werner shook his head. "I can't help. I told you, I haven't seen her in a while."

"But you've known her awhile—a long while. Since your days with the Gimlets, at least."

"Yeah . . . and?"

I smiled encouragingly. "And you're bound to know plenty of things that I don't." Werner shrugged and I pressed on. "Did you stay in the theater after the Gimlets broke up?"

He nodded, and smiled back, happy for the chance to talk about himself. "I'm directing, and the days of scrambling to find a stage and an audience seem like a long time ago. Now I've got more work than I can handle. I'm at the end of a run of one-acts, and next month I'm doing *Hamlet* downtown. Come spring, I'm doing Mamet up in Connecticut, and I've got a big project in Williamstown scheduled for summer. Not enough hours in the fucking day." He looked in the mirror and ran a finger over his eyebrow.

I nodded. "But Holly got out of all that, right? Out of theater and into what . . . film?"

"Video," he said carefully.

"She doing well at it?"

"How the hell should I know? Like I said, I can't help you, March."

I smiled. "Only because you're not trying, Gene. I'm sure you know all there is to know about her—you two were involved for a long time, after all."

Werner stiffened and a ridge of tension rose along his jaw. His voice became a low rumble. "I guess you know a fair amount about her, yourself."

I shrugged. "I've been talking to people."

"Talking to who?"

"Friends, acquaintances, the usual suspects." I made a show of leafing through my notebook. "Why, did I get it wrong about you and her dating?"

He took a deep breath and forced out a laugh. "No, I just don't know if I'd call it *dating,* is all. We'd worked together, we were friends, and sometimes we fucked. But it wasn't an exclusive thing—not for me, anyway."

"Apparently not for Holly, either."

Werner's sculpted brows furrowed. "Come again?"

"I've seen her videos, Gene." Werner straightened, but said nothing. "I understand you have too, and that they took you by surprise."

He pursed his lips and toyed with the small gold hoop in his ear. "They'd surprise anybody," he said slowly.

"Sure," I said. "And you had no idea—"

"Of how fucking crazy she was? No, I didn't. It was a bolt from the goddamn blue."

"I heard you were upset. It must've felt like a real betrayal."

"Heard from who?" he asked. "Who *are* these people?"

"Friends of Holly. How upset were you?"

Werner took a deep breath and ambled to a chair. He settled in it with elaborate nonchalance, and pulled off the rubber band that held his little ponytail. He ran his hands over his shiny hair, and put a smile on his face. It looked uneasy there.

"I was . . ." Werner looked away from me, and back again, with eyes wide. "Those videos were a shock, it's true, but they were also a wake-up call. Holly has always had *issues,* but this was another story entirely. You know what she looks like—stunning, incredibly . . . exciting—but even so, after seeing those things, it was too much. I was sick, and I wanted no part of her. That's why I broke things off."

I kept my voice even and my face still. "You broke things off with her?"

Werner touched his goatee and showed his big teeth. "I only have so much energy, and it frankly wasn't enough to deal with Holly's craziness. It was upsetting, but I got some perspective on it soon enough. And like I said, it was never that big a deal—not for me, at least."

I nodded. "But you were pretty pissed off at the time, right? I heard you guys went at it hammer and tongs last fall."

Werner leaned forward and pointed at me. "You're talking to that old man, aren't you—her fucking neighbor?"

I shook my head. "I haven't met the guy, but back to my question: Were you two fighting a lot last fall?"

"We were both unhappy then."

"Unhappy—like it was the end of more than just a casual thing?"

Werner stood and swept his hair behind him and wrapped it again in his rubber band. He sighed deeply and put on a grave expression. "All that time, and I never knew: it was like she'd lied to me every one of those days. So I was upset—we both were. We yelled, we slammed doors, we said things we regretted later—okay? It wasn't pleasant and I'm not particularly proud of it, but it is what it is."

I tried to look sympathetic, but it was hard work. Werner paced around the living room and I let him, and let him think we were moving on to something else. After a minute or so, I shook him up some more. "I heard it was more than just cruel words and slammed doors, Gene. I heard you hit her."

Werner spun around. There was anger in his face, and maybe a little fear. "Where the fuck did that come from? Because that's bullshit! Sure, we fought, but I never once laid hands on her. It's crap, and I'd be careful about spreading it around."

"I hear you kind of stalked her for a while too, followed her around—"

"Pure crap! Have you been talking to Krug? Because that old queen has always had it in for me, and I've never even met the bastard."

"Imagine," I said. "But I wonder why people thought you were knocking her around."

"How the hell should I know? Maybe if you told me where you heard this garbage—"

"People saw bruises on her, Gene, and she was upset. You know her, or at least, you did back then—where else could she have gotten those bruises? Who else might have upset her?"

"Fuck if I know. Anything could've happened to her in those hotel rooms."

I sighed and let the silence percolate. "Sure," I said finally. "But you don't know any names."

A cunning light came up in Werner's dark eyes. "There was one guy. . . . She hung with him over the summer, and after we ended things, I think she started seeing him. But he's a real psycho, a muscleman type, a bouncer, if you can believe it. Anyway, I think she finally realized what a nasty piece of work he was and wanted to break it off. But she was scared of him—scared of what he might do."

"And this guy would be Jamie Coyle?"

Werner nodded vigorously. "Jamie, yeah, that's him—a real lowlife. You know about him?"

"A little. When did Holly tell you all this?"

"I don't know . . . whenever I saw her last."

"Which was when?"

"A while ago—a month at least."

"And you haven't been in touch since?" He shook his head. "Not last week?" Another shake. "Not the week before?"

"I told you—it was a couple of months ago." I nodded slowly and Werner leaned on the mantel again and looked at me. "Now, if you're through with your questions—"

"Almost. You said that Holly had issues. What kind of issues?"

Werner looked surprised. "Family issues," he said. "Daddy issues. Christ, it's all she ever wrote about. I don't know the details, but her family was screwed up, more than the usual amount. I gather when she was a kid her father chased anything in skirts, and didn't bother to hide it. Now, if that's it . . ."

"One more thing. How well do you know Jamie Coyle?"

He squinted, even more confused. "I don't—not really. I met him a couple of times last summer, at a club Holly went to. He worked there. But I don't think I said ten words to him."

I raised my eyebrows. "No? Then can you think of a reason why he'd be hanging around outside your apartment building?"

Werner went pale, and his casual elbow slipped from the mantel.

"All in all, it's good he gave up the acting," I said.

Mike Metz chuckled. Over the phone I heard him pouring something, and I heard NPR in the background: *Weekend Edition*. It was Sunday morning, and drops of snowmelt fell glittering past my window.

"He was that bad?" Mike asked.

"Worse. Or maybe it's just that he can't improvise. That stuff about his relationship with Holly being no big deal, and that he broke things off with her—it was utter crap."

"What about the business with Jamie Coyle?"

"About Holly being afraid of him? I guess it's possible—Jamie is a scary guy—but I take what Werner says with lots of salt. About the only thing I'm sure of about him is that he's scared himself."

"Scared of whom—Coyle?"

"Him, certainly. Werner nearly wet his pants when I told him that Coyle had had his place staked out. But it's not just Coyle; he was nervous from the start. He clearly didn't want to talk to me, and he could've thrown me out anytime, but he didn't. He was worried enough about something—what I knew, maybe, or what I wanted to know, or who I was working for—that he let me keep talking."

"You think he knows Holly's dead?" Mike said around a mouthful of something.

"That's the question, isn't it? If he saw the pictures in the newspaper, he would've recognized the tattoo, but it's possible he didn't see them. The weather's pushed that and every other story to the back of the paper for the past few days, and it never got much TV time. Of course, it's possible that he knows without having seen the papers."

"Because he killed her."

"That would also explain the worry, though just seeing the pictures in the paper, knowing Holly is dead, might explain it too. If what Krug told me about him is true—the hitting, the stalking, the whole obsessive-lover-spurned thing—then Werner has to know he'd look very good to the cops."

"He looks pretty good to me too," Metz said. "And so does Coyle—maybe good enough to make an ADA think twice about going after your brother."

"I'll try Coyle's PO on Monday, and we'll see how he looks then. And who knows—maybe lawyer Vickers will call back."

"Don't hold your breath. But work fast on Coyle; I want to move on this next week."

"I'll be quick as I can, but David still needs convincing. Last time we talked, he thought the idea of going to the cops was crazy, and maybe you were too. And he wasn't listening too well to reason."

Mike snorted. "Well, something you said sank in. He called me last night, and he was a model of cooperation."

"He called you?"

"He ran down his whereabouts for me on that Tuesday, and answered all my questions about times and places and people. Almost all, anyway."

"What's the 'almost' part?"

"He's still reluctant to talk about Stephanie, or to let me talk to her."

I sighed deeply. "Can he account for his time?"

"Some of it. His day's a little patchy, but with some legwork we can probably fill the gaps. It's the nighttime that's a problem."

"He told me he was home."

"That's what he told me, too. But apparently Stephanie is the only person who can substantiate that."

"And he won't let you talk to her. Great. Does he say why?"

"He says she's out of town and that he'll talk to her when she gets back, though he doesn't say when that will be."

I took another deep breath. Shit. "What does he say about going to the cops?"

"He seems to understand it's the best course."

"Which is not quite the same as agreeing to do it."

"No," Mike said. "But it's getting there."

"Does he understand that we can't talk to the cops until we talk to Stephanie?"

"Yes, though it doesn't seem to translate into actually letting us talk to her. And he's developed a theory that the timing of Holly's death actually works to his advantage."

"What the hell does that mean?"

"His reasoning is, How could he have killed her when, on that Tuesday, he didn't even know who she was. He'd hired you only twenty-four hours before, and you didn't even tell him her name until the following day."

I almost laughed. "Sounds watertight to me—we might as well pack up and call it a day, Mike. Except, maybe, for the fact that *she's* the one who was calling *him*—and visiting his house *and* probably following him around. It won't take the Einstein of cops to work out a scenario where she calls him, they arrange a meeting, and things go wrong. Hell, maybe she didn't even call; maybe she just waylaid him on the street somewhere."

"I explained all that, though without the sarcasm. I'm not sure how much got through."

"So where does that leave us?" I asked.

Mike cleared his throat. "With you and him having another talk, I'm afraid."

I managed not to throw the phone through the window, but hung it up instead. Clare came yawning and stretching from the bedroom, her gray eyes puffy from sleep. She poured a glass of cranberry juice and sat at the end of the sofa and put her feet in my lap. They were cold and white and I rubbed her toes. She picked up the TV remote.

The news had gone from plowing and digging to melting and flooding, and there was footage of water, water everywhere—on roads, in basements, and coursing through storm drains and subway tunnels. Images of JFK came on the screen, where the runways were clear, and long lines of planes were landing and taking off, and the stranded, rumpled, bleary, and unwashed were more or less on their ways. I looked at Clare, who drank her juice and watched in silence. When the images shifted again—to scenes of plows pushing mountains of snow into the river—she looked at me. I opened my mouth to speak, but Clare beat me to it.

"He's not flying in from anywhere, if that's what you're wondering." I had been, and now I was wondering why not. A tiny smile flickered on Clare's lips. "He's not snowbound anywhere, except at home."

I sat up. "No?" I said. My voice was tight.

Clare shook her head. "No."

"Then where does . . ." There was a little rushing sound in my ears. "What did you—"

"I left him."

"You . . ."

"I left him. I walked out."

I nodded, more out of habit than because I understood anything. "You . . . what are you—"

"Don't worry; I'm not planning on moving in. But the storm made it impossible to get a hotel room." She drank some more juice and looked at me over the top of her glass. "I was going to give it a couple of days, but I can start calling the hotels now if you like."

"No . . . I . . . You don't have to do that," I said.

Clare nodded. She went to the kitchen and put her glass in the sink and stood by the windows. Her back was straight and stiff.

"What happened?" I asked. She shook her head but didn't turn around. "You can stay as long as you need to," I said, "as long as you want."

"Which is it," she asked softly, " 'need' or 'want'?"

"Whichever," I said.

She nodded, and watched a wing of snow slide from a rooftop

across the street and break into diamonds on the way down. "It's all coming loose," she said.

Clare went for a walk in the afternoon, and didn't ask for company, and I went for a messy run. My shoes were heavy with water when I got back, and my eyes ached from squinting. Clare was still gone, and still gone when I got out of the shower. I pulled on a pair of jeans and a T-shirt, and opened my laptop and my notebook.

I found Phil Losanto's telephone number on-line, and found him at home, in Yorktown Heights. He had just gotten back from forty-eight hours of skidding across northern Westchester County, covering the county's response to the storm and, according to him, freezing his freaking nuts off. His voice was permanently tired and permanently amused.

"Plus the wife's on my ass now 'cause our drive's the only one on the block that isn't shoveled. Christ, let me get a Pepsi first." There was a lot of noise on his end—a television playing loud cartoons, the piercing trills and beeps of a video game, small children fighting, or playing, or both, and a shrill, exasperated woman yelling at them. My heart went out to Phil.

"You wrote a couple of articles a few years ago about Jamie Coyle."

Phil thought for a while amidst the noise. "Yeah, in Peekskill, right. The kid who beat the crap out of that video store guy. He got sent away for a while."

"And got out about a year ago. You recall much about him?"

"Enough. Why?"

"Your article talked about him being a star athlete, local-hero type. Was that for real, or was it just good copy?"

Losanto snorted. "What, you don't trust the press? No, that was mostly for real. Until the knee thing, the kid was a phenomenal defensive tackle—made all-county in his sophomore year—and he was Golden Gloves champ in his class since he was fourteen. As far as the *hero* part goes . . . that's a different story."

"Don't leave me hanging, Phil."

He laughed. Behind him something glass shattered, the woman yelled, and one of the children shrieked. "Even before he got into the collection business, Coyle was no altar boy. He was a hell-raiser in high school, with a bad temper. He got in a few fights, boosted a few cars, and was generally one of the kids the local cops knew by name."

"Doesn't sound like a criminal mastermind, though."

"No, not a mastermind."

"What happened with the video store guy?"

"Ray Vessic? The usual thing that happens when a guy gets behind and doesn't listen: somebody like Coyle comes around."

"Yeah, but when they do, they usually leave the guy in good enough shape to pay—that's the point of collection, after all. But that guy took a hell of a beating. I was surprised they let Coyle cop to Assault II."

"He had a good lawyer—Jerry Lavin, rest his soul—and there were maybe some other things going on."

"What other things?"

Losanto sighed wearily. "I heard it came up in Coyle's plea negotiations. Apparently Vessic had a sideline going in the back of his store, something a little less mainstream than the latest teen screamer flick."

"Porn?"

"The kid variety. He was selling the shit, ran chat rooms for the fans, and even made some films himself—all in all, a real prince. Coyle tipped the prosecutors to it, and Jerry even managed to sell them on the idea that finding out about the porn was the reason Coyle went off on Vessic. At the end of the day, it bought the kid the D felony deal."

"Good lawyer and good luck for Coyle. You have much faith in the outrage story?"

Losanto snorted again. "Who knows? It makes a good tale, and Jerry, God bless him, was a creative guy, but I don't know." There was another crash at Losanto's end, and more yelling. "And now I better get my ass in there, before I got outrage of my own to deal with."

I put down the phone, pulled my laptop over, and transcribed my notes about Coyle. I read them over, and reread what I already had on him from Arrua, Krug, J.T., Lia, and Werner, and tried to square it all. And couldn't quite do it. Scary, bad-tempered, and violent—I'd seen those qualities in Coyle firsthand, and they didn't jibe with the gentle giant, protector of the weak whom Lia had described. And then there was Coyle's relationship with Holly. According to Krug, Holly was happier than he'd ever seen her, while Werner's spin was that she was scared and wanted out. I knew who I was inclined to believe, but still ... Losanto's story was interesting but ultimately inconclusive. And of course I still had no idea of where Coyle might be or what he wanted with Werner. I shook my head. Maybe Coyle's PO ... maybe tomorrow.

I pushed the laptop away and looked at my dim windows and wondered where Clare had gone. I got up and stretched and looked outside. The sky was drained of color and darkening at its eastern edge, and the cityscape was gray. I saw cars on the street, and more people, though none who looked like Clare returning. Lights were coming on in windows across the street and across town, scattered yellow pinpoints that only made the dusk seem colder.

23

Mike Metz was wrong about Thomas Vickers: he did call back, or rather his frail-sounding secretary did it for him. It was hideously early on Monday, and I was wrapped in a dream, and in a tangle of blankets, and in Clare's long legs. She elbowed me awake and I groped for the telephone.

"Mr. March?" the parchment voice said. "I'm calling from Mr. Vickers's office." I croaked something back at her, I'm not sure what. "Mr. Vickers would like to see you here, this afternoon at three," she said. There was no *Are you available?* and not the slightest thought that I would decline. And I didn't. She gave me the address, on Broadway south of Wall, and rang off.

I looked at the clock: too early to call Mike. I propped myself on my elbow and looked outside. Ridged fangs of ice hung from the tops of my windows and shook in the wind that shook the glass. The sky was a thin, clear blue. Something—a gull—blew sideways across it, east to west and gone. A chill ran through me. I squeezed my eyes shut and opened them again. Dust motes swam, and the last pieces of my dream tumbled past. Something with Holly—her icon's face and kohl eyes and thousand-yard stare, and behind her the shadowed figure of a man, Bluto, maybe. And then it vanished, spinning away, faster than the gull.

When we finally rose, hours later, Clare moved quickly, showering, dressing, breakfasting, and slipping on her coat, all before I'd shaved. I asked her where she was going, and even to me the question sounded odd.

Clare smirked. "To see my lawyer," she said, and she turned up the collar of her long black coat.

I nodded. "Is he a good one?"

"Jay's the best," she said. "Not that there's much for him to do. The pre-nup leaves nothing to the imagination."

"And that's a positive thing?"

"It is to me," she said, and her grin turned chilly.

After she left, I showered and shaved and sat at my laptop with a slice of toast. It took an hour and a half of typing, calling, navigating mazes of telephone menus, and waiting on bad-music hold, for me to find the guy who'd been Jamie Coyle's parole officer. He was in the Division of Parole office in New Rochelle, and his name was Paul Darrow. He had a rich Bronx baritone, and what sounded like a nasty head cold.

"Don't tell me Jamie got himself jammed up again. For chrissakes, he was one of my success stories—one of the few."

"I don't know if he's jammed up, but I came across his name in a case, and I'm trying to find the guy, or at least find out a little more about him."

Darrow coughed and snorted, and somebody spoke to him in Spanish. "I got six customers waiting here already, March, so it's not a real good time."

"When is?"

He laughed. "Next month maybe, or how about next year?"

I chuckled along with him to be polite, and eventually he consulted his calendar and found a slice of it that he could spare. "I got a meeting down in the city this afternoon, if you want to grab a coffee before."

"Fine," I said, and we agreed on a time and place.

I ate more toast and flicked on the news. The storm stories had already begun to fade, coming in fourth behind oil prices, cabinet appointments, and the arrest of a popular action-movie star for exposing himself to the nanny. There was no mention of the Williamsburg Mermaid, not on TV or in the papers. David's luck was holding.

I called Mike Metz to tell him about the meeting with Vickers, and he was quiet for a bit, while the gears turned.

"You touched some kind of nerve," he said.

"And maybe not surprisingly. If Vickers's client really was one of Holly's costars, he might've seen the picture in the papers and recognized the tattoo, and he might find himself in the same kind of leaky boat my brother is in."

"In which case, we need to be very careful around Tommy."

"We? You're coming along."

"I figure you can always use a little help being careful. And besides, it'll be good to see that bastard again."

"You hear any more about the autopsy?"

"Not yet, and I'm assuming the storm slowed things down a little—which is good news for us. Have you spoken to your brother yet?"

"No."

"But you will?"

"I will," I said, without enthusiasm.

I went for a run instead.

I met Paul Darrow at a diner on West Thirty-second Street, not far from the Division of Parole's Manhattan office. The last of the lunch crowd was paying up and the windows were fogged and dripping. The air was heavy with bacon and burnt coffee and, underneath, some kind of cleaning fluid. The booths were gray vinyl, liberally taped.

Darrow was a bald, barrel-shaped black man of about fifty, with a drooping face, a gray mustache, and wary, watery eyes. I knew him by his sneeze. He wore a sagging jacket of hairy gray tweed, a white shirt gone beige, and a shiny striped tie. His coat and hat sat next to him in the booth, and he was hunched over a teacup, breathing the steam. I slid into the seat across.

He looked up and looked me over. "March?" I nodded. "I didn't wait for you." I shrugged and flagged down a waitress and ordered a ginger ale. Darrow sipped at his tea. "You worked that Danes thing, a couple of years ago," he said. It wasn't a question. "And that other thing, upstate." The point being: *I looked you up.*

I nodded. "What can you tell me about Jamie Coyle?"

Darrow shrugged. "What's to say? He's a big, tough kid who, if you looked at him on paper, you'd think, *Back inside in a year—two years tops,* but who somehow managed to turn it around. Unless you calling me up means something different."

I shrugged. "I'm not sure it means anything. I'm looking for his girlfriend, so I'd like to talk to him. I can't seem to find him, though."

Darrow nodded. "His girlfriend, the artist?"

"You know her?"

"He talked about her—a lot. He was real serious about her."

"Real serious how?"

"Serious like how she changed his life, and turned his whole world around."

I raised an eyebrow. "Are you telling me he was saved by the love of a good woman?"

Darrow smiled and sneezed and blew his nose. When he was done, he shook his head. "I'm saying that's how Jamie tells it. To me, it sounded like the girl was pretty, and smart, and had money and some class, and that she wanted more from life than pumping out four kids and riding them on the bus on the weekends to see their daddy in the joint. I don't know that Jamie's met too many girls like that before, or ever. She lives in a different world, and he sees maybe how he can live there too. For his sake, I hope he's right. But as for turning his life around, truth is he mostly did that himself, up in Coxsackie."

"A lot of good time?"

"Yeah. He had trouble to start—that place is no tennis camp, and him being a white boy and all—but he didn't hurt anybody too bad, or get hurt himself, and he went through a lot of the anger management courses, counseling and stuff, and did a lot of college work. He was halfway to a degree by the time he got out. Said he wanted to finish."

"Smart kid?"

"Smarter than he looks, and especially smart when he watches his temper. He's not afraid to work, either; he's ambitious in his own way."

"He have problems with the temper?"

"He used to, but it looked like he had it beat."

"What do you know about his plea?"

"He went for Assault Two."

"Which sounded light, given what he did to that guy."

"What I read, the guy was a real piece of shit."

"Is that why Coyle went off on him?"

Darrow blew his nose again. "I couldn't tell you why Jamie did what he did. But the file says he provided information that took a piece of shit off the street, and that's why he got a deal."

I nodded. And now, the $64,000 question. "You know where I can find him?"

"You try his job?"

"What job is that?"

"He works maintenance at a condo complex in Tarrytown. His uncle is the super, and Jamie has an apartment there, in the basement."

"I didn't know about that gig. I'd heard that he was working in the city somewhere . . . at some club."

Darrow went still, and his eyes went suddenly hard. "What club?" he asked.

I shook my head. "I didn't get the name."

Darrow smacked his hand on the table, and made the mugs jump. "Fuckin' Jamie," he said. "He bitched about wanting extra money for school, but I didn't think he'd be stupid enough to lie."

"Did he do that often?"

Irritation creased Darrow's heavy face. "This is the first time I know about," he said. "The caseloads we get—there's only so much you can check—only so many hours in the day. What are we supposed to do, live in their fucking pockets?"

I drank my soda and nodded. "You said before that Jamie was ambitious. Ambitious how?"

"He was always working a plan—not always the same one, mind you, but Jamie was always shooting for something. Make some money, finish school. Make some money, open a restaurant. Make some money, buy some property."

"The money part was consistent."

He shrugged. "Kid lives in the real world."

I picked up the check, and Darrow and I walked out together. The light was already long and the wind felt like steel on my face. Darrow shivered and sneezed.

There was no oblique way to ask it, so I just asked. "Is Jamie a dangerous guy?"

Darrow turned to me. "Dangerous to who?"

"To anyone."

"You know enough to know that's a bullshit question. You, me, that old guy at the cash register in there—you push the right buttons with anyone, get them scared enough, angry enough, back 'em up against a wall, they're dangerous."

"And Jamie no more so than anybody else?"

"I wouldn't have recommended him for discharge otherwise," Darrow said. He pulled out a handkerchief, ran it under his nose, and squinted at me again. "On the other hand, I didn't know shit about his moonlighting."

Mike Metz was waiting in the lobby of Tommy Vickers's building when I arrived. He was leaning on a column and tapping on his Black-Berry; his face was still pink from the cold, and full of concentration. We signed in at security, which did not quite entail a cavity search, and rode alone to the twenty-seventh floor. On the way, I talked about my meeting with Darrow. He drew a finger along his chin as the elevator crawled upward.

"Coyle's a mixed bag, I guess," he said when I was through. "He's gotten over his anger issues, except for knocking you around, and he was a model parolee, except for lying to his PO. And he was apparently very serious about Holly, maybe enough to get seriously mad at her, or seriously violent."

I watched the numbers change and thought about what Krug had told me—about how happy Holly had been—and what Lia said: "Look, he's a good guy."

"Everyone's a mixed bag," I said. "I'm not sure quite what to make of Coyle." Mike looked at me, one narrow brow raised. The elevator stopped and the doors slid open. We stepped into an empty corridor.

"Your job is to develop alternative theories," he said, "and this guy qualifies. Let the police sort out just how good a theory he is."

Vickers's office was at the end of the hall, a dark wooden door with shiny brass hardware and a brass plate that read "TEV Consulting." We went in, into a good-sized waiting room done up in Hollywood corporate: teak paneling, Oriental rugs, brass lamps, green leather furniture heavy with brass tacks. The prints on the walls were nautical: packet ships and schooners, laden with treasure and headed for some faraway tax haven with no money-laundering statutes on the books and no extradition.

There were double doors ahead, and a big teak desk to the left; behind it was a woman whose hair was younger by decades than the rest of her. She was small and pale and powdered, and her improbable chestnut tresses were pulled in a cruel bun, away from her withered face. She looked from one of us to the other and squinted at her watch.

"Mr. March?" In person, her voice was even more fragile than it sounded on the phone.

"I'm March."

The woman looked at Mike, and looked distressed. "I wasn't expecting—"

A soft, raspy voice interrupted from the direction of the double doors. "It's okay, Edie. There's always room at the table for Mr. Metz."

Thomas Vickers was five foot nine, with a blocky frame covered in well-cut navy wool. His hair was a glossy white helmet on his square head, and his hooded eyes were bright blue. His features were fine but weathered—their edges and peaks sanded by age and shot with veins—and I put him somewhere north of sixty.

He offered Mike a manicured hand. "Long time, Michael," he said.

"I should have called first," Mike said, smiling.

"Nonsense." Vickers turned to me. "March, thanks for coming." His grip was cold and surprisingly delicate. "And for bringing Michael along. I heard you did a lot of work for him; I didn't know this was one of those times. Let's sit." Edie took our coats.

Mike followed Vickers, and I followed Mike—through the double doors and down a corridor lined with law books and silence. We turned a corner and passed a large office. The door was open and I saw a sofa, a big mahogany desk, and a green Oriental rug inside. And I saw a stocky, dark-haired man in black trousers and a chocolate-brown jacket. He was sitting on the sofa, looking at me. I paused and looked back, and he got up and closed the office door. I caught up with Mike and Vickers, and wondered about the tension I'd felt, and the odd sense of déjà vu.

We came to rest in a conference room that looked out on Broadway and Bowling Green and a piece of the darkening harbor. The walls that weren't windows were covered in gray fabric and more nautical prints. The table was an ebony slab with a dozen chairs around it. There was an ebony console against the wall, with china cups and saucers on it. Vickers offered coffee and we declined. We sat at the table.

Vickers smoothed his tie and looked at me. "You never actually said why it is you're interested in Cassandra Z," he said.

I glanced at Mike, who moved his head minutely. "Missing persons," I said.

Vickers nodded. "Cassandra being the person?" I nodded back. "Have you been to the police?"

"Not yet," I said.

Vickers nodded. "Your client would rather not?" he asked. Mike saved me from answering.

"John told me you were going to talk to us about Cassandra, Tommy. Did he get that wrong?"

"No," Vickers sighed, and smiled wearily. "He didn't. You asked me about Cassandra; here's what I can tell you: I was looking for her on behalf of a client; I spoke to the art dealer who represents her—a man named Orlando Krug—and eventually, I spoke to her. That was in December, over a month ago. Neither I nor my client has had any contact with her since." He looked at both of us.

Mike stared out the window, and pursed his lips. I shook my head. "And . . . ?" I said.

"And what?" Vickers asked.

"And that's it? That's what you called us in to say?"

"Actually, I just called you, not that I'm not glad to see Michael."

"But that's all you've got?" He nodded. "Why bother to say anything, then?"

He looked mildly puzzled. "You asked."

"Is that all it takes?" My laugh was short and sharp. "Because if it is, I have plenty of other questions."

Vickers sighed. "You have a reputation for being persistent. I thought I could save us all some time and undue effort, and let you move on to more productive things." He looked at Mike. "I hope I haven't miscalculated."

"Of course not, Tommy," Mike said. "And we appreciate you having us in. Nobody wants to waste time or cause unnecessary trouble, and if we could just follow up on a couple of things, then we'll get out of your hair." Vickers nodded vaguely and Mike smiled wider. "To start, what was it that you wanted to discuss with Cassandra?"

Vickers turned his palms up. "It's a confidential matter, Michael; I'm sure you understand. I imagine your client feels much the same way."

Mike nodded understandingly. "And your client is . . . ?"

Vickers raised a white eyebrow. "A private person," he said.

"Finding himself in one of Cassandra's videos must've come as a surprise, then," I said.

Vickers turned chilly eyes on me and tightened his mouth. "You're missing the important point," he said. "The important point is that I saw her once, over a month ago, and not again. *Once.* That's the important point, son."

My face tightened and I took a deep breath. "What about your client?" I asked.

"My client returned to New York a week ago, after three weeks in Latin America. And he can document his movements during that time." He turned to Mike and smiled. "The itinerary makes it rock-solid, Michael."

"Not really," I said. "If he can afford you, then your client can afford all sorts of other help."

Vickers looked at me as if I'd just crapped on his conference table. When he spoke, it was to Mike, and his voice was dry as kindling. "What the hell is with your friend? I invite him in to talk—as a favor, mind you—and I get this? I heard he was a hothead, but Christ . . . I mean, I could sit here asking you the same questions about *your* client—who he is, what he wants with this girl, and so forth—but am I doing that? No. Instead, I'm trying to help you out. And in return I get this?"

Mike gave him an apologetic shrug and looked at me. "Tommy's right, John, there's no call for us to speculate about things when he's so willing to help," he said. He turned back to Vickers. "January's a nice time to get out of town, and go somewhere warm. Was Latin America a business trip?"

Vickers squinted. "How does that—"

"I'm sure you're right—it probably doesn't matter, and if the police think otherwise, I expect they'll just ask."

The hoods came down over Vickers's blue eyes. "I have nothing to do with the police."

Mike's smile was guileless and his eyes were opened wide. "Of course you don't," he said. "And there's no reason why you should." And we were all quiet for a while.

It was Vickers who broke the silence. "Is that a threat, Michael?" he asked, though he didn't seem much threatened.

"More of a proposal."

"Proposing what, exactly?"

"That you tell us what your client wanted with Cassandra, and we go away and pursue the more productive things that you mentioned."

Vickers smoothed his tie some more. "I don't think so," he said. "If the police have questions, so be it. We can't help them, but if we have to waste time explaining that, then I guess that's the way it is."

Mike nodded. "Talking to the police, dealing with the press, questions about the business . . . all of that takes time." His tone was sympathetic, even regretful.

"I don't think the press—" Vickers began, but I cut him off.

"Your client is in a select group, Tommy: he's the only guy in one of Cassandra's videos to ever come looking for her, much less to find her. That alone makes for some elaborate explaining . . . especially given the timing."

Vickers drummed his fingers on the tabletop for a while. Then he shook his head slowly. "You're making things more complicated than they are, son—more complicated than they have to be—and you're wasting your own time and your client's money doing it. I spoke to this girl a month ago, and not again, and my client hasn't seen or spoken to her in years." He looked at Mike. "I'm asking you to trust me on this, Michael."

Mike's smile was small and bland. "That might be easier to do if we knew why you were looking for Holly in the first place."

Vickers drank off whatever was in his cup, and sighed. "A girl like that—there must be a dozen other people you could talk to, more maybe. You really—"

"A girl like *what*?" I interrupted, and the anger in my voice surprised even me.

Vickers pursed his lips and looked at Mike. "He really can't keep it in his pants, can he? That must cause you problems."

Mike shrugged. "It's the cross I bear," he said coolly. Then he looked at me and twitched an eyebrow.

"I'll meet you out front," I said, and I left the room. Vickers didn't say goodbye, and neither did I.

I paused by the corner office again, on my way back to the waiting room. The door was still shut and I thought about opening it and looking in on the dark-haired man, but I didn't. Instead, I rode the elevator down and waited for Mike in a corner of the lobby. He was buttoning his coat as he approached.

"I'd forgotten what an arrogant bastard that guy is," he said. "And those theatrics—either he's lost his touch, or my standards are higher now than when I was twenty-five." He smiled and ran a hand through his hair. "Your performance was far superior, by the way: no one does 'volatile' better."

"It wasn't entirely an act," I said.

"The best performances never are."

"Did Vickers say anything useful?"

Mike pulled out his BlackBerry and thumbed through messages while he spoke. "Not really. A vague offer to swap client names—a 'You show me yours, I'll show you mine' sort of thing—but nothing sincere. He was never going to tell us shit."

"Then what was the point of his invitation?"

"A calculated risk on Tommy's part, I suppose—a chance to size you up, to dazzle you and befuddle you and maybe find something out. Best case, a chance to sell you on his story and get you to leave his client alone. All of which would've been worth the risk of stirring the pot a little, especially given that you already knew he'd been looking for Cassandra. I suspect he gave up on most of it when you brought me along."

Over Mike's shoulder, I watched the elevators empty. Ranks of dark-coated figures flowed past, girding themselves for the cold. "You buy any of his story?"

"I don't know," Mike said. "Tommy wasn't particularly circumspect when he went looking for Cassandra, which is not what you'd expect if he or his client had meant her harm."

"Maybe they meant no harm when they were just looking; maybe that changed when they actually found her. Or maybe your pal doesn't know everything his client was up to."

Mike looked at me. "Has it occurred to you that maybe we're in the same boat?"

I was about to say something—to concede the point, perhaps, or to ask just how worried he was about David—when an elevator door opened. A fat man emerged, followed by a small blond woman, followed by a stocky, dark-haired man. He swaggered off, and he rolled his shoulders as he went, and he was suddenly more than familiar. I stepped back, into the shadow of a column, and watched him cross the lobby, turning up the collar of his big camel coat as he went. Mike turned to look and I caught his arm.

"What?" he asked.

"That guy—in the tan coat—he was in Vickers's office."

"Yeah, I saw him when we came in. So what?"

"I think he's Vickers's client." The stocky man pushed through the revolving doors and into the crowd on Broadway. He turned right, north.

"His Cassandra client?" Mike asked. "How do you know?"

But I was already past him when the questions came, headed for the doors. I glanced back and answered. "He's Bluto," I said.

It was nearly dark outside, and it took me a few minutes to pick out the swagger and the wide, brown shoulders from the hurrying crowd. I hung back while he waited for the light at Exchange Place, and my cell phone burred. It was Mike.

"You're just following him, right?" he asked.

"What does that mean?"

"It means I know you were pissed at Tommy, and I know how you felt about those videos, and I don't want you getting jammed up with something stupid like an assault charge when you're in the middle of a case. It won't do you or your brother any good." The light changed and Bluto was moving.

"Nothing stupid," I said, and I turned off my phone and followed him across Broadway. He headed west, through Exchange Alley, and north again on Trinity Place. Half a block later he went into an office building.

It was an older structure, circa 1950, built of brown brick and squatter than its neighbors. It was currently incarnated as Trinity Parc Tower, its aging, undistinguished bones only partially hidden beneath a recent veneer of marble and frosted glass. I was grateful that the lobby was shallow, so that I could see the elevators from the street. It also helped that the building directory was up to date, and that the security guards were dullards.

Through the lobby glass, I watched Bluto board an elevator by himself, and watched the floor display climb to 11 and stop. Then I scanned the directory and went inside. I scrawled the name of a twelfth-floor law firm in the sign-in book, and showed my driver's license to the guards, who waved me through with barely a glance.

According to the building directory, three firms shared the eleventh floor: Fenn Partners LLC; MF Securities LLC; and Trading Pit LLC, and apparently they shared the same office too. I stepped off the elevator directly into a reception area, and the three names were spelled out in blue plastic letters on a sign above an unmanned receptionist's desk. There was an arrangement of angular leather chairs and glass coffee tables to the right—the waiting area, also vacant. Behind that, beyond a waist-high partition, was a drab expanse of gray carpet, fluorescent lighting, and cubicles.

The cubicles were low-walled and tiny, and the ones I could see were equipped with narrow desks, swivel chairs, and banks of flat-screen monitors. The monitors glowed and flickered with charts and graphs and numbers, though just then they were playing to mostly empty seats. The few men left in the cubes—and there were only men in them—were stuffing briefcases and donning coats. They paid little attention to one another at the elevators, and none at all to me, and in a few moments I was alone in the waiting room.

There were glossy brochures on the coffee tables and I picked one up and read. After four pages of photos, diagrams, and acronym-laden babble about the latest trading technology, the most current market data, cutting-edge risk management, Nasdaq Level II quotes, extensive training, and low, low, low fees, I knew what I needed to about Trading Pit LLC. It was a day-trading firm—a motel of sorts—that for low, low, low fees, let an individual, a day trader, rent one of its cubes and the use of its trading systems, to earn or burn his money in a clean, well-lighted place. In theory, the firm's systems were better than what one could typically access at home, the fees were lower than trading through a discount broker, at least for high-volume players, the executions were faster, and the environment was more disciplined and professional. Maybe, but I saw more than one screen that displayed the home page of a popular on-line poker site.

The most useful part of the literature was the back page, and the bios and photos of the firm's management. There, at the top of the heap, was Bluto, the founder, chairman, and CEO of Trading Pit LLC: Mitchell Fenn.

According to the brochure, Fenn was a longtime veteran of the securities industry—a former SVP at a big broker-dealer, and director of that firm's trading operations—and he'd left there two years ago to found Trading Pit, piecing it together from the scraps of several other day-trading outfits that hadn't survived the last market downturn. His picture showed a broad, tanned face beneath a head of dark, curly hair. His teeth were large and bright, and his wide smile was hungry. I dropped the brochure on the table and stepped into the maze of cubicles.

I found Fenn at the northwest corner of the floor, in a large, chrome and leather den with views of Ground Zero. He was lounging behind a chrome and glass desk, and talking to a red-haired guy in a shirt and tie, who sat across from him, smiling and nodding. I saw a dusting of gray in Fenn's shiny black curls, and a web of lines around his dark eyes, and closer up, he looked ten years older than he did in his photo—around fifty, maybe. He'd lost the overcoat and jacket, and his blue shirtsleeves were rolled over thick forearms. I stood in the door and he recognized me right away. He was still for a moment, and then the wide, greedy smile appeared.

"Fuck if Tommy wasn't right about you," he said. His voice was deep Brooklyn, and hearing it was a little shock. Some part of me had been expecting synthesized speech. "Fuck if he didn't say I should keep away today. But I didn't listen—I wanted to have a look." He turned to the redhead. "Take a lesson from that, Chris: don't argue with your lawyer."

Chris looked from Fenn to me, and his doughy face was puzzled. He put his big hands on his knees, as if he was about to get up.

"He a friend of yours, Mitch?" he asked. His voice was surprisingly high-pitched, and full of adolescent tough. He ran a hand over his spiky hair, and his stupid blue eyes narrowed.

Fenn smiled wider. "We haven't been introduced, but we've seen each other before—haven't we?"

"I think I've seen a little more of you," I said.

The big smile didn't falter, but it turned colder, and a shade meaner. "Yeah? Hope you didn't get some kind of inferiority complex from it." His laugh was a throaty bark.

"It was something closer to indigestion."

The grin held, but even Chris couldn't miss the radiating anger. He had no idea what was going on, but he stood up anyway. "You want to watch your mouth, buddy," he said. He was maybe an inch taller than I, and heavier by twenty sloppy pounds.

I looked more closely at his face—the freckles, snub nose, thin lips, and chipped front tooth—and I recognized him from the brochure: Christopher Fitz-something, the head sales guy. Which explained his eagerness to impress his boss. I shook my head.

"You don't want an audience for this, Mitch," I said.

Fenn barked out another laugh. "An audience for what? You doing tricks or something?"

Chris took a step toward me and poked a finger in my direction and then at the door. "You, out—now." His face was red, and his fists were clenched. Fenn's dark eyes were shining with expectation.

"You're going to get him hurt," I said to Fenn. Behind Chris's back, he shrugged. Chris took another step.

"There's only one guy gonna get hurt, asshole," he said. Then he put his hands up, to shove me in the chest. I stepped aside and he fell past me, and I hurried him along with a push between the shoulders. I stuck out my foot as he went by, and he stumbled into the hallway, down on one knee and flapping like an ungainly red bird. I shut the door and turned the lock and looked at Fenn. He laughed out loud.

"Tommy said you were a piece of work," he said, and his wide frame shook. Behind me, Chris cursed and worked the doorknob. Then he started pounding.

"You okay, Mitch?" he shouted. "You want security for that asshole, or the cops?"

"No," Fenn called. "No cops. Everything's fine, Chris—I'll catch you tomorrow."

"You sure? I can—"

"Tomorrow, Chris," he repeated, and Chris got the message and went away. Fenn picked up a red rubber ball from his desk and started squeezing it. He shook his head.

"Or was I wrong, and you're going to try and push me around, too? 'Cause I'm telling you, it won't be so easy with me."

"As appealing an idea as that is, I came to talk."

Fenn leaned back in his chair and smiled. If there was relief there, it was hard to tell. "You want to talk, talk to Tommy."

I walked to the desk and slung my coat on one guest seat and sat in the other. "I heard what he had to say. I didn't find it convincing."

"That sounds like something between you and Tommy."

I sighed heavily. "You're going to make me go through the motions?"

Fenn squeezed the rubber ball, and watched his knuckles go white. "Which motions are those?" he asked.

"The ones I make while I'm calling the cops."

"Calling them about what?"

"About you and the Williamsburg Mermaid, for starters."

Fenn was quiet for a while, and studied his fingers on the red ball. "Is that supposed to make me go weak in the knees?" he asked eventually.

"Worry more about the effect it has on the cops, and especially when they see Cassandra's video."

He smirked. "You know, I've never watched the final product. I hope she made me look good."

A little rushing noise started in my ears. "Yeah, you look great choking her, Mitch—almost as good as when you're slapping her around, or burning her breasts with candle wax."

Fenn let go of the ball. It took a small bounce on his desk and came to rest against his phone. He pointed at me, and finally the grin went away. "Fuck you, March—that bitch was a freak, but she was a grown-up freak. She knew what she was getting into, and she liked it, so don't lecture me."

I felt my hands grip the armrests of the chair, and I felt something shift in my face. Fenn pushed his chair back from his desk by half a foot.

"What—she was a friend of yours or something?"

I took a deep breath and let it out slowly. "Don't call her 'bitch' anymore," I said softly.

"Whatever," he said. "My point is, she was no schoolgirl, and the cops will figure that out. And, anyway, I can account for my time."

"Sure, and while they're figuring, and you're accounting, who knows what other agencies will start asking questions—about your business, maybe, and Tommy's, about your clients . . ."

Fenn's eyes narrowed. "What agencies?"

"I don't know," I said, shrugging. "The IRS, maybe, or the SEC—there are all sorts of initials out there, and all just a phone call away."

Fenn's mouth was an angry line, and I could almost see the steam rising from his dark curls as he stared at me. He shook his head. "Tommy wasn't bullshitting you; it's been years since I had any contact with her, and I had nothing to do with what happened."

"Why did you send him looking for her, then?"

He ran a hand across the back of his neck and let out a long breath. "I got a letter a while ago—about three months back—pictures of me and her, from when we were together. A few days later a note came, from somebody squeezing me, or trying to."

"Somebody who?"

Fenn snorted. "Do blackmailers usually sign their letters?"

"You assumed it was Wren?"

"From the photos and the bullshit threats, that's what I thought, but I never knew who the fuck Wren was. That's why I called Tommy."

"What were the threats?"

"The same crap as two years ago," Fenn said. "Sending pictures to the boss, the wife, the in-laws—all that shit." Fenn paused and surprised me with a satisfied smile. "She didn't know that it was all old news, though. That ship sailed a long time ago."

"What does that mean?"

"It means in the last couple years I've become pretty much squeeze-proof."

"Squeeze-proof how?"

Fenn laughed. "Two years ago, I was still married, I was working for somebody else, and I was just putting together the money for this." He gestured around him. "Now I'm single, I'm in charge around here, and I bought out the last of my investors six months back. So if somebody wants to put pictures of me fucking a beautiful girl on the Internet, they can go right ahead. The way we went at it, it'd probably get me more dates."

"Why not ignore the letter, then? Why send Vickers to look for her?"

"That's just what Tommy said—leave it alone—but I said no way. Immune to it or not, I fucking hate the idea of someone trying to shake me down. I hate being harassed; I hate people messing with my privacy. And the fact that there's somebody out there who thinks they can get away with it—who thinks I'm a soft touch—that's a fucking insult."

"So what was Vickers supposed to do once he found her?"

"Send her a fucking message, that's what. Let her know that *I* know who she is, and that she's going to get herself in trouble—serious *legal* trouble—if she keeps screwing around with me." I shook my head. The words were familiar, and so was the reasoning.

"What happened then?" I asked.

"Just what Tommy told you. He tracked her down, they had their talk, and that was it, the one and only time he spoke to her."

"How did she take it?"

"The bit—the girl? Tommy said she was fucking surprised."

"Surprised that he'd tracked her down?"

Fenn shook his head. "Surprised by the whole thing. According to him, she didn't know what the fuck he was talking about. Didn't know about the pictures or the letter, didn't know anything about a squeeze. According to Tommy, it was all a big shock."

"He believed her?"

Fenn shrugged. "I told him this chick could sell ice to Eskimos, but still he bought it."

"But not you?"

"I knew her. I also know that after their talk we never heard another word about pictures or threats or sending cash. To me, that says she took the hint."

"To the cops, it might say you killed her."

Fenn slapped his hand on the desk. His voice was tight and loud. "Don't you listen? I had *no reason* to kill her. Those pictures were no threat to me, they were just an annoyance. She was just an annoyance.

Shit, if I was planning something like that, do you think I would've sent Tommy out looking for her that way? It wasn't exactly a secret what he was doing."

"Maybe things were different once you found her. Something she said, maybe, or something she did . . ."

"What—some kind of a crime of passion? I told you, I never even saw her. And I was out of the country when she died." I shook my head. "You don't believe it," Fenn said, "here—look." He opened a drawer and pulled out a manila envelope and slid it across the desk.

I looked inside. There were fifteen pages, all copies—airline tickets and hotel receipts mostly. Rio, São Paulo, Buenos Aires, Punta del Este, then back to Rio—three weeks, just as Vickers had said. I tossed it back to him.

"These don't mean anything. You could've hired it out."

Fenn shook his head, and the grin began to reappear. "You just can't make up your mind, can you? 'Hired it out' or 'crime of passion'—which is it? Hiring somebody means planning, and if I was planning it, I wouldn't have had Tommy out beating the bushes so loud. And flipping out means I had to be there—which you can see I wasn't. On top of which, I had *no fucking reason* to do anything to this girl besides sue the hell out of her.

"For chrissakes, March, for a guy who's supposed to be smart, you got your head squarely up your ass."

26

Cold and fatigue sat like a yoke on my shoulders, and I leaned heavily in the elevator as it rose. It was only seven o'clock, but it felt like years since I'd left my apartment to meet Paul Darrow. I opened my door to the smell of thyme and warm bread, and to Clare at the kitchen counter, leafing through a shiny magazine. I hung my coat and poured a cranberry juice and looked in the pot that was heating on the stove. A thick stew simmered inside.

"You cooked?" I asked.

Clare smiled. "If by cooking you mean buying it, putting it in the pot, and turning on the heat—then, yes. It's an old family recipe I picked up at the hem of Mother's cocktail dress." I smiled back at her, but it turned into a yawn midway.

"This'll keep," she said. "Why don't you rest for a while?" Which sounded like a fine idea—a deeply brilliant idea—except that Mitchell Fenn's wide smile lit the darkness whenever I closed my eyes, and I knew that I should call Mike Metz. As it happened, I wasn't fifteen minutes tossing on the sofa when he called me. I carried the phone into the bedroom.

I told Mike how it went with Fenn and there was silence when I was done, and then a moment's irritation.

"I thought you were just going to follow him," Mike said.

"An opportunity presented itself," I said, "and, anyway, no blood was spilled."

"That's comforting. Do you buy his story?"

I'd had a slow cab ride home to think about it. "Grudgingly," I said.

"So do I. And it presents an interesting scenario—of someone using Holly's videos for blackmail, and of Holly finding out. Those are circumstances for violence, and it's a story the police will take seriously."

"It suggests someone close to her—close enough to have access to her unedited work, anyway."

"Someone like a boyfriend, for instance."

"That's one possibility."

"With Coyle's record, it's the possibility the cops will focus on. And speaking of which, it's time to call them—past time, really. Have you talked to David about Stephanie?"

"Not yet," I said.

"Jesus," Mike sighed. "You have to do it, John. We need to know—"

"I know, I know—I'll call him tonight."

And I did, right after I got off the phone with Mike. I had no idea of what to say to him, and I was relieved when his recorded voice came on. I thought about just hanging up, but ultimately I left a message. *Call me.*

I came out of the bedroom as Clare was setting a bowl of stew and a loaf of peasant bread on the table. She carried her own bowl over and sat.

"You didn't seem to be doing much resting," she said. I shook my head and tore off a piece of bread and dipped it in the stew. "I won't ask about your day at the office," she said. "'Cause then you'd have to kill me, and you're too tired now."

I smiled. "So thoughtful. How did it go with your lawyer?"

"No surprises," Clare said. "The pre-nup spells it all out, and according to Jay no one's arguing anything. It's a matter of filings and court calendars now."

I nodded. "And afterward?"

A little smile crossed Clare's face. "Afterward what?"

"Do you have . . ."

"Plans?" Clare asked. I nodded. "I've been thinking about going back to gallery work," she said, "or maybe something else. I'm in no rush. And as far as housing goes . . . I figured I'd just move in here." I stopped chewing for half a second—not even that long—but it was long enough for Clare to have her fun.

Her smile was wicked and her cheeks turned pink. "Never a camera when you need one."

I shook my head. "And I called you thoughtful," I muttered, which made her laugh more.

Later, I stretched out next to her in bed, my head against her hip. Clare was sitting up, reading, and her fingers traced my hairline. My eyes were heavy doors.

"I don't mind your staying," I said as they were closing.

"I know," she whispered.

I was blind and deaf, and Clare shook me awake for the telephone. I rubbed sleep from my eyes and looked at the clock, and didn't believe that it was seven a.m. I read the caller ID.

"Shit," I sighed. It was David, and I still had no idea what to say. As it turned out, he did the talking.

The voice on the line was nothing I'd heard from him before: trembling, fragile, and utterly lost. "The police are downstairs, Johnny. They want to come up."

27

Pitt Street runs through the heart of the Lower East Side, several miles south of where my brother lives, and usually a world away—though not that Tuesday morning. That morning, David's world had collapsed to the size of the narrow, windowless room where we sat and waited and watched a clock tick to ten. The Seventh Precinct station house is a new building, but the beige walls around us seemed a hundred years old, and the thick air older still. We were on one side of a metal table, Mike and I, and David in between. He was silent and motionless, and he had the blasted look of a man who's recently survived a terrible storm. Except the storm was just beginning, and survival was very much an open question.

In David's apartment, the dance had been all cordiality and caution, everyone polite and all the threats implicit. The two detectives sent to fetch him, Russo and Conlon, were large and tired-looking and almost bored with the proceedings. They'd been happy to wait until Mike and I arrived before talking to David, and they'd never uttered the word "arrest" or "suspect," never even hinted at them. They kept their explanations of why they'd come vague—something about help with an investigation, a Jane Doe they'd been trying to identify for over a week—and they acted as if a summons to a police station was an unremarkable thing, a bureaucratic nuisance no more important than an expired dog license.

It was only when Mike tested the waters of resistance, suggesting that David appear tomorrow instead, that they'd stirred. And then, without a word spoken—with only glances, furrowed brows, small coughs, and the shifting of feet—David's situation was plain. *We've come, so early in the morning, for you.* And so we went.

In the station house, the politesse thinned further, and in the way cops do—in the way that I used to do—they made us wait. Because waiting works. Worry turns into paranoid fantasy and a case of the sweats, stomach cramps turn into an urgent need to crap, and pretty soon out bursts full-blown terror. It was working on David—I could see it in the pallor and in the moist sheen on his forehead, and I could hear it in the rumblings of his gut—and nothing Mike or I said seemed to help. I wasn't sure how much was even getting through.

Mike squeezed David's shoulder and smiled, relaxed, imperturbable, and entirely confident. "We're going home soon," he said. I was hoping he was right when the door opened and a new cast of characters walked in. There were three of them, a man and two women.

The detectives were Leo McCue and Tina Vines, and they made an odd couple. McCue was about fifty and medium height, with a jutting belly and sagging smudges beneath his spaniel eyes. His mustache, like his hair, was bulky and mostly gray, and his fingers were thick and ragged-nailed. Vines was thirty, tall and precise and with the concave cheeks and restless look of an exercise junkie. Her blond hair was cut short, and her blue eyes were quick and unconvinced of anything. She wore her sleeves rolled, and there was a lot of muscle definition in her forearms.

The ADA was Rita Flores. She was small and rounded and forty, with glossy black hair cut to her shoulders, a full, pretty face, and nearly black eyes. Her suit was blue and careful, her shoes were flat, and it was easy to imagine the kindergarten art on her office wall, and the minivan in her garage—easy to cast her as the reliable car-pooler or the genial soccer mom. Which would have been a bad mistake. She introduced herself and I saw Mike's jaw tighten.

McCue and Vines sat across from us, and Rita Flores took a chair near the door. Vines had a laptop, and she switched it on. McCue smiled and made some noises about everything being informal and thanks for coming down. No one believed a word of it. Vines tapped away at something, and Flores stared at David. McCue went on.

"The autopsy says that, besides being shot in the face, our Jane Doe was beat up pretty bad before she died—probably a few days before, maybe a little longer. And then she was in the water five days so, all in all, she was a mess." He paused to look at us, his gaze lingering on David. Then he continued.

"We pulled prints from her apartment and matched them to Jane Doe's. We pulled DNA too—from a hairbrush—and we're pretty sure that'll confirm the print match. So we know our Jane is Holly Cade." He paused again, waiting for a question, daring us to ask. *Jane Doe? Holly who?*

Mike smiled affably and offered a different query. "Then you don't need Mr. March's help with identification?"

McCue smiled back. "Not with that, but with a few other things," he said, and he looked at Vines.

"Can you tell us something about this?" Vines asked, and she turned the laptop screen toward us and tapped a key. The laptop whirred and a video started playing, dim, but not too dim to see. David and Holly, in the hotel room and with no digital masking. "We hoped you could confirm that that's Holly's pussy you're eating."

"Jesus Christ," David breathed.

Mike put a hand on his arm. "Really, Ms. Flores . . ." he said.

From across the room, Flores raised her hands in a helpless shrug. *These crazy cops. What can you do?* The smile on her face was less than sympathetic.

McCue tapped a thick finger on the screen. "You see that, on her leg, near your face? To me, that looks like a happy red cat, but Tina disagrees. Maybe you can resolve it for us, Mr. March: was there a happy cat on that leg, or were you too busy to notice? And while you're at it, maybe you can explain what your relationship with Holly was—besides the pussy-eating, I mean—and why the fuck you didn't come forward and identify her for us?"

After which, there were theatrics. Mike was shocked and offended: "deliberately embarrassing" . . . "unnecessary" . . . "abusive" . . . "my client is here voluntarily." He slapped the table. McCue and Vines played bad cop and worse cop, respectively: "no sense of responsibility" . . . "something to hide" . . . "bullshit." They pointed and sneered, and Rita Flores said little but somehow assumed the mien of Darth Vader. Only David and I were silent—I because I had nothing to say, and David because he was, for the moment, incapable of speech. He stared at the screen and his face was paper white. I reached over and turned the laptop around, away from him. Rita Flores watched me with glittering eyes.

When Mike felt he'd defended his turf sufficiently, he cleared his throat and became all affability and reason again. "As it turned out, detectives, you preempted our call to you by just a few hours. We were waiting for Mr. March—the other Mr. March—to complete his report."

McCue and Vines spoke together, in a torrent of disbelief, but Flores interrupted them. "By all means, counselor, I'd love to hear what you and the other Mr. March have to say."

And Mike told the story—of David's brief and limited relationship with Cassandra, of the phone calls and threats, of his intent to pursue legal action against her if necessary, of him hiring me and me finding Holly, and of reading in the papers about the Williamsburg Mermaid.

"My client was shocked by the news, and upset and frightened too—and the direction of your investigation would seem to bear out his fears. So we elected to wait a few days before contacting the police, and in that time to do what we could to identify other reasonable avenues that an investigation might pursue. As John's report makes clear, there are several."

He was good at the telling, better than good, and he made the sequence of events—the reasoning, the decisions, and the actions taken—seem entirely logical, if not inevitable. But despite Mike's delivery, the story itself remained a tough sell. He knew it, and so did Rita Flores and the cops.

Flores smiled ruefully. "I've got to get you in front of my law students, counselor, because that was frigging great. Really, you live up to your reputation. But the sad fact is, after all the magic words, it's still just a sow's ear. It's still Holly Cade blackmailing your client, him hiring a PI—his own brother, no less—to find her, and her turning up dead. It's still him with motive and opportunity."

"Are you saying that you consider my client a suspect, Ms. Flores?"

She waved a hand. "This is still just a friendly chat, counselor, and I'm still waiting to hear from your investigator." There was only a little irony in how she said it. Mike turned to me, and so did everyone else.

"It was a dangerous life," I said, and I walked them through my investigation, and all that I'd learned about Holly's anonymous, often extreme, sexual encounters, the secret recordings, the pressure she exerted on her partners, the interrogation sessions, the abusive former boyfriend, the current one who was a violent ex-con, and the possibility that someone had been using her videos for blackmail. I could tell by the glances they exchanged and the notes they took that much of it was news. Rita Flores looked at me again and I felt the weight of her dark eyes.

McCue sighed dramatically and shook his head. "I've heard shit about you, and none of it good, but nobody said you were stupid enough for this—jumping into an active investigation with both feet. . . ." He shook his head some more. "We know you talked to the neighbor, and to the sister in Connecticut, but I want a list of everybody else: names, addresses, phone numbers, everything. We need to figure out how bad you fucked things up."

"I know my business, McCue—I documented everything, and nothing was fucked up."

"Right." Vines snorted. "The fact that you'd mess with an open case tells me you don't know shit. I can only imagine how many witnesses you screwed with."

I took a deep breath. "Check my notes, talk to the people I talked to. I didn't screw with any of them. I didn't lead, coax, or coach anyone."

Vines ignored me. "And God knows what you did to the evidence."

"Evidence of what?" I snapped, and Mike cleared his throat. "I was nowhere near any physical evidence."

"No?" McCue asked. "What about when you tossed Holly's apartment?"

I shook my head. "That wasn't me," I said.

Mike coughed again and looked at Flores. "As John said, we're happy to share information—" Vines snorted. Mike ignored her. "And it seems we've developed some that you haven't come across yet."

"It's not so hard when you know who the vic is," Vines said.

Mike looked at Flores. "I realize there's a lot to think about in what John had to say."

"A lot of speculation," McCue said, "a lot of guesswork."

Mike continued. "A lot of reasonable doubt to look into, and we're pleased to help in any way we can. But we could be more helpful if we knew a little more about the state of the investigation."

McCue's eyebrows leapt to his hairline. "You have some nerve, asking—" Flores cut him off.

"We're all playing our cards close, counselor, and I guess that's only natural at this point." She looked at McCue. "On the other hand, Leo, I don't think there's harm in a little sharing—provided Mr. Metz is willing to do the same."

Mike nodded. "Within reason."

Vines glared and McCue's jaw tightened. "What do you want to know?" he rumbled.

"The video you showed us—where did you get it?"

McCue looked at Flores, who nodded. "We got a DVD in the mail. The footage was on it, and so was a shot of March's driver's license."

"You know where it came from?"

McCue shook his head. "The envelope was postmarked Manhattan, but it had Holly's return address on it."

"Was there anything else inside," Mike asked. "A note, perhaps?" McCue thought for a while, and shook his head.

"An anonymous tip," I said. "That's breathtaking police work."

Vines nearly came out of her chair. "The fuck was that, asshole?"

"It didn't strike you as a little convenient? Maybe even suspicious?"

"Which means we're supposed to ignore it?" McCue's face reddened. "That'd be fucking great police work."

"Not ignore it," Mike said, "but given what you know now, about someone using Holly's videos for blackmail, I'd expect that you'd look at it a little differently."

Vines sneered. "Differently how?"

I answered before Mike could. "You ever consider that maybe your DVD came from the blackmailer—who maybe had something to do with Holly's death, and therefore has every reason to set my brother up to take the heat?"

Vines started to snap back, but Flores cut her off. "We'll look at all of this, counselor, and very closely, I promise," she said. Then she looked at David.

"And now, what about you, Mr. March? We've talked a lot about you today, but we haven't actually heard you talk."

Mike nodded at him, and David looked at Rita Flores. His voice, once he found it, was quiet but even. "Mike and John have laid out the facts, and I can't add to them. But if you want to hear me say I had nothing to do with this woman's death, then I'm saying it. I don't know what happened to her, and I had nothing to do with what happened to her." Flores nodded vaguely and McCue spoke.

"Do you own a gun, Mr. March?"

David didn't flinch. "No."

"Can you account for your time two weeks ago today, Mr. March?" he asked. And David walked them through that day. It was the same story he'd told me, and I knew they would see the same holes.

McCue made notes, and looked up at David. "And your wife can confirm that you were home all evening?" Something in his voice raised the hairs on the back of my neck.

"Yes," David said.

"So she was with you the whole time?" McCue asked. Mike caught the bad vibe too and interrupted.

"I think Mr. March's answer was clear," he said, before David could answer.

McCue swapped looks with Vines and Flores, but went on to other things. "From what you—or your lawyer—said, it sounds like Holly's telephone calls were mostly about wanting to see you again." David nodded. "No other topics of conversation?"

David looked puzzled, and the bad vibe returned. "Only that one, and the . . . threats."

McCue nodded. "So she never mentioned being pregnant?"

The silence afterward was expectant, just waiting to be filled by sounds of rending metal and breaking glass. David's face went from white to gray, and his mouth opened and closed, but nothing came out. I put my hand on his back. Mike looked at Flores and tapped his finger on his chin. His face was blank and his voice was icy.

"You want to explain that?"

She shrugged. "ME said she was pregnant, though not by much—four weeks maybe."

Mike's brow twitched. "Four weeks. She might not have known herself."

"It's hard to ask her, though, so we're asking your client."

David took a noisy breath. "She never said anything like that."

"Then would you mind giving us some DNA," Flores asked, "to eliminate you as the father?"

Mike answered for him. "The question is whether he knew Holly was pregnant, and the answer to that is *no*. I think DNA is a little premature."

"A conversation for another day, then," Flores said. "But back to who knew what about Holly's pregnancy . . ." Flores nodded at Vines, who tapped away on the laptop and turned the screen to face us.

A video played, and this time it was well lit, and the star was fully clothed. It was another hidden camera shot, skewed and looking up from roughly knee height. In the background there were windows covered by a metal gate, and in the foreground there was a woman. She had dark, wiry hair, and big eyes in a pale, pinched face. The sound quality was poor, but Stephanie's words were distinct.

"Leave him alone, you fucking bitch. Leave my husband alone."

A haughty laugh came from somewhere off camera, and I knew that it was Holly's. From across the room, Rita Flores spoke to David. Through the rushing in my ears, her voice sounded much farther away.

"Where is your wife now, Mr. March?" she asked.

Something shattered in the kitchen, a loud piece of crockery, and we heard David curse. Mike Metz shook his head.

"I feel like breaking stuff, myself," he said. His voice was low, and he was staring out of David's living room window at the white and gray patchwork of Central Park. The bare tree limbs were like a fog over the landscape, and something like a fog had settled over my brain since we left the precinct house on Pitt Street. I rubbed my face with both hands but it did no good.

"We're exactly where I didn't want to be," Mike said. "Off balance, surprised, and playing catch-up." He sighed heavily, loosened his tie, and pushed his shirtsleeves to his elbows. "And catching up to Flores won't be easy."

"What was she doing there, anyway?" I asked. "It's early for an ADA to show up."

"She was there to protect her interests," Mike said. "An ugly killing, a wealthy, high-profile suspect, and plenty of sex, all in a bigtime media market like New York: if this gets to a trial, she knows it's six months of cable TV frenzy, minimum, and afterward a book deal and

God knows what else. But she knows it could just as easily turn into a career-killer, and she can't afford any fuckups. So she was there to be careful, and to send a message."

"That being?"

"That she's serious, but that she might be willing to deal; that otherwise this could get seriously ugly for your brother; and—most of all—that she has all the cards."

"That video . . ."

"Fuck that video," he said vehemently. "I don't want a jury ever seeing that thing."

McCue and Vines had only played a snippet for us, but it was enough. Holly was doing some version of her interrogation act, and Stephanie was white, and shaking with anger.

I took a deep breath. "Surely we're a ways from that."

"Not as far as I'd like," he said.

Mike turned and paced the length of the room. It was a long walk, across an expanse of bleached hardwood floor and white carpet, and past low, sleek furniture in glass, polished stone, and white leather. Mike's face was pale and full of concentration.

"The particulars of Holly's life took them by surprise," I said. "That had to buy us something."

"It complicates things for them, so it buys time, though probably not a lot. They'll run down the stuff we gave them—they have to— but unless something jumps out at them, it'll be perfunctory. Make no mistake—it's David they like for this, or Stephanie, or both."

"I got that."

Mike's brows came together. "They're not so sure about you, either."

"I got that too. What do you want to do with this time we bought?"

"The first thing I want you to do is find Jamie Coyle."

I raised an eyebrow. "Coyle's going to be at the top of McCue's list of people to talk to."

"Exactly," Mike said, "and I don't want any more surprises. I want to know what he's got to say, and I don't want to hear it secondhand from Rita Flores."

"The cops won't be happy to see me around."

"Not in the slightest," Mike said, "but I don't think it can be helped."

"Easy for you to say—it's not your license they'll yank."

Mike squinted at me some more. "Your brother's skating on some very thin ice right now—it's not the time to get—"

I cut him off. "I know, I know," I said. "What if Coyle's in the wind?"

Mike looked out the window some more. "The best thing for your brother is a Coyle who confesses. Next best is a Coyle who cuts and runs."

"What about a Coyle who had nothing to do with Holly's death?"

He shook his head. "Bad news. Without a viable alternative, Flores will keep looking where she's looking now."

I stared up Fifth Avenue, and watched a bus slide past the Engineers' Gate at Ninetieth Street. I wasn't sure yet what case there was to make against Coyle, or if there was any at all, but I kept that to myself. Mike seemed to read my mind.

"If you've got someone else in mind, don't keep it secret," he said. "Because Flores is eager, and time is not on our side."

I shook my head. "You think she's going to make things more formal soon?"

"Probably. And after that, it won't keep quiet long. It may not keep quiet as it is. The longer David stays on Flores's radar, the more likely it is the press will get hold of it, one way or another."

"Are the cops releasing the identification?"

"Flores said they've notified the sister, but they're not making an announcement just yet."

We heard the clatter of silverware on tile, and another curse from David. I crossed the room to the hall and looked through the dining room into the kitchen. I saw a shadow move across the floor, but nothing else. I turned to Mike.

"So I look for Coyle; what about you?"

Mike ran a hand through his hair. "The first thing is to sit down with Stephanie, and figure out just what the fuck is going on." I nodded.

David had been very little help on that front. In the cab uptown he'd been blank-faced and silent. Back at his apartment, he'd sent the maid home and stood in the entrance foyer in a freefall of confusion. I'd guided him to the living room and sat him on a sofa. Mike had asked questions and David had groped for answers.

"What did Stephanie know about your affairs?"

"She knew there were other women, I don't know how. We didn't talk about it, not directly. Maybe once . . . I don't know. I didn't think she knew about Wren—she never said anything. I was wrong, I guess."

"Were you together all night that Tuesday?"

"She was here when I got home, but she left a little while later. She said she was going around the corner, to Eighty-sixth Street, to meet . . . I don't remember who, some friend of hers, to see a movie. I'm not sure when she got back—I'd had a couple of drinks, I guess, and I fell asleep. She was here around eleven-thirty, when I woke up, and she seemed fine to me."

"How would she have met Holly?"

"I don't know how they met—maybe Holly called her. I have no fucking idea."

"Do you think Stephanie could have—"

"No, absolutely not. Steph had nothing to do with this. Nothing."

His voice was a monotone, and he'd stared at the carpet the whole time, as if there was something hidden in the weave that only he could see. It was only when Mike asked about Holly being pregnant that David had looked up. His face was flushed, and for an instant there was a tiny, bitter smile.

"It's not me," he'd said.

Mike's voice was gentle. "Condoms fail."

"It's not me."

"And Holly never—"

"She never said a word about it."

"Could she have said something to Stephanie?" Mike had asked.

"I don't know what she said or didn't say, but Steph . . . she wouldn't believe it."

He'd gone to the kitchen after that, to make coffee.

Mike put his hands in his pockets and paced some more. "It didn't help that he lied to McCue," he said.

"About being here with Stephanie all evening? He was confused—he made a mistake."

Mike pursed his lips. "Call it what you want; the cops will see it as an alibi that doesn't stick."

"Whose alibi?"

He shook his head. "That's the question, isn't it?"

Mike and I turned as David reappeared. There was an empty creamer in his hand and a confounded look on his face.

"The coffee machine . . ." he said. His voice was vague and very tired.

"I'll get it," I said.

In the cavern of David's stone and steel kitchen, the remains of a skirmish: coffee beans scattered on the countertop, the coffee grinder empty, unplugged, tipped on its side, a box of filter papers on the floor, with a measuring spoon and David's coat. I picked up his coat and everything else, and I ground the beans. While I was waiting for the coffee to brew, I saw the bottle of vodka, uncapped beside the sink. Shit.

I found a tray and carried the coffee out. Mike and David had migrated to the dining room. They sat at the long oval table, and David stared at himself in the glass top. Mike looked as if he were waiting for an answer, though none seemed forthcoming.

"I'll call her myself, if you like, David, but she's got to be told what happened. And I've got to meet with her."

David sighed and hoisted himself up. "I'll do it, for chrissakes," he said, but he couldn't muster the energy for petulance. He left the room, and Mike looked at me.

"Has he been drinking?" Mike asked. I nodded. "He has a problem with that?"

"I don't know."

He picked up his coffee mug. "Beautiful," he muttered, "fucking beautiful."

David returned red-eyed and told us he hadn't reached Stephanie. Her cell was off, and all her parents would say was that she was out for the day. He'd left a message. Mike gave up on more questioning for the moment. He pulled on his coat and fished in his pockets for his gloves.

"You'll call if you get anything on Coyle?" he asked. I nodded and saw him to the door. "You've got to keep him together," he whispered, but he had no suggestions of how.

I found David in the kitchen, bottle in one hand, glass in the other.

"Maybe not the best idea now," I said.

He went to the fridge and held his glass under the ice dispenser. "Don't start," he said, but there was nothing behind it.

"You have things to do that will go better if you're sober."

"I called Stephanie. She wasn't there."

"I'm talking about calling Ned."

David covered his ice cubes, and then some. He took a gulp and leaned against the kitchen counter and sighed. "I told him I wasn't coming in."

"You need to tell him what's going on."

"What business is it of his?"

"You run M and A, David; Ned runs the firm. He needs to know what's happening, and what may happen. He needs to prepare."

"Prepare for what?" David looked up. His face was blotchy and his eyes were sunken. "What do I tell him to be ready for, Johnny? Me in handcuffs? Or Steph, maybe? Maybe both of us? What the fuck should he expect?" He rubbed his hand back and forth across his forehead.

"Just tell him what's going on."

He stared past my shoulder. "I don't know what's going on," he whispered.

I took the glass from him, and he didn't argue. "Do you want me to call?" I asked, and after a while he nodded. I emptied the glass in the sink and took him by the elbow. We went into the living room and I sat him on a long white sofa. He looked up at me.

"I didn't think . . . it would end up like this." His speech was slurred and his eyelids were teetering. I wasn't sure which *it* he was talking about.

"Don't be dramatic, David. It hasn't ended up like anything, yet. Nothing's ended."

"That video . . . Steph was so angry."

"Nothing's ended," I said again. "There are things we can do."

He took my wrist in his old man's hand, and I could feel the trembling up my arm. "Jesus," he sighed. "I am so tired."

I went to the kitchen to make the call, and when I came out again, David was asleep. His chin was on his chest and his breathing was heavy. Now and then he moaned and twitched, like a dog being chased in his dreams.

29

A jaundiced sunset was seeping through the clouds as I drove into Tarrytown, and it tinted the Hudson in the colors of a faded bruise. It was just past four; I'd come to see Kenny Hagen, maintenance manager of the Van Winkle Court condominiums, and Jamie Coyle's uncle. I turned west off Route 9, onto College Avenue, and worked my way toward the river. Walls of dirty snow were plowed up on the roadsides, and I missed two intersections but eventually found the place. It didn't look worth the trouble.

Van Winkle Court was an ugly circle of two-story garden apartment buildings, eight squat bunkers with mock brick siding and white vinyl trim. Except for a man with a salt spreader, working the footpaths between the buildings, the complex looked abandoned in the waning light. I watched the man roll the spreader to a flight of stairs, bump it down to a basement doorway, and go inside. I got out of my rented Nissan and followed.

I went through a metal door into a low cinderblock corridor. To my right was a storage room, and lots of tools. A short man in a green jacket was inside, parking a salt spreader beside a pile of folded tarpaulins. He looked at me and pulled off his gloves. His accent was heavy Spanish, and his English was limited.

"Help you?" he said.

"Kenny Hagen?"

The man pointed. "Down there Kenny." I nodded and went down the hall.

I found Kenny in the office he shared with a squad of old kitchen ranges. They were dented and scorched, and layered in grease and ancient food, and so was he. Kenny was close to sixty, thin and lined, and his face was ruddy where it wasn't smudged with dirt. His grimy plaid sleeves were rolled over a thermal undershirt, and there was an old Screaming Eagle tattoo on the back of one hand. A dollop of what looked like tomato sauce made a red comma on his chin. He was fiddling with a soldering iron and a little motor when I came in, and the air smelled of hot metal. He looked up from his card-table desk and set the motor down. His eyes were small and blue behind taped wire glasses. He ran a veined hand through his white hair.

"You need something?" he asked. His voice was deeper than his size suggested, and I figured it was the cigarettes. There was a full ashtray on the table, and a pack of Marlboros next to it. He propped the soldering iron on the rim of the ashtray, and fired up a smoke with a white plastic lighter.

"I'm looking for Jamie," I said.

He squinted at me. "Jamie who?"

"Jamie your nephew."

"Uh-huh, and you are who?"

"A friend of a friend. I'm trying to get in touch."

Kenny nodded. "Yeah? Well, so am I. So if you find the prick, give me a shout."

"I thought he worked here."

"Only till I see him next."

There was a plastic chair in front of Kenny's table, and I pulled it out and sat. "Why's that?" I asked.

"How about for not showing up to work for a couple of weeks running, and not calling in to say what's what? How about for not returning my hundred freaking phone calls? How about for screwing over the only relative he has left in the world, who went out on a limb to get him this job in the first place? Those enough reasons for you?" He punctuated his speech with the orange end of his cigarette, and little bits of ash floated in the air when he was done.

I nodded. "You know where he lives?"

"He used to live right here, in the unit at the end of the hall, but he hasn't been around in weeks."

"You have a phone number for him?"

Kenny rattled off Coyle's cell number. "Nobody answers, though."

"Any other family he'd be in touch with, or maybe visit?"

"His old man drank himself to death twenty years ago, and we lost my sister, God bless her, three years back—so, like I said, I'm it."

"How about his friends?"

Kenny pulled a hand down his face, and left a streak of grease along his jawline. He shrugged. "You'd know more about that than me—I didn't think he had any." Kenny paused and made a thinking face. "There was a guy upstate, maybe, a guy he was inside with."

"You have a name?" Kenny blew smoke and shook his head. "A telephone number or address?"

Another head shake. "I don't know—maybe he's somewhere in Buffalo."

I nodded. Buffalo. "You don't know Jamie's girlfriend?"

He lifted his eyebrows. "He has a girlfriend?"

I didn't bother to explain. "Jamie leave anything behind when he took off?"

"Check it out for yourself," Kenny said, and he reached into the pocket of the big orange parka that hung on the back of his chair. He fished out a noisy ring of keys and stepped around the table.

"Come on," he said. He went clinking down the hall, and I followed.

The apartment was dark and small, not even three hundred square feet and all of it visible from the doorway. To the right was a kitchenette, built into what had been a closet. Next to it was a bathroom, hardly larger than the airplane variety. There was a mattress on the floor, laid out beneath a narrow window set high up on the wall. That wall and all the others were a dingy white, and the floor was gray vinyl. The bare ceiling bulb cast a light like dirty water.

Kenny told me to close the door when I was through, and it didn't take me long. But for dust and the smell of heating oil, the place was empty. Kenny was back at his desk when I passed his office, looking at his motor and blowing smoke. I didn't bother to say goodbye.

I got into my rental, pulled out of the Van Winkle lot, and headed back toward Route 9. And stopped when I'd driven fifty yards. There was an alcove in the snow on the other side of the street, a void where a car had been excavated, and I pulled my Nissan in a tight turn and into the snug space. I took out my binoculars and settled in. It was all but dark now, but the path lighting around Van Winkle Court was good enough. I'd be able to see that lying bastard Kenny when he came up the basement stairs.

As an actor, Kenny was right up there with Gene Werner. He'd never pressed me about who I was or how I knew Jamie or what I wanted from him, and he'd never once told me to go away. The line about Jamie's pal in Buffalo was matched in its dubiousness only by the look of surprise he dressed up in when I mentioned Jamie's girl-friend. Above all, Kenny had been just too ready to let me poke around in Jamie's apartment. He'd wanted me to believe that Jamie had moved out—and I did—but I also believed that he was still close by, and that Kenny knew where. I cracked the windows, killed the lights and engine, and zipped my parka to the neck.

As it grew later, traffic picked up at Van Winkle Court, and more lights came on in the brick-faced boxes, but no one came up the base-ment stairs. While I waited and watched, I thought about my conver-sation with Ned.

He'd been surprised to hear from me—it had been eighteen months—but he knew from my tone that I hadn't called to chat. He listened quietly as I explained that David had become involved in a murder investigation, that the victim was a woman David had had a sexual relationship with, that David—or Stephanie—might become a suspect in her death, and that if there was an arrest, the press coverage would be vast and voracious.

The news shocked him—how could it not?—but Ned hadn't risen to the top at Klein & Sons by being panicky or dumb, and he didn't start then. He'd asked smart questions, and had neither pressed me on the ones I wouldn't answer nor pushed me into wild speculation on the ones I couldn't. I heard him taking rapid notes throughout. He asked about lawyers, and something relaxed a little in his voice when I told him that Mike Metz was representing David.

"How is David doing?" he asked.

"That's why I'm calling. I have to go out, but I don't want to leave him alone. He's been drinking."

"Steph isn't there?"

"No, and I'm not sure when she will be. Or if."

"Jesus Christ." He sighed. "I'll send Liz up."

Ned rang off and an hour later my older sister had arrived. I met her in the foyer. She wore a black coat over a black suit, and her blond hair was swept straight back from her forehead. Her heels were low, but tall enough to bring her to my height, and her green eyes were narrow and uncertain. Her usual detached cool had deserted her, and her strong, handsome features were set in a mask of worry. On Liz it looked much like anger, and it reminded me uncomfortably of our mother.

"Where is he?" she asked. She spoke in a husky whisper.

"Asleep, on the sofa. With any luck, he'll stay that way for a while."

"And what should I do with him when he wakes?"

I shrugged. "Hang out. Give him something to eat. Keep him from doing anything stupid."

She shook her head. "That's apparently easier said than done. Will he be surprised to see me?"

"Probably."

"And pissed off?"

"Definitely."

Liz shook her head. "Excellent. Ned said he'd been drinking."

I nodded. "Try not to let him do that anymore."

"Am I supposed to restrain him?"

"Do the best you can."

I pulled on my coat and Liz caught my arm. "Jesus Christ, Johnny, this is dramatic even for you. We don't hear word one for over a year, and all of a sudden you're in the middle of a *murder*—and with David, of all people. What the fuck is going—"

I cut her off. "What can I tell you? Shit happens. Right now I'm trying to keep it from happening to David." I tried to get my arm back, but Liz held on.

" 'Shit happens' isn't good enough. How did he get himself into . . . all *this*?"

"There's no short answer to that," I'd said, "maybe no answer at all. But you can try asking David when he gets up."

There was movement on the basement stairs and I picked up my binoculars. I saw a flash of orange: Kenny Hagen in his big parka walking carefully along a footpath. There was something under his arm, and it took me a moment to make it out. It turned out to be two things: a carton of Marlboros and a box of doughnuts. He walked two buildings south and went down another flight of steps and fished his key ring from his pocket. He fiddled with the lock and went inside. He was in there for twenty minutes by my watch, and when he came out he was empty-handed.

He was descending the stairs to his own basement when a battered brown Ford rolled past me and into the Van Winkle parking lot. Two people got out, and I didn't need the binoculars to recognize McCue's aggressive gut or Vines's cropped blond hair. They headed right for Kenny Hagen's building. Half an hour later, Vines came out. She got into the Ford and started the engine, but didn't go anywhere. In a minute or two the windows fogged, and she became a hazy silhouette behind the wheel.

She sat there for fifteen minutes, and emerged again when a Tarry-town police cruiser pulled into the space beside hers. A uniformed cop got out and shook hands with her, and a minute later another crappy sedan pulled up. A big guy who might have been one of the cops in David's apartment that morning climbed out. He spoke with Vines and the Tarrytown cop, and the three of them walked toward Kenny's basement. And then the big guy bent his head and said something to Vines. She stopped and turned and he pointed at my car, and Vines began to walk—then jog—toward me.

I fired the engine, shoved the car into R, and prayed that no one was coming up the street. The Nissan swerved and slid as I popped out of the space and onto the road, and I saw Vines sprint across the Van Winkle parking lot. Her coat was open and she was reaching inside and I flicked on the car lights and hit the brights. Her hand went to her eyes and I tapped the gas. For one sick instant my wheels whined and spun and rooster tails of sandy brown snow flew up. Then the car shuddered and slewed, and I was gone.

I called Mike from the Saw Mill.

"I don't think she made me, though I'll find out soon enough if she did."

"And Coyle?" Mike asked.

"He's gone, but not far, and I'm pretty sure Uncle Kenny knows where. I'll give it another go tomorrow, assuming McCue and Vines haven't beaten me to him or yanked my license by then."

"Not too early tomorrow, though," Mike said.

"Why not?"

"David finally got in touch with Stephanie. He told her what happened this morning, and explained that there are questions she has to answer. She said she'd come back to town tomorrow morning, to talk."

"It's about time," I said, "but what does it have to do with me?"

There was a long silence at Mike's end, and then he cleared his throat. "She says you're the only one she'll talk to."

30

The maid met me at the door. Her lined face was empty of expression, but her blue eyes were anxious and more than a little curious. I knew how she felt. She led me through the foyer and down a hallway, and left me to wait in a khaki-colored room. The walls were mostly bookshelves, and the furniture was low-slung and leather. The views were of the park, a wedge of the Guggenheim, and blue, blue skies. It was ten-thirty, and traffic was contentious on Fifth Avenue, but no street sounds intruded on the apartment's thick quiet.

David, I knew, was at work, though from the message Liz had left me, I doubted he was working well.

"He started drinking at around six, and there was nothing I could do to stop him. I stayed until eleven, at which point he passed out and I went home. He's a bad drunk, and the whole thing left me wishing I was an only child. You and Ned owe me, and an explanation of what the hell is going on would be a good start."

Around six: that would've been after he'd spoken to Stephanie. I could only imagine how that conversation had gone, and reaching for a bottle wasn't an incomprehensible reaction. And what had he made of Stephanie's insistence on talking only to me? Mike had repeated it twice, and I still didn't get it.

I shook my head and wandered around the room. The bookshelves were filled with slender, buff-colored volumes of identical dimensions. They were all about modern architecture and all in Italian, and to the best of my knowledge David was ignorant of both. Of course, I'd learned lately that when it came to my brother—and his wife—the best of my knowledge wasn't very good. Maybe he was fluent in Italian, and had a thing for I. M. Pei, or maybe Stephanie had. Maybe it was just the decorator. What did I know?

There were photos on some of the shelves: David and Stephanie smiling stiffly at a black-tie function; Stephanie in the yard of their East Hampton place, looking washed out against the red front door; David, Ned, and Liz in the cockpit of Ned's sailboat. They were soaked, and Ned and Liz were grinning widely. The door opened and Stephanie came in.

She was pale and barefoot, and dressed in jeans and a gray wool sweater. She wore her hair loose. It fell in a dark wave to her shoulders, framing her sharp features and softening them. Her eyes were red and shadowed and larger than ever, and her face had lost its typical tics and tensions. She had instead a remote, distracted look, like a convalescent, preoccupied with the waxing and waning of her symptoms and pains. Her steps were stiff and careful across the room, as if her bones were hollow and a sudden gust might carry her away. She curled in a deep chair and tucked her small white feet beneath her. She had a glass of water, and she sipped from it and held it in her lap. There was something almost shy in the way she looked at me.

"It's not a conversation I expected to have," Stephanie said, and managed the thinnest of smiles. There was a tremble in her voice, and a deep fatigue.

"You and me both," I said.

"It's hard to believe the mess he's made of everything—that woman, the videos, and now this. I should be worried about the police, but I keep thinking of TV, of all things—the way the cameras chase people down the street . . . what they'd do to us. I try to think of who would still speak to me, whom I could look in the eye." Stephanie shook her head and picked at a seam on her jeans. "Do you know why I wanted to talk to you?"

"Not because we've been so close."

Stephanie shook her head. "It's more because we never pretended to be," she said. "We've never liked each other—" I started to speak but she waved it away. "Don't bother, John, not now. We've never liked each other, but we've never faked it, either; we've never lied to each other that way. In fact, you're the only one in this nightmare who hasn't lied to me."

"Mike Metz—"

"I don't know Mike Metz from Adam. Maybe he's as good a lawyer as everyone says—I pray to God he is—and maybe when I get to know him I'll trust him. But right now he's just a voice on the phone, and I don't have it in me to talk to a stranger about this, not yet. What I want now is someone I know, and someone who won't bullshit me."

"Even if it's someone you don't particularly like?"

Again a fragile smile. "Strange, huh, trusting a person you don't like?"

"Not the strangest thing."

The little smile turned rueful, and then disappeared. "Not as strange as being married to a person you don't trust, for instance."

"It happens," I said, and I took a deep breath and took out my notebook. "There are questions I have to ask."

She nodded. "And I don't want to be arrested. So if that's the price, go on."

If only it were that simple, I thought, and then I asked and she answered.

"I guess I've known, in a general way, for a while," she said. "I didn't catch him in bed with one of them, or anything, but he gets a certain tone, irritated and guilty at the same time, when I ask an inconvenient question about where he's been or where he'll be. And he has a certain look sometimes when he comes home, furtive and a little smug. It took me a few years to catch on, but eventually I did. I suppose there was a part of me that didn't want to know. Not surprising, I guess.

"I found out about this one not long after New Year's. She left a message—'David, why don't you call?' or something like that. David had seemed more tense than usual, and he'd been drinking more, and I knew something was eating at him. Then I heard that message, and I knew what."

"Did you say anything to him?"

She managed another smile, this one bitter. "You think there'd be much point to that?"

"Probably not."

"I didn't think so, either, but I tried anyway. He actually got angry at me—*he* got angry at *me*—and then he just lied. 'Nothing's wrong, busy with the new job,' things along those lines. I knew it was crap, but . . ." The muscles in Stephanie's jaw tightened as she worked her anger back into its pen.

"How did you meet her?"

Her face darkened, and she shook her head. "She was downstairs, if you can believe it. It was a Thursday night and I was coming back from yoga. I came up to the front door, and there was a woman in the lobby, shouting at the doorman. Her voice was all breathy and theatrical, but it was familiar too, though I didn't know from where. For some reason, I stayed out on the sidewalk and listened. And then I realized she was shouting about David.

" 'Don't lie to me. Don't tell me he's not home when I just saw him go in. March—Apartment Ten-A.' She sounded crazy, and then I knew who it was. She stormed out after that, and passed right by me. I was shocked by how she looked . . . how beautiful she was."

"You spoke to her?"

"Not then."

"Then how—"

"I followed her," Stephanie said, and her cheeks colored.

"Followed her where?"

"To Eighty-sixth Street, and onto the subway, and then I followed when she got off in Brooklyn, all the way back to her apartment." Stephanie saw something in my face and shook her head. "I didn't plan it—it just happened. I couldn't take my eyes off her, and I . . . had to do it."

Shit. "Is that when you spoke to her—at her apartment?"

"That was the next day. All that night, I thought about . . ." She paused, and squeezed her eyes shut, and pinched the bridge of her nose. She said something under her breath—a curse maybe—and looked up. "David was worse than ever that night, snapping at everything I said, and drinking. . . . When it was all abstract, when the women were faceless, it was easier to pretend. But hearing her voice, seeing her—I couldn't take it. I couldn't stop thinking about her, about the two of them, and I had to *do* something. So the next day I went to see her."

"What happened?"

"It was terrible. She was laughing, and . . . I never saw a camera, but David told me she recorded it."

"We only saw a part of it. I need to know the whole thing."

Stephanie hunched her shoulders and drank some water. "I said my name in the intercom, and she knew who I was right away, and started laughing. She let me in to her apartment, and I sat, and for the longest time she didn't say anything. She just stared at me and waited. The apartment was horrible—tiny and dark—and that building . . . But somehow, the way she looked at me, she made me feel—I don't know—as if I were underdressed or something. Finally, I just said what I had to say."

"Which was?"

"I told her to leave David alone. I told her to find her own husband and to stop harassing mine. She didn't say anything for a while; she just kept watching me, as if I were some sort of specimen. And then she laughed again. I got angry—angrier—and said some other things."

"What things?"

"I cursed at her, and she laughed harder. Finally she started talking."

"About what?"

Stephanie looked out the window, at a solitary figure slowly circling the reservoir—a plodding black shape against the blue-white snow. Her face stiffened and ridges appeared at her jawline again. "She asked questions . . . about me and David."

"What questions?"

"She asked why I let my husband fuck other women." The words caught in her throat and a red patch appeared on her neck. "She asked how I could be married to him and let that happen—why I'd married him in the first place if I was going to let him do that. Why I stayed married. Why I put up with it all.

"Then she asked if I'd driven him to it, if a part of me liked the idea . . . liked to picture him . . ." Stephanie's throat closed up and she shook her head and looked at me. "She asked if I even knew what David . . . liked, if he talked to me about what he did with his women. With her. If he ever did those things to me. She said she'd tell me about it, if I wanted. She said she'd teach me."

My stomach twisted and my neck prickled with cold sweat. Stephanie sniffed, and drank some water. "There was more, but I think you get the drift."

"What did you do?" I asked.

The little smile came again, and lingered. Stephanie's eyes held mine. "She was sitting there, smiling, so beautiful . . . it was hideous. She was hideous, and I wanted to kill her. I wanted to hit her with something, or wring her neck, and if I'd had a gun then, I would have shot her right there."

My mouth was dry and it was hard to get the words out. "What did you do?" I asked again.

Her laugh was bitter and angry, an echo of a more familiar Stephanie. "What I did was cry, John. I cried like an infant and I ran out of there. I ran until I found a taxi, and I cried all the way home." Stephanie shook her head and wiped a hand across her eyes.

"When did you see her again?"

"I didn't."

"Never?"

Stephanie squinted at me. "Never."

"You didn't fight, there in her apartment? You didn't hit her?"

"No, for God's sake. I wish I *had* slapped her—I wish I could've—but I didn't touch her."

"There was no violence?"

She sat up and her face hardened. "I said I never touched her."

"Did you threaten her?"

"I . . . I was angry. I yelled and cursed and told her to leave us alone. I might have said some other things—"

"What other things?"

"I don't remember."

"Did you threaten to harm her? To—"

"I told you, I don't remember everything I said."

I nodded. "Did she have any signs of injury that you saw? Any bruises or cuts?"

She squinted again. "No, nothing like that."

"What else did she say to you, besides the questions?"

She shook her head. "That was all. There was nothing else."

I looked at my notes. "Did you tell David what you'd done?"

"I . . . I was embarrassed."

"Did her calls stop?"

"I don't think she called here again, but it didn't seem to help David much. He was worse than ever, almost panicked. I didn't know what to do, and then he went to you."

"How did you know about that?"

Stephanie stared at the rug. "I saw you together, at breakfast. I . . . followed him."

"You've been doing a lot of that."

She colored again. "I'm not proud of it. I was frantic—I didn't know what was happening to him, or what to do. Then I saw the two of you, and I thought that you were involved somehow with all this—that you had somehow dragged David into it. I don't know—I wasn't thinking straight." She looked up at me. "It was pitiful, I know."

I took a deep breath. "Tell me about that Tuesday," I said.

"Which Tuesday?"

"Three weeks ago yesterday. It would've been the Tuesday after you saw Holly—the day before you saw David and me at breakfast. Take me through that day."

And, with starts and stops and stumbling, she did. Like David, she'd spent much of that day downtown—in and out of her office, at meetings, and on conference calls. And as with David, it was her after-work hours that were more difficult to account for. Presumably, there were people from her yoga class who could testify to her presence there, but would the clerks in the shops on upper Madison recall her—another well-dressed woman who'd browsed but hadn't bought? Would they swear to it in court? And then there was her trip to the movies.

"I walked down to Seventy-second and Third. I was supposed to meet Bibi Shea, but I wasn't in the mood, so I called her and canceled."

"So you were by yourself at the movies?"

"I didn't feel like talking." Shit.

"You walked there?" Nod. "It was a cold night."

"I wanted the air."

"Did you pay cash for the ticket?" Another nod. "What was the film?" Stephanie told me the name, and the time she thought the show had started, and the time it had gotten out. She didn't remember the previews. "Did you see anyone you knew?"

"No."

"What was David doing all that time?"

"As far as I know, he was home. He was here when I left, and here when I got back, asleep—or passed out."

I paged through my notebook and ran her through the dates and times once more. Then I looked up.

"Besides her questions, what else did Holly say?"

She shook her head. "You asked me that already, and I told you—she didn't say anything."

"She didn't tell you anything?"

Stephanie shook her head impatiently. "No."

I took a deep breath. "She didn't tell you she was pregnant?"

Stephanie's brows came together and her lips pursed. "No," she said after a while.

"The police dropped that on us yesterday. David didn't mention it?"

Stephanie touched her fingers to her neck. Her smile surprised me. "It must've slipped his mind," she said, and she chuckled bitterly.

"They want to know if he could be the father. And I imagine they're wondering how you would've reacted to that news."

"Did David have an answer?"

"He said it wasn't his, and that if Holly had said so, you wouldn't have believed it."

"He wasn't lying about that; I wouldn't have believed it."

"Because he's sterile?"

Stephanie's brow went up and she nodded slowly at me. "It's not the word the doctors used, but it amounts to the same thing. His sperm count is low, and the few that he has don't swim, and they die if you look at them funny. He told you?"

"David doesn't tell me much. I guessed."

"We got tested a few years ago. We'd been trying and . . ." She shook her head.

"I'm sorry."

"For what?" she said quickly, and her eyes narrowed. "Clearly, it's worked out for the best."

I paged through my notebook one last time. Stephanie stood and dug a brown plastic bottle from the pocket of her jeans. She popped the lid, and tipped a white pill out.

"He's got vodka; I've got Ativan. But at least mine's prescription." She put the pill on her tongue and drained her glass and set it on an end table. "Are you through?"

"I am," I said. But Stephanie wasn't. She folded herself in the chair again and looked at me.

"Did he say anything about why?" she asked.

"Why?"

"Why this whole thing. Why these women? Why the lying? Why he's bound and determined to turn his life—our lives—into shit?" Her voice was firm and steady, as if she'd rehearsed her questions. She didn't wait for an answer.

"You know what surprised me as much as finding out about the women? It was realizing that David wanted me to find him out. He was like a kid with a secret, squirming to tell. I don't know if he wanted to see what I would do—if I would get mad, or leave, or forgive him—I don't know what he wanted. I just know there's a part of him that's been waiting for all this."

"For all what?"

"For this. For some kind of punishment."

"Punishment for . . . what?"

"You think I understand it?" she said, shaking her head. "But he's been this way as long as I've known him—one part thinking that he's forever been shortchanged, and another that thinks any good thing that happens is more than he deserves. And that's the part that's been waiting—to get caught, to be punished." Stephanie closed her eyes and rubbed her temples. "It's a twisted quid pro quo with him: every good thing matched with some self-inflicted pain. I should have known something big was coming when he finally got the M and A job." She looked up and studied my face.

"You have no clue, do you?" she asked. I shook my head. "Of course you don't—how could you? All you Marches, in your own little worlds."

"Have you talked to David about this?"

"Not for years now," Stephanie said, and her mouth curved angrily. "Maybe Holly had better luck—she was good with the questions. I'm still working on the one she asked me: why I put up with it."

"Why do you?"

If she'd told me to go to hell, or just kept stiff-faced and silent, it wouldn't have surprised me, but I didn't expect the quiet, level voice, or the answer that I got.

"It's the deal I made, isn't it? Or what's left of it. It's what I've negotiated down to." Her hands found each other in her lap, and they held on tight, but her voice stayed even. "When you look back on it—when you look at it all together—it seems crazy, I know. Crazy to stay. But it didn't happen all together. It was a gradual process, like erosion.

"Little by little, things turn out to be less than you thought—every year, always a little less. So one day you realize there won't be any children, and another day you realize your husband doesn't really like you. Later on, you find you don't like him much, either, and wonder if maybe he's not a little crazy. And that takes the sting out a bit when you think about the children you won't have, and when you find out about the other women. It helps you care a bit less.

"It's a slow whittling away, but with each new disappointment, with each hope you abandon, you strike a new bargain with yourself. You'll trade up to a larger apartment, you think, maybe in a better building, or you'll buy a larger beach house. You'll spend an extra week on St. Bart's this year, or throw yourself a bigger birthday party. You'll go for the seven-sixty Beemer, instead of the five-fifty. And after a while, leaving becomes . . . tricky. Apartments, houses, vacations, all the friends and acquaintances . . . In the end it comes down to money, I guess, and that leaving is so expensive and complicated. So scary.

"There were times I thought I'd reached the end of my rope—I thought so when I heard her voice on the telephone—but each time I found the rope had no end. There's always another strand you convince yourself to cling to, however frayed. And it just keeps unraveling, miles of it, year after year . . . down, down, down."

Outside, the sun had shifted in the sky, and a bright beam came through the window. The unfiltered light fell on Stephanie's face and turned it to a mask, taut, Kabuki white, and brittle. Only her will, and maybe the Ativan, kept it from crumbling. She looked at me.

"I'm used to the erosion, John, but this is . . . too fast. We're not ready for it, David and I—we're not ready."

31

I was on hold for Mike Metz when Clare came through the door. She had a cell phone in her ear and newspapers under her arm.

"Yeah, Amy, Berkeley's heaven on earth, you've been saying it for years. But it's so crunchy granola, and besides, what would—" Amy, whoever Amy was, was saying something, and Clare put down her papers and slipped off her coat while she listened. She smiled at me and ran a hand through her hair, which rippled like a silk sheet. She pulled up the sleeves of her black turtleneck, and her arms were white and smooth. Mike Metz came on the line.

"You spoke to her?" he asked. He sounded slightly out of breath. I carried the phone into the bedroom, along with my notebook, and I told it all to Mike. When I was through, he had questions, and when I'd answered all of those he was quiet.

"So no one has an alibi for anything," he said finally. "That's great."

"She's not in bad shape for business hours; neither is David."

"It's not business hours I'm worried about. The ME is placing time of death somewhere between seven p.m. Tuesday and midnight Wednesday."

"That's new."

"I just got off the phone with my friend. They're basing it mostly on stomach contents. The cops found someone who claims to have seen Holly at a diner near her apartment at around five Tuesday afternoon."

"Stomach content isn't very precise."

"Nope. So it would help if David and Stephanie could account for even some of that time period. Unfortunately, they can't. Add to that Stephanie saying she wanted to kill Holly, and it's almost more good news than I can handle."

"I'm guessing you'll counsel her against putting things quite that way when she talks to the cops."

"Assuming she'll take my advice."

"She knows she has to," I said. "And by the time I left, she seemed ready. She's scared out of her mind—she and David both."

"An entirely reasonable response, all things considered. We need to come up with a viable alternative soon—either that, or consider whether they need separate counsel."

"Christ! What're you going to do, hang one of them out to dry, to defend the other?"

"If it comes to a trial, we'll be looking for reasonable doubt where we can find it."

"There's got to be a better place than with each other."

Mike went silent, and I could almost hear him weighing something. After nearly a minute, he decided to say it. "Have you considered the possibility that the cops may be looking in the right place?"

"David? You've got to be kidding. Why the hell would he hire me, if he was planning something like that? Or keep me on the job afterward, if it wasn't planned? It doesn't make sense."

"I'm not talking about David."

It was my turn to be quiet. I thought of Stephanie, ashen, exhausted, and medicated in her chair, and I tried to picture it. But it was a stupid exercise, I knew: my ability to imagine her pulling a trigger had nothing to do with whether she actually could.

"Any word on Coyle?" I asked finally.

"I haven't heard anything about him being picked up. And you—any word from the cops?"

"No one's thrown me in a holding cell yet."

"Are you headed up to Tarrytown again?"

"This evening. I want to see where Uncle Kenny was going with those doughnuts."

Clare was off the phone when I came out of the bedroom, standing at the kitchen counter with the newspaper spread before her. Apartment listings.

"Shopping?"

"Getting the lay of the land, anyway. I don't want to overstay my welcome, after all."

I went into the kitchen and poured myself a seltzer. "I'm not complaining," I said. "Who's Amy?"

Clare smiled. "My sister—my big sister—who knows all there is to know about divorce, real estate, career planning, you name it. I try to listen politely, but it doesn't always work out."

"She lives out west?"

Clare turned and leaned against the counter. She crossed her arms beneath her breasts. "In the Bay Area," she said. "How are things with your brother?"

I shook my head. "Not improving."

"You've put in some long days on this—and nights."

"Tonight will be another."

"He must appreciate the effort."

"He's got other things on his mind," I said. "And so far the effort hasn't done much good."

"I'm sorry," Clare said. Her gray eyes held mine, and there was no irony in them. She put her hand on my cheek. I kissed her palm, and I thought again of Stephanie—her hands clutched together in her lap, her desperate fingers.

"Why did you stay?" I asked.

Clare's brows knit. "Stay where?"

"With your husband. Why did you stay so long?" Clare's face stiffened and her hand withdrew. I caught her wrist. "I'm not making trouble," I said.

She pulled her hand free. "Yeah," she said, "it's just your great timing again."

I stepped closer and took her around the waist. Clare brought her fists to my chest. "I just want to know," I said softly.

She raised an eyebrow. "Mr. Curious," she said, but her fists uncurled. She wriggled away and drank from my glass and looked at me over the rim. "Staying was easy," she said. "It was the path of least resistance. He may be self-indulgent, and completely self-absorbed, but he's not a mean bastard, not in the usual ways. As long as he could do his thing, and so long as I showed up on his arm when he wanted me there, he was happy to let me do mine.

"And the perks didn't hurt, either—the real estate and the vacations and the rest. I'd be lying if I said I hadn't thought twice about walking away from all of that. How does the song go? 'Money changes everything.' I didn't have a lot of it growing up, and it definitely changes the calculus of leaving."

"Still, you left."

She drank some seltzer and put the glass down. "As far as I know, you only get this one life, and I wasn't getting any younger. And it turned out I still had some ideas about marriage that I wasn't ready to trade for another Hermès bag." A crooked smile crossed her face. "Who knew I was so fucking noble?" she said, and she turned back to her newspaper.

I came up behind her and put my face into her hair. I slid a hand under her shirt and across her warm belly, and I slid my fingers down the waistband of her low-slung jeans. "There's something about all that integrity . . ." I said softly.

She shuddered, and rolled her ass against me, and unbuttoned her jeans. "Mr. Curious," she whispered, and she slid my hand lower.

I drove north with the first wave of rush hour. The sky was purple going to black, and the traffic was stop-and-go into Yonkers and again in Tarrytown as I made my way along Route 9. I parked three long blocks from Van Winkle Court and took a cold, roundabout walk to the condo complex. I kept my eyes open the whole way; if there were cops staked out, I didn't spot them.

Hagen's basement door was locked, and there were no lights on in the windows that I thought were his. I followed the path he'd taken the night before and went two buildings south and tried the basement door there. Locked. I circled the building and checked the basement windows. I saw an empty laundry room through one. The rest were dark, and one was painted black. Yellow light seeped through a crack in the frame. I went back to the basement door and looked over the Van Winkle Court footpaths. No one. I pulled a small pry bar from the pocket of my parka and slipped it in the door jamb. I barely leaned and the door popped open with a sound like a cough. I put the pry bar away and took out a flashlight.

Inside, I smelled damp cement and laundry soap. I listened for a moment and heard mechanical ticks and water in pipes and the rush of air in ductwork, but nothing else. There was a dark corridor ahead, and I walked in what I thought was the direction of the painted window. There was a fine grit on the concrete floor, and I tried to move quietly on it.

The hallway branched. To the right, light spilled from a wide doorway. The laundry room. To the left was darkness. I went left. I passed by a dented metal door, and the reek of rotted vegetables and dirty diapers. Garbage room. I kept going. At the end of the hall, opposite a small mountain of bundled newspaper and flattened cardboard boxes, there was another metal door. There was a lock in the knob, another, heftier one above it, and a seam of light at the sill. I leaned closer and, faintly, I smelled coffee. And cigarettes.

I took the pry bar from my pocket and found the darkest shadows I could beside a tall stack of newspaper. I held the pry bar high and let it drop. It made a shattering clang on the cement; I picked it up and waited.

Almost instantly, a shadow moved across the threshold. Adrenaline surged into my arms and legs, and my heart spun like a flywheel. And then, nothing . . . for what seemed a very long time. Sweat prickled on my chest and slid down my ribs, and the shadow shifted again. I heard a metallic scraping, and I held my breath. The seam of light slowly widened and spread up the doorframe, and I saw a sliver of crew-cut head, one blue eye and a pinch of nose. I got all my weight behind the kick.

I hit the door above the knob, and there was a sound of crumpled metal, splintered wood, and a wetter sort of crunch. There was a barked, startled curse and the door flew wide and then rebounded, but Coyle was down against the far wall and I was in. His hand was to his face and blood was streaming between his fingers. I caught a glimpse of cot and card table, utility sink, lamp and folding chair, coffee pot—and then, somehow, he was coming up fast and a big fist caught me under the ribs.

Air came out of me in a shout and I covered up and threw an elbow at his neck. It went off his shoulder and I went back, into the doorframe. Coyle grabbed a hunk of my jacket and hauled me forward, toward a waiting haymaker. I tucked my chin down and drove off the wall and ducked under the blow and smacked him in the cheek with my forehead. He cursed again and we both went over. I kneed him somewhere and he cuffed me on the ear and a flare went off behind my eyes. I scrambled up but Coyle got there first and dug a thumb at my throat. I gagged and yanked the pry bar from my pocket and swung it at his thigh. He roared and went down, but on the way he grabbed my wrist and dragged me into his forearm. Stars lit and the pry bar went flying and so did I, into the card table and into a corner. It took a moment for my vision to clear, another to realize that the hot wet patch down my back was coffee and not blood, and one more to register that Coyle was gone. I hauled myself up and shook my head and lunged out the door.

The cold air was like a slap as I came up the basement steps, and I picked up Coyle headed south, toward a cluster of Dumpsters on a square of hardtop. He wasn't moving well and the path was treacherous; he slipped more than once. I didn't push it, but kept him in sight, a muscular figure lurching under sodium lights, past the Dumpsters, through a tangle of bushes, and onto an icy street. My limbs loosened as I trotted along, and my pulse steadied, and after a little while the pain in my ribs dimmed.

On the street, Coyle turned west. I lengthened my stride and trimmed the distance between us. He glanced over his shoulder a few times and sprinted forward a few paces after each look, but smoking had robbed his wind and he couldn't keep it up. When he saw I was closing, he cursed.

"Fuck you, asshole," he shouted over his shoulder, and "Get the fuck out of here." It screwed up his breathing even more.

We rounded a curve and the road ahead became an overpass spanning the Metro-North train tracks. Coyle put his head down and charged at it. But when he got there, he didn't cross. Instead, he vaulted the metal railing and slid down the embankment. Shit. I ran faster and followed.

The embankment was steep and snow-covered, and I went down along the trail Coyle had made, mostly on my ass. I skidded at the bottom onto a badly plowed service road that ran parallel to the train tracks, and that was separated from them by a high schoolyard fence. I looked north and south. The road was empty. There was no sign of Coyle, but snowy prints led beneath the overpass. I took a slow, deep breath and pulled the flashlight from my jacket pocket, and the Glock from its holster behind my back. I flicked on the light.

The beam disappeared into the darkness beneath the bridge, and I walked forward, listening for ragged breathing. My ears were straining when I saw a bright yellow light to the north. I stopped, and heard a rising and falling air horn. Train. The light grew brighter, and swept across the rails, and the rush and rumble widened, and swallowed every other sound. So I never heard him coming.

He charged from the left and lifted me off the ground, and if not for the schoolyard fence I'd have been on my way to Grand Central, pasted to the front of a Hudson Line train. As it was, I was doing only slightly better. The flashlight vanished and so did my breath, in a burning bellow, but I held on to the Glock and brought it up in both hands as I bounced off the fence. It wasn't above my waist before Coyle was on me—both hands wrapped around my own, fingers behind the trigger and over the slide. His bristled, block head ground into my eye socket, and his extra forty pounds drove me back.

My boots scrabbled over the icy hardtop and only the fencing kept me from going over. Coyle was pushing and grunting, and the smell of cigarettes, burnt coffee, and sweat was smothering. My heels were sliding away when I brought my knee up hard—and connected. Coyle roared, and for an instant sagged, and then he twisted and yanked and the Glock came out of my hands. I heard my fingers break before I felt the pain.

We spun apart, and I caught myself on the fence and nearly screamed when I did. I came up panting and so did Coyle, holding the Glock in his big palm, looking down at it, bleeding from his nose, his mouth, and the split in his eyebrow. Looking at me. Looking at the gun. My arms and legs were shaking with fatigue and adrenaline, and

I gathered what juice I had left for . . . I wasn't sure what. Coyle stared for a long minute, and then a fat tear fell from his eye onto the Glock. His voice was choked and his words were squeezed between gasped breaths.

"Fuck it, man—fuck it all. You want me so bad, take me. Take me in, send me upstate, send me straight to hell if you want. I don't give a shit. I just can't do this anymore." He slumped against the fence and slid to the ground. He tossed the Glock in the snow at my feet.

32

There was a corner of Coyle's room that we hadn't trashed, and in it was a pint-sized refrigerator. It held two midget ice trays, and Coyle took one and sat on the cot and fashioned an icepack out of a T-shirt. I took the other and sat on the folding chair. I did the best I could with some paper towels, but it was tough going with three broken fingers, two on the right hand and one on the left. They were already beginning to swell and discolor.

Coyle held the icepack to his brow. "It's a big surprise, I ran?" His soft voice was scratchy and tired. "The cops bring me in—with my record, it's like they won the lottery. Who are they gonna like better than me?"

A couple of names came to mind, but I kept them to myself and nodded. He adjusted his ice and winced. Meltwater and blood ran down his face. Coyle's sweatshirt and jeans were filthy and sodden, and so was he, and beneath the dirt, the fatigue, and the still-suspicious glances, there were other things: fear, confusion, and a deep and grueling sadness. He had, for the moment, spent his anger and panic and blind motion; now he was lost and drifting. I'd told him who I was, and a story about what I wanted, the main points of which were that I wasn't a cop, wasn't working with the cops, and had no particular interest in helping them out. He didn't care much, to the extent he had energy to care at all. Elbows on his knees, he seemed to wither and deflate before my eyes. I wanted him to use the air he had left talking to me. Under the cot, only slightly crushed in the mêlée, were Uncle Kenny's doughnuts in a cardboard box. I managed to drag them over without whimpering.

"You mind?" I asked. Coyle looked at me and shook his head. I picked a glazed one and offered him the box. He shook his head again. I got up and righted the card table, and found the little coffeemaker miraculously intact underneath.

"You have any coffee?" I asked. Coyle pointed to a cabinet over the sink. I found filter papers and Folger's and some foam cups inside. He watched while I fumbled with the fixings. When the coffee was brewing, I turned around.

"Tell me about Holly," I said quietly. Coyle's mouth tightened and his chin trembled, and he stayed silent. The aroma of coffee filled the room, masking for the moment the stink of sweat and cigarettes and wet clothing. Coyle stared nowhere, a faraway, convict gaze, and I thought I'd lost him even before we started. Then he looked at me and decided something. And then—with eyes on the walls, the floor or someplace over my shoulder, and with a voice hoarse and sometimes shaky—he spoke.

They'd met last spring, at the 9:30 Club, on a night Jamie Coyle had been on the door. Holly and Gene Werner wanted in, and Coyle had given Holly the free pass he gave all beautiful women. But something about Werner had rubbed him the wrong way.

"Fucking Weenie. Maybe it was the way he was looking at himself in the window, or maybe it was how he grabbed her arm. I don't know, the prick just pissed me off." Holly had interceded on Werner's behalf, which made Werner mad. That had pleased Coyle—that, and Holly's smile.

"Man, she could melt you. I mean, she was a prizewinner—you had to stare—but that smile . . . It made something bubble in your chest. She was like nobody I ever knew."

She'd turned into a regular, occasionally with Werner, but most times not.

"She'd come early sometimes, sometimes late. She'd have a drink or two, always bourbon and ginger ale, and maybe she'd dance. Mostly though it was people watching. Guys would try to work her, girls too sometimes, but Holly was always in her own head, and she could give a damn.

"She'd always come by to shoot the shit, though; it didn't matter if I was on the door or behind the bar or wherever. A lot of times she'd talk about the crowd. She'd make up things about this guy or that girl, whole stories about their lives. Real funny shit sometimes, and sometimes strange stuff—I didn't always get it all. Other times she'd talk about next to nothing, the weather or whatever, or she'd ask about my job—how I knew who was gonna be a problem, and how big a problem they'd be, how I knew who would back down, and how much pushing it would take, that kind of stuff. And then there were times she'd just hang out, and not say anything at all."

All he'd known of Holly's work at that point was some vague talk about movies. "A director or a cameraman or something like that." In July, she'd approached him about freelancing, and he found out more.

"She said it was security work for her, while she was making her movies—like a bodyguard. Then she gave me the details—the where and when and why—and my fucking jaw hit the floor. I told her no way. The money was fine and all, but the whole setup was fucked, like she was scamming these guys and she wanted muscle. That kind of thing, it goes bad in a heartbeat—a fucking shitstorm waiting to happen. Where I was in my life—where I'd been—no way I wanted any part of that.

"Holly was cool with it. She didn't push and she didn't try to work me—she never pulled that kind of bullshit. She just asked me to take a look at one of her movies. So I did.

"I gotta tell you, it fucking blew me away. I never saw anything like it before. She was . . . amazing. The way she looked, the things she said—it could make your heart explode just watching. And the way she tore that guy apart at the end, the way she got all in his head—Jesus. I saw one, and then she showed me the rest. Fucking amazing.

"It was weird watching her with those guys—it was fucked up—but Holly wasn't embarrassed. It was a thing she did to make her movies, she said—'part of the process,' like figuring out where to put the cameras, and the lights, and the editing and shit. It was just a role she played, and she was in charge the whole time. That's what she said.

"I asked her why she did it, why she made those movies when she had enough talent to do whatever. She told me these were the stories she wanted to tell, and these were the questions she wanted to answer. I said, to me it seemed like always the same story. She thought that was funny, and said I was right, and that it was always the same questions too."

After he'd watched the videos, Holly had offered him the job once more. And because of what he'd seen—the strangeness of her work, its power, her passion for it, and the risks she took to make it—but mostly because he was by then half in love with her, Coyle accepted.

She'd called on him only three times, and while each session had had its tense moments, he'd never had to intervene. He didn't like the idea of her having sex with other men—it made him sick and crazy when he thought of it, he said, and he tried not to think of it—but he never stood in judgment of her.

"I learned upstate, everybody does their own time, and they do it their own way. I knew a lot of screwed-up people inside—on the street too—and the things they did to manage, to get through the day, were way more funky than anything Holly did. And they had less to show for it. Everybody does their own time."

Gene Werner was less enlightened. He'd found out about Holly's videos in late August, and—as Orlando Krug had told me—he'd made her life hell. It was only because Holly had insisted, that Coyle refrained from kicking his ass.

"He was up in her face all the time, and it was making her crazy. A couple of nights at the club, he made big scenes—yelling, breaking glasses, that kind of bullshit. He was a real asshole, and I was about to take him in the alley, but Holly stopped me. She didn't give a shit what happened to Weenie, she said, she just didn't want me getting jammed up for smacking him. She put her hand on my chest, and no shit it made me dizzy."

He did as Holly asked that night, but Werner didn't let up, and a week or so later, with no word to Holly, Coyle had paid him a visit. "I didn't lay a finger on the guy. I didn't even raise my voice. I just said some shit about fucking up his face, and that did the trick."

That was in September. By October, Holly and Coyle had become lovers. It started one Wednesday, when Holly came into the 9:30 Club for the first time in a week, and stayed until closing. "She asked me to take her home," Coyle said. "Then she asked me to stay." His voice was nearly a whisper.

"Some weeks we'd see each other four, five nights, other weeks once or not at all. Some days she'd call me up two, three times, other days she wouldn't call. It depended on her work. When she was working, her head was in another place. She needed space and she needed quiet. And she didn't ever like to be pushed."

Coyle's eyes lit with memories of Holly as he spoke, and each time a smile would crease his broad face. But then his sadness would reassert itself: his eyes would empty and his face would go blank. There were no more happy memories when I asked him about the last time he'd heard from Holly, and about the days since.

"It was a Sunday," he said. I asked him the date and he gave it to me. It was the Sunday before she died: two days after Stephanie had visited her. "She was working on a project and I hadn't seen her for like two weeks. We were gonna get together that night, but she called in the morning to say no—she didn't say why. I was pissed—I wanted to see her—but you couldn't press Holly, and it wasn't the first time she did something like that.

"I tried her Monday and got no answer. I tried again Tuesday and Wednesday. By then I was worried. On Thursday I went over. There was nobody there, but her place was wrecked, and I was freaked. I wasn't there ten minutes when you knocked."

"You didn't call the cops," I said.

"And you think I don't fucking kick myself about it? But I don't deal with the cops—and besides, I didn't know then what the hell was happening. Maybe her place got robbed; maybe she'd already reported it."

"She wouldn't have mentioned it to you?"

"Holly kept a lot of shit to herself."

"You see any signs of a break-in?"

Coyle's brow creased and blood welled in his cut. He shook his head. "No."

I nodded. "You call anybody? Her family maybe, or friends?"

"I don't know the family; I don't know any friends, either. She talked about her art dealer—Krug—a few times, but I never met him."

"So what did you do after her place?"

Coyle's face colored. "You freaked me out. I didn't think you were a cop, but I wasn't sure, and I didn't know what the fuck you wanted—I didn't know what to do. So I came back here and called her some more. Then I went looking for that prick Werner."

The coffee was done and I filled two cups without scalding myself. We had no choice but to take it black. "Why Werner?" I asked.

Coyle shrugged and it looked like it hurt. "Holly was talking about him three, four weeks before. She was pissed off about something, and she was gonna talk to him about whatever it was."

"You didn't ask?"

Coyle colored again and he looked at the floor. "You don't . . . You didn't know her. You couldn't push her—she told what she wanted to tell, and otherwise she kept her mouth shut. She didn't tell me what was up with her and Werner. But I didn't trust that little fuck, and I was gonna find out."

"What did you think was up?" He shook his head and kept quiet. "You spoke to her on Sunday, and you went to her place on Thursday," I said. "Where were you in between?"

"Up here."

"Doing what?"

"Working."

"On what?"

Coyle scowled, and thought about it. "The usual shit. Monday and Tuesday, Kenny had me painting. Then there was a plumbing problem in the D unit—we were at that till like nine or ten Tuesday night. Wednesday was garbage day. You want me to go on?"

"You didn't work at the club?"

"It's closed Sundays and Mondays."

"What about Tuesday and Wednesday?"

"I called in sick," Coyle said.

I raised an eyebrow. "That's not what J.T. said."

His scowl deepened. "So I blew it off. So what?"

"Why?"

Coyle looked at the ceiling. His chin quivered and so did his voice. "I thought Holly might be there and . . . I was pissed at her." He swallowed. "Jesus Christ . . . I didn't want to see her."

I nodded. "What did you think was up with her and Werner?" I asked again.

"I didn't think—"

"Did you think she was seeing him again?"

His face darkened and his big hand clenched around what was left of the ice pack; for a moment I thought we were going to go at it again, but he had no heart for it. "Fuck you," he said quietly. "I didn't know what to think."

I nodded, and thought about dates. If Holly had been talking about Werner three or four weeks before her death, that would've been in December. "Did Holly say anything about someone looking for her?" I asked. "Anything about a lawyer coming to see her?"

Coyle looked confused. He shook his head. "Nothing."

"When did you realize that Holly was . . ."

Coyle stared at his hands, at the soaked T-shirt and his coffee cup—at things I couldn't see. He dropped his T-shirt on the floor. "I saw the paper. I saw the picture . . . her tattoo."

"And after that?"

"After that I didn't know what to do. I went back to looking for Werner. I don't know why, or what I would've done if I found him, but I didn't know what else to do. Then I ran into you again.

"After that, I went by her apartment a few times. I wanted to go in, but I didn't. I just . . . looked at the building. Then I saw cops there, and split. I figured it was just a matter of time before they came around here, and I thought about taking off—but where am I supposed to go? The last few months, every plan I had had to do with her." Coyle shook his head and sighed. "I should've known better. Jesus, has it been two weeks since I saw that picture? It seems like a hundred years, or yesterday."

"What plans did you make?"

"We talked about maybe moving in together, and maybe getting out of the city. Holly liked Philly—she said space was cheap there. She had in mind making different kinds of films—documentaries, maybe—or writing more plays."

Coyle made a fist and examined it. Then he rubbed it over his eyes. "We talked about kids too, if you can believe it. It surprised the hell out of me Holly wanted them, but she did. She said she might be ready soon, if that was all right by me. I said sure, why not."

I thought about Holly's pregnancy, and I looked at Coyle—hunched and staring a hole in the concrete floor—and didn't ask.

If he'd known about it, I was pretty sure he would've said; if he didn't . . . it wasn't in me to tell him. I drank some of my coffee. It was cold.

"Holly ever talk about the guys from her videos? She ever worry about anything coming back at her?"

He looked up. Life came into his dirty, wrung-out face. "You think that's what happened? You think one of them—"

I shook my head. "It's a question, that's all. I want to know if she ever talked about any of them, if any of them scared her."

His shoulders slumped. "No, she never talked about them, not to me, and I didn't ask. If she worried, it was only about the ones she was gonna question. That's why she asked me to back her up those times. But even those she didn't worry much about. Not enough, as far as I was concerned. She was in charge, she would say. She was always in charge."

Coyle went back to studying the floor, and I thought more about Holly and her work. "You told Holly that the story in her videos was always the same. You said that she agreed with you, and that she said the questions she wanted to answer were all the same too." Coyle looked at me and nodded uncertainly. "What were they?" I asked.

"What was what?"

"The story she wanted to tell, the questions she wanted to answer—what were they?"

He shook his head slowly. "The story was always about a married guy fucking around, and the questions were all about why—why he did it, why he'd screw over his wife and kids that way. It was always the same thing, always about her family."

"That's what happened to her family?"

"That's what she said. Her dad was a real asshole, I guess— couldn't keep it in his pants, and didn't bother keeping it a secret from anyone, including her mom. The whole time they were growing up, he was fucking around—his secretary, neighbors, even some of Holly's teachers. The mom and dad went at it pretty good, I guess, and all the time. Her mom never left him, though. After all the yelling and shit, she just took it and took it, right up until the time she got in the tub, ate a few bottles of pills, and opened her veins. Holly came home from school and found her. She was, like, fourteen."

"Christ."

Coyle nodded. "It's fucked-up shit."

"You never met the sister?"

He shook his head. "Holly never invited me when she went up there," he said. "I asked a few times, but she said no."

I squinted. "How often did she go?"

"I don't know—once or twice a month, maybe. I didn't keep track."

Once or twice a month. "I heard she didn't have much to do with her family."

"She didn't. She and the sister didn't get along, so when she went up there, it was mostly to see her dad. He's in some kind of a home, and pretty out of it—too out of it to fight with much, I guess."

I nodded. I thought about Holly's apartment, and the video camera boxes on the floor. "Did Holly do all her editing at home?"

"Yeah—she had her computer, and software for the editing, and for burning the disks. But all that stuff was gone when I got there."

I thought about the videos, about watching them in Todd Herring's screening room. And then I thought of something else. "The reliquaries—the little cabinets that went with the videos—Holly didn't make those in the apartment, did she?"

Coyle shook his head. "She did that in her studio."

"Her studio?"

"That's what she called it. It was just a locker in one of those self-storage places—not much more than a giant closet—but she had a workbench in there, and woodworking tools and shit." Coyle gave me the name of the place and the address. It was in Greenpoint, Brooklyn. He didn't have a key, but he knew the unit number.

I looked down at my hands. They were throbbing and ugly, and the pain was making it hard to concentrate. A trip to the emergency room was in my near future, and I wondered about driving. I asked Coyle how I could reach him, and he sighed and gave me Kenny's cell number. His lassitude was contagious; a wave of fatigue washed over me, and washed away what little buzz I'd gotten from the caffeine and the sugar. I hoisted myself up and pulled on my jacket. Coyle sighed again and dragged himself off the cot and to the sink. He ran the water and leaned at the edge—all out of air. I was surprised when he spoke.

"It was just a matter of time," he said softly.

"What was a matter of time?"

"I felt lucky to be with her—too lucky, like it was all a mistake, like I got somebody else's good luck by accident. It was like finding a wallet full of cash—you know somebody's gonna come around looking for it eventually. It was all borrowed time." Bent over the sink, his broad back shook. His voice was small and choked.

"You ask these fucking questions I can't answer, and I realize I didn't know a damn thing about her. I had no part in her life. I didn't know her family, her friends—I don't even know where she's gonna be buried, or when, or who's gonna do it. Will there be a wake or something? If I showed up, would anybody but the cops know who I was?"

Coyle leaned into the sink and began to retch. I closed the door behind me.

33

It was gray and raw on Thursday morning, and the clouds scudding above the midtown skyline were full of ice or sleet or stone. In Mike Metz's office, it didn't feel much warmer. I'd told him what Jamie Coyle had said, and that I'd basically believed it, and Mike was silent on the other side of his wide ebony desk. Behind his steepled fingers, his narrow face was blank, but his eyes were skeptical and irritated.

"Grief isn't innocence," he said finally. "Plenty of killers grieve for their victims; they love feeling sorry for themselves, and that's another way to do it. This guy has a history of violence"—Mike pointed to my bruised face, and my taped and splinted fingers—"and he all but admitted he'd been worried that Holly was seeing Werner again."

"He didn't quite admit to that," I said, "and he has an alibi. I spoke to the uncle, and it seems to hold water."

"This would be the same uncle who's been lying to you and the cops about Coyle's whereabouts? How long do you think his corroboration will last?"

"There were apparently other people who saw him that Tuesday night." Mike scowled and shook his head. "Besides which, the guy had my gun, and plenty of time to use it, and instead he gave it back."

"Which means that with you he had time to think, and with Holly the passions ran higher."

"You're reaching."

"And you're *not*, and you should be. It's your brother on the line, and his wife."

"If Coyle is no good for Holly's killing, then I don't think I'm doing David or Stephanie any favors by making it easier for the cops to find him. If it takes them a couple of days longer to sit him down and figure out he's clean, then that's a couple of days more I have to find a viable alternative."

"That's assuming you're right about Coyle, and assuming the cops didn't already hear about his great alibi from the uncle."

"According to Kenny, they didn't ask and he didn't tell," I said, and drank some water. My aluminum splint made a bright sound on the glass. "Coyle loved her and he's grieving, and he hasn't hotfooted it out of town, though he's had ample opportunity. On top of which, he's got a better alibi than either David or Stephanie has."

Mike's skepticism was undiminished. "He was our best bet. I think he still is."

"He's not going anywhere, Mike, and if I—"

"How do you know he's not going anywhere?"

I shook my head. "He would've gone by now. Look, if I found him, the cops will too, and if they haven't in a couple of days, we'll call and give them a hint. In the meantime, Coyle gave me some things to chase."

"Werner?"

"Coyle says Holly saw him sometime in December. That would've been right around the time Vickers came to see her."

"You're thinking he had something to do with the blackmail scheme?"

"The timing could work, and apparently Holly was upset about something then."

"If you believe Coyle," Mike said.

I shrugged. "Besides Werner, there's the storage locker."

He held up a hand. "And I already know more than I want to about that."

I smiled. "Coward."

He didn't smile back, but pointed across the desk. "Just keep the word 'tampering' in mind, and be fucking careful."

"Always," I said. "You talk to David lately?"

Mike nodded. "I call; he doesn't say much. I gather he's sticking close to home."

"Was he sober?"

Mike shrugged. "He doesn't say much," he repeated.

"And Stephanie?"

"She's agreed to see me this afternoon."

"That's progress."

"Not enough," Mike said, "and I'm hoping it's not too late."

"What happened?"

"Only the inevitable. McCue called; they want her down at Pitt Street tomorrow morning, to talk."

"Still informally?"

"That's what they say."

I walked from Mike's office down to Grand Central, and caught a 7 train into Queens. I changed to the G in Long Island City, took it south into Brooklyn, and got off at Greenpoint Avenue. I walked east on Greenpoint, north on McGuinness Boulevard, and east again on Freeman.

Creek Self-Store was on Freeman Street, in half of an old brick factory building, on a block that, perhaps because of its proximity to Newtown Creek and to an enormous sewage treatment plant, bore not the slightest gentrifying trace. The cold air made my fingers ache, but it kept the odor down.

I pushed through wired-glass doors into a small lobby. There was a wooden bench, well polished by the seats of many pants, and wall posters with tables of container sizes and prices, and lists of rules and restrictions, most of which amounted to "No Nuclear Waste" and "No Livestock." There was another pair of wired-glass doors straight ahead and a teller's window to the left.

Behind the bars was a twentysomething Latina with a gold stud in her nose. She was working on an early lunch or a late breakfast and the lobby smelled of eggs and fried onions. She handed me a clipboard and some forms, and pointed me at the bench. I sat, and fished a pen from my backpack. I took my time on the forms—with my fingers, I had no choice—and I had a good look around the lobby and behind the counter. There was a little office to the right behind the counter, with a fat, bald guy in it. He was busying himself with what looked like a Bud tallboy in a paper bag, and what looked like celebrity poker on the television. On a table beside the girl there were three small video monitors. One showed an oddly angled view of the front doors and another showed a flickering image of a loading dock; the third was gray static. Wholly satisfactory security arrangements, as far as I was concerned. I took out my wallet and brought the forms to the counter.

I followed the bald guy's slow shuffle onto a freight elevator. We went up two floors, and I followed him some more, through a dimly lit maze of numbered metal overhead doors. We stopped at unit 137, a lovely ten-by-ten affair with walls of corrugated orange plastic and fluorescent lights in a wire cage on the ceiling. He departed; I waited until I heard the freight elevator close, and then I waited some more. The air was cold—about sixty degrees—and it smelled of plaster dust and plastic. In the silence after the elevator, I heard faint music, hip-hop, but I couldn't tell from where.

I closed unit 137, found the stairway, and walked down one flight. Holly's unit was number 58, and I wandered for a while before I located it. I passed a few people along the way: a bickering couple hauling boxes in; another, better-humored couple, hauling boxes out; a painter standing in the open doorway of his unit, mixing greens and whites on a palette; a middle-aged woman with tears in her eyes, pushing a dolly. None of them paid me any mind. Unit 58 was at the dead end of a silent corridor, and I was relieved to see no police seals or crime scene tape anywhere nearby. The hasp was set into the floor and there was a medium-sized lock on it. It was more tarnished than the replacement I'd brought in my backpack, but I doubted anyone around here would notice. I put my backpack down and looked up the corridor. No one. I reached inside and pulled out my bolt cutters.

They were hard to maneuver with broken fingers, and I was noisier than I wanted to be, but in five minutes the lock was scrap. I put the pieces in my backpack, along with the cutters, and rolled up the door. I went inside and rolled it shut behind me.

The fluorescents blinked light onto a fifteen-by-ten-foot space, with yellow plastic walls and a bare concrete floor. There was a workbench along one wall, with vises mounted on either end, a rolling stool underneath, and tools stacked neatly on shelves in the back: hammers, handsaws, chisels, planes, clamps, T-squares, bottles of wood glue, small cans of varnish and shellac. A place for everything. There were metal shelves against the back wall, with a router, a sander, and electric drills and drill bits on them; in the far corner, next to a shop-vac, was a small table saw. Opposite the workbench was a large cardboard box full of wood. I took some slow breaths, to drive my heart rate down, and I took a pair of vinyl gloves from my pocket. I worked them carefully over my splints and started with the box.

It was big—the dimensions of a refrigerator lying on its side—but it held only wood: maple burl, walnut, ebony, and teak boards, in three- and five-foot lengths, and smaller bits and pieces at the bottom. I moved on to the metal shelves, where I found spotless and quite pricey power tools and nothing else. The table saw was well oiled but held no secrets, and the shop vac was ignorant of everything but some wood shavings in the can. There was a layer of dust over things, and nothing seemed to have been disturbed recently. By the time I'd finished with the workbench, I'd concluded only that Holly had had expensive taste in her equipment, and that she'd taken excellent care of it. I pushed the rolling stool back under the workbench and heard a bump. I rolled it out again, knelt down, and looked underneath. I needed my penlight to see them: two cardboard filing boxes, side by side and up against the corrugated plastic wall. I pulled them out and opened one.

It was filled with plastic bags. They were the self-sealing variety, like evidence bags, and in them were souvenirs from Holly's video encounters—items of the sort I'd seen in her reliquaries, though these were going nowhere now. Used condoms, stockings, soiled underwear—his and hers—neckties, cigar butts, washcloths, a pillowcase, some matchbooks, six inches of rubber tubing: a sordid lost-and-found. Each bag was labeled in black marker with a date and a location, in a firm, precise hand. I read the labels and realized that the items on top must have come from her sessions with David. While it was comforting to know that he'd practiced safe sex, the trophies made me uneasy, and my eyes skidded away. I picked through the box delicately, enough to see that it was bags of mementoes, top to bottom, and nothing more. I closed it. My heart was pounding, and I waited a moment and took a deep breath before I opened the second one.

It held memories of a different sort. There was a zippered black nylon case inside, filled with plastic sleeves. Each sleeve held several DVDs and was labeled in Holly's neat print: "Interview #1"; "Interview #2"; "Interview #3," all the way up to 12. Nestled next to the binder were twelve external computer disk drives, each one the size of a thin paperback. Like the DVDs, each was labeled: "January 31 backup"; "February 28 backup," all the way up to last December 31.

I sat on the stool and looked down at the locker. Mike Metz's voice sounded in my head: "Just keep the word 'tampering' in mind, and be fucking careful." He was accompanied by Detective Vines: "And God knows what you did to the evidence." I tapped my foot on the concrete floor.

"Shit," I whispered.

34

It was past seven when Clare came in, and I closed the lid on my laptop. She stood in the doorway and took off her coat. Her brow was furrowed for a moment, and then a smile spread on her face as a blush rose on mine.

"The last time I saw anyone move that fast, and look that guilty, was when I walked in on my cousin Roger, in the bathroom. He was fourteen, and I forgot to knock." She unwound her long scarf. "Keep it up, and you'll go blind."

"It's work," I said.

"Roger said he was just reading the interview."

I pointed at the bags she'd brought with her. "Dinner?"

"I've got cold sesame noodles, hot-and-sour soup, steamed dumplings, and broccoli with garlic sauce . . . assuming you can tear yourself away." I didn't have much appetite, but I was glad for the break.

Back at Creek Self-Store, I'd stared for several minutes at Holly's file box, and then I'd said fuck it. I'd returned one box to its place under the workbench, emptied the other one, and snapped the lock that I'd brought with me onto the door of unit 58. I put the empty file box in a Dumpster near the stairs, and took the elevator down. My backpack was considerably bulkier on the way out, but no one at the front desk seemed to notice.

When I got home, I fired up my laptop and connected Holly's December 31 backup disk to it. I'd been going through files and watching videos ever since, and I'd sat through two painful hours of Holly and my brother when Clare walked in. I'd watched the scene McCue and Vines had shown us, and many others, and they left me covered in a skin of sweat and embarrassment. The only solace to be had was in the fact that David hadn't hit her. As it turned out, my brother's appetites seemed to lie in quite the opposite direction.

Which was cold comfort. I imagined the video playing in a courtroom—to jurors, to the press, to what family and friends were there. I imagined it playing on television. The humiliation would be crippling, and it wouldn't take a prosecutor half as bright as Rita Flores to turn that footage into a basis for blackmail and a motive for murder. If the cops had seen what I'd seen, it was no surprise they liked David for Holly's death.

Clare called me to the kitchen counter and dinner, and she eyed my bruises as we ate. She'd been openmouthed and staring when I'd come back in tatters the night before, and she'd stood unmoving for nearly a minute. Then she'd put on her coat and walked with me to the ER at St. Vincent's. "Fucking crazy" had been her only comment, and she'd made it two hours later, when we were walking home again. I took it as rhetorical, and kept my mouth shut.

We were drinking tea, and she put out orange slices and fortune cookies. Her eyes went to my splints.

"Nothing new since last night," I said.

She nodded. "Slow day, huh?"

"It doesn't happen that often."

"No? I guess I've just been lucky to see so much of it."

"It comes with the job now and then."

"You say it like you're talking about carpal tunnel syndrome or something. Coming home cut and bruised and broken, it's not quite the same thing."

"It doesn't happen—"

Clare stopped me. " 'Doesn't happen often,' 'part of the job'—I heard you the first time. And I'm not asking you to justify it. You love it—that much is clear."

"You think I love getting beat up?"

"No." She smiled. "I don't think you're quite that twisted. I meant your work—it's clear you love your work. Enough so that you're willing to get the crap beat out of you on a semiregular basis to do it."

I shrugged. "I don't know that I'm cut out for much else."

Clare squinted at me. "What bullshit!" she said. "There are a zillion other things you could do, or you could sit around and do nothing at all. But you don't—because you love your work. You love running around town, and digging around on-line, and talking to people, and finding things out. And I think there's a part of you that likes being— very quietly—the smartest guy in the room. Mostly, though, I think you want to help people, as corny as that sounds. I think you want to do good. You love your work, and you get all morose and weird— weirder—when you don't do it. So don't be shy about saying so. I guess all I'm saying is: be careful."

I looked at her. Her hair had fallen forward, and soft shadows lay across the planes and angles of her face. Through a blond curtain, her gray eyes were shining, and larger than I'd ever seen them.

"I didn't realize you'd given it so much thought."

"Go figure," she said, and she ran a fingertip around my ear.

"I don't know how much good I've done lately, though."

"For your brother?" she asked. I nodded. "You're still at it?"

"For what it's worth."

She smiled. "I'll put coffee on."

Clare made a large pot and I went back to my laptop. I got through another hour of Holly and David, and then I walked around the room and tried to force some oxygen into my lungs. It had been more of the same, and maybe more embarrassing toward the end. At least he hadn't hit her.

There were other hotel clips on the disk, though they were much shorter than the ones with David. They showed Holly with two other men, one tall and bald, the other pale and very hairy, and from the dates on the video files, in March and May of the previous year, I guessed that they were outtakes of earlier works, and that these guys had already had their final interviews. There was nothing in the sequences to make either man a more likely suspect than David, and nothing to identify them.

Clare ran a hand over the back of my neck and went into the bathroom. I heard water running in the tub and I thought about joining her, but didn't. I clicked on another folder and found another video file, this one dated from last summer.

I played it, and I thought of some things Jamie Coyle had said: "She'd always come by to shoot the shit, though—it didn't matter if I was on the door or behind the bar or wherever." And: "She had in mind making different kinds of films—documentaries, maybe . . ." I wondered if this clip was Holly's first attempt.

It was more hidden-camera work, most likely taken from a handbag, and it was all about Jamie Coyle. The camera looked up at him, and there was something worshipful and larger than life in the perspective. The soundtrack was muddy and the background filled with club clatter—music, laughter, glassware, the hum and buzz of many bodies—but Coyle's voice was close and intimate, and so was Holly's as she interviewed him.

"What about that guy?" she asked. "Do you think he'll cause problems?"

"That guy there—with all the gel and the soul patch? He's coming up all hard and loud, and he's had too many mojitos, but he's no trouble. Just look at his hands—the guy's got a fucking manicure, and my mother had thicker wrists. Plus he's got a BlackBerry on his belt. A guy with a BlackBerry and a manicure, nine times out of ten he's gonna do what you tell him."

She asked about how he decided who to let in, and how the VIPs behaved, and what about the girls who waited tables, and in his answers Coyle was relaxed and funny and supremely competent, or at least Holly had made him seem that way. Her infatuation with her subject was obvious, and I wondered if Coyle had ever seen the video. Maybe when this was all over . . .

When that video ended, I clicked on a folder labeled "Brookfield," and found a dozen more. I played one and let out a deep breath.

He was the husk of a handsome man—thick hair gone white, rheumy blue eyes, a strong, straight nose cratered and darkened by broken blood vessels, white skin sagging from high cheekbones, graceful fingers clawed, mottled, shaking. His voice was still strong and sonorous, which made his bewilderment all the sadder and more frightening. Fredrick Cade, Holly's father. I knew for sure when she called him Daddy.

There were no hidden-camera shots here; it was all hand held, and Holly's point of view. She panned around a room that was a cross between hospital and Holiday Inn—oxygen tank, IV stand, pink wallpaper, blond wood trim, bright, bland fabrics—and came to rest again on her father, wrapped in a plaid robe and sitting in a chair.

"It's me, Daddy, it's Holly. Look this way, Daddy—here, into the camera. No, goddammit, over here! That's right, at me. Now, tell me about Mrs. Manton. Do you remember her, Daddy—my seventh-grade teacher? Tell me about you and Mrs. Manton."

In the hotel rooms, with the faceless men, Holly's questions were instruments of contempt and punishment and power, and with Coyle, they were tokens of affection. But this was . . . something else—petulance, pleading curiosity, a child's desperate search for attention. Fredrick Cade couldn't answer her, of course—I wasn't sure he even knew who she was—but Holly kept at it. Most of the short clips ended with the camera focused on the vinyl floor, and with the sound of her ragged breaths. A lump formed in my throat as I watched, and a dull ache grew in my chest.

Not all of Holly's questions to her father were about his other women, though. In several of the clips she asked about her mother, and in others she questioned him about something called Redtails. Didn't he remember that Mommy promised it to her? How could he not remember? Why would he give it away? Fredrick just looked at her. I wrote the word in my notebook, with a question mark beside it.

I pushed the laptop away and stood by the window. Sixteenth Street was quiet, Clare was asleep, and my coffee was long cold. And useless anyway. My eyes were filled with grit, and my bones were heavy with a fatigue that was beyond the power of caffeine to cure, beyond even sleep. I thought of what Clare had said—"You love the work; you love finding out." Not so much just then.

I'd found out more than I wanted to about David and Stephanie: the orthodox façade of success and self-satisfaction they labored to maintain; the unhappiness and anger and self-loathing that lay behind it; what a desperate, fragile structure it was. More than I wanted to know, but nothing that would help them.

I'd learned much about Holly too—about her obsessions and anger, her cruelty and taste for retribution, her prodigious talents, her bleak artistic vision and her terrible commitment to it, her secretiveness, and dangerous faith in her own ability to control things. I'd learned much, but not yet who killed her. "The smartest guy in the room." It was a tough sell just then, even standing all alone.

My fingers were aching and my back was stiff, and I wanted to go to bed. Instead, I returned to the laptop and Holly's files. That was when I found the video of Gene Werner.

35

But for the stage lights, the tiny theater was dark, and but for Claudius, Hamlet, Laertes, and the director, it was empty. They were gathered at stage left, near a frail-looking table. I was quiet coming in, and they didn't look up as I took a seat in the last row. The air was warm and old, and there was a chemical smell in it, like antifreeze.

> *King:*   *Yo, playahs, the O.G. drinks to Hammy!*
>   *Let's light it up*
>   *And you judging muthafuckahs bear a wary eye.*
>
> *Hamlet:* *Come on, bitch.*
>
> *Laertes:* *You come on, dawg.*

Gene Werner watched as Hamlet and Laertes circled each other, foils wobbling in their uncertain hands. "No, you idiots," he shouted, "you're fencing, not skipping. You're fighting for your fucking lives!" Werner's own foil whipped through the air and snicked Laertes's leg.

The actor dropped his sword and spun. "Screw you, Gene—you do that one more time, you'll be fighting for your own fucking life."

Werner's laugh was rich and haughty, and it carried easily to the back of the house. "That's right, Sean, get angry! And Greg, keep your fucking arm *up*. The way you hold that thing, you look like a faggot houseboy, mincing around the den with a goddamn feather duster. You're the fucking prince of the 'hood, for chrissakes—the *lead*. This play is all about you!"

Hamlet's face was shiny, and there were rings of sweat under his arms. He wiped his forehead and flipped Werner the bird. Claudius hitched up his baggy jeans and laughed, and the actors took their places to run it through again. Werner walked to the front of the stage and peered into the darkness. I didn't think he could see me in the thick shadow, but some actor radar had made him exquisitely sensitive to the presence of an audience. I kept still, he turned back to his players, and the rehearsal continued.

I'd spent most of the morning in Brooklyn, where I'd paid another visit to Holly's neighbor, Jorge Arrua. I'd spent the afternoon back in my apartment, reading through my notes and drawing up a timeline. I'd called Mike Metz several times throughout the day, and heard every time from his secretary that he was still downtown, at the Seventh Precinct house, with Stephanie.

When I'd finished the timeline, I'd gone hunting, on-line and on the telephone, for Gene Werner. I remembered what he'd told me about his upcoming directing projects, and I'd found one of them, a hip-hop interpretation of *Hamlet,* mentioned on the website of the Little Gidding Theatre. According to the site, the production was due to premiere in a month, and I'd called an information number and learned that rehearsals were taking place all afternoon, in the basement space on West Thirteenth Street.

Werner's nasty laugh rolled over the rows of folding chairs. "What part of 'switch swords' don't you get, Greg? It means he takes yours and you take his and then you start fighting again. Watch."

Werner put the tip of his foil under the guard of Hamlet's, and lifted it from the stage with a flourish. He caught it midair and offered it—grip first—to Hamlet, who took it hesitantly. Werner raised his weapon, and before Hamlet could do the same he shouted "En garde!" He batted Hamlet's blade aside, stepped in, and locked the guard of Hamlet's foil against his own. Werner grabbed the smaller man by his shirtfront and grinned down at him. Then he planted his sneaker behind the actor's heel and pushed. Hamlet went down with an echoing thump and Werner laughed.

He hadn't been laughing much on Holly's video, nor had he been nearly so well groomed. It was an untitled, unedited work, shot in her apartment, with a single hidden camera, and Werner was its hapless star. He was unshaven and rumpled, his hair greasy-looking, and his eyes full of fear and anger. Holly, mostly unseen, was at her inquisitorial best. Her voice was a finely calibrated mix—wheedling, sympathetic, seductive, and patient.

"I made you angry, didn't I?" she said from someplace. "You felt like I lied to you."

"How else was I *supposed* to feel? Jesus, Holly, I *loved* you. How could you do it to me?"

"It wasn't about you, Gene."

"Not *about* me? All that time we were together, and you're fucking these guys you don't even know—making these *porn* flicks—how is that not about me?"

"It's my project—my work. It has nothing to do with anyone but me."

Werner shook his head, eyes wide. "Nothing to do with . . . And you wonder why I was angry. You're un-fucking-believable."

"I wonder less about the anger than I do about the theft," Holly said.

A sheepish grin ran across Werner's face. "What are you talking about?" he said. He tried for puzzled and irritated, but neither worked.

Holly was relaxed, almost amused. "Come on, baby, we know each other too long for games."

"It turned out I didn't know shit about you," he said.

"You knew me," Holly said. "You still do." Her voice was lazy and insinuating, and Werner reacted to it like a dog to a whistle—attentive and hungry.

"I thought I did," he said slowly.

"Was it just money, baby, or was it something else? Say it wasn't just about the money."

He made a pouting face. "I was angry, Holly—*fucking heartbroken.*"

A clash of blades and another fall brought me back to the theater and to the action onstage. Laertes was rubbing his wrist, and Hamlet was dusting himself off. Claudius was laughing.

"The hell with you," Hamlet said. "I don't need a gig so bad I'm going to be a punching bag for anyone."

Werner laughed some more and swept a hand through his shiny hair. "Your choice, Greggers. I'll have ten guys here in an hour to audition for your part, and not one of them will be too lazy or delicate to learn stage combat. But, as I said, it's your call. So what'll it be—stay or go?" He crossed his arms on his chest and smiled down on Hamlet.

The actor looked at him. "Screw you," he said softly, but he picked up his foil and took his position for another run-through.

They stumbled through the fifth-act fight scene many times during the next hour, with no joy and no appreciable improvement in technique. Only Werner seemed to take pleasure in the process, full as it was of occasions for him to berate and abuse his colleagues. I was surprised that when the actors left for the day, exiting stage right, they left him still alive. When their voices faded, and a heavy door opened and closed somewhere backstage, I took a deep breath, and stood.

Werner was collecting the foils, and he heard me coming. He shielded his eyes from the stage lights and looked up the aisle. He took a step back when he recognized me.

"What are you doing here?" he said. No haughtiness now.

"I'm here to see you." My heart was pounding, and I took some easy breaths, to slow things down.

"Technically, the theater is closed."

"There was no one around to stop me."

"Yeah, well—I've got someplace to be, so I have to lock up."

I reached the stage, and jumped up. Werner took another step back. "This won't take long."

"What won't take long?" he said. His jaw was grim and jutting.

"I came to talk, Gene. About the video."

"We talked about Holly's videos already, and I told you what I knew. I have nothing else to say about those things; I don't even like thinking about them."

"I'm not talking about the videos of her and those men."

Werner swallowed hard and shrugged. He managed a casual stride to the little table, where he put the foils down, all but his own. "Then what the hell *are* you talking about?"

"Come on, Gene, we can be grown-ups, right? We can at least not waste each other's time."

Werner forced a smile. He smoothed his shiny hair and tugged on his little ponytail. Then he sent his blade through a series of blurring, humming arcs, and finished with his arm extended and the sword pointed at me. Somewhere along the line, the plastic button had come off the end, and the bare, wicked tip was motionless and level with my eye. Werner smiled wider and chuckled. He whipped the foil down.

"There's nothing like the feel of a blade," he said. He walked toward me, stopping when he was two arm's lengths away. He pointed with his foil at my splints, and smiled.

"Fucked up your hands, huh?"

"A run-in with your pal Jamie Coyle," I said. Color drained from Werner's face. He opened his mouth to speak, but didn't. "I saw the video, Gene."

Werner frowned. He backed away two steps and began practicing lunges at half speed. He coiled and uncoiled himself—precise, flowing, and graceful each time. Each time, the tip of his foil came to a quivering halt twelve inches from my chest. "What video is this?"

"You never answered her question—whether or not it was just about money."

"I don't know what you're saying." He took the lunges up to three-quarter speed. The blade became a blur again.

"Holly made a backup, Gene. I have you on disk, confessing to her that you lifted unedited copies of her videos from her apartment, and that you tried to blackmail Mitchell Fenn with them."

Werner stopped lunging and stood very still. His head was tilted as if he were straining to hear something. After a minute, he smiled in a way he might have thought was ingratiating. "Backup," he said quietly. He tapped the sword against his leg and paced in a slow circle at center stage.

"It was a prank," he said. "The whole thing with the videos and

Fenn—the blackmail—it was just a prank." I raised an eyebrow, and Werner chuckled ruefully. "It was stupid, I admit, but I wasn't thinking straight at the time. I was . . ." He looked down at the stage and then up at me, his lower lip all but quivering. "I was *heartbroken* over her, for chrissakes. Can you understand that? I went a little nuts then, and I wanted to get even somehow."

"And blackmailing Fenn seemed like just the thing?"

"That wasn't serious—I would never have taken his money. I just . . ." Again his gaze dipped to the floor and back up. "Look, I'm not proud of this, but . . . I wanted it to come back at Holly. I wanted her to see what she was doing was *crazy*. That it had consequences."

Consequences. I nodded, as if it made any sense. "And, what—you counted on Fenn tracing it back to her?"

Werner was eager. "Yes, exactly. And when he did, it scared the hell out of her."

"And then Holly figured out that you were behind it—that you'd kept a set of her house keys, and you'd stolen her disks."

More nodding. "And I was glad she figured it out. I wanted her to know what she'd done to me. And I wanted her to know the risk she was taking. She thought she was immune somehow. She thought she could control everything—but she couldn't."

"Apparently not," I said. "So you weren't surprised when Holly called you—when she wanted to see you?"

"Not surprised," Werner said. He stopped pacing and assumed a splay-footed stance. He bent his legs and raised the foil, and his face was a picture of concentration as he carved long shapes in the air.

"The reason I ask is that, on the video, you seemed surprised when she told you what she wanted to talk about."

Werner frowned. "I wasn't surprised."

I shook my head. "Definitely surprised, Gene, and nervous too—sweating, pale. There were times I thought you might puke."

Werner's brow wrinkled. "I wasn't sweating."

I shook my head some more. "And you say that you wanted her to know what you'd done, but that isn't true, is it? I mean, you didn't own up to anything at all; you made Holly work to get it out of you."

"I was nervous. It was a stupid prank, and I knew it. I was embarrassed at first—flustered. But then I told her all of it."

"You certainly did," I said, and Werner's eyes narrowed. "When did Holly tell you she'd recorded it?" I asked.

Werner's frown deepened. "What are you talking about?"

"Come on, Gene—it's a simple question: when did Holly tell you she'd recorded your conversation? Did she tell you on the spot, or after the fact? Or maybe she didn't tell you at all; maybe it just dawned on you at some point."

"I don't know—"

"Don't play games, Gene—when did you find out?"

Werner windmilled his sword arm, like a batter in the on-deck circle. The blade whistled through the air. "I'm not playing games, and I don't see why I have to tell you a goddamn thing."

I smiled to myself. "You don't have to say shit to me, Gene, but the police are another story. I imagine they've been around to see you already, and maybe you've already gone over this with them. Or maybe not. In which case, I'd be happy to mention it."

He walked toward me, his arm still spinning. He stopped maybe six feet away, with a nasty grin on. "You know the cops pretty well, huh?"

My eyebrows went up. "What do you mean by that, Gene?"

Werner colored, and waved an impatient hand. "Nothing."

"Then why'd you say it?"

"No reason," he said, and turned away. "And if you must know, Holly told me about the video. She told me she'd recorded it."

I smiled. "When was that?"

"I don't remember—a week later; maybe longer than that."

"The date on the file was December twenty-seventh. A week or so later puts it in January. Was it in January when she told you about it?" Werner shrugged. "And she played it for you?"

He made a show of thinking about it. "Yeah, she played it for me."

"When was that?"

He hesitated. "After she called. After New Year's, I guess."

"And that was the last time you saw her?" Werner nodded. "You remember the date?"

He scowled and made an elaborate check of his watch. "I have to leave," he said.

"Of course you do. Just let me go over the facts once more, to be sure. Holly recorded your confession on December twenty-seventh. Sometime after that—in early January, say—she told you about the recording, after which, on the Saturday before she was killed, you went to her apartment, beat the crap out of her, and walked off with her computer and her video equipment. Is that about right?"

Werner's mouth fell open, but no sound came out. "What . . . what the fuck are you talking about?" he said finally.

We were getting there. I took a deep breath, and smiled big at Werner. "I have the video of you confessing to blackmail, Gene, and of Holly throwing you out of her apartment afterwards. It's plain how pissed you were when you finally figured out she wasn't taking you back. I can only imagine how you stewed over that, and all the more, I expect, when you found out she'd recorded the whole episode."

Werner straightened his shoulders and shook his arms out. He ran a hand over his chin, as if to make sure it was still there. He hung a lopsided smile on his face. "You can make what you want out of that video, but I was there. I know what really happened. And as for that other stuff, it's bullshit and you know it, and you can go fuck yourself. I never touched Hol—"

"You have a history of knocking her around. She told people."

"Who'd she tell—Krug? Coyle? I told you that faggot has it in for me, and so does that fucking ape." Werner's face burned. He swung his arm in a big figure eight. A little bit closer now.

"You shoved her in the video, Gene."

"I tripped. I tripped and fell and bumped into her." His jagged smile grew, and the sword whirred through the air.

"You knocked her halfway across the room, for chrissakes."

"You have your story, and I have mine."

"Except that I also have a witness, Gene, who puts you in Holly's apartment the Saturday before she died, in the middle of a noisy fight." He stopped slashing and brought the foil to his side. His mouth was an angry line, and his jaw was like a millstone. I continued. "On top of which, you were seen leaving there, carrying what looked like a computer and video equipment."

Werner's fingers whitened on the sword grip. He bared his large teeth and his arm came up in a blur. The blade whipped the air, and I felt the draft on my face. Almost there.

I smiled. "You want to watch that, Gene. I'm not one of your actors, and I take a punch better than Holly."

He snapped the foil to his side. "Besides 'Fuck off,' I have nothing else to say to you."

Almost . . .

"I guess I'll do my talking elsewhere, then."

"You're so full of shit—you won't go to the cops. You can't."

"No? Now why would that be, Gene?" Werner worried his lower lip, but didn't answer. "I wasn't actually thinking of the cops, though. I was thinking more of having this chat with Jamie Coyle."

Werner's voice was a whisper. "You son of a—"

"So what happened after that Saturday, Gene? Did you not find the video in the stuff you'd taken? Or did you maybe get scared about the beating you'd given her? You really lost it, didn't you? You drew blood; you left marks." Werner's face went from white to red. His hands were fists and he brought the sword up.

Almost . . .

"Were you scared she'd go to the cops—or maybe that she'd tell Coyle about it? Three long nights of worrying; you must've been out of your mind by the time you saw her again. But what I can't figure out is whether you went there planning to finish the job, or whether things just got away from you."

Werner drew his arm back, and his blade was pointed at my neck. "Fucker," he spat, and he uncoiled.

There.

The blade slashed my arm, and despite the padding of my coat, I felt the sting. I pivoted, and kicked Werner—hard—on his left thigh. I was fast and I got weight behind it, and I caught him just above the knee. He crumpled like a puppet.

His bellow echoed in the empty theater. I kicked the sword away and watched him roll on the stage for a while, crying and clutching at his leg. When he stopped thrashing, I pulled the Glock from behind my back. I couldn't hold it well enough to shoot straight, but Werner didn't know that, and I made sure he got a good look.

"It'll pass," I said. "Yelling doesn't help."

His handsome face was red and twisted, but he managed some gasping curses. I squatted by his head. "You haven't answered my question yet: did you go there to finish the job, or did things get out of hand?"

"You're craz—" A cramp rolled through his leg, and squeezed the air from him.

"My question, Gene."

"You're saying I killed her. You're saying I killed Holly." His deep voice was cracking.

I laughed a little. "Well, of course I am."

"But I didn't—"

"You beat the shit out of her, Gene, and think hard before you tell me otherwise."

"I—"

"Think hard."

Sweat ran from Werner's hairline. His ponytail was gone, and strands of hair were stuck to the side of his face. "It . . . it got out of hand. She told me she'd recorded me, about Fenn, and I wanted the video. But Holly wouldn't give it to me. She just laughed."

"And you hit her."

Werner grimaced and squeezed his leg. "She wouldn't give it to me, and she kept laughing."

I stood up, and let out a dusty breath. "You beat the shit out of her."

"You don't know what it was like—what she was like. She was so beautiful . . . you had to have her. But she didn't care—however much you felt for her, however much you wanted her, it didn't matter. You could never get at her—she was always in control. She kept laughing and . . . I lost it. Even when I hit her, she laughed the whole time."

I walked away from him, across the stage, and ground my teeth together. "You took her computer?"

"The computer, the cameras, the disks . . ."

"Your video was there?" Werner nodded. "And you found the video of my brother too, and his wife." Fear crowded out pain on Werner's face, and he propped himself on his elbow and tried to slide backward. "Think, Gene," I said quietly. "You found video of my brother?" He nodded. "And after I came to see you, what happened then?"

"I . . . I got scared. I recognized your name, and I looked you up. I saw that you were his brother. I figured you were trying to get him off the hook for Holly . . . that you were looking for someone else."

"Someone like you."

Werner shook his head. "I was afraid if the police knew I'd . . . if they knew about Fenn, and that Holly and I had fought, they'd think that I'd . . . killed her."

"And we couldn't have that, could we? So you fed them my brother and his wife. You sent them that disk." He scuttled back, like a wounded crab. I followed, and my shadow fell across him. "You sent them that disk," I said again. He nodded.

I sighed. "Talk to me about that Tuesday night," I said after a while.

"What about it?"

"We're almost through here—don't get stupid now. Tell me what happened."

Werner looked confused. "Nothing . . . nothing happened."

I stepped closer. "Goddammit, Gene—"

"For chrissakes, I'm telling you the truth! Nothing happened that night!" His face was white and his eyes were wild with panic. "I didn't see her or talk to her or anything. I had nothing to do with what happened. It's like I told the cops."

I shook my head. "What line did you feed the cops?"

"They asked me to account for my time that Tuesday night, and I did."

"With what bullshit?"

"It wasn't bullshit."

I crouched beside him. He tried to slide away but I caught his arm. My voice was a low rumble. "Don't insult me, Gene."

"I'm not! I was at the theater all night—the Morningside Lyceum, by Columbia. I'm directing and one of my leads was out sick that night. I had to fill in. I got to the theater before six, and all night I was either onstage, or backstage with the cast and crew. We didn't get out of there till ten-thirty or eleven, and then a bunch of us went to eat. I didn't get home until one, and I wasn't alone." He swallowed and squeezed his eyes shut, and he looked like he might throw up.

"You fucking beat her!"

"I know—Jesus, I know what I did. But I swear to God I didn't kill her."

"Then who did, Gene? Who killed Holly?"

Werner looked at me. His mouth was trembling and his face was breaking down. "I don't know," he said, and his voice was a choked thing. "I watched those videos, and afterward I thought . . . I swear to God I thought it was your brother."

36

There weren't many lawyers still toiling at Paley, Clay and Quick on Friday night, and certainly no other partners, and the corridors were dim and quiet as I made my way to Mike Metz's office. He was sprawled on the sofa with his feet on the coffee table. His sleeves were rolled and his tie was loose, and his face was pale and bleak. There were papers in his lap, but his gaze was out the window, at the Midtown towers bright against the inky sky. I hung my coat on the hook and dropped into a chair. He didn't look up.

"You were downtown for a long time," I said.

"There was a lot of sitting and waiting," he said. His voice was ancient.

"How did it go?"

He rubbed his eyes. "Stephanie was nervous, even with the drugs, and the cops were cops. McCue played hard-ass, which was typecasting, and Vines tried gal-pal rapport, which was almost funny. They went at her a dozen different ways about her movements Tuesday night—when she left home, what route she took walking, the weather—they even quizzed her on the movie. And of course they wanted to talk all about her trips to Brooklyn, and Holly being pregnant. All in a very informal way."

"How did she do?"

"I'd give her a B, maybe a B-minus. She was fuzzy about a few things on Tuesday night, and the anger came through when they played the video of her talking to Holly."

"They didn't show her the stuff with David, did they?"

"They tried to—Vines claimed she clicked on the wrong file—but I stopped it."

"How was Flores?"

Mike shook his head. "Hard to read. She asked some questions, but I couldn't tell you if she liked the answers. Mostly she just watched."

"Trying to figure out how Stephanie would play to a jury, no doubt."

"No doubt."

"You have a view on that?"

Mike sighed. "Neither one of them would elicit a whole lot of compassion. David comes across as cold and arrogant, and Stephanie is wrapped way too tight—you get uncomfortable just watching her. And, of course, they have too much money." He dragged a hand down his face and looked at me. "Still, I'm hoping we won't get to that," he said. "Tell me I'm not kidding myself."

I told him about watching Holly's videos, saying nothing about their provenance, and about my conversation with Gene Werner. He didn't interrupt, but shook his head and sighed at several points. When I was done, he rose and stood by the big window. He put his palm on the glass, on the palm of his reflection.

"You checked the alibi?" he asked.

"I've started making calls. The only one I've spoken to so far is the manager at the Lyceum, and he confirmed the basic story—that Werner filled in for an actor that night, and that he was in the theater from around six until close to eleven. He even remembers Werner leaving with a bunch of the actors afterward."

"You know if the cops confront him, Werner will deny everything—especially when he finds out you have no witness. He'll claim he never said anything about a fight with Holly, or he'll claim that you coerced him. And he's probably out dumping her equipment as we speak, if he hasn't already."

"Already dumped, apparently. He says he got rid of everything right after he sent the disk to the cops."

"You believe him?"

"Not even about the day of the week, but it's a reasonable thing to have done."

Mike sighed again. "Too bad your witness story was bullshit."

I nodded. "I did what I could with Arrua. He remembers ruckuses at Holly's, and maybe one around that time, but he's vague on dates. And he swears he didn't see anyone."

Mike nodded. "How did you know Saturday was the day Werner went there?"

"An educated guess. Stephanie told me Holly was fine on Friday—no bruises—and Coyle got a call from Holly on Sunday morning, telling him not to come over, no explanation why. I figured it was because she didn't want him seeing her injuries—she didn't want him going after Werner and maybe landing himself in jail again. That made it Saturday."

"A good guess," Mike said.

"A thimbleful of luck, in a large ocean of crap."

Mike was quiet for a while, staring out. His narrow frame was perfectly still, and his pale face floated above the city like a ghost. "You've noticed that, have you?"

My jaw tightened. "I've noticed that all I've managed to discover in the last forty-eight hours is that our two best alternatives are non-starters, if that's what you mean. I've also noticed that we're fresh out of other candidates."

Mike turned around. "Which leaves us where we started, with David and Stephanie."

I took a deep breath and pain pulsed in my fingers. "Where is Flores going with this?" I asked.

"I don't know what she's going to do," Mike said. "There are plenty of reasons why a case against either of them would be a dog to prosecute: no witnesses, no physical evidence, the victim's lifestyle, her history—the list goes on. An ADA as smart as Flores wouldn't usually be in a hurry to roll the dice over something like this. But we don't have 'usually' here. Here we have sex tapes, adultery, a beautiful white victim, and wealthy, prominent, unsympathetic suspects—a cable television wet dream. Flores is ambitious, and . . ." He shook his head. "I just don't know."

"Best guess, then."

"I'm not in the guessing business."

"As a favor to a friend."

Mike looked at me with bloodshot eyes. "I don't know if it's any favor," he said, "but best guess is we're circling the drain."

His words stayed with me in the taxi home, and they were with me still as I sat at the table, staring stupidly at my notes. My memories of Pitt Street, and of Rita Flores—her stares and questions and body language, her nods to Vines and McCue—took on an ever more menacing cast, and it was hard to shake the feeling that there was doom written all over this thing. There was nothing yet certain about the case going to indictment, I told myself, much less to trial, and nothing sure in what a jury might do, even if the case did go that far. But if it did, I knew, there would be one all too predictable outcome—public humiliation for David and Stephanie, and professional and personal ruin. I remembered something Stephanie had said: "There's a part of him that's been waiting for all this . . . to get caught, to be punished." Was this what David had had in mind when he'd answered those ads?

I opened my laptop. I could wonder and worry all night, and it wouldn't be of any use to David or Stephanie—not that there was much useful to be done at this point. There were more calls to be made, to check on Werner's alibi, but Friday night isn't the best time to reach people, and especially not theater people. There were loose ends in my notes to tie off. And there were the other backup disks, and the DVDs, that I'd taken from unit 58 at Creek Self-Store—hours of depressing video, sitting on my kitchen counter. I knew I should watch them, but just then, I couldn't bring myself to do it. *Circling the drain.*

I sighed, and tapped my splints on the table, and thought of something else Mike had said: "Have you considered the possibility that the cops may be looking in the right place?" It was a reasonable question, a prudent question, the right one to ask. It was the kind of question I'd asked before, about plenty of other clients. But not about this one, not seriously. Was that because I thought I knew the answer, or because I didn't want to know?

"Shit," I said out loud, and I heard a key in the lock.

Clare opened the door and stood at the threshold, looking at me. After a while, she shook her head. "Get your coat on," she said. "If there's a long night of brooding ahead, you're at least getting some air and a meal first."

She walked me south and west, to Doctor Wu's, the New York branch of a trendy LA burger joint, and a favorite of the fashion crowd. It's usually impossible to get a table there any evening, much less a Friday, but Clare worked some magic and we were seated in ten minutes.

I ordered a ginger ale and Clare had wine, and the candlelight wrapped around us, and the chatter of the crowd covered us like a tent. The warmth and darkness and noise of the place made for a kind of privacy, and I was drifting into silence and fatigue and the scramble of my own head when Clare took my wrist. I looked up. Her hair was loose around her shoulders, and nearly white against her black sweater. Her face was luminous, and her fingers were smooth and cool.

I thought she was going to ask questions—where had I been, how was the case, what was wrong with me—and I had no answers, nor even the breath to try. But Clare asked nothing. Instead, she smiled, and talked about, of all things, real estate: the twelve apartments she'd seen that day, the outrageous asking prices, the hideous furnishings, the bizarre owners, the fascist co-op boards, and the freakish real estate agents. It was a wry, flowing monologue, interrupted only by the waitress and our food, and I didn't have to do anything except laugh, which—after a while—I did.

On the walk home, Clare leaned close and took my hand. Her perfume was light on the icy air. "I should work," I said.

She shook her head. "It'll keep."

I awoke two hours before dawn, in the ashes of a dream. It was something with Holly and David and Stephanie and Jamie Coyle, but the narrative was lost. I stood by the windows and looked at the frozen city, and salvaged what pieces I could: Holly's voice, pleading, laughing, cruel, and sad; her shadowed eyes; her bare, shining back; David's angry mouth; his fingers tugging at the skin over his Adam's apple; Stephanie's hands, twisting in her lap; Coyle, bent over his sink; a pall of sadness over them all. I turned the fragments over and around in my head, but I couldn't make them fit. I pulled on jeans and a sweat-shirt and opened my laptop.

Clare got up at nine-thirty, and she moved slowly but methodi-cally around the apartment—breakfast, newspaper, shower. I was working my way through Holly's DVDs, and she put a hand in my hair as she passed.

I'd gotten through three so far, *Interviews Nine, Ten,* and *Eleven,* the final and the unedited versions I'd found in the binder. The men were there, unmasked, in all their glory, and so were their names, addresses and places of business. I'd never seen *Nine* before, but *Ten* and *Eleven* were, respectively, the tall bald guy and the pale, hairy guy I'd watched the night before. Chaz Monroe had been right about her later work being more extreme, and each of these men would be worth a visit.

Not that there was anything to suggest that one of them had come looking for Holly months after the fact. Still, it was possible some-thing had stirred one of them up, perhaps in the way that Mitchell Fenn had been stirred. Cowering on the stage of the Little Gidding Theatre, Werner had sworn up and down that Fenn had been his only foray into blackmail, but doubting him came easy. I sighed. This had the feel of grasping at straws. I was reaching for another disk when the intercom sounded.

I went to the screen just as David's image emerged. He was wrapped in a coat that looked too large, and he was stabbing at the intercom button again and again. I buzzed him in and opened my apartment door. I knew when he stepped off the elevator that he was drunk.

His steps were slow and deliberate, and though they didn't wander, they seemed to require a great deal of concentration. He wore jeans and a pink oxford shirt under his big coat; the clothes looked slept in, and maybe more than once. His face was unshaven and the stubble on his chin was gray. His hair was tangled and cowlicked. He walked past me into the apartment, smelling of sweat and cigarettes. I looked at my watch; it was just eleven. Great.

"You have orange juice?" he said. His voice was dry and tired.

"In the fridge," I said. He tried to help himself, and I looked on. His hands shook and his attention faltered, and it was like watching a slow-motion car wreck. After a while I went into the kitchen and poured it for him. "What are you doing?" I asked.

He was annoyed. "Drinking orange juice—what's it look like?"

"What are you doing here, David? What are you doing wandering around drunk on a Saturday morning?"

He took a drink and slopped juice down his shirtfront. He seemed not to notice. "This isn't drunk—this isn't even a decent buzz."

"I'm going to get you a taxi. You need to go home."

David snorted. "You are the last fucking person on earth to tell me what I need, Johnny."

Great. "You need to go home," I said again.

He pointed at me, and lost more juice. "What I *needed* was for you to do one thing—one stinking thing—and look at what you turned it into." His voice got louder.

I shook my head. "You're not making sense."

"No? Then let me make it clear: you destroyed my life, Johnny. I needed you to take care of one problem, and you turned it into a disaster—a total fucking disaster. Jesus Christ, you're more of a screw-up than any of us ever thought—and that's saying some—" He looked over my shoulder, at Clare coming out of the bathroom. She was wearing a long towel, and her hair was loose and wet.

"Bad time?" she asked.

David laughed and looked at me. "If that's not the story of my fucking life! Here I am with my whole world on fire, and you're lounging around with her, getting blow jobs!"

I hit him. I didn't think twice about it. I didn't even think once. I just whipped my forearm into the side of his head and down he went. A spray of orange juice covered the kitchen wall, and the glass broke into three neat pieces at his feet.

Clare looked at me, and looked at David, and looked at me again. Her face was blank and her eyes were cold and empty. "Jesus Christ," she said softly. She shook her head and went into the bedroom and closed the door. Shit.

I knelt by David, and he moaned and brushed my hands off. He muttered something and got his legs beneath him and caught hold of the countertop. I tried to help him, but he jerked away.

"Get off me, you fucking psycho," he said, leaning against the counter. One side of his face was red and there was a cut at the corner of his mouth.

"Let me get you some ice."

He waved a hand. "Fuck you. You fucking stay away from me." His voice was trembling; tears were welling in his eyes. Shit.

"Sit down and put some ice on that, and I'll get you something to drink."

He waved some more. His sleeve was soaked with juice. "You go to hell," he said, and lurched toward the door.

"Just sit down, dammit!" I reached for his arm; he shrank back.

"Or what—you're going to hit me again?"

I put my hands up and took a deep breath. I softened my voice and spoke slowly. "I'm sorry that I hit you, David. I'm not going to do it again. I just want you to please sit down." His lip was swelling and his eyes were red, and he said nothing for a while, but finally shuffled to the table.

I took his coat and fixed an ice pack, and I poured him another orange juice. While he drank, I checked his head for cuts. David tolerated my ministrations without a word, but his eyes followed my every move. I was pouring him a second glass when Clare appeared. Her black coat was on her arm. She didn't look at David as she crossed the room, and she barely looked at me. She stopped at the door.

"Are you boys going to be all right on your own?" Her smile was thin and her tone was chilly. I nodded. "Let's hope so," she said, and left.

I threw away the broken glass and poured myself a seltzer. I drank it, and David and I looked at each other over the kitchen counter. And said nothing. He was hunched in his chair, tugging absently on a scrap of skin at his neck, when the phone rang. We both jumped. It was Mike Metz.

"I got a call from Stephanie," he said.

"If she's looking for David, he's here with me. I was—"

"She's not the one looking. She's at the house in East Hampton, and the police are executing a search warrant there right now. They're doing the same at the apartment, and they want some of David's DNA."

37

There shouldn't have been traffic. It was early Sunday morning and the sky was bright, and I should have been doing an easy seventy instead of grinding through a three-lanes-into-one merge. I crawled a few feet forward and rocked to a halt. In the car ahead, the driver pounded his steering wheel and slapped his palm on the dash. The guy behind me pulled at his hair and mouthed obscenities. There was a Mercedes SUV on my right, angling sharply into the front bumper of my rent-a-car. There was a doughy blond guy at the wheel, and he looked over with what he thought was a hard stare. Then he glanced into my car, at the passenger seat, and blanched. He hit the brakes and someone leaned on a horn. I reached over and covered the Glock with my notebook. Taillights flared as far ahead as I could see. I took a slow, deep breath and told myself that I was nearly there.

My mistake had been in not starting at the beginning, with the DVDs in the plastic sleeve labeled "Interview #1." If I had, I might have made this drive yesterday. As it was, I didn't watch those disks until seven on Saturday night.

I'd ridden uptown with David after Mike's call, and he was silent and blank-eyed in the back of the taxi. We met Mike on the sidewalk in front of David's building.

"They're up there now," Mike said. "McCue, Conlon, a lab guy, and a uniform. They'll be a while."

The doorman watched through the glass, staring at David's swollen lip and bruised face and rumpled clothing. We went inside and he nodded nervously. "Mr. March," he said, and he explained, in low, anxious tones, about having to let the police in. David walked past him and into the elevator with no sign of having heard a word. Mike followed, and I did too, but when I tried to step into the car, David put a hand on my chest.

"Not you," he said quietly. Mike raised an eyebrow and began to speak, but I shook my head. David pressed the button and the elevator door slid closed. I watched the numbers climb until they reached David's floor. When I turned around, the doorman was looking at me and scratching his jaw. I'd walked slowly home from there.

It was midafternoon when I got in. The light had begun to wane, and the apartment was empty. The phone was ringing. It was Mike, and he'd sounded tired.

"They just left," he said. "David's lying down."

"How did it go?"

"Slowly. They collected stuff for comparison—fiber samples, hair samples, paint samples—and they swabbed David. Mostly, though, they were looking for a gun. They didn't find one."

"How did David take it?"

"Like a mannequin—a mannequin with a fat lip. What happened to his face?"

I ignored the question. "How did it go out in East Hampton?"

"Pretty much the same way. I sent an associate to be with Stephanie, and he told me Vines was running the show out there."

"And . . . ?"

"And no gun."

"That's something."

"Barely," Mike said. "In case we had any doubts, the warrants mean Flores is serious—pretty much, as serious as it gets. Worse still, she's managed to convince a couple of judges that there's probable cause."

"Shit," I said.

"And plenty more where that came from. So if there are unturned stones out there, I'd get to turning them goddamn quick, because I expect a call from Flores Monday morning—a formal call."

"Shit," I said again. Mike was quiet, but stayed on the line. "What is it?" I asked.

"I have to go soon, and . . . you may not want to leave David alone just now."

"Stephanie isn't coming back to town?"

"Not tonight, she told me, and I got the impression she meant not tomorrow, either, and maybe not the next day."

"I'll call Ned," I said, and I did.

I explained what I could, as briefly as I could, to my brother, who said he would go right over. I hung up the phone and looked at the black nylon case, still on the table, and at the DVDs—all the unturned stones—still inside. I wondered whether the cops had yet discovered unit 58 at Creek Self-Store, and said "Fuck it" again. I flicked on my laptop and opened another sleeve. It had taken me hours to make my way to the "Interview #1" DVDs, and to the unlabeled disk that was tucked into the sleeve with them.

A tow truck eased by on the shoulder, and ten minutes later, traffic began to dissolve. Ten minutes after that, I was doing seventy. The sun climbed in the empty sky, and my head filled, yet again, with thoughts of family: brothers, sisters, David's bruised and empty face, his words in the elevator. *Not you.*

I got to the house before noon. I'd called the night before, and I was expected, but something prickled on my neck when I saw the red door standing wide. Curtains were open, but I saw no movement inside as I pulled up the drive. I climbed out of the car and listened, and heard nothing but icy branches creaking in a small wind. A knot tightened in my stomach.

I looked down at my fingers, and wiggled them in their splints. I peeled the tape off my right hand and pulled the splints off. Underneath, my fingers were bruised and swollen. I reached into the car and took the Glock off the seat, and very slowly wrapped my hand around the grip. It hurt like hell, and I wasn't at all sure I could hang on through the recoil, but it was better than nothing. I slipped the gun into its holster behind my back and headed up the path. I slipped it out again when I approached the door.

There were footprints in the pristine snow, and handprints, and shapes that a body might make if it ran, fell, and then crawled. Scattered on the trampled patch, in dashes, spidery lines, and fat, ragged dots like rotted berries was blood. I called out, but there was no answer. The blood trail led to the path, up the stone steps, to the front door, and inside. My pulse was racing, and I followed.

The heating system was cycling loudly, but it was no warmer in the entry hall than on the front steps. I wondered how long the door had been open, and I called out again. Again, no answer. There were scuff marks on the polished wood floor, and the Persian rugs were twisted and askew. The rusty droplets led to the left, through the living room, down a hallway, and past the study. Besides the rush of air in the ducts, the rooms were silent.

I followed the trail to a pair of French doors and the conservatory. It was a long glass room with a peaked glass ceiling and a brick floor laid in a herringbone pattern. Warm air wafted through the open doors, along with an odor. It was not a garden smell, and it was not pleasant. I held my gun down along my leg, and stepped across the threshold.

Big container plants—fruit trees and dusty shrubbery in round terra-cotta pots—lined the room, and made an enclosure around an Oriental rug, a long wicker sofa, a glass-and-wicker coffee table, and a wicker chair. Nicole Cade was sitting on the sofa with her legs folded under her. She wore jeans and a purple sweatshirt, and a distracted look on her wind-beaten face. Her sleeves were pushed up over her sinewy arms, and there was a short-barreled Smith & Wesson in her hand. Herbert Deering was on the chair. He was leaning heavily to his left, and on the floor beneath him was a pool of blood.

38

Deering was alive. He moved a paper-white hand when I stepped into the room, and opened cloudy, terrified eyes. His desiccated lips parted, and a groan came out. A sheen of sweat covered his gray face, and his thin hair was plastered to his head. His right arm cradled his gut, and his right hand was pressed to a wet patch on his left side. Blood soaked the left side of his plaid shirt from armpit to waist. His khakis were stained with something else. Deering's breaths were rapid, shallow, and uneven, and if he hadn't already crossed into shock, he was right at the edge. I looked at Nicole. She hadn't moved, except to point the gun at her husband.

"He said you were coming. He told me last night." Her voice was shaky, and she had trouble with the volume. One of her legs was quivering, and strands of tired red hair fell across her face. There were sooty circles under her eyes, and red patches on her neck and bony cheeks. The gun was black and hammerless, and Nicole ran a nervous thumbnail over the top of the rubber grip.

"That's what started it—that you were coming. He said you were coming to talk more about Holly, and that you had questions about

Redtails, and Dad. I asked him how you knew about Redtails, and . . . he came apart."

I nodded, and put on my most earnest face. "Uh-huh. We should call an ambulance now, okay? We should get you some help here."

She shook her head absently. "He said he couldn't take it any more—the lying. He said it was making him crazy, and that he was glad it was over, that he was exhausted. Can you believe he wanted me to feel sorry for him? Feel *sorry,* for chrissakes!"

I nodded some more. "We should call an ambulance now, Nicole, and get all this taken care of." I eased my cell phone from my jacket pocket.

Nicole pointed the gun at me. "No calls," she said. She was quite certain. "He falls apart—crying, hysterical—and I'm supposed to take care of him. *Comfort him!* He was grabbing my arm, kissing my hands, burying his face in my shoulder, begging forgiveness. Like I'm supposed to make everything all right." She looked down at the gun in her hand and almost smiled.

"When I brought Daddy's gun down, he knew that wasn't going to happen. He ran around the house, screaming like a girl. He wet his *pants,* for chrissakes. I should've left him in the snow all night."

"You shot . . . Herbert was shot last night?"

She nodded vaguely. I looked at Deering again and saw what might have been a blood-soaked dishtowel clutched in his right hand. He opened his mouth and managed a parched whisper.

"I'm sorry, Nikki, I—"

The gun swung back to Deering and I gritted my teeth. "I don't want to hear from you, Herb. Not one word!"

I took a slow breath, and tried to keep my voice conversational. "When's the last time you ate, Nikki?" I said.

She ignored the question, but turned back to me. She held the gun out for me to see. "This is what he used, you know—*my father's* gun. The little bastard took it from my lingerie drawer." She turned to Deering again, and her face darkened. "So on top of everything else, you're a thief too!"

She pointed the gun at him again, her bony fingers white on the grip. My heart was pounding, and my ribs were shaking in my chest. I gulped some air. "Let me get you something, Nikki—some water, something to eat. . . ." I took half a step backward, and the S&W swung over again, following me like a camera lens.

"Stay here," Nicole said. She squinted at me, as if recognizing me for the first time. "What did you want from him? Why did you want to talk about Redtails?"

I fought to keep my voice steady. "Holly mentioned it, on some videos she made when she visited your father. I wanted to know what it was, and why she didn't want it sold. And I wanted to ask about those visits. Herbert told me she never saw him, but apparently she did."

"Is that a surprise—that he lied to you? Is that a big *shock*? Lying is what he does." Deering shifted on the chair and another groan came from him, from deep in his chest. Pain rippled across his face and Nicole pointed the gun at him.

"What is Redtails, Nicole?" I asked. Even to me, it sounded desperate and too loud.

Nicole's lipless mouth split into a nasty grin, and something like a laugh came out. She looked at Deering. "You idiot. You thought he knew something! You came crying to me with your confessions because he was coming here, and you thought he knew. And it turns out he doesn't know anything. You stupid, pathetic idiot."

Her knuckles whitened on the gun again, and I cleared my throat. "What is Redtails?" I repeated softly.

She shook her head. "It's a cabin. Not even a cabin, more like a falling-down shack. One room, an outhouse, and a sagging porch— but she could never get over the place." She turned back to Deering again. "And that's what this is all about, isn't it, Herbert." There was loathing in her tone and on her face. Deering stayed silent.

"It's a house?" I asked.

"It's a shack, I told you—a fucking shack, on a big piece of land. *Redtails*—Holly gave it that name, like it was a manor house or something. She was six or seven, and we saw a pair of hawks up there one weekend—that's when she came up with it. And just because it was Mother's, just because Mother went there when she was a girl, and it was in her family for who knows how long, Holly was fixated on the place. But Mother didn't leave it to Holly, did she? No—she left it to Daddy, to do with what he wants."

A bead of sweat rolled down my ribs, and my fingers ached on the grips of the Glock. Deering was looking at me, and looking for—what—compassion? Rescue? He kept shifting in his chair, and every time he did, Nicole pointed the gun at him and I held my breath.

"And now your father wants to sell?" I asked.

Nicole frowned. "Daddy's not up to dealing with that kind of thing right now; that's why he turned those decisions over to me. I'm the one who wants to sell, and why not? The kind of care he needs—it's goddamn expensive, and more so every year. Developers will pay a lot of money for five hundred acres in Columbia County right now. That made Holly even crazier—the idea that the money would pay for Daddy's care."

I nodded. "You argued with Holly about it?"

"We didn't talk."

"You didn't see her when she visited your father?"

Disgust became anger on Nicole's face. "If I could've arranged it, I wouldn't have let her visit. The way she carried on with him, with those questions and taping everything—going on about Mother, how what she did to herself was Daddy's fault . . . As far as I was concerned, Holly was abusing him with all that. Nobody agreed with me, but I certainly wasn't going to stand around and watch it." She turned to Deering again and held the gun in front of her, in both hands. My grip on the Glock tightened. I watched Nicole's fingers and concentrated on keeping my arm loose.

"No, it wasn't Holly I argued with about the property," Nicole said. "It was him. And now I know why."

I thought about the video I'd seen last night—the footage on the unmarked disk—and thought that I knew why too. But I needed to hear them say it. Slowly, so as not to spook Nicole, I rolled my shoulders and worked the kinks from my neck. Nicole brought the gun to bear on me again.

"Why does Herbert care about the property?" I asked.

Nicole's weathered face darkened. She drew back her lips and looked at Deering. "Why don't you tell him, Herbert? Go ahead—tell him why."

Deering tried again to sit up, but a wave of pain washed across him and he slumped lower in the chair. His eyes wandered awhile before they found me. When they did, they were forlorn.

"Tell him!" Nicole shouted. Her shrill voice echoed off the glass.

"She forced me," Deering said. His voice was barely a whisper now, barely more than rustling leaves. "Holly forced me."

"Forced you how, Herbert?" Nicole said, as if she were speaking to a very slow, very trying child.

Deering closed his eyes. "She'd made a video. She said I had to convince Nikki not to sell Redtails, and that if I didn't—if I couldn't—she'd show it. She'd show it to Nikki."

"Tell him what was on the video, Herbert." She pointed the gun in encouragement.

Deering slumped lower, and his head lolled to the side. "It was a video of me and Holly. We were . . . in bed."

I nodded slowly. Having seen the video last night, I understood how Herbert Deering might be driven to distraction—might be driven well beyond—by the thought of his wife watching it. I also understood why he'd offered such a pallid description of the footage: "in bed."

I'd begun to think of the video as Holly's test reel, because it incorporated so many essential elements of her later work: graphic, edgy sex, themes of dominance and submission, and a wrenching, punitive interrogation at the end. But there were differences, too. The technical ones were comparatively minor—brighter lighting, murkier sound, the use of a single camera. The important distinction was in the lack of anonymity: the fact that Deering was unmasked—face and voice—throughout, and the fact that he and Holly knew each other outside the confines of the hotel room. So, besides the vivid renderings of Deering's lust for Holly, the video also documented his many declarations of love for her, his lengthy discourses on Nicole's sexual deficiencies—on her deficiencies in general—and, near the end, his proposal of marriage to his sister-in-law.

Nicole chuckled grimly. "Of course, Herbert couldn't give away water in the desert, and all his babbling to me about Redtails—'Let's hang on a little longer, it'll be worth even more next year'—just made me angry. It made me push the deal along faster."

"What happened then?" I asked.

Nicole looked at Deering. "Go on, Herbert—tell."

He shook his head. "No, Nikki—"

"You do as I say, you prick!" she said, and she took aim squarely at

Deering's head. He squeezed his eyes shut, and Nicole looked at him with fresh disgust. "You tell him, or I swear to Christ I will shoot you again!"

Deering kept his eyes closed, and his words were nearly lost in the dry rasp of his breathing. "I went to see her, down in the city. I went to explain that Nikki wouldn't . . . that I couldn't convince her. I went to ask her—to beg her—not to do this. I—"

Nicole interrupted with another harsh laugh. "But you brought the gun along, didn't you, you prick? You stole Daddy's gun from me and brought it with you."

He nodded weakly. "It was nighttime and we walked near the water, and Holly was in a bad way. Something happened, an accident or something, and she was bruised. And she was in a terrible mood—angry. I tried to explain about Nikki, but she wouldn't listen. She yelled and threatened—said she'd send Nikki the video that night. And she called me names—stupid, useless, an ape . . .

"And then I hit her. I hit her with the back of my hand. I didn't plan it—it just happened, and she fell down. I tried to help her, but she pushed me away, and when she got up, she was holding a brick. She cursed at me and threw it and it almost hit me. Then she picked up something else, a broken bottle, and she was screaming at me and calling me names, and . . ." Deering's head dropped and his shoulders shook.

"Christ, just say it, Herbert—say what happened next."

He didn't look up, but he said it. "I took out the gun . . . and I shot her."

I let out a deep breath, and something unwound in my gut. Nicole stared at her husband, like a bluejay at a worm. "What happened after that?" I asked.

"I took her things . . . her clothes . . . and I threw them in a storm drain. I put her . . . her body . . . in the river. Then I went to her apartment, to look for the disk, but I couldn't. . . . It was a mess, torn apart, so I got out and went home.

"You came by the next day, and ever since, I've been . . . crazy. I can't sleep, I can't think straight." Deering pressed his right hand harder against his side, and folded around his wound. The pool beneath his chair was larger now.

Nicole snorted. "Hell of a guy, isn't he?" she said. There was a wild light in her blue eyes.

I looked at her. "Let me call an ambulance, Nicole—for your sake as much as his. If he dies—"

She ignored me. "I knew Holly. I knew what she was like, how selfish she was, how self-indulgent and sick, that there was nothing she wasn't capable of. Holly didn't surprise me. But him . . ." She turned to Deering and brought the gun up again, in a two-handed grip. "You surprised me, Herbert. I thought I knew what you were about—not Superman, maybe, not the brightest bulb, but not a guy who'd fuck my evil sister, either. It turns out you were full of surprises. Live and learn, I guess."

"Let me make a call, Nicole—for you. You don't want to sit here and watch him bleed out."

She laughed, an unlovely, crazy sound. "You sure about that?"

"He's not worth it, Nicole. Come on." She looked at me and sighed, and let her hands fall to her lap. She took a deep breath and a shiver ran through her. Her face seemed to collapse on itself, and she looked a thousand years old. "Come on," I said again.

She ran a hand across the back of her neck, and what was left of her ponytail was gone. Her hair fell forward in a tangle, and caught the winter light, which brightened it and made it somehow richer. For an instant, as she turned her head, it looked like Holly's hair, and she looked more than a little like Holly. Nicole found a calm, exhausted smile. Her voice was quiet and even.

"You're right—I don't want to watch him bleed out," she said. "It's taking too damn long." Then she shot him twice, and blew his chest apart.

39

"I'm sick of looking at you," Leo McCue said, and he ran a thumb over his mustache, and closed the door of the interview room. I started to say something and Mike kicked me under the table. McCue made us a quorum: me, Mike Metz, Rita Flores, Tina Vines, and the fat man himself, gathered yet again at the Seventh Precinct station house. It was early enough on Thursday morning that we were all drinking coffee and rubbing sleep from our eyes. McCue was right: we'd seen entirely too much of each other lately.

It had started on Sunday, in the brick bunker on Route 7 that housed the Wilton PD. I'd spent the day there, surrounded by predictably frosty Connecticut law enforcement types—a couple of Wilton detectives, the Wilton chief, and a guy from the state's attorney's office—and when I hadn't been sitting and waiting, I'd been answering questions and giving statements.

I'd kept my story simple, and almost true: that I'd come to Wilton in an attempt to tie up some loose ends in an investigation—specifically, that I'd wanted to discuss with Deering his apparently false claims that Holly never visited her father, and that I'd wanted to ask him what "Redtails" was. I hadn't mentioned the fact that I also wanted to discuss the video I'd seen the night before, of Deering and his sister-in-law fucking like bunnies. Everything else I told the cops about what had happened at the Cade house, from the time I pulled up, to when the first cars responded to my 911, was as complete and accurate as I could make it. And it was happily consistent with the story Nicole had repeated—with a notable lack of remorse, and over the strenuous objections of her attorneys—several times that day.

Mike Metz had joined me sometime in the midafternoon, and sometime after that, the Connecticut guys had thawed enough to offer me a refill on the bad coffee. For a little while, it looked like we might get out of there before dark. We were sitting in the day room, at a cafeteria table, under buzzing fluorescent lights, when McCue and Vines swept in and sucked all the air from the place.

Vines perched on a desk, and knocked over photos of someone's kids. McCue opened his mouth, and an avalanche of commands and condescension tumbled out. The Connecticut guys, for their part, were amazingly patient. McCue was told that it would be some time before he and Vines could interview Nicole, and even more time before he could look at the crime scene. Going through Herbert Deering's personal effects would take longer still. Demands that Nicole's gun be turned over to the NYPD for testing were met with amazed laughter. Maybe just to get McCue out of his face, the Wilton chief had agreed to let him talk to me.

We'd gone into a small, airless room, McCue, Vines, Mike, and I, and they took me over the same ground I'd covered with the Wilton cops. I told them the same story, but they'd pushed back harder. "What the hell gave you the right to question Deering?" "Who the hell else have you been talking to?" "What did we say about fucking around in an active investigation?" They snarled and snapped, but even they knew that the game had changed. Their big case, while still plenty lurid, was effectively closed. Mike had summed it up for them.

"We all know how it can go sometimes with investigations, Detective," he said, smiling. "A direction suggests itself, and—right or wrong—resources follow it. And the more man-hours you spend, the more likely it is you can find things that reinforce your leanings, or that seem to, and that justify sending even more resources in the same direction. And so other possibilities get less attention. No one's talking about conspiracy here, Detective, or prosecutorial misconduct, or even mismanagement—no one has used those words—it's just a thing that happens sometimes. Call it an echo chamber, or group-think. It's just everyone's good fortune that John is somewhat independent minded. It saved a lot of awkwardness all around."

Vines had gnashed her teeth and McCue had darkened to a coronary red, but a little while later, they'd cut me loose. Though not for long.

The evaporation of their high-profile trial, and all its attendant career fantasies, left McCue, Vines, and Flores frustrated and angry, and made me a target of opportunity. So it was back to Pitt Street on Monday, and Tuesday, and again on Wednesday. Nominally, the cops were still investigating the death of Holly Cade, but in fact they were fishing. Whom had I spoken to; what had I found; what did I know and when did I know it—anything that even hinted at obstruction.

I said as little as possible, and let Mike do most of the dancing, which he did better than anyone else I knew. He invoked attorney work-product confidentiality when he had to, and raised before them, more or less subtly, the specter of public embarrassment, and in the end I said not a word about Jamie Coyle, computer backups, DVDs, or unit 58 at Creek Self-Store—which, to my knowledge, they still haven't discovered. When McCue made the clumsy suggestion that the DVD of David and Holly and Stephanie might somehow find its way to the Internet, Mike laughed, and cut him off at the knees.

"Better sell the condo in Florida now, Detective, and cash in the pension, and somebody should tell the mayor that the department's going to overrun the budget on civil settlements this year."

As the week wore on, it was obvious they were losing steam. Mike attributed some of it to the mounting forensic evidence that supported Deering's confession: the E-ZPass records of his car crossing the Triborough Bridge on the night Holly died; the ballistics report on Nicole Cade's gun, which matched it to the bullets that killed Holly; and the souvenirs found in the spare tire well of Deering's station wagon—Holly's bra and panties, and the keys to her apartment, all in a plastic grocery bag. Deering had done it, and we all knew there was less and less excuse for the cops to grill me.

Mike ascribed most of their waning enthusiasm, though, to the press. Because there weren't many murders in the Wilton zip code, Deering's had started out as a good-sized story. It had grown larger, and taken a gothic turn, when local reporters recalled the suicide, years earlier and in the same house, of Nicole's mother. It achieved the status of minor frenzy when it was revealed that the murder victim had himself confessed to shooting his sister-in-law, one Holly Cade, also known as the Williamsburg Mermaid. Mike had explained it as we walked into the station house that morning.

"The bigger the story gets, the less Flores and company want it known that their investigation was headed entirely in the wrong direction. They want to mark Holly's case closed, and they want you to go away." Which was fine with me, but there was a lecture to sit through first.

McCue's voice was a low growl as he wrapped up, and his face was dark. "Bottom line is: you got fucking lucky on this. Things broke your way. But God help you if you think you got over on us, because you didn't. You think we don't know the shit you've done? You think we don't know about you going to Coyle's place, or that you kicked the crap out of Werner? You're not getting over on us, and I swear to God if I see that smirk again, I'm going to come across the table and slap it off your face." He pointed a finger at me and I started to stand, and Mike held my arm. Rita Flores nodded, and offered her own admonitions.

"That's right, counselor, sit him down—that's good advice you're giving. And you explain to him that next time—if he's so foolish that there is a next time—pulling his license is just for starters. There'll be charges, civil and criminal both, if my office has anything to say about it, and I won't care if he's captured Jack the fucking Ripper." She looked at me, and her eyes were like nail heads. "You get that, March?" I nodded. "Great. Now clear out while I talk to your boss."

I got up and took a long look at McCue, and hoped it would be for the last time. I had no doubt he was hoping the same. As it happened, we were both disappointed.

I waited for Mike on Pitt Street, under stony skies, in the penetrating cold. He came out smiling, and patting his overcoat pocket.

"You got it?" I asked.

He nodded, and slipped the disk out of his pocket and handed it to me. "Flores promised there were no copies."

"Do you believe her?"

"I believe that if we keep our end of the deal—to keep quiet and keep away from the press—we won't have to find out."

"What about Werner?" I asked. "Are they going to go after him for the assault?"

Mike shook his head. "I tried," he said. "But with no witnesses, no evidence, and only your coerced confession to go on, it's a nonstarter for them."

"He beat the shit—"

"It's a nonstarter, John."

I sighed and nodded my head. "So we're done?"

"With these guys. You've got some trips to New Haven in your future."

"What do you think will happen with Nicole?"

He shrugged. "I imagine her lawyer is thinking about some sort of diminished-capacity argument, and I imagine the state's attorney has figured that out too. My guess is they'll deal it down, but how far, I have no clue."

"She didn't seem all that diminished to me," I said. "Mostly, she seemed pissed off."

"Having your husband fuck your sister and then shoot her dead has that effect."

"I don't think it was the shooting she minded."

Clare was at the table when I got home, finishing her breakfast and looking through the real estate listings. I hadn't seen much of her in the past few days—she'd been all over town, and Brooklyn too, looking at apartments—but she'd waited up for me on Sunday night, rigid and white-faced on the sofa when I came in.

"There was news on TV," she'd said. "A guy shot in Wilton." She slipped her hands under my shirt. They were smooth and freezing. "They didn't give his name."

"It wasn't me," I said.

"Your guy, though?" I nodded. "I had a feeling, I don't know why. Did you . . . ?"

"I was a witness." I put my face into her pale hair. Soap, perfume, and underneath, something warmer. "I should've called you," I'd said.

"I wasn't asking," she'd whispered.

"Still . . ."

Clare tapped the newspaper—the Metro section—and slid it across to me. "Another thing about your thing," she said.

I scanned the article. It was the fifth story that week, and mostly a rehash of other reports: another portrait of the Williamsburg Mermaid as a troubled young hipster, actress, and failed playwright, and liberally seasoned with rumors of sadomasochistic sex tapes. Cassandra Z was mentioned yet again. I looked at my backpack, sitting in the corner and bulging with DVDs and backup disks.

"You want to come to Brooklyn?" Clare asked. "Check out some apartments?"

I shook my head. "I've got chores."

I spent the afternoon erasing Holly's backups and breaking DVDs—not easy to do with splints on. In between, I fielded phone calls. The first was from Ned.

"I've followed the story in the papers," he said.

"They're getting it about half right."

"It sounds like this Holly was quite a disturbed person."

"She was a lot of things," I said. "Disturbed was one of them."

"David's lucky this worked out. He's lucky he had you to help him. He owes you a huge thanks."

I laughed. "I'm sure he'll get around to it."

"He hasn't—"

"Don't worry about it. Is he back at work yet?"

Ned was quiet for a moment. "He didn't tell you?"

I sighed. "Tell me what?"

"David is taking a leave of absence. Six months."

"Whose decision was that?"

"I thought it would be a good idea, and Stephanie agreed."

"And David?"

"He came around eventually," Ned said, and I laughed again. "Speaking of which, I'm hoping you'll come around too—literally, I mean. Your nephews miss you, and so do Janine and I."

"Sure, Ned, once things settle down, we'll see."

"I want to do more than see, John. I want you to come over."

I took a deep breath. "Sure," I said, and hung up.

Chaz Monroe called me not long after. He, too, had been following the stories in the papers, and there were sly undertones in his raspy voice. "I didn't think you were really a buyer," he said. "But not to worry, I forgive the lies. And at least yours were in the line of duty or something."

"I'm relieved."

"Indeed." He chuckled. "So, it turns out she was an actress. Well, that's no surprise, and neither is the fact that she was a playwright. I'm just amazed she never had more conventional success—she was fucking remarkable."

"She had other things on her mind, I guess."

"Apparently. And so do I, of course. These stories have brought buyers out of the woodwork, and I guess it's more than Don Orlando can handle—or wants to handle—because my phone's been ringing off the hook. So, if you know of anyone looking to sell—"

"I thought you knew all the owners of Cassandra's works, or knew of them."

Monroe hesitated. "I was thinking more of *undocumented* work—anything you might have *stumbled* across. . . . Prices are only going up."

I almost laughed. "I'll keep an eye out," I said. I hung up and snapped another DVD in two.

I was erasing the last of Holly's backup disks when Orlando Krug called. He sounded old and tired, and his accent was more pronounced. "It was really her brother-in-law?" he asked.

"It was," I said.

"The police are sure? It wasn't Werner?"

"It was Herbert Deering, Mr. Krug."

"But why? The papers hinted at some sort of affair . . ." I didn't say anything, and Krug got the hint.

"I understand, you can't speak of it. It's just that I read the newspapers, and the person they describe . . . it's not the Holly I knew."

"They don't know her. They have column inches to fill, so they write things."

I heard Krug sip at something. "I've wondered lately just how well I knew her myself."

"You're the one who told me that she wasn't easy to know. She was complicated—not just one thing."

"She was very unhappy," he said.

"And angry, and lost."

"And cruel, Mr. March. Not to me—never—but what she did to those men . . ."

"She was talented, too—maybe brilliant. And driven."

Krug's laugh was bitter. " 'Obsessed' is a better word, or perhaps 'mad.' She just couldn't let go."

"She told Jamie Coyle there was a story she wanted to tell, and questions she wanted to answer."

"Do you think she found her answers?"

"I'm the wrong guy to ask about closure, Mr. Krug. But I think, sometimes, for some people, the questions come to loom less large. The answers don't matter so much."

He sipped his drink again. "I wonder if Holly would have reached that point," he said.

"She was happy with Jamie, I think. Maybe she was getting there." It was the only comfort I could offer. We rang off.

I didn't know if it was the fallout of Krug's sadness and fatigue, or my own string of sleepless nights, or simply the dull light in the low, beaten sky, but a tidal weariness swept over me and filled my limbs with lead. I listened to the whirr of the disk drive—Holly's work being whisked away—and looked at the shiny plastic shards in my garbage pail. Holly, Wren, Cassandra—all that anger and sadness, all that cruelty and control, all the searching, and for what? I lay down on the sofa, and as my eyes fell shut, I thought of something else Jamie Coyle had said: "Everybody does their own time, and they do it their own way."

As I had every day since Sunday, I dreamed of Deering's body. He was lumpy and twisted on the bricks, like a gutted scarecrow, and there was a terrible intimacy to the sound he made as he hit the floor. His face was deserted; the fear and surprise and everything else packed up and gone. Nicole's words were the only lyrics—"It's taking too damn long"—but the voice in my head was Holly's.

Clare's voice woke me. She was in the kitchen, talking on her cell phone and putting takeout in the oven. She spoke softly, but firmly.

"I said I'd think about it, Amy, and that's what I'm doing."

I went into the bathroom and splashed water on my face, and when I came out she was off the phone. "Your sister?" I asked, and she nodded. "How was Brooklyn?"

She shrugged. "Far. I'm looking at some places in TriBeCa tomorrow."

"No rush," I said, and Clare nodded again.

Jamie Coyle called after dinner. I recognized the soft voice immediately, though his reason for calling took me by surprise.

"I wanted to say thanks," he said.

"For what?"

"I been reading the papers, and reading between the lines, and it seems like that asshole would never have got his if not for you."

"I got lucky," I said. "The cops would've found him eventually—they just wasted time looking in the wrong place. I did too, for that matter."

Coyle snorted. "You were the guy working at it, though. So, thanks."

"And to you too, for the information. Without it—"

"Yeah, whatever," Coyle grunted.

"What are you doing now?" I asked.

"Nobody's looking for me for anything, so I'm back working for Kenny—but I'm not sure how long. A guy I know out in Vegas tells me there's work there, and I can crash on his couch. I'm just waiting for the service . . . for Holly. She had a cousin down in Virginia that's arranging it. I spoke to her yesterday."

I glanced at the table, at the disk I'd made before I'd erased Holly's backups: her hidden-camera interviews with Coyle. "I have something you might want—a keepsake." He asked what it was and I told him. He was quiet for a while.

"I don't know," he said finally. "All I do is think about her. I get angry sometimes, and I get this pain . . . in my chest. It feels like someone carved me out with a spoon. I don't know if I can listen to her voice."

I thought of the hollow in my own chest, still there after five years, and of the gasping, suffocating feeling that still took me by surprise. I wasn't going to tell him it would pass. "You might want it later," I said.

"Send it, then," Coyle said quietly. I mailed the disk that night.

On Friday, there were two more Mermaid stories in the tabloids, both featuring a come-hither headshot of Holly that someone had dug up from somewhere. One piece, relying on a leak from the coroner's office, revealed that Holly had been beaten before she died, and that she had been pregnant. The other aired rumors that her sex tape costars had included some of the city's more prominent real estate and financial types. No names were named, but it no doubt made a lot of people nervous.

I'd just finished reading the articles, and Clare had just left for TriBeCa, when my intercom sounded. Stephanie's face appeared on the screen, with David fidgeting behind her. I buzzed them up.

Stephanie wore a sweater and yoga pants, and she carried a shearling coat on her arm. She was expertly made up, and her dark hair was tied loosely with a velvet ribbon. David was pale and freshly barbered, and he paced by the door with the naked, skittish look of a newly shorn sheep. A newly shorn sheep looking for a drink.

"We're on our way to the airport," Stephanie said. Her voice was tight. "We're going away for a while."

"Ned told me."

David scowled and stared at me. "Ned told you what?"

"Only that you were taking a leave. It sounded like a good idea."

"Swell," David said, and tugged on a patch of skin over his Adam's apple.

Stephanie colored and shook her head. She extended a nervous hand and squeezed my arm. "We wanted to say goodbye, and we wanted to thank you." I nodded at her, and we managed a clumsy exchange of smiles.

Stephanie looked at David. He frowned and jammed his hands in his pockets. His eyes were on the floor. "Yeah, thanks," he said, and a muscle twitched on his jaw. Stephanie pursed her lips.

"Where are you headed?" I asked.

"Vail for a few weeks, and then the islands."

"Sounds nice."

David snorted. "We wouldn't be going anywhere if—"

Stephanie's hand shot out and wrapped around David's wrist. Her fingers were white and her nails were sharp, and David jerked his hand away as if from a flame. He glared at her, but when he spoke his voice was low and tired. "I'll be in the car," he said, and walked out.

Stephanie shook her head and sighed. "He doesn't mean anything. He's still upset over all this—in some sort of shock."

"He should talk to someone, Stephanie. He needs help."

She colored again, and her face stiffened. She nodded, too fast. "And he'll get it. Some time off, a change of scene, a little fresh air and exercise—this trip will really help him."

I shook my head. "He needs more than a trip."

"And he'll get it, John, don't worry. David will be fine."

"And what about you?"

Stephanie frowned and looked at her hands. They were perfectly manicured, the nails like pink pearls. "Me? I'm a little on edge still, but some skiing and a seaweed wrap and I'll be A-okay." She looked up at me, and her eyes were huge and shining. She squeezed my arm again. "Don't worry about us, John, we'll be fine. Even keel again in no time."

I started to say something and stopped, and Stephanie looked relieved. And then she was gone—a nervous laugh, a brittle smile, and quick steps out the door. I went to the windows and looked down and saw David, standing near a black Town Car. In a moment, Stephanie appeared. She came up beside him, and put a hand on his back. His head inclined toward hers and his arm circled her waist, and they stood together for a moment. Then they got into the car, and the car pulled away. I watched it round the corner and I heard Jamie Coyle's voice again. "Everybody does their own time."

Epilogue

In March, Clare found a place to live. It wasn't in Manhattan, and it wasn't in Brooklyn. It was a Craftsman bungalow on Rose Street, in North Berkeley. She sat cross-legged on the sofa when she told me, and she put her hand on my cheek.

"If I stayed in New York, I'd end up staying with you," she said.

"And that would be a bad thing?"

She shook her head. "Not a bad thing, honey, but an easy one. It's comfortable, and companionable, and we have a lot of fun—and, Christ, you give me all the space in the known universe. Hanging out with you is the simplest thing in the world. It's like being back in college, the path of least resistance. But I've gone down that path already, and it's not what I'm looking for anymore."

"What are you looking for? And how do you know—"

"I want kids, John," she said, and there was humming silence afterward. She let it hum for a while, and then she smiled. "I'm thirty-five years old, and I want to have a baby. And I want it to be with someone who wants to raise children, who's ready for that." I started to speak and she put a hand to my mouth. "That's not you, John—not now."

I held her hands and sat there until the room was dark around us, but I couldn't tell her otherwise.

I saw Leo McCue again in April, two weeks after Clare moved, and two days after Gene Werner's body was found under the Williamsburg Bridge. McCue was fatter than ever, and his mustache was badly overgrown. He pushed a paper coffee cup across the interrogation table to me.

"Hell of a coincidence, don't you think?" he said. "Him under the bridge, not a hundred yards from where we found her. I remembered what a hard-on you had for this guy at the end, so naturally I wondered if you'd aced him."

"Naturally. What happened to him?"

McCue drank some coffee and grimaced. "Somebody beat the crap out of him, and capped it off by snapping his neck. Let me see your hands." I held them out and McCue inspected them. "Soft as a baby's ass," he said.

"And no cuts or bruises. Sorry to disappoint."

McCue shrugged. "A shot in the dark," he said. "And I'm guessing you can account for your time."

I sighed. "Only if you tell me what time I'm supposed to account for." He told me, and took it well when he heard I'd been in a roomful of bankers on the evening in question.

"Like I said, a shot in the dark. You come across anybody in your travels who'd want to punch his ticket?"

I shook my head. "Nope."

"But if you think of somebody, I'm your first call, right?"

"Sure," I said, and I headed for the door. I was halfway out when McCue spoke again.

"How's that brother of yours doing, by the way?" he asked. "His wife give him back his balls yet?"

"Fuck you," I said, and left. His laughter followed me down the hall.

The next day I drove up to Tarrytown. The Van Winkle Court condominiums were still there, and so was Uncle Kenny, but Jamie Coyle was long gone.

ALSO BY PETER SPIEGELMAN

BLACK MAPS

John March walked away from his family's merchant bank for the life of a rural deputy sheriff—a life that would explode in personal tragedy and professional disaster. Three years later, March is back in New York City, working as a private investigator and still running from his grief and guilt. When he takes the case of Rick Pierro, a wealthy investment banker threatened by blackmail, March is swiftly drawn into a web of Wall Street insiders and outcasts, and back to a world he thought he'd left behind. The more he learns about Pierro's connections to a notorious international bank that made billions in blood money, the darker the terrain becomes. Soon March's own life is in danger, as he follows a trail of blood and shattered lives to a ruthless and depraved extortionist.

Crime Fiction/978-1-4000-3359-1

DEATH'S LITTLE HELPERS

In this masterful follow-up, private investigator John March finds himself drawn into a web of corruption that extends from the halls of high finance to the dark underworld of organized crime. Gregory Danes was once Master of the Universe, a hotshot Wall Street analyst whose stock picks moved markets. Now his career is on the rocks, and he's gone missing. So too have the big alimony checks his ex-wife expects each month. His ex, a fashionable painter, calls March to track him down, but the seemingly straightforward missing-person case soon takes a vicious turn. And when March's own family is threatened, he realizes that Danes is involved in something far more lethal that insider trading.

Crime Fiction/978-1-4000-3360-7